Home for the Hollandaise

ERIN LUCY

Chapter 1

I wore these heels to impress, and the pain in my toes tells me they're making an impression, just the wrong kind. As a former runway model, I've worn some doozies. Seven-inch, florescent-yellow ballet boots. Ten-inch platforms with shark fins. Heels carved out of lava rock, dipped in resin, and covered with Swarovski crystals. Don't ask me. I didn't get it either.

After walking to the subway station, the train, and then through Newark Liberty International Airport in these three-inchers, my feet were already mincemeat, reminding me why I gave up heels the same day I gave up modeling. Now my feet are throbbing in time with my temples as I watch luggage wind around United's baggage carousel at Indianapolis International Airport.

With each anxious heartbeat, my vision shimmies like I'm standing on the New Madrid Fault during a tremor. I follow an army-green duffel bag, a black garment bag, a plastic suitcase decorated with Hello Kitty stickers. This is the sixth rotation, and my pink leather Samsonite still hasn't joined the mix.

I expected to leave Newark at five fifteen this morning. Instead, my plane sat on the runway for two hours while United struggled to find a pilot, thus ruining my plans to grab a lox plate and everything bagel from Shapiro's in Indy by seven o'clock.

It's ten o'clock, I'm starving, and my suitcase is apparently en route to the International Space Station. I hope the astronauts enjoy my never-worn Victoria's Secret lace cheekies. Seven pairs for thirty-five dollars. I couldn't pass up that deal.

A muscular gentleman in army fatigues grabs the green duffel bag. Somebody else claims the stickered suitcase. My luggage is nowhere in sight.

I tromp over to the customer service desk, tell the red-haired lady named Mauve my unfortunate news, and await her sympathetic reply.

"Go to the Baggage Recovery Center on our website," Mauve says, "click on 'Report lost items,' and fill out the form." She's either good at hiding her concern, or she doesn't give a flip about my lost cheekies. "We'll deliver it to you if we find it."

"What do you mean *if*?" I narrow my eyes at Mauve's fake eyelashes.

"You've heard the news lately, haven't you? We're all struggling here, honey."

I want to spit back, *Don't call people 'honey.' It's disrespectful to bees.*

"Thank you," I mumble instead. I clutch my sterling silver bee pendant and retreat to a quiet corner to follow Mauve's instructions.

After filling out the form, I rush to Civic Plaza. The broad, circular atrium offers many food options, but I already know what I want. I grab my lox plate and my bagel and find an empty table, set my carry-on on the tabletop—careful not to jostle it—and unzip the top compartment. The travel terrarium is nestled between a change of clothes and my toiletry bag. I pull it free and peer inside.

Jupiter, my *Phidippus Regius*, or Regal Jumping Spider, is nestled in one corner, his bottom four eyes glaring at me beneath a distinct monobrow.

"Sorry. Geez. You think you've had a bad day? Let me tell you about mine."

Jupiter waves his furry pedipalps to let me know he's had a much worse day, which included an encounter with a TSA agent who didn't think he had a permit to board the plane and several air pressure changes that nearly split his exoskeleton.

"You're alive, okay?" I answer. "I saved you from the grumpy dude who wanted to flush you down the toilet. Show some appreciation."

Jupiter is probably as hungry as I am. Hungrier. I unzip a secret compartment in my carry-on and pull out a baggie of wriggling mealworms, pinch a couple between my fingers, and drop them in front of Jupiter's jaws. He pounces and goes to work.

Satisfied that my pet is going to survive this ordeal, I set him aside and focus on my food, devouring three bites of veggies and smoked salmon with barely a breath in between.

The food will satisfy my gnawing hunger, but it won't fix my frustration. I should have stuffed a few workout suits and a pair of Five Below flip-flops into a surplus military tote and called it a day. Except that wouldn't do. Cold Spring expects more from the girl who moved away and made it semi-big. I need to look the part.

About ninety-seven percent of lost luggage is returned to its owner within two days. I've traveled enough to know the statistics. Odds are I won't be wearing this navy pantsuit and matching pumps every day for the next six weeks. Thankfully.

I spread cream cheese onto my untoasted bagel and tear off a bite. A few minutes later, my plate is clean and I'm ready to pick up my rental car.

"I booked the rental car on Priceline," I say to the woman at the Enterprise desk when she tells me she doesn't have my reservation. "I received a confirmation number."

"Do you have it?"

I grab my phone and show her the email. She types in the number and pounds on her keyboard while biting her bottom lip. The screen casts a glare on her glasses, but I can read her eyebrows as they cinch together.

"This reservation was for yesterday," she says.

"What? No. I—"

I turn my phone around and check the date. She's right.

Part of my job as a bookings agent is making sure our models arrive at their destinations on time with proper travel arrangements to get them where they need to go. My job keeps me busy. So busy I can't tend to my own business.

"What do I do now?" I ask the polite lady who shows more concern than Mauve did.

Dumb question. I do this for a *living*. But for some reason my mind is blank. Maybe it's the Indiana air and its lingering dust from recent soybean harvests and dying foliage, or maybe it's the flat landscape that crawls endlessly to the horizon without beaches to designate the edge of civilization. I grew up here, but after ten years in New York City, returning home always feels so foreign. I forget myself. Or do I remember myself? Or both?

I don't have time for existential questions. I need to get home, check on the café, and slip back into the self that knows how to navigate small towns, straight highways, and county roads that divide farmland into square miles.

"You could call a taxi or an Uber," the woman says.

"You're right. Never mind. I don't know why I'm so frazzled. Probably just wonky blood sugar. Sorry to bother you."

I wave my phone at the lady and let the next person in line have my place.

Once again, I retreat to a quiet corner to lick my wounds.

You're not going to believe this, I text my boyfriend, Hayden.

I wait for him to respond even though I know he's at a photo shoot in Lower Manhattan this morning. When he doesn't, I add: **I'm stuck at the Indianapolis airport. Taxi service here**

is non-existent. I guess I'm calling an Uber. Wish me luck. Hopefully I don't get a talker.

Gary is a talker.

The farther I sink into the second-row, gray leather bucket seat in his Chrysler Pacifica, the louder he speaks. I already know about his granddaughter's preschool Thanksgiving program on Tuesday, his wife's lifelong struggle with rosacea, and his dog's skin tag removal that came back benign. And we're still on I-465.

Trees buzz by on the right and left interrupted by frequent billboards advertising everything from the Law Offices of Keller and Keller to the Uranus Fudge Factory. We approach a series of towering overpasses that gleam white in the November sun and curve gracefully above and beneath each other like a well-imagined sculpture.

If I didn't know any better, I'd think we were in the middle of nowhere. Indianapolis's downtown boasts a mere handful of skyscrapers. From I-465's outer loop, none are visible, even though we're technically in the city.

"What size do you wear?" Gary says.

"Um."

"My wife is tall and thin like you. My house is ten minutes from here. We could stop by and find you some clothes to wear until your luggage shows up."

"Er."

He flips on his turn signal and merges into the right lane. We still have forty-five minutes until we reach Cold Spring. I can't fathom what Gary is going to say next. His Hoosier hospitality seems to know no bounds.

"That's okay," I say. "I'm fine. I'll run by Target or something."

"No Targets that far north. They closed down the one in Winford."

"Really?"

"Yep."

I wrinkle my nose. "I'll try Old Navy."

"Nope. That's closed too."

"Really?"

"Yep. You've got Ross or Marshalls or Kohl's or Goodwill. So, what brings you home?"

Gary's conversation is like a winding creek. It curves right. It juts left. It loops back on itself.

"My dad's getting a pacemaker and my mom is getting her hip replaced. They need me to run the café while they recover."

Gary leans forward and grips the wheel. "Does your dad run Eat and Treats?"

"Nope. That's the new place by the interstate. My mom and dad's café is downtown."

"Welp, the pancakes à la mode at Eat and Treats will have you rolling home."

Who puts ice cream on pancakes? That's what syrup is for. "I'll have to try it."

"Cold Spring is a unique place," Gary says while tapping his fingers to "HandClap," by Fitz and Tantrums, which he just turned up.

Urban sprawl streams past my window. Steel-framed light industrial buildings share acreage with strip malls housing various small businesses that, despite their humble signs, are the heartbeat of America's economy.

"Most pop music nowadays is crap," Gary says when the song ends, "but that's a good one. Do you mind the volume?"

"No. Not at all." Because it's just loud enough to hinder conversation.

Gary quiets down as songs stream by. My view shifts from architecturally bland buildings to wide swaths of farmland, most of it flat with gentle swells here and there. Large rolls of hay dot dormant fields. Wire fencerows delineate properties and add biodiversity as native weeds and saplings take root along them.

My rib cage expands. Just a little. It's nice being able to see to the horizon instead of being boxed in by buildings. But I'm not getting used to this. I've made a good life in New York City and I'm not giving it up for a few corn fields and a view.

Chapter 2

I plunk the heel of my Coach Waverly pump against Main Street's weathered asphalt, clutching my carry-on as I offer a thanks to Gary.

"Sorry about all the travel mix-ups," he says. "I hope they find your luggage."

"Me too. Thanks for the ride." I shift my weight and exit the van, stepping onto the curb.

Instead of throwing the van into Drive, he rolls down his window. "That's your café?" He points to the building across the street.

The brick façade on my parent's building, locally known as the Coleman Building, is weathered, the mortar deterioration looking more pronounced than I remember. The two-story building was constructed in 1890 by the Odd Fellows and Morton Coleman. An I.O.O.F plaque sits just below the decorative cornice, a reminder that the building was used as the Odd Fellows' lodge for seven decades before my Grandpa Jerry bought it for my Grandma Delores so she could fulfill her dream of opening a restaurant.

Two sets of windows allow light into the upstairs meeting room that hasn't seen a gathering since 1964. Long storefront windows flank the first-floor entrance. Above them, the café's signage occupies a small portion of the available advertising real estate. Faded Christmas lights border the handmade wooden sign, some rendered white with age. Peeling green paint surrounds the storefront windows, and a sad little Christmas tree with tarnished glass bulbs stands just outside the front door.

"Yep. That's it," I answer.

"I can see why I missed it. Might need to work on the curb appeal." He chuckles, which softens his criticism. A little. "It's like that show 'Diners, Drive-Ins, and Dives' with what's his name."

"Guy Fieri."

I'm pretty sure Gary just called my parents' place a dive.

"I may stop by sometime," he continues. "I'm sure it's great inside."

I haven't been inside the café in over three years. I've been immersed in my job, shuffling models to the UK, Paris, and Milan, only finding short pockets of time to visit my parents, usually during Christmas when the restaurant was closed.

"I'm only here for six weeks. Maybe seven."

"You might be seeing my face." Gary points at himself.

"Great." I step back into the grass to give him more room to maneuver. My heel sinks into the damp earth and I teeter backward, plunging my other heel into the soft soil as I try to right myself. A second later, I'm on my butt, soiling my Anne Klein trousers with the remnants of last night's rainfall.

Gary throws open his car door and dives toward me. With his help, I pull myself upright and extract my shoes from the ground.

"You dress fancy for an airplane ride," he says.

I know Gary well enough after our hour-long ride to know he'll think I'm silly for trying to outdress everyone in Cold Spring. With my water-soaked rear feeling the full extent of November's forty-degree chill, *I* think I'm silly.

"I dress for success," I say. "You never know when you might discover the next supermodel."

"In Indiana?"

"Sure. Why not? Good genes can happen anywhere."

"I guess."

He's not convinced. I don't feel like telling him I was born in Indiana and had my own somewhat impressive modeling career. I was discovered in New York City while attending Columbia University, but that doesn't matter.

Gary helps me over to the asphalt where my heels won't bore any new holes.

"Thanks again," I say.

"No problem. Get ya a pair of Crocs."

"I might."

He hops back into his Pacifica. I shuffle to the open parallel spot behind him and wave as he pulls away.

This side of the street is one way heading west, but you never know when a sophomore Driver's Ed student might try to head east into oncoming traffic. Not that I know anyone who has done that. I've heard rumors. I look both ways before crossing the one-way street. Just in case.

"And here I go," I say as I grab the antique brass door handle. I haven't run the café since high school. This should be...fine. Yes. It will be fine. I'll stay in the kitchen as much as possible. No one will notice I'm here.

"Edith Tucker!"

The shopkeeper bells barely have a chance to ding-a-ling before someone calls my name.

A grand staircase splits the building's first floor. The café is to the left. Our bakery is to the right where we sell donuts, muffins, and other pastries from seven o'clock to noon.

I peer into the dimly lit dining room. *We need better lighting in there.*

I've always thought we needed better lighting. With the high tin ceilings casting shadows on the space, the room's southern exposure doesn't cut it.

"Edith. Get over here," says Dottie.

Some things never change. The three elderly ladies, collectively known as the Silver Sweethearts, are always here by eleven o'clock. They order the eggs Benedict and rave over it like it's the first time they've tasted Grandma Tucker's top secret hollandaise sauce recipe.

All three women wave me over. Why did I think I could hide?

"We should move the Prime Meridian to this table," I say as I approach their customary round table next to the vintage silver Christmas tree. All the café regulars know to leave this spot open for the three matriarchs. "I could set my atomic watch to your lunchtime. If I had a watch."

"Who has watches these days?" Mabel, the oldest and tallest of the Sweethearts, says. "We all have these phones." She picks up her cell phone and lets it drop. "It's like an appendage now. Whenever I misplace it, I get phantom pains."

"I get pains every time I move," Dottie says.

"Those are real," Mabel answers. "Phantom pains are a psychological phenomenon."

"I still have a watch," Jean says. "I wind it every day."

"We *know*," Dottie says.

"Well." Jean slips her hands under the table and starts winding.

"Eadie Tucker," Dottie says. She spins around in her seat and outstretches her hands. "Let me look at you."

Dottie is the youngest and plumpest of the bunch. Gentle rolls of fat on her arms and midsection hide the svelte body of a former dancer. She did a stint on Broadway before touring the country with a professional dance troupe. When her dancing days were over, she opened a studio in Cold Spring and spent years teaching kids to tap and adults to ballroom dance.

When I was in high school, she still did the choreography for the Cold Spring Crooners, of which I was never a part. Mugging for a camera for two hours straight? Sure. I can do that. Singing and dancing in front of hundreds of people? No. Never. What a nightmare.

"I still look like me," I say.

"You look wiser and more mature," Dottie says with an approving nod.

"I do? I'm not sure I like that. Maybe my anti-aging regimen isn't working."

"Oh please," Mabel waves a bony hand at me. "I'm eighty-two years old. You're still a single cell yet to divide."

"Isn't that a strange thing to say," Jean mumbles, still winding her watch under the table.

Mabel leans toward her short, curly-haired friend. "What I mean is, the sperm hasn't even reached the egg."

Mabel taught science classes at the high school for forty years, including Anatomy and Physiology. She knows more about the human body than most people want to know, but she's happy to inform people anyway.

"I know what you *mean*," Jean says. "I had five children." She rests her forearms on the table. A plethora of gold bracelets adorn her wrists. "I just don't think Eadie appreciates being compared to an egg in a woman's vagina."

"A human egg is fertilized in a woman's fallopian tube."

"Do we have to be so graphic ladies?" Dottie cuts in, then she refocuses on me. "I'm sorry Mabel compared you to an ovum."

"I've been called worse things by angry New Yorkers," I say.

Mabel smooths her cropped hair with one hand and anchors the other on the thick-framed, blue glasses hanging from her neck. "You know what I mean, Eadie. You look fabulous. And *young*."

I open my mouth to answer, but Dottie beats me to it.

"You're here to take over while your father's out," she says matter-of-factly.

"And Mom," I say. "She has her hip replacement surgery in three weeks."

"Oh," Dottie shakes her head. "She's never here anymore."

"She isn't?"

"Don't you know?"

I don't know. Should I know?

"Eadie was on the cover of *Vogue* and walked the runway during New York Fashion Week," Mabel says to Jean.

Jean shoots her friend an exasperated look. "I know. I was alive last year too."

"Actually, the *Vogue* cover was three years ago," I say. "And it wasn't just me. There were five of us."

Dottie's chunky gold wedding ring bangs against the wood as she slaps the table. "That was three years ago? Really? Well, you are getting old. My goodness. We all are. How does time move so fast?"

"When did my mom stop working here?" I ask, trying not to sound like the clueless daughter that I apparently am.

"She can't stand more than an hour," Jean says to her brightly colored scarf as she rearranges it.

"And if she does," Dottie adds, "she's couchbound for the rest of the day so it's not worth the trouble. She has to do things in fits and spurts. Don't you talk to your parents?" Dottie says, her innocent expression and pink cheeks camouflaging her subtle judgment.

Mabel slides on her reading glasses and picks up her book. She's reading Emily Henry's latest. Not what one might expect an eighty-two-year-old former science teacher to read, but she's always preferred romance. "Leave the girl alone," she says after cracking her book open. "It's none of our business." She finishes her statement by shooting Dottie the stink-eye.

Dottie fluffs a curl on her forehead and huffs. "I just asked if they talk."

"You did it in that way you do when you're trying to needle people for information," Jean says softly.

"It was just a question. You don't mind questions do you, Eadie?"

"Not at all."

Dottie spins back to the table. "*See*?"

"Eadie, dear?" Mabel lowers her glasses and peers over them. "We ordered forty-five minutes ago. After you're settled in back there, would you mind checking on our eggs?"

I shift my bag behind me. "Absolutely. Sorry about that. I'll make sure they're right out."

Subtle nerves tickle my stomach. The lunch rush nerves. I remember this feeling.

"No hurry," Mabel says. She sticks her nose in her book while Jean and Dottie chatter about last week's town council meeting.

Deep breaths. I'll put my bag in the office. Check on Jupiter. Center myself and then—

"How long has it been since someone watered that tree?"

Chapter 3

The wilted Christmas tree in the corner sets off alarm bells in my head. Its dead limbs support hastily hung ornaments, and its needles litter the surrounding floor.

Years ago, Grandma started a tradition of displaying a live tree year-round, compliments of North Pole Nurseries, a local family-owned Christmas tree farm. After Grandma passed, I encouraged Dad to end the tradition by buying a lifelike artificial tree. He walked away mumbling something about his mother rolling in her grave. I mumbled something about Grandma jumping out of her grave and throttling him if the café burned down, especially if people were inside.

I walk over and reach into the dry tree stand. By the looks of the tree, it's been dry for weeks, and now we have a major fire hazard on our hands. After I fix whatever disaster is happening in the kitchen, I'm sending this tree to the woodchipper.

"Eadie, dear," Dottie calls. "Your pants are wet. Did you have an accident?" She giggles.

I look over my shoulder. "I did. Thank you for noticing."

"Do you need a Depends?" Dottie says loud enough for the entire restaurant to hear.

I roll my eyes playfully as I walk back over to her. "I fell in the grass."

Dottie giggles again and shrugs. "I have a pullup for my great-granddaughter in my purse. I'm ready for any emergency. Do you want it?"

"Let me check on your lunch," I say, shaking my head while giving Dottie's shoulder a pat.

The dining room's outdated decor looms large as I hurry to the kitchen. Of the four artificial Christmas trees in the room, three have burned-out strands of lights. Above the kitchen pass-through, the Santa Claus tapestry has faded to pink.

I've been away too long.

The only sign of life in the kitchen is the young woman scribbling in a notebook by the utility sink. Her messy pixie cut matches her dark eyeliner and black lipstick. A vintage apron covers her Ramones T-shirt and distressed wide-legged jeans.

When I worked here in high school, I knew all the staff. I owned the kitchen, checking orders, making sure the line was stocked, telling people decades older than me to step it up or else. Some days I even manned the cook station.

"Hello?"

The young woman pops her head up and closes her notebook. "Do you work here?"

This seems to miff her. "Uh...yeah."

Managers get more done with kindness, I remind myself. I thrust out my hand. "I'm Eadie, Weston's daughter. I'll be in charge here for the next few weeks."

"I figured," she says while sliding off the stool. She grabs my hand and gives it a weak shake. "I'm Lexis."

I wonder what the Silver Sweethearts think of her black lipstick? And ear gauges? And tongue piercing?

"Where's Annette?" I ask. "She usually works Saturdays."

Lexis slides back onto her stool and scratches the "Believe" tattoo on her forearm. "She took the day off. Her dog ate a rock again. He's in surgery."

My jaw drops. "This has happened more than once?"

"Yep. And a chocolate bar. And a sock. And a magnet."

"Oh. Wow. So..." I hope the pup is going to be okay, but I need to get back to business. "Why aren't you serving customers?"

"There's no food to serve. Obvi," Lexis says dully.

I cross my arms and shift my weight, sweeping my eyes around the empty kitchen. "And there's no food because why?" I say it calmly. Kindly.

"We ran out of eggs."

I should have flown home yesterday. Last week.

"Um," I say as I try not to panic. "The restaurant's name is Home for the Hollandaise."

Lexis looks at me like I'm an idiot. Her facial expressions seem a little one-note.

Maybe I should have provided more context. "I mean, how does a restaurant with a signature hollandaise sauce run out of eggs?"

Lexis shrugs.

"Do we have a cook, at least?"

"He's out back having a smoke."

I set my bag on the stainless-steel shelving unit behind me. "Don't worry. I've got this under control."

"I'm not worried," Lexis says.

Obvi.

I head to the back of the kitchen and exit through the service door. Our small, crumbling employee parking lot greets me. It abuts the alley, which provides access for the buildings along this side of Main Street and the homes one street over.

A couple of dumpsters sit to my right. To my left, our cook (I presume) sits on a retired park bench smoking a cigarette. His scruffy beard and loosely netted man bun give him a hippie vibe.

"Who's buying the eggs?" I blurt. "Do I need to go get eggs?"

He regards me like I don't belong in a dilapidated parking lot behind a deteriorating building in small-town Indiana. It might have something to do with the pantsuit and the three-inch heels.

Which is why I wore them. I wanted to stand out. As if being five feet ten inches—half of it neck—doesn't scream *she doesn't belong here*. It did in high school, which is why I left this place.

When his skepticism subsides, he takes a puff of his cigarette and then says, "They should be here in five minutes or so."

"How? Who? Where?"

"Reid went to scour the grocery stores."

A tiny shock needles through my veins. "Who's Reid?" I ask cautiously. I know a Reid. Surely my hippie cook is referring to a *different* Reid.

"Reid's the general manager."

"When did my dad hire a general manager?" I nearly yell. Dad doesn't need a general manager. He does the accounting, the hiring and firing, the ordering. By the looks of the place, Dad can't *afford* a general manager.

"I don't know. Ask him. I assume you're his daughter."

For some reason, his comment makes me realize I'm freezing. I wrap my arms around myself and turn my back to the wind to ward off the chill. "Yes. Sorry. I'm Eadie. I'll be in charge for the next several weeks. And you are?"

"Reid."

"*You're* Reid?"

"No. I'm Wyatt. Reid just turned into the alley."

I spin around as a Dodge Charger pulls up behind me. The throaty engine cuts and Reid, the Egg Man, steps out.

A puff of relief relaxes my arms. *Not* my Reid. Thank goodness.

He's bearded like Wyatt, but his beard is close-cut and well-trimmed on his neck. His dark-rimmed glasses match his brown hair but don't obscure his ocean-blue eyes.

His smile pierces through me and tickles my stomach.

Geez, Eadie, you have a boyfriend.

Yes. My boyfriend. Hayden.

I imagine Hayden's pouty lips, steel-gray eyes, chiseled model features, and wavy hair. He and I are perfect for each other. He's everything I've ever wanted. The yin to my yang. The concave to my convex.

I clear my throat.

"Eadie?" Reid says.

His voice is lower than Hayden's.

"Yes. I'm Weston's daughter. Do you have the eggs? We've never gotten a bad review from the Silver Sweethearts. I don't want today to be the first."

"Eadie. It's Reid."

"Um. Yeah. Reid, the Egg Man. You come bearing eggs."

"Reid Avory."

My stomach drops through the asphalt and bores a hole all the way to the Eastern Hemisphere.

How is the gorgeous lumberjack in front of me scrawny Reid Avory from high school? The Reid Avory who sat by quietly while his jock friends called me "Walking Stick." The Reid who played along when they thought it was funny to call me Eadie Tucker with an "F."

Oh, and that time he invited me to the Valentine's dance only to humiliate me by dumping raw eggs and feathers onto my head. Yeah. Reid Avory. Egg Man, indeed.

But that was ten years ago. I'm totally over the bullying. *Totally*.

"Hey," Reid says. "Let's just get it out of the way. I—"

"We're out of eggs!"

"I'm really sorry, I—"

"I'm really freezing and customers have been waiting for an hour, so prove your worth."

My dad hired Reid Avory as the general manager for a café that specializes in breakfast food, and this guy can't manage to stock enough eggs?

I'm over Reid, the bully. But Reid, the general manager, has some explaining to do.

Chapter 4

"How do you run out of eggs? How does that happen?"

Reid and I are hovering by the kitchen pass-through, waiting for Wyatt to make it through the backlog of orders. As soon as the Silver Sweethearts' dishes are ready, I'll personally deliver them to the ladies and let them know their meals are on the house.

"Your dad doesn't want to let go of inventory," Reid says. "I didn't realize we were low on eggs until this morning."

"Why did he hire you if you don't know how to monitor the stock?"

"I do. I just haven't been."

"What *do* you do then?"

"Accounting mostly. Your mom and dad are slowing down. They need help."

His words grate on my already frazzled nerves. "What's that supposed to mean?"

Reid steps back and raises his hands in defense. "Nothing. Nothing at all. I'm just a guy standing in front of a girl who seems grumpy."

I relax my stance and run my hand through my shoulder-length bob. "It's been a long day. I've been up since four. My pants are wet. Does anyone clean around here? Also, I have customers waiting for eggs Benedict and we have no eggs."

"*Had*. We had no eggs."

With my heels on, Reid is shorter than me. His blue flannel shirt has a fashionable vibe, loose enough for comfort, but tight enough to display muscular contours. The top and bottom buttons are undone, revealing the form-fitting T-shirt underneath. He's rolled up the sleeves, giving me a full view of his muscular forearms. Way more than I want to see.

"I wish you weren't here." I cross my arms.

"Um. Thanks?"

"You being here means Dad doesn't think he can take care of this place by himself."

"He's getting a pacemaker put in on Monday. So... I think it's pretty clear he needs help."

There's that grating tone again. I narrow my eyes. "Can he even afford to pay you?"

"That's something you'll have to take up with him."

"You're the accountant. You should know."

"He can afford me for now."

I glance around the kitchen. A decades-old patina covers the dual stainless-steel gas ranges. The cooktops need scouring. The shelves are a disarray of plates, bowls, and cups. Not to mention the dusty cobwebs in the corners. They won't pass inspection.

"I've been here less than an hour and I can already tell you have no idea what you're doing."

"I've been wanting to streamline things for two years."

Two years?

I glare at Reid so hard I nearly burn holes through his eye sockets. "You've been taking my dad's money for two years, and this place is still a wreck?"

"It's not a wreck. It's—"

"There are cobwebs in the kitchen!"

"Your dad is stubborn. I didn't want to overstep my bounds. He made it clear he wanted me in the back office, so I respected his wishes. I've been taking over duties bit by bit."

"The tree in the dining room is going to spontaneously combust!"

Reid slouches. "You're right. That's on me. Your mom used to water it, and your dad keeps forgetting. That's his thing, you know. That tree. I should have kept a better eye on it."

"Get rid of it today."

"I will."

"Don't replace it."

"I will."

I scrunch my lips. The pecking order needs to be established, and fast. A general manager may be higher than a kitchen manager in rank, but I'm the owner's daughter. My opinion takes precedence.

"*Don't* replace it."

Reid shifts his weight to one foot, crosses his arms, and holds my stare.

"If we get a bad review on Yelp today, I'm blaming you."

"You haven't been around. You don't know the dynamics. It's complicated."

"I worked here every summer for four years."

"Ten years ago. Things have changed."

"Obvi."

"Is that what people say in New York?"

There's an edge to his voice and I want to take a metal file and sheer it off. Instead, I say, "Do we have enough eggs to make it through today?"

"We should."

"What about Monday? And Tuesday. And Wednesday. And—"

"Do you want to know what happened to the eggs or do you want to keep looking down your nose while lecturing me?"

Instead of lowering my chin, I raise it a millimeter. "What happened, Egg Man?"

"Is that my name now?"

"Better than 'Walking Stick.'"

"You're still mad about that. Okay. Fine. Like I said, your dad wouldn't let me take over restocking. He missed the email from our supplier telling us the shipment was canceled because they had to cull half of their flock."

I gasp. "Why?"

"A virus. They didn't specify."

I lean against the stainless-steel countertop and cover my face with my hands. "How many birds?" I ask, my voice muffled.

"Hundreds."

The softest spot in my heart belongs to bugs, but all the animal kingdom reserves a special place in there. I hate it when animals suffer.

"Your dad is particular about his eggs."

"I know."

"They were free-range birds. Your Grandma's hollandaise sauce recipe requires dark orange yolks."

"I know."

"So it wasn't easy to find a new supplier."

I lower my hands. "What about Dad's chickens?"

My dad has had a chicken coop my entire life. At one point he had fifty chickens. I'm not sure how many he has now.

"I collected the eggs this morning, but it wasn't enough. I ran around town buying the best quality eggs I could find, including stopping by local farmers to see what they could give me. I know what goes on around here, and I care. I lined up a new supplier that should live up to your dad's standards. Deliveries start Monday."

"Table fifteen up," Wyatt calls.

It's the Silver Sweethearts table. "Got it," I yell. I look over at Lexis who is back on her stool scribbling in her notebook. "Lexis, can you come with me and refill their waters?"

"Sure, boss," she says, her tone as dull as her expression.

"Is everyone disrespectful around here?" I mumble.

"You have to earn their respect," Reid says in a low voice. "Especially Lexis's."

"Thanks for the tip, Egg Man."

Reid bristles. "I'll let you take it from here."

First order of business: ditch the pumps and go barefoot. The health department isn't here. This is about survival.

Half an hour later, Wyatt has cleared the backlog and a few parties are waiting in the bakery for their turns in the dining room. The pace is steady for a couple more hours while I fall into an easy rhythm. Muscle memory guides me along the well-worn path from Wyatt to the pass-through where Lexis grabs the food and serves our customers.

At two thirty, half an hour before closing, the dining room thins out, and I have a moment to think.

"Jupiter!"

Lexis casts me a confused look as she grabs the plates for table four. "Uh... Neptune?"

"I forgot about him! He's been in the dark all day!"

The random weirdness of my comment seems to intrigue Lexis. She lifts a shoulder before carrying the plates away.

I run around to the shelves and grab my bag, tear open the zipper, and peer inside. Jupiter is looking up at me, his eyes glittering in the bright fluorescents. "Sorry buddy. Let me get you out of there."

With the dining room slowly emptying, I trust Lexis can handle the remaining crowd. Tucking my bag under my arm, I round the prep station and beeline into the office.

The twelve-by-twelve office is dark, windowless, cramped, and it stinks like rancid oil. A halo of light surrounds Reid's body as he scrolls through something on his computer screen.

"No lights?" I flip the switch expecting the round ceiling light to turn on. Nothing happens. I flip it a few more times. Maybe it needs to be primed like a water pump.

"It doesn't work," Reid says without spinning around.

"Why am I not surprised?"

"We use desk lamps." He reaches over and turns his on.

Dad's desk is opposite Reid's. It looked better in the dark. Now I can see his clutter in its fullness.

"Dad's organizational skills haven't improved," I say. "In fact, they've gotten worse."

"Oh. It's organized. He knows where to find everything in that mess." Reid still hasn't turned around to look at me.

"Well, it can't stay this way." I scoot a pile of papers to the side, pull out Jupiter's terrarium and set it on the desk, and then I go to work consolidating invoices, pamphlets, magazines, almost any and every kind of paper you can imagine.

Reid spins around and lurches forward in his chair. "I mean it. He knows where everything is. If you move it—"

I pick up a two-inch stack of paper, many of the pieces curled at the corners, and plop it onto the pile I've created.

"—he won't be able to find anything," Reid finishes. He settles back in his chair and slowly swivels to his computer.

"I'll sort through everything, file what needs filing, and throw away the junk. Like this." I grab an ad for Egyptian cotton table linens. The glossy paper is warped by a coffee ring. It pops away from the desktop and leaves behind a patch of the image.

"He's not going to like it," Reid cautions.

"I'm his daughter. He won't mind."

"You know him better than I do. I only work with him every day."

I straighten and scowl at the back of Reid's head. "He changed my diapers."

"Yep. You've got that on me."

I want to bark out a snarky response, but Reid and I were just reacquainted today. Ten years have passed. We're relative strangers. And I have been a bit difficult.

"Would he be happier if you looked through it?" I ask.

Reid peers over his shoulder at me. "Maybe."

"Fine."

I've finally uncovered Dad's desk lamp, so I flip it on and scoot Jupiter under the light.

"What's that?" Reid leans in for a closer look.

"Jupiter."

"Jupiter is a gas giant that's one-tenth the size of the sun."

I smirk at him. "I thought I was the nerd."

Reid's face relaxes. "It's a bug, isn't it? You're still into bugs."

"Jupiter is an arachnid, which technically isn't a bug. But they're both arthropods."

"You're right. You are the nerd."

Chapter 5

"I don't think so. No. That's not a pet," Reid says as he looks down at the fuzzy spider crawling on my hand.

"He's hairy. Dogs are hairy. Cats are hairy. Hairy is cute."

"Bigfoot is hairy, and people are afraid of him."

"Do you think I'd let Bigfoot crawl around on my hand? Think about it. There's a fatal flaw in your reasoning. I don't own a shrink ray."

"Your eyes are shrink rays," Reid mutters.

"I like spiders," a voice says behind me. Lexis is leaning on the doorjamb with her arms folded.

"Do you want to meet him?" I beckon her into the office with a tilt of my head.

"Sure." She enters tentatively, stops a couple of feet away, and leans over.

"Here, let me put him in the light." I sit in Dad's office chair and position Jupiter under the desk lamp. Lexis edges closer and peers at him. He waves his pedipalps at her and dances back-and-forth on my knuckle.

"He's showing off," I say.

"Does he have a personality?"

"Yes. He's very persnickety. Do you want to hold him?"

Lexis's face brightens. I think I'm gaining her respect.

She holds out her hand and I carefully deposit Jupiter onto her palm. He goes crazy for a second, eliciting a yelp from Lexis, but he finally calms down. As Lexis studies his details, I rattle off facts about jumping spiders.

"Jumpin' Jupiter," Lexis says when I'm finished.

"Yes!" I look over my shoulder at Reid. "She gets it."

"You two are weird."

"That's a microaggression," Lexis counters.

"He's good at those," I quip.

"Fine." Reid jumps to his feet. "Give me the spider."

I shoot him a skeptical look. "Are you sure you can handle it? Jupiter is delicate."

"Bugs wear their skeletons on the outside," Reid says. "They can fall from the ceiling to the floor and scurry away unscathed."

"He's not a bug," Lexis says. "He's an arachnid. It's different. Haven't you seen *Spiderman* or read any of the billions of comics written about him?"

I'm liking this girl more and more.

"Also." Her voice gains confidence as she banters with Reid. "Do you know how small a nerve is?"

Reid looks at Lexis blankly. He's not following her line of reasoning, but I am.

"Small enough to fit inside a spider," she announces.

"Spiders have one nerve?" Reid says it with a laugh.

"No, dummy. My point is, spiders can feel pain."

"That's debatable."

"Hold out your hand." Lexis glances at me. "Are you okay with this?"

"As long as he doesn't squeal. Jupiter doesn't like high-pitched noises."

"I *won't* squeal," Reid says.

I'm not sure about this. His muscles are as stiff as the Statue of David. "Go ahead," I say despite my misgivings.

Lexis carefully transfers Jupiter onto Reid's knuckle. His shoulders seize the moment Jupiter's scopulae touch his skin. I step in closer, ever the protective spider mom.

"How is it?" Lexis asks.

"Do these bite?"

"All spiders bite," I say.

"Are they venomous?"

"Only when they sense fear."

Reid narrows his eyes at me. I step closer.

"Here. Give him to me." I wave Reid over, but he jerks his hand away.

"No. I'm fine. This isn't as bad as I thought it would be."

"Embrace your fears," Lexis says. "It makes you a stronger person."

"Yeah. It does." Reid lifts Jupiter to his face and sniffs.

"What are you doing?" I say distrustfully. "He doesn't like that."

"Doesn't like wh—?"

Jupiter leaps onto Reid's nose. Reid squeals like a baby dolphin. In response, Jupiter jumps to Reid's forehead while Reid flails his arms like he's falling from a ten-story building.

"Stand still!" I yell, a thousand pounds of tension in my voice.

"Get it off!"

"I'm trying. Don't move. You're making him jump!"

Reid bends over. "I think he's in my hair. Is he in my hair?" He combs his quivering fingers through his thick mane of brown waves.

"I knew I shouldn't have let you hold him," I growl.

"I'm sorry." Lexis shrinks back through the open doorway.

I've lost sight of Jupiter, so I join Reid and claw through his very thick, very soft hair. "It's not your fault," I assure Lexis. "It's—There he is! Jupiter, c'mere. No!"

My pet spider jumps to the floor. Before I can catch him, he hops like a bunny across the tile and scurries under Reid's desk. I drop to the floor and squint. "I can hardly see because it's so freaking dark in here! Can someone turn on the light?"

Lexis drops to her knees beside me and angles her phone's flashlight into the darkness. "Do you see him?"

"No." The weight of this day, everything about it makes my voice wobble.

"We'll find him," Lexis says softly.

"I'm—I'm sorry," Reid stammers behind me. "He just started jumping everywhere."

"He's a jumping spider!" Lexis and I holler in unison.

"Can we move the desk?" Reid asks.

I stand to help him. "Carefully."

For the next ten minutes, the three of us scour the office, looking in nooks and crannies and corners and cracks. As the minutes pass, the effort seems increasingly hopeless. Eventually, I drop into Dad's office chair, fold myself in half at the waist, and cover my face.

I'm not going to cry. Yet.

"How long can he live outside of his cage?" Lexis asks.

"A few days? Maybe? I'm not sure. I've always been extra careful." My voice catches in my throat. I take a deep breath through my nose and release it through my mouth.

"I could get you a new one," Reid says.

I lift my head and glare at him. "I've had Jupiter for a year and a half."

"Oh." He falls back against the desk and shoves his hands in his pockets. "I just can't imagine getting that attached to a spider."

His comment sets off a rocket in my core. I shoot out of my seat and grab my bag. "I'm assuming you know how to close this place up?" I say to Lexis.

"Sure." She slouches and interlocks her hands in front of her.

"I'm going home," I say. "I need a nap."

"Do you need a ride?" Reid asks.

"I'll walk."

"In your heels?"

"I've walked up and down runways in worse."

"Do you have a coat?"

I spin toward Reid. "Do you have a plane ticket ho—?" My coat hits me in the face. I wrangle it off my head. "Did you have to throw it?"

"It was a reflex. Like when you're at a haunted house and you get spooked. Sorry."

"What spooked you?" I drill my eyes into his.

"Um. Nothing." He scratches his head. "I have to balance the register drawer. While I'm at it, I'll keep an eye out for the..."

"For Ms. Tucker's pet," Lexis finishes, emphasis on the word "pet."

I drop my bag to slide on my coat. "You don't have to call me 'Ms.' It makes me shudder."

"Sorry."

"It's Eadie."

Lexis nods and backs out of the doorway to let me through.

"See you Monday," I say as I cross the threshold.

Chapter 6

A cold front moved in an hour ago, creating a ceiling of white and gray clouds that are releasing miniature snowflakes, their random paths determined by the whims of nature. A fifteen-mile-an-hour wind is refreshing in the heat of the summer. Today, it's a numbing slap in the face. I pull up my hood and tighten the strings, which gives me some reprieve.

Cold Spring's most dominant and memorable feature is the Spring Creek Canal. It runs through the center of town with Main Street flanking both sides. Broad strips of grass and maple trees line the canal, the mature trees towering over the water at even intervals.

Twenty years ago, the town received a grant to beautify the canal. Its banks were bricked, and metal railings, sidewalks, antique lamps, and benches were installed, giving the waterway a romantic European feel.

The canal cuts across a wide bend in Spring Creek. It was built in 1859 to transport goods and materials to and from the region's factories and mills. After the construction, Cold Spring quickly became a hub for manufacturers to store their goods. Warehouses built up along the south side of Main Street, earning the title "Warehouse Row."

The warehouses are currently home to shops like Ned's Tool Shed, a mom-and-pop hardware store, and The Bean Mill, which makes the county's best lattes. The upper floors of many of the old warehouses are empty. At one time, a proposal was brought before the town council to convert several of the buildings into condos. I don't know what came of it.

Most of the retail spaces on this side of the street are occupied, an improvement since the last time I was in town. Cold Spring has seasonal festivals all year round that attract out-of-towners, but the main tourist season is during summer when people can peruse the shops unencumbered by coats, hats, and gloves. During the cold months, the shops work harder to make ends meet, but the lack of empty storefronts indicates the town's economy might be improving.

My parents' 1940s bungalow is on Marsh Street, two blocks down, three blocks over. As my feet pound against the concrete in these heels, I realize how long the day has been and how I want to slide into a cozy pair of slippers right this moment.

By the time I reach Cross Street, I've passed Bound to Read, a cozy-looking used bookstore, Bloomfields, the local flower shop, and a new record store called The Vinyl Depot. A few stores dot Cross Street, downtown's secondary thoroughfare. As I pass a store called The Garment Swap, I glance in the glowing window and stop in my tracks.

"Gracelyn?"

We stare at each other through the window for a moment, both of our mouths agape. Seconds later, I burst through the door and run to my high school friend. She rounds the check-out counter and accepts my exuberant hug.

"What are you doing here?" she squeals.

I step back and look at her. "What are *you* doing here? Is this your store?"

Gracelyn's cheeks blush with pride. She stands a little straighter and nods.

"That's amazing!"

I sweep my eyes across the chic, freshly painted retail space. "You sell used clothing?"

"New and used. I started with a clothing exchange, and now I'm sticking my toe into retail sales with a small inventory."

Gracelyn's store reflects her style, relaxed but sophisticated. Her low ponytail curls around the front and rests on her collarbone like an accessory to her linen tunic and charm necklace.

When we were growing up, she always had an eye for style, out-doing me in every way, which—to be fair—wasn't hard. My go-to style back then was witty science T-shirts and a few pairs of joggers that I rotated through. Gracelyn always came to school with a full ensemble, from the makeup to the jewelry to the shoes.

We met in fourth grade when her parents moved to town. Her mom started teaching at one of the elementaries and her dad commuted to a job in Indianapolis that easily paid the bills, hence Gracelyn's extensive wardrobe. I was never jealous. She never made me feel less-than. And she bit back at anyone who made fun of my "noodle arms" and "ostrich neck."

After graduation, we lost touch, mostly my fault. I got lost in New York City, quite literally at times, sucked in by the promise of a glamorous modeling career, which I now know is anything but.

"Oh, my goodness, you were on the cover of *Vogue*." Gracelyn covers her mouth.

I shrug, remembering that day in the hot California desert. For ten hours, I wore a Victorian dress with a hoop skirt under layers of fabric and a corset that was cinched so tightly that I had acid reflux for days. Glamorous indeed.

Gracelyn runs around the counter and pulls out a copy of the three-year-old June issue. "I still have it! Can you sign it?"

"Gracelyn, no. I can't do that. I—"

"Please?" Her brown eyes become pleading.

I concede, which makes Gracelyn inordinately happy. We spend the next ten minutes catching up on the last ten years. I spend five more minutes bragging about Hayden, showing her pictures that elicit gushing and swooning.

"He's everything you dreamed of," she says. "You said you were going to leave Cold Spring and find a guy that put all the men here to shame. Do you remember that time we put Jaden's picture on my dad's dartboard and spent forever trying to pierce out his eyes?"

I laugh. "Did we ever manage to?"

"I think we gave up and sent the picture through the paper shredder. Then we taped the strips back together into a Franken-Jaden."

Her comment jogs my memory and I double over. "We were such dorks."

"I still am."

"Same."

When I tell her why I'm in town, concern etches the skin around her eyes. I assure her my mom and dad's procedures are routine. Mostly. Then I tell her about my luggage fiasco, and she starts zooming through the clothing racks pulling shirts, pants, sweaters, pajamas. She stuffs them into a bag and hands it to me.

"No charge."

"Gracelyn."

"No charge," she says emphatically.

"I can pay."

"Just bring me some of your secondhand clothes sometime. I'm sure your closet is overflowing with name-brand treasures."

"It is," I say with zero humility and then we burst out laughing.

I eye a pair of fuzzy, pink slippers on display behind the counter. "How much are those?" I point.

Gracelyn grabs them. "Yes. You need these. Um…" She examines them for a moment. "Ten bucks."

"Deal."

I pay. We say our goodbyes for now. Gracelyn promises to visit Home for the Hollandaise, and then I'm back in the needling cold wondering why I suddenly feel upset despite my jovial conversation with Gracelyn.

Then I remember.

Reid Avory lost Jupiter. I'm spiderless. A spider widow.

I set my jaw and double my pace.

That nap can't come soon enough.

Chapter 7

Marsh Street, with its aging sidewalks and mature trees, is a typical Cold Spring thoroughfare. Several years ago, the road surface was restored to its original brick, an effort to increase the town's charm and make it more appealing to Indianapolis residents looking to relocate or spend the afternoon in small-town America. The houses along the street range from mid-century bungalows to one-hundred-year-old brightly sided Victorians with complementary trim colors designed to make each house stand out from the others.

By the time I reach my parents' house, my feet feel like they've been ravaged by a rabid porcupine. I stagger up the steps to their brown-brick bungalow, clutching the masonry railing for support.

My luggage is sitting by the front door. If I wasn't exhausted, I'd be ecstatic. I settle for being mildly pleased that my Converse All Stars will be accompanying me to church tomorrow instead of these three-inch torture devices. In anticipation, I pull them off and throw them into the bag from The Garment Swap.

The cold concrete soothes my throbbing feet. I close my eyes and enjoy the mini spa treatment before pushing through the front door.

The dogs bark in greeting. Koda and Tully, my mom and dad's Golden Retrievers come running, their claws clicking against the wood floor. Nine-year-old Tully settles quickly and perches at my feet while Koda jumps for my hands.

"Whoa. Settle down."

I land a few pets on Koda's head, and then I kneel and give Tully a good squeeze. She licks my cheek eagerly, showing off the new gray hairs around her nose.

Mom dries her hands with a towel as she limps in from the kitchen. Her pure white hair is pulled back in a ponytail giving her youthful, rosy skin all the attention.

"I thought you were never coming," she says.

"I closed the café."

Mom waves dismissively. "You didn't have to do that."

"I told Dad I would."

She scoffs and then leans in for a hug. "A Tucker doesn't have to be there every day of the year. How was your flight?" she asks when she lets go, leaving a hint of her light floral perfume on my clothing.

"Honestly?"

"Was it horrendous?"

"Pretty much."

"I've been hearing about the airlines on the news. It sounds like they're imploding."

"Mauve thinks so."

This garners a confused look from Mom, so I explain my day to her as briefly as possible, stopping before Jupiter's jumping incident. I don't feel like rehashing it. It's too raw.

"You've been up since four?"

I nod. "Do you mind if I take a nap? We can catch up later."

"Sure."

"Where's Dad?"

"He's asleep in the den."

"Is he feeling okay?"

"As well as he can."

I'm too tired to probe her with more questions. Instead, I drag my suitcase up the steps and make a hard left into my old bedroom. Mom redecorated it after I graduated from high school, turning it into a proper guest room. She left one of my insect terrariums under the window, filling it with succulents and old logs. Jupiter was going to have a palace.

A sense of overwhelm rises from my gut. I collapse onto the bed and cover my face. Tears spurt from my eyes, but I don't sob. I just let them flow into my palms and wipe my eyes when I think I've shed enough.

It's not just losing Jupiter. It's the out-of-date café. My dad going into surgery. Mom needing a new hip. My parents aging while I've been gallivanting in Paris, London, and L.A.

Rather than think about it all, I peel back the covers, slide into bed, and descend into sleep.

I wake up at quarter till six with thoughts swarming my head. Is Jupiter safe in that dusty old office? Will he find food and water? What does Mom mean when she says Dad's feeling "as well as he can?" Is he worse off than I realize?

While I've been living at breakneck speed in New York City, my parents have been living at a slower pace, slowly growing older without me. I've been missing out on time with them. Time that is running shorter by the day.

What if something goes wrong during Dad's surgery? Am I prepared for the worst?

The tiny kernel of dread in my stomach tells me I'm not prepared. Not at all.

I shove the comforter off my legs and plant my feet onto the chilly floor. A thin ribbon of cold streams through a crack in the old window, making me shiver. Using the throw blanket as a shawl, I tiptoe over to The Garment Swap bag, quickly change into a sweatshirt and pajama pants, and then slide my feet into the fuzzy, pink slippers.

After diving back under the covers, I grab my phone from the nightstand and send Hayden a text. Surely, he's home by now, sitting on the couch with a seltzer and a HelloFresh meal.

Hey. I'm finally home. It was a rough day. I lost Jupiter at the café. I have no idea where he is. Super bummed.

I expect an *OMG, you lost Jupiter?* Or an *I'm sorry you had a bad day*, but my screen remains blank.

Long days are common in the modeling world. He's probably still on set. Yes. That's it. He's not ignoring me.

I let it go for now and head downstairs. When I round the newel post, I find Dad reclined in the living room watching a documentary about aliens.

"Hey, Dad." I run over and bend down to give him a hug. He feels sturdy, like I remember.

"Hey there, Lovebug. Long time no see."

"I know, Dad. I'm sorry."

"Don't worry. I know you have all kinds of things to do and places to be."

"Nowhere is more important than being here. How's your heart?"

Dad scratches his mottled scalp. A couple of years ago, he had a basal cell carcinoma removed leaving a taut, pink scar. "They got me on all kinds of medicines to keep it running. But I should be good as new once I get my device."

"You'll be the bionic man."

He rests a hand on the slight swell of his stomach. "I suppose."

"What's for dinner? It smells good in here."

"I think your mom's got some meatloaf in the oven. And some funeral potatoes."

"That sounds ominous."

"Your mom always did like to have contingency plans."

I swat Dad's arm. "Ha ha. Very funny. I guess I'll go in to help."

"She'd appreciate that. Glad to have you home."

Like the house's windows, the kitchen isn't up to modern standards. The 1980s cabinets are sturdy and styled plainly, which, to my frugal parents, means there's no need to upgrade. The white subway tile backsplash and penny tiles give the room a historic charm.

Mom bends over and pulls the meatloaf from the oven. "Hey, hon," she says in her IU sweatshirt and black sweatpants, her hair still pulled back in a neat ponytail. She walks the loaf pan over to the counter, wincing and limping.

"Let me take over."

"No, no, I got it." She limps to the Crock-pot and pulls off the lid. "Actually, can you set the table? We're eating in the dining room tonight."

"Sure." I grab plates, silverware, and napkins, and flip the switch to illuminate the dining room.

The Craftsman decor creates a warm and inviting atmosphere. Grandma collected the furniture during her golden years, single-handedly furnishing half of Mom and Dad's house. The table pairs with the buffet, both made of solid oak with a natural finish and clean lines. An antique chandelier bathes our faces in a soft glow as we sit and prepare to eat.

Dad sits at the head of the table and studies his place setting, picking up his fork, inspecting it like he's a caveman who has never seen silver utensils before. I furrow my brow at him. "Dad?"

"Eadie set the table," Mom says. "She put the fork on the right side of the plate."

His eyes flicker with recognition. Without a word, he centers his plate and swaps the knife with the fork, carefully placing them equidistant from the plate. "The fork goes on the left," he grumbles.

I raise an eyebrow at Mom, but she looks down at her food.

Dad's always been a little particular. When I was younger, he collected guns and spent hours in the basement taking them apart and cleaning them. Meanwhile, his den upstairs was a mess of books, loose papers, and boxes full of items he bought online but never got around to opening. In contrast, he kept the chicken coop so clean you could eat off the floor. That's saying a lot considering the number of chickens meandering in and out of the coop. His particularness has always been selective, and I guess nothing has changed.

I dish out my food and take a drink of lemonade before launching into a discussion. "You didn't tell me you hired a general manager."

"Did we have to?" Mom asks.

"I guess not. But I expected to be top of the pecking order."

"You're always top of the pecking order," Dad says. "You're a Tucker. We own the place. Reid answers to you, not the other way around."

"Yeah. Reid." I set down my fork. "I was surprised to see him."

"You know Reid from church," Mom says. "You two went to camp together."

"He also bullied me in high school. Or he enabled it." I pick up my fork again and shovel in a bite of potatoes. The rich cheese warms my palette and satisfies my hunger.

"Reid Avory?" Mom says, looking incredulous. "He bullied you?"

"His friends did, and he did nothing to stop it. Anyway... He said he's been working at the café for two years."

Mom dabs the corners of her mouth with her napkin. "If it's been that long it doesn't feel like it."

"It looks like it's been two years since anyone cleaned the cobwebs from the ceiling."

"Reid knows I like doing things a certain way," Dad says, his eyes focused on his food rather than me.

"The Health Department likes things done a certain way too."

"We have no problems with the Health Department," Dad replies.

"He's right," Mom says. "We've never gotten a bad report."

"The kitchen's never had cobwebs."

Dad's hands tighten around his silverware. He glares at me with a strange detachment. I shrink back and glance at Mom for support. She shakes her head.

"You have strong opinions after a single visit," Dad says, "when the rest of us have been there day after day taking care of things while you were gone."

I open my mouth, but no sound comes out. Tears threaten to emerge, but I fight them back. "You're right. I'm sorry, Dad. I know you work hard. I shouldn't be asking so many questions."

Dad's boiling expression lingers for a moment before his demeanor dissolves into remorse mixed with confusion. He glances at Mom and then back at me.

"I—" he falters. "I'm sorry, Lovebug. I guess I'm a little punchy. You're right. The kitchen needs a scrub. You can ask as many questions as you want." He refocuses on his meatloaf.

I rub my napkin between my thumb and forefinger. Mom delicately works through her food, her head down too, offering me no insight into Dad's outburst.

I take another drink as the uncomfortable mood in the room renders us all mute. Halfway through my meatloaf, I decide it's safe to talk again. I distract them with a play-by-play of my day, including the antics at the airport, talkative Gary, falling on my butt in the grass, and easing back into my role as kitchen manager. As I recount my adventures, their expressions and postures relax.

The rest of dinner goes smoothly. A niggling sense that something isn't quite right with Dad hampers my enjoyment of Mom's food, but I keep my worries to myself.

It's nine thirty, I'm in bed, and Hayden still hasn't texted me back. There's no way he's still at the photo shoot. I need to find out what's up.

Instead of texting him, I hit the FaceTime option. His phone rings while I rap my fingers against the comforter. On the seventh ring, his face appears. The odd angle of the camera makes his chin ginormous and his eyes small pools of shadow.

It doesn't matter how camera-ready a face is, FaceTime and poor lighting can make a person look downright homely. He never minds unflattering angles, but I do. I scoot onto my right hip to capture the lamplight on both sides of my face, and I adjust my camera angle to show Hayden my best side.

"Long day?" I ask.

"Yeah, I suppose." He's lounging on the couch with his TV chattering in the background.

How do you "suppose" you have a long day? Either you do or you don't. I know better than to unleash into analytics with Hayden though, so instead, I say, "Did you get my texts?"

"Yeah."

I wait for more, but he just scratches his forehead and yawns.

"You seem tired."

"Yeah, I am." He sits up and leans into the camera.

"I *suppose* that means you had a long day?"

He nods, unloosing a dark brown curl that falls onto his forehead. Despite gravity tugging on his cheeks, this angle provides a better view of his squared-off chin and sharp cheekbones. His sleepy expression makes me want to crawl into bed with him and snuggle. Just snuggle. We haven't done anything more than that, and he's okay waiting.

When I ask him how his photo shoot went, he tells me he spent five hours in a plastic bubble.

"What?" I spurt. "Did you run out of oxygen?"

"No, I was wearing the bubble."

I try to imagine Hayden as a human balloon. "Were you wearing clothes underneath?"

"Just underwear." He smirks, sending a shiver through me. Man, I love his dimples.

Hayden and I met on a photo shoot in Cancun. I was still modeling at the time, and we spent an entire day in the aqua-blue ocean, him scantily clad in a Speedo and me in a revealing string bikini. I clutched onto his biceps all day while the waves buffeted our bodies, both of us pouting into the camera like broody lovers.

"Why didn't you text me back?" I ask.

"I was wearing a bubble."

The thought of Hayden trying to look sultry as a human bubble makes me laugh hysterically. His smirk turns into a full smile as he watches me belly laugh.

"Did you take potty breaks?" I say after I've calmed down enough to talk.

"Nope. I couldn't get to my phone either. Sorry." He threads his fingers through his hair and his curls tumble seductively back into place.

That's the problem with dating a drop-dead gorgeous male model. The luxurious hair. The sizzling stare. The strikingly geometric bone structure highlighted by plump, pouty lips. It's an equation that adds up to "chick magnet."

My boyfriend is a chick magnet in New York City without me for six weeks. Or seven.

"You lost Jupiter?" he asks in a knee-buckling baritone.

"I didn't lose him. Reid did. But I let Reid have him so…"

"Who's Reid?"

"My parents' general manager. He's supposed to be running the café, but the place is so disorganized. I don't have much confidence in him."

"If your parents have a general manager, why do they need you to fill in?"

"To clean up the place, apparently. Starting with the cobwebs."

Hayden winces. "The kitchen has cobwebs?"

"And an overabundance of disorganization."

"How long are you going to be gone?"

"Didn't I tell you?" I glance at Jupiter's home away from home, the bug palace under the drafty window. If—I mean, *when* I find Jupiter, I'll have to move the terrarium to the other side of the room and buy a heat lamp.

"Eight weeks?"

"No. Six. I'll be back after Christmas."

Hayden rubs his face. "Are we going to call every day?"

"Do you want to?"

Hayden tilts his forehead toward the phone. "Don't start."

"What? We don't have to talk if you're going to get sick of me."

He rolls his eyes.

"Just tell me what you want."

"I want you back here. It's the holiday season. I don't want to go to all the parties by myself."

We frequently attend parties with top models in the business, and I'm usually there to run defense when they unabashedly vie for ownership of Haden's rare beauty. "Just don't lock eyes with any gorgeous women."

Hayden laughs. "It's kind of a job requirement. It's how I met you."

Exactly.

"Just hang out with men."

"I might be safer with women."

"Hayden!"

"You know what I mean. It's equal opportunity these days. I've got offers coming from both sides."

My chest constricts. I force a laugh. "Just make sure you don't take anyone up on them."

"Sure."

"Sure meaning 'yes' or 'no?'"

Hayden flashes me an are-you-joking-face.

No, I'm not. I'm not joking at all. My chest still feels tight.

"I'm not going to take anyone up on any offers," he says softly with a reassuring smile. I lap it up. It's the first time we've really connected today. This temporary long-distance thing might be harder than I thought.

I always wanted to land a gorgeous guy, someone to put all my high school classmates to shame. I fantasized about walking into our ten- or fifteen-year reunion looking hot with a hottie on my arm. My former bullies are so ashamed that they crawl under the table and wail.

It's a fantasy. It can be a little over the top.

However, I didn't realize dating a gorgeous, sought-after guy would feel so complicated.

"Okay. Well. I'm tired," Hayden says.

And there goes our connection. But I'm tired too, so I don't balk.

We both say "I love you" and end the call. It's something we've only been saying for a few months. He likes to take things slowly which works for me. Why rush when we have the rest of our lives?

Yeah. He doesn't know it yet, but he's the one. And I'm committed to waiting patiently until he figures it out.

Chapter 8

I park Mom's 1999 Chevy Lumina behind the café, grab the old floor lamp that I found in Mom and Dad's attic, and hurry from the car to the service door. I can't believe the car still runs. Mom and Dad have a newer Equinox. The Lumina is just a back-up in case they need to be two separate places at once. It only has fifty-thousand miles on it and not a speck of rust.

It's five thirty in the morning. I'm the first to arrive, so I flip on the light, my eyes peeled for a furry spider no bigger than a quarter.

I spent two hours here after church yesterday searching for Jupiter. This is an old building. Corners don't match up, plaster is cracked. He could be in the walls making a nest from one-hundred-dred-year-old newspapers.

"Jupiter," I call.

He's responded to his name before. It was a controlled experiment with repeatable results. If he's nearby, he might come running.

People don't understand the bond between a woman and her spider. They think all eight-legged creatures are disposable. When they see one on the ceiling, their first instinct is to kill it instead of scooping it up and releasing it outside.

Who are we to say a spider's life has no value? What if giant aliens came to earth and started squashing us? There would be moral outrage.

I sigh. Jupiter is still hiding.

I flip the switch in the office before remembering the overhead light doesn't work which is why I'm holding a brass floor lamp from 1987. I turn on my desk lamp and shove boxes out of the corner to set the lamp near an outlet, and then I turn it on to properly light the room.

"Jupiter," I try again. Maybe the light woke him up.

I grab my phone, turn on the flashlight, get down on my hands and knees, and study the dust bunnies under Reid's desk for the umpteenth time.

"Still can't find him?"

I yelp and spin around, my bum landing on the floor like I'm getting ready for the crabwalk.

Speaking of my bum, seconds ago it was facing the office doorway, poised in the air, putting me in a rather compromising position. And Reid saw it all.

"What are you doing here?" I ask.

"I work here. What's with the new lamp?"

"I was looking for Jupiter under your desk."

"I saw that. I saw…" He makes a circle with his thumbs and forefingers. "…all that."

"I had no idea you'd be here this early."

"I'm always here this early."

"The dining room doesn't open until seven."

"I need fifteen minutes of quiet before the staff starts coming in."

I can see up Reid's nose. This angle isn't working for me. He offers his hand to help me up.

"I got it." I push myself to my feet and brush the dust off my black capris.

In my Converse All Stars, Reid and I are the same height. He's wearing a fitted flannel again so I can see the swell of his pecs, sleeves rolled up to his elbows revealing his veiny forearms and his muscular hands. My stomach flutters, betraying me.

I duck my head and round him to catch a breath of fresh air in the kitchen.

"What are you doing?" he asks, following.

"Are we going to do this?"

"Do what?"

"Keep tabs on each other."

"We're the only two here. It's natural to talk."

"I'm making coffee."

"I usually make the coffee."

I turn around, my stomach fluttering again at the sight of his rugged build, at the way his hands are stuffed confidently into his jeans pockets. He wasn't built like this in high school. Not even close.

"Dad says I'm in charge."

Reid lifts his hands and turns on his heel. "Fine." He disappears into the office. "I like mine black."

I don't even want coffee. But I couldn't tell him I needed to get out of that office because the sight of his hands made me short of breath. I wonder if Hayden is awake yet?

I hover by the coffee maker as it brews, pour Reid a mug, and head back into the office. After depositing the mug on Reid's desk, I sit in front of Dad's computer and wait for it to boot up.

"You're not drinking any?" Reid asks.

"I changed my mind."

This office is way too small.

The password screen flashes on my monitor, and I stare at it for several moments trying to decode Dad's brain. What would he set his password to? Password123?

I try it. No dice.

Reid clears his throat. I look over my shoulder. He's holding a green Post-it note with Dad's password on it. "He told me to give you this."

I swipe it from him and turn back around.

"You're welcome," I hear him say under his breath.

"You owe me," I mumble back as I gaze at Jupiter's empty terrarium.

"I spent three hours looking for your bug last night."

I furrow my brow at the computer screen. "What would you have done if you found him? Squealed like a piggy?"

Reid's chair squeaks as he swivels to face me. I don't turn around. Instead, I pull up Dad's Restaurant365 app and poke around until I find the inventory module.

"I got it," Reid says.

"Got what?"

"The inventory. We're good for the next three weeks."

"Are you sure about that, Egg Man?"

He doesn't answer. His chair squeaks as he swivels back around. I have nothing else to do but look at the numbers, so I become acquainted with our stock and recent invoices to get a better idea of our turnover.

"Well, hey there!"

I turn to find Annette beaming at me from the doorway. She's dressed in black pants and a black shirt as usual. I stand and give her a hug, her curly gray hair tickling my nose as she pulls me in tight.

"I didn't think I'd see you today," she says while pulling her apron over her head. "How's your dad?"

"He starts surgery prep in a few minutes."

"My dad got a pacemaker in 2010. It's fairly noninvasive. I'm sure he'll be fine. And how are you Miss Big City Girl?"

I give her a brief update on my life, emphasizing how well my love life is going.

"He's a model?" Annette gasps.

"Want to see him?"

"Of course!" She looks at Reid. "Don't judge. Old women need their kicks too."

I pull up a few pictures on my phone.

Annette's cheeks go slack. "He. Is. A. God."

I snicker. "I don't think he'd agree with you."

"He's an Adonis, then."

I flick my eyes at Reid just in time to catch him rolling his.

"Yes. He really is," I say.

"You've done good for yourself, girl. We need to have dinner and catch up. I want to hear about your travels."

"Sure," I say. "That would be fun."

"Well, I need to help Wyatt with food prep. What time's your dad's surgery?"

"Eight."

"Okay. I'll say a prayer before then."

"Thanks, Annette."

When she's gone, I smirk at my computer screen. Seeing Reid roll his eyes felt good. Really good.

He and I work back-to-back for the next hour without speaking. I mostly click around in Dad's folders to get an idea of how he has things organized. By the time the breakfast rush starts, I feel like I'm starting to get my bearings.

At seven o'clock the dining room begins filling up. I take my position in the kitchen and facilitate the fulfillment of customer orders. Annette's such a pro that she doesn't need me, but Wyatt takes some prodding. Whenever there's a break, I check the food prep area to make sure we're not running low on any key ingredients. Like eggs.

"Your phone buzzed," Reid says at eight o'clock. He walks over and hands me my phone. "Your dad's going into surgery."

"You read my text?"

"It popped up on the screen. Sorry."

"Oh." I grab the phone and look at Mom's text.

They just took him back.

I feel a twinge of guilt.

"You should go," Reid says. "I can take it from here."

The dining room is full, and customers are waiting. Does Egg Man know how to run the kitchen, or has he spent the last two years hiding in the office? I narrow my eyes at him. "Are you sure you can handle it?"

"Here we go again. You doubt me." He settles into his default pose, a relaxed stance with his hands in his pockets.

"I've never seen you run the kitchen, so I don't know if you're competent."

"I am. I have it all under control."

"Like that time you sank Gracelyn's RC boat in Lake Turtle?"

"You remember that?"

"I remember a lot of things."

Like that time in Spanish class when Kara Hoffman said, "At least my boobs aren't as small as Eadie's," and he ignored me while chuckling along with her.

I was sitting right behind them.

Reid's eyebrows pinch toward the center.

"Yeah. At least I know how to stock eggs," I quip.

That was the worst burn in the history of mankind. I've never been good at defending myself. Except I don't need to defend myself. Not anymore. Reid's being friendly and offering to help.

"Dad doesn't want me there," I quickly add.

"Can he stop you?"

I remember Dad's angry outburst at the dinner table a couple of nights ago. It was so out of character for him, and I still haven't made sense of it. Will he chew me out for leaving the cafe in Reid's hands?"

"He likes a Tucker to be in the kitchen," I say.

"I know. Come back this afternoon. You don't even have to tell him you were there. Just be there for your mom."

I glance at Mom's text again.

"Table four is waiting," Annette says from the other side of the kitchen pass-through.

"I got it," Reid says. "Wyatt! Table four. Status."

"Under the warmer," Wyatt answers.

"Make sure the food isn't overcooked," I say.

"I will." He places a finger on each of my shoulders and turns me toward the door. "Go."

Benevolence Hospital has been a fixture in Winford since 1915 when the brick hospital was built on a flat rectangle of land between

John and Morris Streets. Since then, wings, additions, pavilions, and annexes have been built claiming every square foot of land.

Cohesiveness of design can't be expected over a one-hundred-year span of building projects. The hospital's central high-rise retains its historical charm, while the structures radiating from it vary in style from 1950s utilitarian to twenty-first-century modern.

I enter through the front doors following the signs to the surgery center. Mom is sitting in a corner of the waiting room looking rather small and overwhelmed in the medium-sized room. The décor is plain with off-white walls, vinyl-padded benches, and pastel artwork from the 1990s. Not very inviting.

"Mom," I say as I approach.

She looks up at me and her spine straightens, adding a few inches to her height. "I thought you weren't coming."

The relief on her face tells me all I need to know. She needs my support. Reid was right.

"I didn't want you to sit here by yourself."

We hug and then settle onto one of the stiff benches.

"I was trying to read, and then I couldn't concentrate, so I'm just sitting here watching the TV but not really paying attention."

I put my arm around her. "Are you worrying?"

"Trying not to. But anesthesia is riskier the older you get, and they *are* messing with his heart."

"Yeah."

She pats my knee. "I'm glad you're here."

"How long is the surgery supposed to take?"

"About an hour, and then he'll spend a while in recovery."

"He comes home tonight though, right?"

"Assuming everything goes well."

"It will."

My phone buzzes in my purse. I ignore it, but it buzzes a few more times.

"You better check it," Mom says.

"Okay." I let go of her shoulder and dig for my phone.

Whitney, my best friend and colleague at Iconic Models, is texting me. She's in our fifth-floor office at Hudson Yards, where I would be on a normal Monday morning.

OMG.

You.

Are.

Missing.

Out.

I laugh and text back, **On what?**

DONUTS.

From where? I type.

The Doughnut Den.

Nooooooo. Are you eating a Two-Tiered Turbinado Turtle?

As we speak, Whitney types, ending it with a drooling emoji.

That's so unfair, I answer. **Did Tabitha treat everyone?**

Yup.

sigh

Tabitha is the owner of Iconic Models. She's the one who insists we come into the office four days a week when we could do most of our jobs from home. I don't mind it. I love sharing space with my coworkers while I work, enjoying the camaraderie of going out to eat and hanging out in the breakroom after a long day of endless phone calls.

She's been a very accommodating boss, agreeing to hold my position without pay for several weeks while I take care of my parents. I'm going to owe her something big after this.

How are things? Whitney texts.

Dad's in surgery. I'm in the waiting room with Mom.

Oh no! I'll quit bugging you then. Call me when he's out, K?

Sure.

Mom turns a page while letting out a heavy breath.

I toss my phone into my purse and grab a well-worn *People* magazine from the table next to me. As I flip open the cover, Mom breathes heavily again.

"What?" I ask.

Mom looks at me, feigning surprise. I know this schtick. She played it a thousand times when I was a teenager. "Nothing. I'm just reading."

"Something is bothering you."

She purses her lips, still pretending to read.

I squint at the Contents trying to find the page number for the exclusive Chris Pine article. Why yes, I'd love to hear the best advice Chris's mother gave him.

"It's just," Mom says. She clears her throat. "I hardly know anything about your life in New York. I worry about you being so far away. And you never text."

Guilt presses against my chest. She's right. I haven't communicated with them nearly enough. I leave work exhausted with limited brainpower. Hayden gets the remainder of my social mojo, and then I'm off to sleep to do it all over again the next day. "I'm sorry. I'll do better."

We meet eyes for a moment, and then she goes back to her pretend reading.

"I've built a good life in New York. I have a job, a boyfriend, a lease."

"Hmm."

An older couple enters the room. The wife is pushing her husband in a wheelchair. He has a dowager's hump and a tremor in both hands. I glance at Mom, at her sturdy spine, calm hands, and age-defying skin. Will she still be healthy a decade from now? Two decades?

"You really love Hayden, then," Mom says.

"Yeah. Of course. We've been together for two years."

Mom looks at me, her eyes penetrating like she's spinning through the numbers on a padlock, trying to unlock something in my brain.

"What are you thinking?" I ask.

"Oh, I don't know." She bobs her head left and right like she's listening to music.

"What was that?" I ask.

"What was what?

"You did this." I mimic her head bobbing.

"I guess I'm just thinking of a song."

"I think you're giddy that you still get to play Mom to your twenty-eight-year-old."

She lowers her book, looks at me, and brushes my hair behind my shoulder. "Would that be so bad?"

I smile back at her. "No, Mom. It's fine. I'm fine. I'm happy in New York."

"Okay. Then I guess that's all that matters."

We both go back to "reading." Another heavy sigh tells me she's not done mothering yet.

"Reid has been so helpful at the café," she says.

I know through the grapevine that Reid is divorced and single, which makes the timing of Mom's comment suspicious. He married his high school sweetheart, none other than Kara Hoffman. They were stuck together like magnets during our time at Cold Spring High School. What happened to the happy couple, I wonder? Not that I care. That much.

"Don't you dare try to hook me up with Reid Avory while I'm here," I say.

She looks at me, aghast. "I'm not. I was just making conversation."

"In high school, he laughed at my flat chest with his snobby little girlfriend. Among other things that I don't want to talk about." Mom doesn't know about the Valentine's dance incident. They were at a church function when I came home covered in raw eggs and feathers.

Mom gives me the side-eye. "Are you sure you're remembering it correctly?"

"You don't forget something like that. Not when you're already self-conscious about your conspicuous lack of mammaries."

"Your grandmother had small breasts and she breastfed seven babies. It's not all about the size."

"In high school it is."

"Well." Mom leans back in her chair. "I'm sorry he said that to you. I'm sure it was hurtful."

I close my magazine and drop it back onto the table.

"Maybe Reid has changed," I say. "Maybe not. Either way, I know how to act professionally."

"Of course. You have a boyfriend, and Reid is just your very handsome coworker." She winks at me.

"Mother," I warn.

"I'm *kidding*."

I'm not so sure she is, but my doubts are cut off by Dad's surgeon, who pushes through the swinging doors and heads over to us. He rubs his palms together and smiles. "All finished. He did great."

"I don't want to rehash it," Whitney says.

"I need to know what happened so I can target my advice to your specific needs."

I'm in my car in Benevolence Hospital's parking lot attempting to give Whitney dating advice per her request, but I can't provide adequate counsel when she's hemming and hawing about the details. Right now, all I know is she's considering nunship after her disaster of a date last Saturday.

Whitney sighs. "Okay. Fine. We ended up in his apartment, and we were...you know...and I had cream sauce on my pasta for dinner."

She's lactose intolerant so I have a hunch where this is going. "And you farted."

"Worse," Whitney answers.

I'm immediately horrified for her. "Did you make it to the bathroom in time?"

"Mostly."

"Whitney! Why did you have cream sauce?"

"Have you ever had a craving?" Whitney asks. "Like a really strong craving?"

"Not on a blind date."

"I ran out the door without saying goodbye."

"Did you get dressed first?"

"Of course," Whitney says. "My clothes were in the bathroom. We showered together first."

Pinpoint raindrops begin speckling the windshield, falling from bland, gray clouds that promise more of the same for the next several hours.

"So...it was going *really* well," I say, "but then your intestines ruined it."

"Not really."

"It wasn't going great, and you *still* ended up showering with him and doing...you know...?"

"Have you ever had a craving? Like a really strong craving?"

"Whitney! You said you were going to stop doing this."

"I know."

I lean against my headrest and press my phone closer to my ear as the tiny raindrops increase, turning the outside world into a pointillistic painting. "Okay. I have enough information to formulate advice."

"I'm all ears," Whitney says sullenly.

"Do not, I repeat, do not consume lactose in any amount on a date. Or ever. And do not go home with a guy on the first date."

"That feels more like a lecture than advice."

"It is."

"Don't worry. I'm trading dating for a nun's habit."

I roll my eyes toward the detached headliner. "You can't be celibate for the rest of your life."

"Yeah. That's probably too big of an ask. Besides, I hate hats."

"Nuns don't wear hats. They wear a coif and a veil."

"That sounds worse."

"Just take a break from men."

"Gladly. I reject all forms of dating until the end of the year, at least. No holiday parties for me. No Hallmark moments where the guy shows up the week before Christmas to fix my plumbing and we fall in love." She makes a gagging noise.

"You're not going home for Christmas this year?" Whitney's from Boston. She normally goes home for a couple of weeks in December.

"My parents are going on a Mediterranean cruise for their 35th anniversary. They said I could go with them, but I didn't want to be a killjoy and ruin their sexy time."

"So you're going to be alone in the city?"

"Yup."

I pull a dog hair from my capris and flick it to the floor. An idea is forming, but I give it a few more seconds to percolate before saying, "Hayden is going to be alone in the city too."

"Yeah?"

"Why don't you go to the office party together, and to whatever parties he's invited to? He was complaining the other night about having to go alone."

"Wouldn't that be weird?" Skepticism laces Whitney's voice.

"Only if you make it weird. It would kill two birds with one stone. You wouldn't have to be alone, and you could keep flirtatious women away from him."

"Are you worried he's going to cheat?"

I grab the steering wheel and dig my thumbnail into the rubber. "I just don't want women fawning all over him. They do that, you know. And he said he didn't want to go to his holiday parties alone, so..."

I listen to Whitney's fingernails click against her desk. "I guess it would be better than being alone for the next month and a half," she says finally. "Talk to Hayden. See what he thinks. If he's game, I suppose I can monitor him for you."

"Two birds with one stone."

"Right. I'll keep the gorgeous women away from him. Not that you need to worry, Miss Gorgeous."

I glance at myself in the rearview mirror, catching only my broad forehead and the halo of frizzy hair created by my short jaunt through the light rain. "Yeah. Sure."

Chapter 9

I get back in time for the lunch rush. Annette handles the workload effortlessly, and Wyatt manages to keep up. While they're waiting for their food, the Silver Sweethearts call me to their table to gush about how smoothly things are running and to fawn over Reid.

"Isn't Reid so handsome?" Dottie says for the third time. She's looking plump and festive in her fall, pumpkin-themed sweater.

"I have a boyfriend, so I haven't really noticed."

Mabel presses her hand to her bony chest, her long fingers complementing her tall stature. She anchors her turquoise beaded necklace as she leans over to Jean. "She hasn't noticed. Honey, *I've* noticed and I'm eighty-two years old."

"Do you want to see pictures of my boyfriend?" I ask to divert their attention. I grab my phone from my back pocket and pull up my best picture of Hayden. They take turns gawking at it. "Okay. So, now you see. I'm taken. No more trying to set me up."

The rest of the day flies by. Reid and I hardly cross paths. He leaves early for an eye doctor appointment, and I'm left helping Annette and Wyatt close up the café.

When I get home, I text Mom to see when the hospital is letting Dad come home. She tells me they'll be back at around seven thirty, and then she informs me Dad wants Subway, so don't bother fixing dinner. That leaves me four hours of free time. I'm already bored.

I plop onto the couch and text Hayden. **Dad's surgery went well**.

As I patiently await his response, Tully brushes against my leg and looks up at me with sad eyes. Her guilt trip works. I give her a kiss and a good scratch-down, making sure to hit the spot that makes her hind leg thump.

Hayden doesn't respond, so I try again. **He wants Subway for dinner, so I guess I'm off the hook.**

He doesn't have a photo shoot today. What's he doing? Grocery shopping? Working out? Sleeping? Gallivanting with a Victoria's Secret model? Shacking up with his new girlfriend?

Rather than dream up more worst-case scenarios, I drive to the PetSmart in Winford to buy a heat lamp, feeling positive that Jupiter is going to survive his ordeal in the wilderness. When I get home, I take the succulents out of the terrarium, line them up on the windowsill, and then scoot the tank to the other side of the room.

I find the lid in the closet, so I pop it on and position the heat lamp on the screen in anticipation of Jupiter's arrival. Afterward, I sit on my bed and stare at my phone, reading and rereading my last two texts to Hayden.

I don't need to know what he's doing every second of every day. It's fine. There are plenty of chores to do around here, bookshelves to dust, floors to sweep, clothes to fold.

As I'm flinging Mom's static feather duster around the house, I open the door to Dad's den and about have a heart attack. No wonder Dad needs a pacemaker. This room is shocking.

Boxes cover the floor, some open, some waiting to be opened. Dusty books and magazines languish in stacks that are three and four feet high. A large telescope sits in the corner surrounded by piles of accessories and other electronics.

How could he let it get this bad? I've watched the show *Hoarders* once or twice on A&E, and this qualifies as a hoard. At least he's kept it contained.

"Help Dad clean out his den" goes on my mental to-do list.

I turn my back to the mess and close the door on it, but the sight continues to stress me as I sweep the dog hair off the floors.

Before heading out to check on the chickens, I glance at my phone. Still no response from Hayden.

I pull one of Mom's coats from the coatrack by the back door and slide my arms into it. The weather isn't bad today, in the forties, I'd guess, feels warm to a Northerner, especially when the sun is out, like it is today.

The houses on this side of the street have large backyards because of the stream running along the property line. Well before Cold Spring was established in 1820, a flood carved out the soil, creating a small valley that isn't conducive to permanent structures.

Dad put the chicken coop back there, leveling it with stilts and adding a ramp so the chickens can move in and out of the enclosure. He flattened an area of the yard, reinforcing the slope with a retaining wall, to give them a place to exercise and peck for worms and bugs.

I enter the gate to the clucking of a healthy flock. Dad chooses high-producing breeds like the white Leghorn and burnt umber Rhode Island Red. I do a quick headcount and come up with twenty chickens.

The chickens have always been Dad's thing, but Mom makes sure they have plenty of entertainment, including a slide, a couple of swings, and a rope bridge. I never had a swing set growing up. The chickens did. But it's okay. They were my pets, and I loved them.

"Hey chickie, chickie," I say to the birds gathered around my feet. They regard me with interest as I check their water and food. A quick peek into their enclosure tells me the bedding will do for another day or two. Several eggs have been laid since yesterday. I grab a carton from the storage bin and fill it with eggs.

"You guys did good." I give one of the Leghorns a head pat. She clucks to the sound of my cell phone notification. It could be Mom with an update. Or Hayden.

I grab my phone out of my pocket and check the text. Hayden finally responded.

Glad everything went okay.

I want to ask him where he's been, but I play it cool. **How has your day been?**

Fine, he answers. **Played a few games of rugby with the guys.**

See? I didn't have to nag. I don't have to worry. I trust him.

I set down the egg carton and lower myself onto one of the chicken swings. Mom built them well. They're human grade.

Can we talk? I ask.

Sure.

I tap his number. While I wait for him to answer, the chickens swarm me, pecking on my shoelace, hopping up on my lap. One clucks loudly like I took her spot.

"What is going on there?" Hayden asks after greeting me.

"I'm in the chicken coop. I sat down and suddenly they're all very interested in me."

"You're sitting in a chicken coop...with chicken poop?"

I laugh at his city-boy skepticism. "No. I mean yes. They poop. Dad keeps it really clean."

"Okay." Hayden doesn't sound convinced.

"Anyway... I talked to Whitney today."

"You talk to her every day."

"Sure, but not about the same stuff."

Hayden laughs.

"What?"

"Nothing." I can hear the smile in his voice. "Go on."

"She's swearing off dating until the end of the year."

"Me too."

"Exactly!" He said it as a joke, but it's spot on. "You should drag her to your holiday parties."

Muffled noises travel through my phone. I think Hayden changed ears.

"Am I friends with Whitney?"

"You're both friends with me. So...yes."

The clucking, rubbing, and pecking are wearing on my nerves. I pick up the bowl of eggs in one hand and, with much shifting and balancing, manage to undo the latch and let myself out of the coop. I'm halfway up the slope before Hayden responds.

"You're trying to keep tabs on me," he says.

The bowl slips off my hip, and the eggs roll into the grass, their shells remaining intact. "You said the other day you didn't want to go to your Christmas parties alone. I just thought—"

"We've talked about this."

"What?"

"You."

I pick up the eggs one by one and gently set them in the bowl. "I'm not being paranoid. This isn't that. I just feel bad that you're both going to be alone during the holidays."

Hayden sighs. "If you don't trust me, why are we even doing this?"

"You keep saying 'this' without context. Can you be more specific?"

"Why are we dating? Why are you hanging out with a guy you think is a two-timing jerk?"

My jaw drops. "You're...not a jerk."

"Then don't treat me like one."

I lug the bowl back up to my hip and walk the rest of the way to the house, pausing at the bench swing on the back patio. A gentle prodding of the cushions tells me they're dry and safe to sit on. I set my bowl down first and then perch on the edge of the swing.

"I've seen you looking at other girls," I say.

"Guilty," he says without hesitation. "Every day when I walk down the sidewalks of New York, I look at other females."

"Not like that. I've seen you look. And then look again. Like you're interested."

Hayden sniffs. If I had to guess, I'd say he's looking up at the ceiling and running his hand through his hair. "I'm a guy, Eadie."

Wrong answer. I want to spit something back at him, but I take a deep breath instead, settle into the swing, and push myself gently with my heels. A crow caws from high atop one of the trees along the property line.

"I'm sorry if you ever caught me looking at other girls." His voice softens. "I won't do it again. I promise. You can trust me, Eadie."

His soothing tone, laced with sincerity, is a magic balm for my worries. "Okay."

"If it makes you feel better," he continues, "I'll let Whitney keep an eye on me."

"That's *not* why I suggested it." Well, maybe a little. "Seriously. I just thought you two could keep each other company while I'm gone."

"Are we that lost without you?"

"Yes."

Hayden's deep laugh resonates through the phone. "Fine. Send me her phone number. I'll try to make it as unweird as possible."

"I'll text you."

"Eadie."

"What?"

"Don't worry. You'll be home by January, and nothing will have changed between us. Okay?"

I smile into the phone. "Looking forward to it."

"Me too."

We say our goodbyes. I wrap my arms around myself and continue swinging, enjoying the warmth generated by Hayden's soft, husky voice.

January can't come soon enough.

Chapter 10

When Mom and Dad get home, we eat our sub sandwiches in the living room, Dad in the recliner, and Mom and me on the couch.

"You okay, Mom? You look a little pale," I say as I wad up my sub wrapper.

She presses her hand to her forehead. "Long, stressful day, I guess. I'm wiped out."

"Why don't you go to bed?"

She doesn't argue.

While Mom gets ready for bed, I help Dad to their first-floor bedroom. I pile pillows behind his back and pull up the covers.

"Thanks, Lovebug," he says as I kiss him on the forehead.

The next morning, Mom is sick with the works: fever, sore throat, queasy stomach. I try not to panic that she slept by Dad the entire night. A call to the doctor doesn't ease my concern. He advises me to keep them separated, monitor Dad for symptoms, and if he comes down with anything, call the doctor's office immediately.

I tell Dad I'm letting Reid and Annette hold down the fort at the café, and he doesn't argue. He's weak, a normal side effect of the anesthesia he tells me, and he's quite happy to let me bring him chicken soup, fresh orange juice, and ice cream whenever his cravings hit. I do the same for Mom, filling her up with broth and saltines, applesauce and bananas.

Mom's flu and Covid tests come back negative, a relief, and by Wednesday she's sitting up in bed and begging me to let her resume normal activities. I convince her to rest another day.

On Thursday, Dad still hasn't come down with Mom's illness, so I feel safe handing her the reins and returning to the café. I arrive at quarter till six with the lights already on, faint music emanating from the office, and the warm smell of yeasted donuts wafting in from the bakery.

Something's off. My eyes zero in on the space above one of the stoves. The range hood is gone. I throw my hands to my head. "What happened?"

I hear shuffling papers and Reid's squeaky chair. He exits the office, clapping his hands in front of his chest and rubbing his palms together.

"What happened to the range hood?" I ask.

"It's fine. Just a little fire. Everything is taken care of."

My arms drop to my sides and my purse smacks the floor. "What. Happened?"

"Yeah. Um." Reid leans against the wall, his hand on his head and his elbow supporting his weight. "It happened yesterday during the lunch rush. Wyatt started a grease fire. You know how these things go. And the fire suppression system worked great along with the fire extinguisher. Nobody was hurt. We sent everyone home. No biggie."

"Why didn't you call me?"

"You were busy with your dad. I was going to call you today if you didn't come in."

I slap my hands to my head again and spin in a circle. "It was so bad that you had to clear the dining room?"

"Bad enough. Yeah. I'm not taking any chances."

"Yeah, of course not." A bolt of panic sears through me. "What about Jupiter? Is he okay? Spiders don't like smoke."

"Still no sign of him."

"What if he ran outside too? He'll freeze to death."

"I'm sure he knows to stay where it's warm."

I slump, unconvinced.

"I've already had a remediation team come in. Everything's fine except for the range hood. The electrical is shot. Anyway. It's toast ...so..."

"So, insurance is going to cover it."

"Um..."

I roll my eyes so hard that they hurt. "Please tell me Dad amended his insurance policy. I warned him about this."

"No." Reid takes a few steps toward me. "I tried to get him to, but—"

"The plan doesn't cover depreciation on the appliances."

"It does as of yesterday afternoon. I decided it was time to overrule his stubbornness."

"How much is a new hood?"

Reid grabs the hood above the second range. "For one comparable to this, I'd say five to seven."

"Thousand?" Disbelief shoots my voice up an octave.

"That's the low end."

I start pacing. "The washer and dryer are from 1980. They're going to die soon. The walk-in freezer is ancient. The pantry door won't shut. The food warmer runs too hot." I stop at the food prep sink. "This faucet won't stop dripping." I grab the handle and flap it up and down a few times trying to stop the incessant trickle of water.

"Whoa." Reid darts over and pushes my hand away. "At least it still works."

I brush past him, snatch my purse off the floor, and disappear into the office. My heart is pumping double-time. All I see when I look around the café is money. Money that Dad doesn't have or he would have spent it modernizing this place.

I drop into my chair, lean back, and loosely shade my eyes. Reid's shoes pad against the tiles as he enters our little cave. He clicks off the music, sits, and swings around to face me.

"Can we afford to replace the hood?" I ask.

"Do you want me to be honest?"

"Yes."

"No."

I angle my hand to peek at him. "What about the other repairs? The ones I mentioned."

"We'd need to take out a loan."

I sit up straight. "And then what? My parents are past retirement age. Is this going to ruin their retirement plans?"

Reid leans onto the armrest and covers his mouth.

When he doesn't answer, I continue, "How are they going to pay off a loan *and* retire?"

"Keeping this cafe open and running is their retirement plan," Reid says softly. "They have no retirement savings."

I recline in my chair again and cover my face with both hands. I should have known. I should have *asked*. But whenever I *did* ask Dad about his finances, he cut me off saying I didn't need to worry about it. Well, now I'm worried about it.

I groan. "It just keeps getting worse, doesn't it?"

"We dodged a major bullet yesterday."

His words adjust my perspective. If the entire café had burned, and Dad didn't have proper insurance coverage, it could have been a disaster. Why didn't he upgrade his insurance plan? Why didn't he save for retirement?

This isn't just about him. It's about Mom too. What will they do if their health problems keep mounting? Will they have to work here until they die, assuming they *can* work?

That's not an option. They deserve to enjoy their later years.

I lower my hands and lean forward. "How about they quit working here, we hire one manager to replace them both, and then they live off the café's profits?"

Reid also leans forward closing the gap between us. He looks at me, worry clouding his blue eyes. I brace myself for his next sentence.

"He can't afford to hire a manager."

The words don't compute. Dad can't afford to hire a manager to replace him, and yet he hired Reid. "No. That doesn't make sense." I sit up and wave away his comments. "He hired *you*."

"Eadie, his finances were a wreck when I started. I barely squeezed out enough to pay the back taxes."

My expression droops. I anchor an arm across my stomach and rest my chin on my opposite fist. Dad wasn't paying his taxes?

"You haven't talked to your dad about any of this?" he asks.

My sigh tells him all he needs to know. He looks down and follows with his own sigh.

There's a knock on the door. "Hey, you two." Gwen, our baker and bakery manager, lets herself into the office. She leans against my desk and crosses her arms across her plump stomach.

"Hey Gwen," I answer. "It smells good over there."

"As always," Reid adds.

"That's my job," she says.

Her apron and gray pants are generously dusted with flour and powdered sugar, and her hands are pink from hours of kneading. She starts at four thirty in the morning to prepare the day's donuts and pastries. Twenty years as our only baker have made her an expert at quickly churning out product.

"We have a problem," she says.

I can't help the groan that escapes my lips. Not another problem. I don't think I can handle it.

Gwen shoots me a confused look. She thinks I'm overreacting. If she only knew. But I'd never burden our employees with the café's financial woes.

"It's not that bad," she reassures. "We can manage it."

"What's up?" Reid asks. He's still leaned over with his elbows on his knees like there's no sense relinquishing his discouraged pose before he hears Gwen's bad news.

I resume my reclined position and shield my eyes from reality.

"You two look like a mouse stole your cheese," she says.

I'm not that partial to cheese. "More like someone stole my donut."

"I have plenty of those. They're baked fresh. Would one cheer you up?"

"I don't think so," I respond. "No offense. I love your glazed donuts. You know that. Just tell us the problem."

"You're stressed about the fire, aren't you?" Gwen says.

"A little."

"Makes sense," she continues, "but my problem may solve yours. A little anyway. We've received too many pumpkin roll orders for Thanksgiving. I'm not going to have time to bake them all myself."

I drop my hand and feel a smile coming on. "We've received more orders than usual?"

"Yep. About three hundred more."

Reid sits up and shifts his gaze between me and Gwen. His eyes brighten. "Five dollars profit per roll. That's fifteen hundred dollars."

"Actually, I'm due for a discount on the flour and sugar, so it should be around six dollars profit per roll."

I shift my focus to Reid. "Can you find us a used range hood for eighteen hundred dollars?"

"I can try."

"Reid and I will help you bake them," I say, turning back to Gwen. "Won't we, Reid?"

"Um. Sure. I'm not a good cook but..."

"It's not rocket science. Just follow the recipe," Gwen says.

"I always do but somehow I still manage to screw things up."

I rest my hand on Reid's forearm and feel a zing through my arm. My breath catches. Reid is an electric eel. How did I not know this? I always assumed he was just a regular human male.

"I'll make sure you don't screw anything up," I say and then release his arm. Residual tingling dances through my hand. That was a legitimate shock. I wonder what other tricks he has up his sleeve. Or under his sleeve. Or under that flannel if I were to pop the buttons open.

Now my whole body is tingling. I try to get a grip by clutching my armrests.

"You'll have to work after hours the Tuesday and/or Wednesday before Thanksgiving."

"Sure," I say to the floor. I can't look at Reid. He might have felt something too—a transference of power, or the *Zap!* of a bug zapper. Those things are inhumane.

Reid clears his throat. "Yeah. Um. I can do that."

"Sounds like a plan," Gwen says. "You two get back to worrying or whatever you were doing."

"Thanks, Gwen," I mumble, and then I spin toward my computer so fast I feel like I'm on a carnival ride. I'm a little woozy even.

Reid's retreat is slower. His chair makes a long *Screech!* as he reorients his body toward his computer.

"Um. By the way," he says. His voice sounds tight. "Wyatt quit. The fire singed his beard. He wasn't happy about it."

I burst out laughing. When all hope feels lost, laugh. Right? I peek over my shoulder at Reid. He's peeking over his shoulder at me with a delicious grin on his face that recharges the tingling in my body.

He *does* have more tricks up his sleeve.

How very...interesting.

Chapter 11

I was in Faith Fusion, the sixth through eighth grade class at Cold Spring Christian Church when a short boy with glasses entered the room and introduced himself to the class as Reid Avory. That Saturday, he and his parents had moved into their new house on Elmwood. His dad, a mechanical engineer, had just hired on with a small firm in Winford, his mom sold dōTERRA, and his dog's name was Mug.

That's all I knew about Reid Avory for months. Young Reid didn't talk. He listened, he watched, he participated in crafts and sporting activities, all with clamped lips.

Gracelyn took pity on him. "He's so shy. I feel bad. He never talks in class either." By class, she meant her sixth-grade homeroom at Cold Spring Elementary. She and Reid were in Mrs. Arnold's class, while I lucked into everyone's least favorite, Mrs. Brewer's. "We're supposed to be like Christ," she said. "We can't just let him sit in a corner alone."

"He's not in a corner," I answered.

"Figuratively." Gracelyn's vocabulary and spelling were always on point. She made it to the state spelling bee three years in a row.

"Also, I tried to talk to him," I added. "I asked him why he named his dog Mug."

"What did he say?"

"Because Mug is a pug. That's it. No further explanation."

That day, Gracelyn and I committed to helping Reid crawl out of his shell. We sat next to him during Bible study time. We joined him at the craft table. We defended him from attack in every game of Capture the Flag.

He started to smile, then he threw out interjections like "Sweet!" or "Bro!" By the time church camp rolled around, we were an official trio. Quiet Reid became the Reid of Many Words. We spent most of camp dreaming up pranks, successfully pulling them on our campmates, and receiving the retaliation that we deserved.

Somehow among the joking, we learned about God and about what Jesus did for us. We listened to testimonies that brought us to tears and unexpected conviction, and we were all baptized in the murky waters of Beaver Creek.

Our friendship flourished through middle school and through two more weeklong stays at church camp. And then Reid joined the football team.

"You're going to get pummeled," I said while leaning against a brick column on Reid's porch. The heavy masonry porch anchored the front of his parents' navy farmhouse-style home, which had splashes of orange in the trim.

During middle school, Reid had grown a foot, but he was still all bones and no muscle.

"We start weight training next week," Reid answered from his lazy pose on the porch swing.

"Seriously, Reid," Gracelyn said. "Have you seen Jaden Moore? You're going to be playing against guys that are his size."

"He's big but I'm fast," Reid said with a shrug.

"You better be," Gracelyn continued, "because one tackle by Jaden will squish you like a bug."

"Hey." I raised a hand. "Don't bring insect murder into this."

"Sorry," Gracelyn mumbled.

"I knew you guys wouldn't understand," Reid said. "It's just something I gotta do."

"I gotta go to the bathroom. That's what I gotta do." Gracelyn hopped off the ledge and darted into Reid's house.

That left me alone with Reid to pick his brain. He was always more apt to go deep with me. Not that Gracelyn was judgy or anything. She was pretty, slender, well-dressed, destined to be popular. Reid and I were tall, lanky, shy, destined to be angst-ridden. We connected on a nerd level.

I propped my feet up on the ledge and watched the trail of tiny ants climbing toward the eave. "This is about you trying to fit in, isn't it?" I said without looking at him.

"Not at all, Grasshopper," he said casually—a little too casually—using his nickname for me for added effect. "I just want to try a sport."

"Football? You said you're fast. Why not try track?"

"Because football sounds more interesting."

"Because all the popular guys play football, and all the popular girls are cheerleaders." I peeked at Reid long enough to catch the tiny grin on his face. "I knew it."

"What?" He shifted his weight and stretched longways on the swing, propping up his head with his hands.

"Reid Avory wants to be popular." A cooling breeze fluttered my hair while I scratched the bug bite on my ankle. No hard feelings. Mosquitos have to eat too.

"Don't you?" he asked.

"Honestly?"

"No. Lie to me."

I swung my legs over the ledge and leaned forward to add weight to my glare. Reid peeked at me from behind his bent elbow and then went back to staring at the beadboard ceiling. "No," I said with finality. "Popular girls get all kinds of attention. I don't want attention. I just want to hang with you two, Hermoine, and my chickens." Hermoine was my pet praying mantis.

Reid sat up, clasped his hands between his knees, and met my gaze. "You have to want more than that."

"No, I don't."

"We're going into high school. In four years, we'll be going to college. This is the big time. We need to make our mark."

"People train their dogs not to do that. And I'm a female, see. I'm not territorial. But if you try to mess with me, I might eat you."

Reid rolled his eyes. "You don't get it."

That was the first time I felt a barrier between us. Subtle, but still notable. He'd always thought my obsession with bugs was cool. He thought my chickens were cool. He thought *I* was cool. Didn't he? Suddenly, a part of me was unsure. Reid was drifting away, only by millimeters, but still away. At this rate, in four years we'd be miles apart.

"What don't I get?" I said.

"You're going to get steamrolled in high school."

"Excuse me?"

"*I'm* going to get steamrolled if I don't change." He thumped his fingertips against his chest.

"We don't have to change just because we're going to a new school."

"Nobody is going to want to hear about your ant farm or your hissing cockroach or your millipede."

I had a bug zoo. My parents were awesome. Mom refused to hold Millicent though (the millipede).

"I thought you liked hearing about them," I said.

"It's just going to be different. The problem is you don't realize *how* different."

I hopped off the porch wall and took a wide stance in front of Reid. "There is no problem. I'm not going to change who I am to be more popular. I like who I am. I thought you liked me too."

Reid tucked his chin so I could only see the top of his head. He scratched his cheek and scuffed the toe of his shoe across the concrete.

"Whew!" Gracelyn said as she exited the house. "It's hot out here. You guys wanna go to the park? We could look for pill bugs."

Reid looked up at me. We narrowed our eyes at each other. "Do you want to?" I challenged. Customarily, after we each found a pill bug, we rolled them down the slide to see which landed first. Was it bug abuse? Maybe. But God designed them to roll.

He slapped his palms to his knees. "Actually, I'm kind of tired. I think I'll rest up for the first day of practice tomorrow."

Gracelyn shrugged. "Your loss. Eadie?"

"Sure, I'll go to the park and look for bugs and I don't care who makes fun of me for it." I shot Reid a parting glare and skipped down the stairs.

"Who would make fun of you?" Gracelyn asked when she matched my stride.

"The 'new' Reid, I guess."

"He's going to get destroyed at practice tomorrow."

"That's the price you pay for popularity."

And he did get destroyed. A month into the football season, he tore his rotator cuff and was sidelined. But it didn't matter. The football players already accepted him into their clique, the cheerleaders knew him as the running back, and the old Reid made way for the new Reid who had no room in his life for me and Gracelyn.

Reid was somewhat right about high school, though. There were opportunities for growth and change that hadn't been available in middle school. As I expanded my interests, my friend circle naturally widened. I didn't have to join a sports team or become a cheerleader. It was a natural progression as I became involved in activities like the Future Scientists Club, Robotics, and Drama Club's backstage support team.

Even though Gracelyn and I were involved in different clubs, we remained supportive friends, but Reid and I only grew further apart as his football buddies, led by Jaden Moore, targeted me with their "nerd," "walking stick," and "gazelle" jokes, lobbing them at me during lunch, passing periods, after school, and any other opportunity they could find.

"You should report them for bullying," Gracelyn once said when we were sitting on a bench in front of the school's main entrance. Spring had arrived in full force, giving us hints of the scorching summer to come. In four weeks, we'd officially be seniors.

"It's fine," I said. Mostly. My faith was strong, and I knew my worth, but the verbal abuse wore on me sometimes.

"No, it's not. Jaden is a piece of crap. I'd like to punch him in the face. He thinks he's so handsome, but he's not. He looks like a pig."

I chuckled. "A wild boar."

"Yes! What is he trying to grow on his face? A beard? It looks like his face is balding."

"He thinks it makes him more intimidating."

"To five-year-olds maybe." Gracelyn switched her backpack to the opposite side. The angled sun beat down on our shoulders despite our location under the covered entryway. "Why doesn't Reid ever stand up for you?"

"He's indoctrinated," I answered.

"Or he's a coward."

"Both."

"Well, I don't like it. He knows better. The three of us were baptized on the same day."

Earlier during lunch, I had walked by the "football" table and Jaden yelled out, "Eadie Tucker!" But with an "F" instead of a "T." Instead of ignoring Jaden like I normally did, I gave him my iciest glare. He feigned fear and tapped Reid. "She's gonna jump me. You better protect me from those toothpicks." Also known as my arms.

Reid just hung his head over his lunch tray and shrugged.

"I think he's insecure," I said while circling my wrist with my opposite hand. My thumb and index finger overlapped by an inch.

"Did you hear he broke up with Kara?"

I rolled my eyes. "Again?"

"She slapped him in study hall."

The thought of someone, anyone slapping Reid Avory filled me with a strange sense of glee. My lips spread into a broad smile. "No way."

"Yep. She has detention."

"What about him?"

"He didn't hit back, so I guess he's innocent."

I propped my fingers under my chin and mused. "Maybe they're finally over, then."

"Doubt it."

Gracelyn was right. Reid and Kara were back together the next day, smiling and cuddling on the gym bleachers after lunch. Despite my mixed feelings for Reid, I didn't wish the snobby, manipulative Kara Hoffman on him. She fancied herself the queen of our class. She knew she wasn't pretty enough to hold the title, so instead of handing it over to Gracelyn, who was arguably prettier than all of us, she embarked on a perpetual campaign to tear down her competition. As popular and well-liked as Gracelyn was, even she incurred Kara's wrath sometimes.

Our senior year rolled by without much fanfare. The Cold Spring Woodrats' football team sucked as usual, finishing the season with a 3-7 record. I worked at Home for the Hollandaise over Christmas and made some money to pay for Future Scientists' spring break trip to Cape Canaveral. A bomb cyclone dropped ten inches of snow in January, closing school for two days. And then another bomb dropped.

Reid and Kara were over. For good. According to the buzz in the hallways, *he* broke up with *her* and told her not to bother crawling back to him. I felt like a proud mom. My boy was growing up. He was finally committing to the change he'd aspired to before our freshman year.

When I approached him to congratulate him on his loss, he said, "Do you want to go to the Valentine's dance with me?"

I didn't feel like a mom anymore. I felt like a nervous teenage girl who had never realized that she might have a slight crush on Reid and always had.

I didn't convene with Gracelyn before answering. The trajectory of my life might have been different if I had. Instead, I blurted out, "Yes" and sealed my fate.

It would be the first and last date of my high school career, an evening that would change my life forever.

Chapter 12

Luckily, we have another cook, Brandon, a clean-cut dad in his mid-thirties who goes to school in the evenings and attends Mom and Dad's church on Sundays. He and Wyatt coordinated their schedules, each putting in thirty hours a week, filling in if the other was sick.

We have to hire a new cook quickly. If Brandon gets sick, it will shut us down. Also, Saturday is Cold Spring's Fall Festival, one of our busiest days of the season. We need two cooks on the line to keep up with the dining room and takeout orders.

Reid assures me he already has two Zoom interviews set up for this afternoon. "You're welcome to sit in on them if you want."

I flash him a warning look.

He coughs. "I mean, a Tucker should be present."

"I have the final say."

"Of course," Reid says like someone is squeezing his neck.

"Do you have a problem with that?"

I've pushed him too far. He glares at me. I glare back. It's better to glare than gawk, which I want to do after the electrical storm he whipped up in me earlier. But I told Hayden not to look at women twice, so I can't either. Look at men, that is. In *that* way. I'm in complete control of this situation.

"I get it," Reid says. "Message sent and received."

"Excellent," I say and then exit the room to manage the morning rush.

I like working with Brandon. He cooks with relaxed ease despite being four burners and a griddle down. The morning rush speeds by effortlessly. Brandon, Annette, and I perform like a professional production of *The Nutcracker*. We deliver meal after scrumptious meal to the tables in minutes, and happy customers fill our cash register while offering Annette generous tips. She deserves every penny.

I might be overstating our talent. I'm giddy. I'm in the flow.

My workdays at Iconic Models are never like this. Whitney and I meet up every day at two o'clock for a mandatory walk to the coffee shop downstairs, the caffeine injection necessary for motivation and morale.

Today I work through two o'clock without a blip in energy even though I forgot to eat lunch. At two forty-five I realize I'm hungry. Brandon fixes me a grilled cheese, egg, and avocado sandwich, and I put it down in half a dozen bites while fulfilling the day's final orders.

"Are you good?" I ask Annette at five till when the dining room is empty except for an older gentleman with a newspaper and a hearty appetite. He just finished his meal and ordered two slices of apple pie to go. "I need to sit in on some interviews."

"Sure, boss," she says. "I'll close up."

Being called "boss" isn't half bad. Much better than being called a "minion" or a "cog." So many cogs in New York City, turning the world but missing out on the big picture.

I peer through the front window, my eyes focused on the slow-moving canal, its current once responsible for spinning the waterwheels that powered the industries that built this small town.

Maybe I do need coffee.

I quickly brew myself a fresh batch, fill two mugs, and carry them to the office.

Reid has already started the first Zoom call with a gentleman named Marlon. They're talking about his past felonies and how prison changed him. I force my skeptical eyebrows to stay put as I set down our mugs, pull my chair next to Reid, and settle in for the interview.

"I spent five years in Plainfield Correctional Facility, where I worked in the kitchen seven days a week. They offered me culinary classes, so I know my way around a commercial kitchen." Marlon tugs on his beard as he talks. His heavily cratered skin is a mosaic of highlights and shadows and the upside-down cross on his forehead looks DIY. Did he get it in the slammer or is it a remnant of his criminal days?

"And why were you in prison again?" I ask.

"Felony robbery. Repeat offender. I was a druggie and I needed money for my fix. But that's all over with now. I got out six months ago and I have good references." He leans over and grabs something. "Here." He pulls up a bandana, covers his forehead tattoo, and ties it behind his head. "I thought you should be aware of my ink, but these days I prefer to keep it hidden. It sends the wrong message."

I nod. He's right about that.

We continue the interview for fifteen more minutes to get a better sense of Marlon's skills, and then we sign off. I look at Reid and let my right eyebrow—the one that tends to be more skeptical—creep up my forehead.

"He's a felon," I say.

"He's also a trained high-volume cook."

"With an upside-down cross tattoo and a sordid past."

Reid leans an elbow on his desk and taps his chin. "Who's that guy we talk about in church? The one who forgives people's sins and gives them a second chance at life?"

I reach over and tug on Reid's hand to stop the tapping. "I'm not sure I want to be here alone with a felon. I mean, I can forgive, but should I forget?"

Reid looks at me thoughtfully. He's considering something. Something outside of this conversation. And I think it has to do with a Valentine's dance that ended with me covered in raw eggs and feathers.

"He's just one candidate," I add hastily. "We have another."

"Two more, actually. I scheduled another interview. It's tonight at seven."

"I need to be included."

"I need your phone number so I can text you the link."

Sharing my phone number with Reid means he'll no longer have to go through my dad. He'll have access to me indefinitely. He could send me texts at any moment, at any hour, while I'm putting on my pants or blowing my nose.

"Don't send me random memes," I say.

"What if it's a bug-related meme?"

"I don't know how to answer that."

"Fine. I'll name your contact card 'DO NOT TEXT. EVER.'"

"Unless it's work-related," I clarify.

We both grab our phones and exchange numbers.

The next interview goes smoothly. The guy's name is Jake, and he doesn't admit to any felonies. I assume that means he has none. He has experience at IHOP, Red Lobster, and Sonic. Never went to high school. Likes to lose himself in cooking. He's the clear frontrunner.

When I convey this sentiment to Reid, he doesn't look convinced.

"I'm not ready to decide," he says.

"I am."

"We have another interview tonight. Let's hear the third guy out and then we can think about it."

I shift in my chair to face Reid directly. "We need a range hood, and we need a new cook by Saturday."

"Why?"

"Saturday is the Fall Festival." Surely I don't have to tell him it's one of our busiest days this quarter.

He lets out a forceful sigh. "I forgot."

"Please tell me you've been in here all day looking for used range hoods."

Reid backhands a stress ball across his desk. "That's one thing I was doing."

"Did you have any luck?"

"A couple possibilities, but..." He lets out another sigh, this one longer.

"But this is an emergency."

"I bet Marlon could help me install one."

"Or we could hire a professional."

Reid and I continue to go back and forth. Eventually, I convince him to make the used range hood priority number one. He's going to spend the rest of the day finding an installer on the assumption that he'll be able to locate the hood this evening. I promise to comb the internet too.

"I'll let you know if I find anything," I say as I head out of the office.

When I get home, Mom's looking a little tired. I shoo her out of the kitchen and tell her to go rest on the couch while I take care of the chickens, do a load of laundry, and cook a pot of white chicken chili. My chores are done, my parents are fed, and the kitchen counters are clean before six thirty.

Fifteen minutes before our third Zoom call, I take a bowl of chili upstairs and settle onto my bed to eat while the minutes tick by.

The interview goes smoothly. Bruce's experience is stellar. Almost too good. Why would he want to work in a café forty-five minutes from some of the best restaurants in Indiana? When I ask him, he hems and haws before saying he only wants to work daytime hours. Fair enough.

After we end the call, Reid and I text our thoughts to each other.

I want to hire Jake, I text. **The IHOP guy. He knows breakfast.**

Let's think about it for a little bit and then decide, Reid responds.

I watch the digital clock on the dresser. After three minutes, I text back, **Okay. We waited a little bit. I want to hire Jake.**

When Reid doesn't answer, I put my boss hat on and double down. **We're hiring Jake.**

Okay then.

Have you found a range hood within our budget?

Actually, I have. It's being delivered tomorrow morning.

I take off my boss hat and go into full girly mode. I shower Reid with unicorn, rainbow, and ladybug emojis.

I know. I rock, Reid replies.

If only I had Jupiter to celebrate with.

I know. I suck, he backpedals.

I glance at the empty terrarium by the closet. I haven't had much time to think about Jupiter this week, but I haven't given up all hope. He's a resourceful spider. And truthfully, I wasn't the best spider momma. He was agitated from traveling. I never should have taken him out of the terrarium, much less let him crawl around on unfamiliar knuckles.

Sorry. That was mean, I text. **It's not your fault**.

Yes, it is.

No, it really isn't. Anyway. Goodnight, Egg Man. Thanks for your hard work.

Goodnight. <smiley emoji>

Before setting my phone down, I click on Hayden's last message and shoot him a quick text to see how his day went. I watch fifteen silent minutes pass on the clock before setting my phone face down on the nightstand and heading downstairs to visit with my parents.

When I finally settle in for sleep, I check my phone again. Hayden still hasn't responded. The anxiety, worry, and doubt about his whereabouts usually creep in now, but my sleepiness is stronger than a Xanax.

I shut off the light and curl onto my right side, my favorite sleeping position. The next couple of days are going to be busy. I need all the sleep I can get.

Chapter 13

I wake up Saturday morning on a mission to organize the café's walk-in pantry. Before I leave Indiana, Home for the Hollandaise is going to be orderly. The pantry seems the obvious place to start my makeover. It's a mess, but it's a contained mess. I can turn it around in an hour or two.

At a frosty five thirty in the morning and under an inky black, starless sky, I hurry to the service door and let myself in, instantly relieved by the welcoming warmth and reassuring rumble of the heater. I drop my coat and purse in the office, shove my phone and earbuds into my pocket, grab my DYMO, and waste no time heading to the pantry.

Before moving items around, I try to come up with a game plan. There is no rhyme or reason to this mess. Cans are next to jars which are next to bags of flour that are beside spices. Loaves of bread are tucked anywhere there is a gap, and oil jugs protrude from the bottom shelves, impeding movement. No problem. With my DYMO handheld label maker at the ready, I'm unstoppable. Chaos will soon become order.

Dry goods shouldn't sit next to anything that might leak. That's just common sense. For safety reasons, heavier items should be on the lower shelves. Loaves of wheat bread shouldn't be stuffed into random nooks. They belong next to the wheat flour because the two share a common ancestor.

I begin sliding, swapping, turning cans so the labels are facing out, checking expiration dates, all to the tune of the Harry Styles channel on Spotify. Everything is going well until I feel a tap on my shoulder while I'm sniffing an open ketchup bottle.

My hand involuntarily squeezes, and a tomato geyser hits me in the face, some of it tunneling up my nose so far that I sneeze, which sprays tomato-y saliva all over the canned goods I just organized.

I hear Reid's laughter before I turn around. Something is dripping from my nose. I don't know if it's mucous or tomato juice.

"Do you need a napkin?" Reid snickers.

I pull my earbuds out of my ears and tuck them into my pocket. "You scared the heck out of me."

"You don't need to get here this early. I can supervise prep."

"I was organizing," I say with a grand gesture.

When Reid glances at the shelves, his eyes go wide. "Why?"

"Because it's a disaster in here."

Reid rolls his eyes. "I wish you would have talked to me first."

A glob of ketchup slides down my cheek. I catch it before it drops onto my shirt. "I look like I just got home from Fight Club, so... You can stand here and enjoy my work while I wash my face. I printed labels and everything. See?" I point to the bread label which is next to the flour label.

"Huh. Yeah."

I expected him to be more impressed.

The bathroom is on the other side of the building, behind the bakery. As I'm passing through, the aroma of freshly baked donuts mingles with the vinegar scent of ketchup—not a match made in heaven.

Gwen looks at me with alarm. "Oh, honey!" She runs over and puts a hand on my elbow. "What happened? Did you fall? Are you missing teeth?"

"Nope. Nothing like that. I just squirted ketchup on my face."

"That's *ketchup*?" Gwen laughs.

I must look terrible.

"Yeah," I say. "Reid jump scared me in the pantry."

"Well, why would he do that?"

"Excellent question. I think it was an accident, but he seemed to enjoy the ramifications." I gesture at my face.

Gwen chuckles again and drops her hand. "You go wash that off before more gets on your shirt."

Her comment prompts me to look down. "I had to wear white today, didn't I?"

"It doesn't look *that* bad."

She's lying. I'm going to have to go home and change.

Several splashes of water at the bathroom sink rinse away most of the damage and a final swipe with a scratchy paper towel removes the rest. When I return to the office, Reid isn't there. He must be in the pantry enjoying my work or continuing what I started. I slather lotion onto my face, my skin drinking it thirstily, and then sneak back over to the pantry.

While poking my head in to jump scare Reid, I catch a glimpse of his handiwork and gasp. "What are you doing!"

He leaps at the sound of my voice. "Gah. You scared me."

"You're *un*-organizing my organization."

Reid palms a can of condensed milk and slides it next to a sack of flour. I stomp over to him, grab the can, and set it back on the second shelf. "Wet goods do not go next to dry goods."

"Cans are dry goods."

"Not if they leak. Then your flour is ruined."

"Have you ever, once in your life, had a can leak on you?"

"It could happen."

I quickly undo what he undid while I was gone, placing items above the labels I studiously created and printed. He grabs my forearms. Not too tightly, but enough to render me immobile.

"It may look disorganized to you," he says, "but it's organized to us." He takes a small step to the right so that he's directly in front of me. We've never been this close as adults, less than a foot away. If I wasn't angry at him, I might wilt under his gentle, authoritative touch.

His blue eyes search my face. Waiting to see if I accept his faulty logic, perhaps?

I jerk my arms out of his grip. "Who's 'us?'"

"Brandon, me, Wyatt, Annette, Lexis. Your *dad*."

Why is he emphasizing my dad when he's on leave? And Wyatt no longer works here. There are black holes in his logic that I refuse to be sucked into. "Wyatt quit. And I added *labels*. We're all adults here. We can change and adapt. This is called improving processes."

Reid sighs heavily. "Some things can't be changed."

"We have a new cook starting today. He's going to get lost in here."

"He'll get used to it."

"I'm really questioning your managerial skills right now, Reid."

"This..." He gestures to the shelves, "...is not your problem. You're only here for a few weeks. The rest of us are here all day, every day. Just trust me on this, okay?"

"No offense, but you all look like you could use a little help. I used to be in charge of this pantry, and it never looked like this. Everything had its place. Everything was organized."

Reid crosses his arms. "There's more than one way to organize a pantry."

I cross mine, holding his challenging gaze. "Some ways are better than others. *Much* better."

"I appreciate your enthusiasm, but—"

"You're mistaking enthusiasm with desperation. I desperately have to get this place into better shape before I leave. Dad can't come back to this mess that you're supposedly managing." I don't try to soften my voice.

Reid's lips shrink into a line. I wait for the line to separate and form words, but he looks down instead, his arms still folded, hands clutching his biceps.

"Does this mean I can't organize anything?" I ask, softening my voice a bit.

After a pause, Reid responds without looking up, "I'd prefer it if you didn't."

"Can I *clean*?"

He glances up at me and then turns back to the shelves, quickly undoing more of my work. "Sure."

I throw up my hands, spin around, and march out of the pantry. And into the arms of a very rough-looking felon.

"Whoa!" Marlon lets go of me and steps back, his hands up in surrender. "Didn't expect that. I was just following the noise."

I slowly rotate toward Reid, who hurriedly tosses a package of paper towels onto the top shelf. Every muscle in my face hardens as my eyes eviscerate him. "Where's Jake?" I mouth with my head cocked like I'm a demon-possessed girl in *The Exorcist*.

Reid's fear is palpable.

"What do you folks want me to do?" Marlon asks. "I'm ready to get this show on the road."

Reid approaches, eyeing me worriedly. As he scoots by, he whispers, "I'll explain in a minute."

"Hey, man," he says to Marlon. I hear the slap of their bro high five. "Brandon should be here soon. He'll be getting you up to speed. Today's going to be a little crazy."

"No problem," Marlon says. "I can do crazy."

I scrunch my lips and scowl at the back of the pantry. Great. The felon is good at being crazy. I hired Jake. Where's *Jake*?

Reid taps me on the shoulder. "Hey, I need to talk to you in the office."

I take a breath, turn around, and offer Marlon a little salute before rounding him, keeping a wide berth. Reid follows me into the office and closes the door behind himself.

"I told you to hire Jake," I say, not minding my volume.

Reid gestures for me to quiet down. "I know, and I tried. But Jake declined the offer, so I offered the job to Bruce. Bruce accepted, and then he called me this morning and told me he quit."

"Bruce quit before he started?"

"Yeah. Anyway, today is a big day. We need two cooks. I called Marlon and he said he'd be here within ten minutes."

"He's a felon," I hiss.

"I'll check his references today, and if they're bad, we can fire him."

"*You* can fire him."

"He seems like a nice guy."

"What if you fire him and then he holds us hostage at gunpoint?"

Reid reaches over and rests his hand on my arm. I feel a tiny zap through my shirt. "That's not going to happen."

"How do *you* know?"

"Because I'm a good judge of character." Reid steps closer, his hand still lightly pressed against my arm, his fingertips sending little zings of electricity. "Don't worry. It's going to be okay."

I'm not sure how he knows it's going to be okay, but his hushed baritone voice is strangely convincing. "You better not be wrong about this," I whisper. "I don't want to be on the front page of the *Cold Spring Times*. Also, why are you touching me?"

Reid lets go. "Sorry." He steps back, takes a wide stance, and raises his hands like he's about to tell me that owning a time-share will be the best investment I've ever made. "Trust me." When I don't answer, he repeats, "Will you trust me, Eadie?"

"I—I'm just not sure I can trust Marlon."

He dips his head to get a better look at my eyes. "People deserve second chances." His imploring expression tells me we're not only talking about Marlon. I look down at his hands and then into the void between us.

"I smell like ketchup."

Reid leans against his desk and laughs.

"It's not funny. You ruined my shirt. I have to go home and change."

"Why were you sniffing ketchup?"

"I couldn't find an expiration date. I was checking it for freshness."

"Is it fresh?"

I grab my shirt and sniff. "Ketchup never goes bad," I say with a shrug. "I guess I'm outa here." I grab my coat and start to put it on.

"Wait. Will any shirt do?"

"I mean. No? I have modesty standards."

Reid grabs the collar of his white T-shirt that's mostly covered by a green and blue flannel. "You could cinch it at your waist. I've seen girls do that. Or women."

"Are you giving me fashion advice?"

"Yeah. I guess I am. Kind of ironic, huh? Do you want it?" He tugs at his shirt.

It's cold outside. The Lumina's heater won't warm up until I make the full circuit to home and back again. I could cinch his T-shirt to the side like the girls do.

"Sure, I can make it work," I say.

Reid stands and begins unbuttoning his flannel.

"Oh. We're doing it here?"

"No. I don't have to. I can leave."

"It's fine. If you had any idea how many half-naked men I've seen."

Reid pauses and raises an eyebrow at me.

"Photo shoots. Fashion shows. Sometimes you have to change clothes in a hurry. Anyway..." I sink into my chair and swivel around so my back is facing Reid, and then I wave at him with the back of my hand. "Continue."

I hear the rustling of fabric while he disrobes. A moment later, a flash of white crosses my vision.

Reid's waving his T-shirt in front of my face. "Truce?" he says.

I turn around to roll my eyes at him, but instead, my pupils zero in on his navel and the abs surrounding it and the light feathering of hair covering it all. My eyes scoot upwards. Yeah, he has hair on his chest too.

Male models usually wax or shave. Hayden does both and there's nothing I hate more than going in for a cuddle against a full-body Brillo pad. I never complain to Hayden because it's a job requirement. Reid doesn't have to bother with that nonsense. Obviously.

His arm goes still. The white flag continues to swing limply between us, losing momentum as Reid stares at me while I stare at his chest.

A blush explodes behind my breastbone and rushes up my neck like a tomato geyser. A millisecond later, I'm all red, even my arms, and there's no place to hide.

I grab the T-shirt, duck my head, and dart out of the room. "I'll change in the bathroom," I squeak out as the door swings closed behind me.

While I'm limping to the bathroom, I conjure mental images of Hayden. My *boyfriend* looks hot bare-chested. Combine bare-chested with an unbuttoned flannel... Oh, that's extreme hotness. Like weak-in-the-knees hotness. So hot it makes me limp.

I bust into the bathroom, grip the sink, and look at myself sternly in the mirror. Hayden doesn't have to know that happened. No one has to know.

Is it hot in here?

I lean over, splash myself with cold water, and then refocus on my dripping face. *Don't be silly. Nothing happened. Why are you so worked up?*

More cold water. I splash five times for good measure.

I'm not worked up. I'm fine. He was just giving me his shirt.

I retreat to a bathroom stall and swap my tomato-stained blouse with Reid's T-shirt. The T-shirt that was hugging his pecs five minutes ago.

A blush blossoms in my chest again. I anchor my forearms on the stall door and rest my forehead against my palms.

You have a boyfriend, Eadie. You love your boyfriend. He's amazing and wonderful and everything you ever wanted. So get a grip and get to work. That's what you're here for. To WORK.

My little pep talk helps. I exit the stall in Reid's shirt, cinch it at the waist, and try not to let the scent of Reid's cologne distract me from the long workday ahead.

Chapter 14

Reid met me at my door for the Valentine's dance wearing black slacks, a turquoise tie, and a simple white oxford, the ensemble making my eighteen-year-old heart do a flip. Even so, I almost didn't open the door for him. Reid was part of the "cool" crowd, a jock, the object of swoons and crushes. It didn't matter that we'd once run around town together during the summers, taking breaks only to steal free sodas from my parents' café.

Was this an olive branch? An attempt at an apology? An act of pity?

Those questions niggled me as we walked through unseasonably warm air to Reid's dull-gray Honda. He opened the passenger door for me, and I slid in, careful not to let my skirt drag against the brick street.

"Wanna go to the park?" he asked when he was strapped into the driver's seat. "We can get someone to take our picture."

Reid and I hadn't talked much before that evening. We'd set a time to meet, agreed to dine at Dolce Vita in Winford. Our text messages hadn't evolved much beyond logistics, even though I had questions. So many questions.

"Sure, that sounds fine," I said.

As we pulled away from the curb, reality hit me. This was a *date*. A D-A-T-E. The word gripped my stomach and squeezed it into contortions. Reid, Gracelyn, and I used to talk for hours in the park as we lounged next to Turtle Lake, never at a loss for words. But that was years ago.

I peeked at him as he drove his car through the quaint streets of Cold Spring. His thinness persisted despite his regular weight training regimen. Any muscles he had were well hidden beneath his white oxford and his loose-fitting pants. I pinned my hands between my knees as Reid's silence curled itself around my neck and rendered me mute.

Cold Spring Park, the town's only community park, was four blocks from my house. In a few dozen breaths, we were there. Reid parked the car and we exited along with another couple, who had just pulled in beside us.

The broad, tree-dotted park offered multiple play areas for various age ranges. Its main feature was the sparkling Turtle Lake, an 800-acre lake, most of which was state-owned. Several dozen of our peers were gathered around the lakeside pavilion, taking turns posing and smiling for smartphones.

"Oh," I said, my body hitting an invisible wall.

Reid continued a few steps before realizing I'd frozen in place.

He turned, looking confused. "You coming?"

"I'm not sure. There's so many people."

"Yeah. It's kind of tradition when the weather is nice. You didn't come here before prom last year?"

"I didn't go to prom."

Reid's eyebrows dropped. "Oh."

"Can we…" I walked backward on my toes so that my heels didn't puncture the ground and then redirected my steps to a swing set surrounded by the previous year's mulch. Satisfied that the swings were clean, I settled into the highest one and let my feet dangle.

Reid came up beside me and sat. "Remember when we used to spend all day here?"

I nodded.

"Why does that feel so long ago?" He looked up into the canopy of naked tree limbs.

"Because we've changed," I said looking down at my feet.

A sixty-five-degree breeze rustled the grass which had come out of dormancy and started greening during the week of warm weather.

"Not necessarily for the better." He gave up on the trees, bent over, grabbed a rock among the mulch, and tossed it several feet. It took a surprise turn at the last minute and landed in a patch of well-fertilized grass. Both of our gazes remained fixed on the crowded turf.

His openness reminded me of old Reid. The Reid who once sat quietly beside me while we watched the wind make ripples on Turtle

Lake. The Reid who thought my hissing cockroaches were cool. The Reid who went inner tubing with me during church camp.

Gracelyn had been relegated to the eighth-grade girl's cabin with an upset stomach, leaving Reid and me alone on the water. As the creek's gentle current carried us along, my lighter weight outpaced his. To remain side-by-side, we grabbed each other's hands and held on. I still remember the texture of his palm, the zing as we connected, the reassuring warmth of his skin as we floated through the sun-dappled water, our heads lulled back in comfortable silence.

When I was growing up, my mom sometimes quipped that I was bad at recognizing my emotions. When they barreled into me full force and I still couldn't put a name on them, my immune system stopped working. Once it was mono, another time it was pneumonia, and then it was recurrent migraines. Mom had to sit on the edge of my sickbed and tell me what was *really* bothering me. I was worried about starting middle school, I was afraid to start my period, I was grieving the death of Grandma.

How long had I been harboring this unknown crush on Reid? How could I not have known? The realization jostled me so much that a wall crashed down and my next words tumbled through. "Why don't you ever have my back?"

Reid stopped his lazy swinging and closed his eyes, his face still pointed toward the errant rock. A breeze lifted his tie and flapped it against his stomach. He peeked at me out of the corner of his eye. "I had this idea that I wanted to be popular, and it overtook everything else."

His bangs also flapped in the breeze as gravity pulled on them. He took his eyes off me, refocused on the ground, his slumped shoulders and downcast demeanor meant to communicate what? Shame? Regret?

We sat in silence while the girls in fancy dresses squealed and laughed.

"It was never about you," Reid said. He lifted his head and met my eyes directly. His posture was more confident. "It was all about me. I was a scrawny shy kid. I was the one who felt like a loser. I thought I had to prove myself."

"And with me around, you thought proving yourself would be impossible. I get it."

"Eadie, I've always thought you were beautiful."

I felt like I'd swallowed a bug, specifically a *Titanus Giganteus*, commonly called a titan beetle, which is found in South American rainforests. What the bug was doing in Indiana, I didn't know, but it was halfway down my gullet so there was no way to bag it, tag it, and conduct research.

I swallowed to regain the use of my vocal cords, but I had no idea what to say.

"I've had a crush on you since sixth grade," Reid said.

Now I *really* didn't know what to say. I swished my dress and the chiffon spoke for me, the rustling giving voice to my uncomfortable nervousness.

"Sorry," Reid said, ducking his head.

"No. Um." I cleared my throat. "I...thought you had a girlfriend."

He looked at me and grinned. "I did."

"And you had a...a crush on me *while* you had a girlfriend?"

"Don't tell Kara."

"And you let Jaden call me Eadie Tucker with an 'F' while you had a crush on me while you had a girlfriend?"

Reid reached up and mussed his hair. "Now that you say it out loud it sounds kinda dumb."

"Which part?"

"The part where I didn't tell Jaden and Kara to eff off."

I stand, feeling too antsy to stay in one place. "That's a lot, Reid. I'm going to have to think about this. Until then, let's get these dumb pictures out of the way. Do you have your phone?"

"That's the Eadie I remember," Reid said, chuckling. He stood and grabbed my hand.

Once again, I froze, not from doubt this time, but from the heat of his touch. It traveled up my arm and lit my insides in a way I'd never experienced. Rather than retreat from the emotion, I stared at it headlong. I wasn't sure what to call it, but I was darn sure I wanted more of it.

Together, Reid and I made our way to the pavilion where a large crowd of students and parents still gathered. We chose a spot close to the lake, enjoying the gentle lapping of the waves against the pebbled shore while we waited. When it was our turn for pictures, Reid handed his phone to one of the parents. We ascended the steps and positioned ourselves beneath the string lights, immersing ourselves in the glow as dusk began to settle in. He put his arm around my waist, and I felt the unfamiliar but welcome full-body warmth of his nearness.

And then something hit me. Cold. Wet. Coating my hair and arms. I looked at Reid. He was dry, void of the gooey liquid that was running down my arms.

I heard laughter from above. Words. In my shock, they were jumbled. A second later, something else hit me, soft and heavy, pricking me here and there. Feathers.

I'd just been tarred and feathered. But the tar was eggs. Whoever dumped them on me jumped down from the rafters and started making clucking noises.

"That was perfect, man." It was Jaden's voice. He came up behind Reid and slapped him on the shoulders.

"Reid," I managed, my voice tremulous.

Kara appeared from the crowd of onlookers, some of whom looked shocked, especially the parents, others who were laughing. Kara looked gleeful. "Oh my God, Reid," she said as she bounded the steps. "That was epic. We did it!" She jumped into Reid's arms, straddling his waist.

Shock, embarrassment, betrayal washed over me, joining the raw eggs and feathers that were ruining my dress. The emotions were jumbled, each competing for expression, I couldn't piece them apart. I didn't try. They coalesced in my stomach, reacting with one another to form a new emotion: anger.

"I never should have trusted you, Reid," I said in a voice so low, cold, and gravelly that I didn't recognize it.

He shoved Kara away, but she pranced back to him and clung to his neck.

"You're such a liar, Reid Avory," I growled. "You can go to hell. You all can go to hell!" I yelled. At Jaden and Kara. At the crowd gaping at me like a school of fish. At Cold Spring and its stupid cliques and pathetic jocks and worthless bullies.

I ran down the steps and across the grass, taking the quickest route to my house. My heels fought me with each step. They could go to hell too. I tore them off my feet and threw them at a tree.

"Eadie!"

Reid's voice was distant. *Good. Keep it that way.*

Eadie, I've always thought you were beautiful. The words echoed through my head, generating a sneer.

I never wanted to see his immature, conniving, lying face again. In fact, I would stay ten feet away from every teenage male in Cold Spring. They didn't deserve me. I was better than them, meant for something better. Some*one* better. And I would find him. Make no mistake.

Reid, Jaden, and Kara may have wanted to end me with their most "epic" prank, but the joke was on them. I was just getting started.

Chapter 15

Novembers in Indiana can be brutal with gray skies, needling precipitation, and forty-mile-an-hour sustained winds, but forty-eight hours later it can be sixty-eight degrees, sunny and positively blissful. When such glorious weather coincides with the Cold Spring Fall Festival, expect record attendance. When all those craft-hunting, holiday-cheer-seeking shoppers spend the morning stopping at every booth along the Spring Creek Canal, they become very hungry.

Believe me, I'm thankful, but also harried, overwhelmed, and exhausted. It's so busy that out-of-towners stole the Silver Sweethearts' table. Not one to disappoint our most devoted customers, I had Lexis set up a table and chairs in the kitchen fitted with a tablecloth and centerpiece to make them feel more welcome.

They haven't commented on the kitchen's disorganization. Thankfully, I dusted away the corner cobwebs days ago.

"Oh, this is fun," Dottie says as Lexis darts past with a bottle of mustard.

"It's certainly warm back here," Jean says over the din of the fryer. She unties the knot in her scarf and lets the two ends hang loosely.

Amid the commotion, Mabel quietly turns the pages of her book, catching her glasses now and then as they threaten to slide off her sweaty nose. "It's fine. Just fine," she says. "As long as I get my food."

Marlon is holding his own at the cook station fixing our more traditional fare like grilled cheese sandwiches, pancakes and eggs, and the occasional hamburger. I keep Brandon on our signature plates, especially our eggs Benedict and loaded breakfast fries with hollandaise sauce.

Annette and Lexis have already walked ten miles apiece traveling from the dining room to the kitchen pass-through, taking and delivering to-go orders, and sprinting back and forth from the drink station. I'm doing my best to make sure everyone gets what they ordered, cooked to their specifications.

"Eadie, dear," I hear Dottie call behind me.

I hurry over to find out what she needs.

She's holding a limp piece of bacon. Its ends droop toward her plate. "I don't think this bacon is quite done."

"Oh, don't bother her with that," Mabel scoffs, swiping a hand at her friend. "Eadie has bigger problems. Just eat your eggs. They're perfectly poached."

Dottie looks conflicted. She wiggles in her seat. "I like to dip my crispy bacon in the yolk."

"Of course, Dottie. I'll get you another order."

"I like the shirt," Mabel calls with one hand in the air, still looking down at her food. "It's very New York chic."

I tug on Reid's shirt. Despite the smells of the kitchen—frying oil, fresh onions, crisping bacon—I still get the occasional whiff of Reid's cologne, and it takes me back to the moment in the office when my eyes were level with his abs. I wasn't joking. I've seen tons of half-naked men up close and personal. Textbook hot men. But it's Reid's half-naked chest that I can't seem to get out of my mind. For some odd reason, this annoys me. Very much.

I stomp over to Marlon. "I need an order of bacon."

"Yup," Marlon answers.

It's only been a few hours, but I already know that's his signature phrase. I think it's the only word he's said since we opened our doors this morning. I'm not complaining. He's putting out good dishes at record speeds. Cooking for a bunch of unruly prisoners taught him how to be cool under pressure. I'm impressed.

"Just a few minutes," I holler over at Dottie.

She waves. "Thank you, dear."

When I glance through the pass-through I see six empty, un-cleared tables and a throng of hungry customers waiting to be seated. Lexis and Annette are both at tables taking orders.

I hastily grab a cart, wheel it into the dining room, and start clearing the tables. "I'll be right with you," I say when I'm within earshot of the waiting crowd.

On my way back to the kitchen, Lexis catches up to me and whispers into my ear. "I'm sorry. We're having trouble keeping up. There are so many to-go orders."

"It's okay, you're doing great. We'll get to everyone."

Lexis responds with a faint smile and then heads over to fulfill her drink orders.

I roll the dirty dishes back to Alex, the high school junior who helps us on busy Saturdays. He starts scraping plates and emptying glasses, while I retrieve Dottie's freshly cooked bacon and deliver it to her.

When I return to my post, Reid is there managing the queue and doing quality control.

"What are you doing?" I ask.

He slides a plate of loaded fries to Annette who grabs it and shuttles it to her table. "I'm helping."

Reid wants me to trust him. He wants me to forgive him. How am I supposed to forgive him when he conspired against me and humiliated me in front of my classmates?

That was ten years ago, Eadie. Also, you're wearing his shirt.

Why am I mad? Earlier he was sending shockwaves of heat through me. Now I just want him out of my sight.

I need Mom to decipher my emotions like she did when I was younger, to help me sort them out so my repressed psychological issues don't turn into typhoid or smallpox or dengue fever. They don't intend to be carriers, those poor mosquitos.

"Help by scooting back into the office and counting money," I say, a hard edge to my voice.

I have a boyfriend. Why did Reid Avory's bare chest make me blush? I've seen so many man-chests. They're like vanilla ice cream to me. Kinda sweet but an easy pass.

"You weren't here. Orders were stacking up," Reid says.

"Well, I'm back now. Bye."

Reid turns to me and anchors his fist on the counter. "We're busy. You need help. I'll count money later."

I can smell his cologne. It's on me, released on warm currents as my body temperature rises. "I'm in charge. We're good."

Reid looks out over the dining room. "Six tables are empty, and three need cleared. Customers are backed up into the bakery."

"Then why don't *you* play greeter and busboy and go take care of it."

His nostrils flare. I watch his jaw muscles bulge under his skin. "I thought we declared a truce."

"You declared a truce."

"Eadie—"

"What?"

"Do we have to keep going back and forth like this?"

"I don't know. Do we? Customers are waiting."

He looks away. Takes a deep breath. And then snaps his attention back to me. His eyes are narrowed beneath a deeply furrowed brow. "Fine. I'll go play busboy for the big city girl who knows *everything* about everything."

"Oh really? Spoken like a washed-up high school football player who's stuck in his hometown with a crap job and an ex high school sweetheart."

Pain tinges the anger in Reid's eyes. His breaths come faster. "So that's what you think." He wads up a napkin in his fist, squeezes, and then tosses it across the counter before walking away.

"Don't mess with me, Reid Avory," I mutter. I grab his napkin and toss it into the trashcan by the door.

The Silver Sweethearts enjoy their meal, but they're in a bigger hurry to leave than usual.

"Thanks, Eadie," Mabel says with a kiss on my cheek. "We're going to go wander through the booths."

"Don't buy too much."

I give Dottie a hug and exchange grins with Annette as they head out of the kitchen.

Noon rolls by with no lull in customers. Reid plays the happy host, oozing with small-town hospitality as he leads people to their tables. None of us break to eat, the stream of customers unrelenting.

At two thirty, clouds pass over the sun. I watch as a stiff wind rattles the naked maple trees along the canal. Half an hour later, a cold front passes through, bringing a torrent of rain and sending frantic people through our doors.

We normally close at three o'clock, but I poll the crew and everyone agrees to work another hour or so. I text Gwen and ask her how we're looking on donuts. She baked extra for the festival and has plenty more to spare, so rather than let them go to waste, I tell her to hand them out to the waiting customers. This buys us a little grace.

The rain passes, leaving behind much colder weather and an end to the festivities on Main Street. As a result, the dining room slows down and eventually begins to clear out. At five o'clock, two hours after our normal closing time, all but two tables are empty, cleared, and wiped down with mild detergent in preparation for Monday morning.

"I have to meet my dad for dinner," Reid says while gripping his coat.

"You can leave."

"I know. I was just telling you."

Since our little tiff, I've been ignoring him, avoiding every opportunity to glance in his general direction.

"Gee, thanks," I say.

He clenches his jaw, narrows his eyes at me, and then ducks toward the service door. I guess he's still mad. Let him be. I'm not here to make friends. I'm here to do a job for Dad, and today I nailed it. We all did.

The family of four pushes back their chairs, the dad helping his two young daughters into their coats while the mother picks random bits of trash from the floor beneath the table.

I hurry into the dining room. "You don't have to do that."

She glances up at me. "My girls made a mess. I don't want to leave it for you."

"We pay people to clean up. It's fine. Really."

"Mommy, are we coming back to see Santa?" The tallest of the girls looks up at her mother. Her thin, blonde ponytail swishes back and forth as she rocks in her untied canvas shoes.

"Oh. I don't know." She looks down at her daughter and then at me. "When will he be here?"

"December 2nd," I say. "For our Christmas by the Canal celebration. There will be crafts, holiday snacks, and a parade followed by the tree lighting."

"Can we sit on Santa's lap?" The girl jumps up and down, prompting her sister to join in. Together, they repeat, "can we, can we, can we" until their dad breaks down.

"Fine," he says. "Now let your mother tie your shoes. We need to head home."

"Thanks for stopping by." I give them a wave and a smile before heading to the other occupied table. "Can I get you more water?" I ask the graying gentleman and his lovely silver-haired companion.

He waves me away. "We don't want to keep you."

"You're still eating. Enjoy. Take all the time you want. If you want a dessert, though, you better order now. I'm sending my cooks home."

"I don't think we'll have room," the woman says. Goosebumps cover her sun-damaged arms, the black and white tank dress she chose for the day no longer weather-appropriate. "This sauce is magnificent." She gestures to her half-eaten eggs Benedict. "What's in it?"

"It was my grandmother's secret recipe."

"Oh? And who was your grandmother?"

"Delores Tucker. She started this place in 1964."

The lady looks past her companion thoughtfully. "The name doesn't ring a bell, but then again, my mom knew so many people. She graduated from Cold Spring High School and was on the town council for decades. I'm sure they knew each other."

"Do you live nearby?" I ask.

"John and I are from Winford, high school sweethearts, but no, we live on the southside of Indy."

"We rarely make it up here," John says. He wipes his mouth with his napkin and takes a sip of water. "We decided it was such a nice day, heck, let's see if there's anything going on. Sure enough, you guys were having your thing, so we drove up."

"We had a wonderful time. This town is so unique. So quaint. Like a European village. And this hollandaise sauce. I need the recipe."

"You'd never use it," John interjects. He looks at me mischievously. "Shari never cooks. She wouldn't even know how to crack the eggs."

"Not true." Shari rolls her eyes at her husband, smiling all the while.

"We need to tell Megan about this place," John says to Shari. He points at her. "The 'Hidden Gems' column. I bet she could twist someone's arm."

Shari's expression brightens at the suggestion. "Our daughter Megan used to work for *The Indy Insider*. They feature a restaurant in the surrounding Indianapolis area every month. A hidden gem they call it. It's featured in their print magazine and goes out to their newsletter subscribers, over two hundred thousand of them. It might drive some business here. Do you want me to hook you up with her?"

I pull out a chair from a nearby table and drop into it. "That would be amazing. Every little bit helps. If you haven't noticed, we're due for a dining room upgrade."

Shari shrugs. I can tell she's torn between being honest and saving my feelings. "The place is looking a little faded, but the food is *wonderful*. And your location in this historic building by the canal. There's so much potential here. You need to contact Food Network and have that blond-haired gentleman visit. The one who drives the red car and wears his sunglasses on the back of his head."

"Guy Fieri," I say.

"Give the lady Megan's phone number," John says. "She wants to go home."

"Oh. Yes. Do you have your phone with you?"

I run to the kitchen to grab it. When I return, Shari recites Megan's phone number while I add her as a contact.

"I'll let her know you're going to contact her," Shari says. "Actually. Here. Let me do it before I forget."

As she texts her daughter, I refill their water. Soon after, they finish their meals, I take their payment, and thank them for stopping by.

"We'll be back," Shari says. "I'd like to take a canal ride in the summer."

"Definitely," I answer, thanking them again as they turn to leave.

Back in the kitchen, Annette and Lexis are collapsed at the Silver Sweethearts' table. Annette is leaning back, eyes closed, fanning herself with a paper plate. Lexis's arms are puddled on the table, her head in the center of them.

I walk over and rest my hand on Lexis's shoulder. "You both did amazing today."

Annette puffs out an exhausted breath. "Do we get a raise?"

"I wish. You get to take home all your tips."

"I made bank," Lexis says, her voice muffled against the white plastic tabletop.

Annette opens an eye and peers at me. "You're pretty good at this, you know?"

I pull out one of the metal folding chairs and sink into it. "I guess I like bossing people around. I forgot about that side of myself."

"I saw you giving Reid the what-for." Annette opens both eyes and scoots higher in her chair, still fanning herself.

I grab a napkin from the dispenser in the center of the table and dab my nose and forehead. "I was being managerial."

Lexis pops her head up. "A general manager is higher than a kitchen manager."

"I'm a *Tucker*."

Her shoulders hitch, and then she drops her head back to the table.

"That's right," Annette says. "You get to boss that blue-eyed, bearded lumberjack all day long while available bachelorettes in Cold Spring salivate for the chance."

Lexis pops up again and squints at Annette. "I'm single and I'm not salivating."

"He's not your type," Annette says dismissively.

I hold up a hand. "He's not mine either. New York model boyfriend, remember?" Also, I vowed never to date a guy from Cold Spring, especially not the one who inspired that vow.

"Sure, I remember," Annette says, relaxing into her seat. "But Reid has eyes for you."

My cheeks flame, two gas burners set on "High." Why does the thought of Reid "eyeing" me ignite a bonfire in my body? I'm mad at him. And he's mad at me. We're *mad*. And I'm spoken for. Reid can take his eyes and shove them onto someone *else*.

Lexis unfolds and slumps against her seatback. "Who says that?"

"Says what?" Annette says. The two women seem unfazed by the blazing inferno beside them.

"He 'has eyes' for her," Lexis says with a scowl. "Who says that?"

Annette props her elbows on the table and leans into them. "I'm old, honey."

Lexis rolls her eyes. "You're telling Eadie to cheat on her boyfriend."

"No, I'm not," Annette says, suddenly demure. Until she winks at me and the innocent act unravels. "All I know is, if I was Eadie's age, I might..." She taps a purple acrylic nail against the table.

"He's our *boss*," Lexis says.

"Our cute boss."

I raise a hand again. "Totally smokin' hot, to-die-for pecs-of-steel model boyfriend. Not interested in Hoosier men. At all. Like ever."

Annette swats my arm. "Why are you blushing? I'm teasing you. This is how I get when I'm exhausted. A little loopy and loose-tongued."

Was Annette kidding, then? Does Reid "have eyes" for me, or not?

No way am I clarifying it with her. Thankfully, my phone chimes, ending the conversation. "Night ladies," I say before taking my blushing cheeks to the office.

I settle in front of my computer and check my phone. To my surprise, Megan texted me.

Hello. My mom and dad gave me your number.

Yes, I text back. **They just left.**

They loved Home for the Holidays.

Home for the Hollandaise, I correct.

A moment passes.

You're kidding me, Megan finally responds. **That's so freaking adorable. So, I don't work for The Indy Insider anymore, but I still have lunch with the managing editor every Friday. I can drop the name of your café.**

That would be wonderful, I reply.

Actually, let me give you her email address. Send her a note. Tell her you know me and intro your café. I'll talk your place up next Friday.

A minute later, she sends the email address: **gigi.smalls@thein dyinsider.com.**

Best of luck, she finishes. **I may pop up there sometime. My parents are picky so you must have something special.**

I text back my most heartfelt thanks and smack my mouse to wake up the computer. Wasting no time, I pull up my Gmail and craft a quick, succinct email to Gigi. Next, I pull out my phone, go to my settings and turn on my Gmail notifications.

The moment Gigi responds—*if* she responds—I'll know.

Chapter 16

The first thing I do when I get home is run to my room and rip off Reid's T-shirt. After flinging it into the wicker clothes basket, I dig through my meager pile of shirts, deciding on a long-sleeved Ralph Lauren T-shirt in a neutral gray. With the fresh scent of my fabric softener replacing the stale scents of Reid's cologne and day-old fryer oil, I sit on the end of my bed and stare at my phone.

Hayden hasn't texted me today. I'm not surprised. I'd be an idiot not to notice that *I* always text him first. Here I am again, kicking off today's digital interaction.

I could tell him about how I killed it in the kitchen today, how I'm becoming quite the boss babe, how I assigned my high school bully to busboy duty. Instead, I address the small, yet weighty dark spot in my chest.

I miss Jupiter, I text.

Hayden has always supported my entomology obsession, buying me my bee necklace, my grasshopper slippers, my ladybug scarf. Only once did he say I have a bug fetish, which I quickly corrected, and we might have been fighting at the time. I can't remember.

So, I guess he's either crossed the rainbow bridge, I continue, **or he's living it up in the walls of the Coleman Building.**

Hayden is a dog man, proud owner of a skittish chihuahua named Simon. He crates Simon when I'm over because the dog bares his teeth at me and foams at the mouth like I'm storming his castle, which I kind of am.

I can't blame Jupiter, I add. **I'm sure there's a lot to see.**

A new starry-eyed couple in New York City is never at a loss for something to do. When we started dating, Hayden and I enjoyed Broadway musicals together, visited the aquarium, explored Little Greece, cruised the harbor. Lately, we've been staying in, surfing Netflix, and ordering DoorDash.

Last summer, I wanted to rent kayaks, stargaze at the High Line, visit the Brooklyn Botanic Garden. We never got around to any of it.

You there?

I tap my phone screen with my thumbnail for a minute or two, waiting for a response. Who knows what Hayden does on a Saturday afternoon in New York City while I'm here in Indiana, hemmed in by corn and soybean fields? Gallivanting in Chinatown, perhaps, or taking Simon on a walk in Central Park? Is he alone or with someone?

My mind flips through the various gorgeous female models he might have encountered on the job this week. I groan when I reach Ella Fernandez, one of the most sought-after models in the business, also represented by Hayden's agency. She's taller than me, bustier, fuller-lipped with a perpetual sultry gaze. It's only a matter of time until the two of them connect in front of the camera, him shirtless, her in a flirty bra.

I groan again before standing to engage in a more productive activity. When I hit the bottom of the stairs, I'm greeted by the sound of Mom's Dyson Ball vacuum. She's sucking up dog hair in the living room, making long swipes while her white linen bell sleeve flutters beneath her thin arm. Dad's reclined in his chair, feet up and fingers resting on his forehead to cover his eyes. The television blares in tandem with the Dyson's shrill motor.

Mom pauses her task to expel a deep, rattling cough. I walk over to the outlet and pull out the vacuum's cord. The machine goes silent.

"Thank the Lord God Almighty," Dad declares. "Are you finally done, woman?"

"It just shut off," Mom says with a confused inflection as she futilely clicks the switch.

"Mother," I say to announce my presence. "Your cough sounds horrendous."

Mom jumps in surprise and then peers at me over her shoulder. Her eyes drop to the limp power cord in my hand. "Plug it back in. I'm almost done."

"Sit down. I'll finish it for you."

"No," Dad moans with his fingertips still pressed to his forehead.

"Or I can do it after you two go to bed," I offer.

Mom limps over to me as hurriedly as her hip will allow and snatches the cord from my hand. "If I don't sweep every day the dog hair becomes atrocious." She leans over to plug the vacuum back in. One of her joints pops as she stands, but she's unfazed, carefully redirecting herself to the vacuum that's chipping away at Dad's sanity.

I decide to leave it alone. For now. I don't like the sound of Mom's cough. She's pushing herself too hard, and I'm the only person who can remedy that.

As I head through the dining room, the Dyson starts up to the sound of Dad's groaning displeasure. Mom feels compelled to sweep every day, understandably with two Golden Retrievers. To give her a break while I'm home, I add sweeping to my mental daily to-do list. It's fine. I'd rather sweep up dog hair, check on the chickens, and cook my parents dinner than worry about Hayden hooking up with Ella Fernandez.

I check my phone for texts before setting it on the kitchen table. No word from him yet. Maybe he'll text while I'm feeding the chickens.

He doesn't. Chicken duty took ten minutes.

Mom has been writing the weekly menu on the white board beside the refrigerator. I go over to check tonight's meal. Her grocery list is scrawled on a piece of paper that's attached to the fridge. A quick comparison of the list with the menu tells me I have some shopping to do.

I pull off the list and stuff it in my pocket, grab my phone, and return to the living room to announce my plans to visit the Winford Meijer.

"I was going to have the groceries delivered," Mom says.

The vacuum sits upright in the center of the living room, the cord wrapped around its handle. Mom is collapsed on the couch with one foot propped on the cushions, the other brushing the floor. She dissolves into a round of coughs that seem to originate from the bottom of her lungs. I don't like the sound.

"Are you okay, Mom?" I ask when her hacking subsides.

"It's just a post-viral cough. Nothing to worry about."

"Do you want cough syrup?"

"It's on the list. Here," she says, reaching out. I hand her the list, and she reads through it, nodding. "You don't have to go. Let me order," she says when she's finished.

"Delivery is too expensive."

And traipsing through the grocery aisles will keep my mind off the fact that Hayden is ignoring me. Or he's too busy to respond. Or both. Why am I fretting? He's probably at the grocery store testing the cantaloupe for ripeness and filling his cart with chicken, salmon, and eggs—the protein he needs to recover from the strenuous work-outs that keep his muscles taut and defined.

"It won't take me long," I add. "I'll be back in time to fix dinner."

Before leaving, I grab a pillow and a blanket from the built-ins under the stairs and deposit them on Mom's lap. "Lay back and rest," I say. She doesn't argue.

Her list isn't long. In forty-five minutes, I'm in and out of Meijer with her items and several of my own including vanilla Greek yogurt and blueberries.

It's nearly eight o'clock by the time I return home. Mom is cozied up on the couch watching the news, and Dad is asleep in his chair. Tonight's dinner isn't going to be fancy. I bought a few cans of low-sodium Progresso soup, and I'll pair it with grilled cheese. Hopefully, Mom won't mind that I'm not following her menu plan.

When the soup is warm and the sandwiches are hot, I carry the food to my parents, tapping lightly on my dad to wake him. He gives me a confused, bleary-eyed look before realizing my intention.

Mom doesn't complain about my decision to forgo lasagna. When they're both settled in with their soup and sandwiches, I carry my portion into the living room and sink into the blue and white mission chair next to Dad.

Between bites, I fill them in on my successful day at the café. Dad's slumped posture straightens a little when I give them my best guess of how many people came through the doors. The slight burst of energy doesn't last, and he resumes struggling to lift the spoon to his lips without spilling soup onto his lap.

He's been sleeping through the days, looking lethargic in his waking hours, concentrating harder than usual to complete simple tasks. The longer it continues, the more I worry. I mentioned my concerns to Mom, but she said he's still feeling the after-effects of the anesthesia. I trust she checked with his doctor before drawing that conclusion.

When we're done eating, I pile Dad's dishes on mine and approach Mom for hers, but she shoos me away.

"I've got it," she says. She pushes off the couch to take some of the strain off her hip and follows me into the kitchen.

We're handwashing the bowls and plates when I hear Dad shuffle in behind us.

"Hey Dad," I call over my shoulder. "Whatcha need?"

He doesn't answer, so I turn around and find him looking lost and purposeless like he's forgotten his own name.

I dry my hands and walk over to him. "Dad?"

He angles his head my way and brushes his eyes across mine without a hint of recognition.

"Wes," Mom says. She grabs his elbow and begins ushering him to the kitchen table. He doesn't put up a fight, his feet shuffling across the tile like he's on slick ice.

We manage to lower him into a chair. Mom grabs his shoulders and bends until her face is inches from his. "Weston."

He gives her a confused look, tilting his head to the side.

"He did this earlier," Mom says, "but it passed."

"Mother! Why didn't you tell me? I'm calling 911." My voice is rising.

"Hush. You don't need to be so loud."

I look down and Dad is shaking his head at me as his eyes sharpen.

"Dad!"

"Why are you yelling at me, Lovebug?"

I meet eyes with Mom. "Should I still call 911?"

Dad pushes us away and eases to his feet. "No one's calling 911."

"What if it's a stroke?" I say, still laser-focused on Mom.

"It's not a stroke," she says.

"How do you know?"

"I'm not having a stroke," Dad says.

Mom tries to support him as he walks, but he swipes her hands away.

"I guess I came in for some ice cream." He heads to the fridge.

"We don't have any," I say. "It wasn't on the grocery list."

"Well, put it on there!" He hobbles to the counter, grabs a pad of paper, and tries to pick up a pencil, but it slips out of his hand and skitters across the floor.

I obey my natural inclination to swoop in and offer support. Unlike Mom's attempt to help, he doesn't swat at me. Instead, he lets me turn him toward the doorway and help him back to the living room. When he's settled in his recliner, I say, "Do you want me to run to Dairy Queen?"

"Large M&M Blizzard," he says.

Mom's hovering behind me. I turn to her and whisper, "Call the doctor tomorrow." She nods. "Do you want anything?" I ask in my normal voice.

She shakes her head, sighs, and heads back to the couch, her worry seemingly gone.

When my parents are settled in bed, I head upstairs, wash my face, and change into a short-sleeved jersey pajama set. A cursory glance at my phone before climbing into bed tells me all I need to know. Hayden hasn't responded. Every excuse I made for him this evening flies out the window. I can't think of a valid reason why my boyfriend would ignore me all day.

Unless... Was he hit by a car? Did he fall through a manhole? Or choke on a grape? How would I know if he was seriously injured? Or worse? Because something horrible must have happened for him not to text. That's the only explanation.

I climb into bed fully aware that I'm blowing this way out of proportion. I dial back my catastrophizing and force myself to be practical. He's probably at a photo shoot. Which still annoys me. Why didn't he tell me he had to work today?

It's ten thirty, but I risk a text to Whitney. **Are you awake?**

She responds immediately. See? How hard was that?

I'm binge watching The Walking Dead, she says.

I ask if we can FaceTime, and my phone starts ringing. I accept her call.

"Hey, girlie," Whitney says. She's wrapped in her favorite pink Comfy. The carefully placed curls in her brunette hair are limp from a day of wear, but her blue eyes are bright and inquisitive. "How's the Midwest?"

"It has its ups and downs." I prop my back against the walnut headboard and tug the comforter to my waist.

"I thought Indiana was flat," Whitney quips.

"Ha ha. It's flat up here, but down south it's hilly. You should come and visit."

"Does Cold Spring have a Saks Fifth Avenue?"

"No."

"A Fresh and Fit Market?"

"No."

Whitney makes a face. "No thanks."

"You get used to it. Anyway—"

"What's wrong?" she cuts in. "Your elevens are showing."

I rub between my eyebrows and relax my worry muscles to smoothen the skin.

"You need to get preventative Botox before it's too late."

"Hayden hasn't texted me all day," I say, ignoring her Botox comment. She's been nagging me about it for months, but I have no intention of injecting botulism into my face.

Whitney lowers her phone and readjusts the camera angle. "Did he go on a day trip with the guys?"

"He doesn't go on day trips with 'the guys.' Have you two talked?"

"Not today."

"Have you made any holiday event plans?"

"Oh. Yeah." She shifts her weight and tugs the Comfy to her chin. "We're heading to his parents' place for Thanksgiving."

My jaw drops. "Uh..."

Hayden's parents live in Northern Maine. It's an eight-hour drive, probably longer during a holiday weekend.

Whitney scoots to the edge of the couch and peers down at me. Her shoulder-length hair falls forward and surrounds her face. "Is that okay?"

"Sure. It's just... That's a long trip, and then to turn around that evening and come home..."

"We're staying until Saturday. Oh my gawd, Eadie. You're not okay with this. I can see it in your face. I can cancel."

I mind my expression, trying to make it less...shocked. Hayden never invited *me* to his parents' house for Thanksgiving. For the last two years, we've flown to Indiana and spent the day with my parents.

"You said you wanted me to keep an eye on him. I thought it would be okay," Whitney adds. "We're sleeping in separate bedrooms. His parents have a mother-in-law suite in the backyard. It's a tiny home that they built for his grandma, but she passed away, and now it's sitting there empty."

"I know."

"Anyway, he's sleeping out there. I get his sister's old bedroom."

I don't know why I'm hesitating. She's right. He'll be with her, which will keep him off the streets. Not like he's a thug or anything, but I'll be able to enjoy my Thanksgiving without worrying that he's hooking up with Ella Fernandez or eating alone for that matter. Not that he would ever hook up with someone. Why am I so paranoid?

"Yeah. That sounds great actually," I say. "You can make him respond to my texts."

Whitney leans back, relieved. She lifts her phone to give me an unencumbered view of her fresh complexion and impeccably shaped eyebrows.

"You know you don't have anything to worry about, though, right?" she says. "Hayden adores you. And you're drop-dead gorgeous. You put ninety-nine-point-nine percent of the single women in New York City to shame."

I drop my forehead to my hand. "I guess it's the point-one percent that worries me. He happens to work in a profession that is swarming with the point-one-ers."

Whitney lets out a bubbly laugh. "You need to spend more time looking in the mirror, missy. Besides, think about it. If you don't trust Hayden, why are you two together?"

I mull over her comment, really *think* about what my deal is. The words "walking stick" and "ostrich" echo through my mind. Graduating from high school doesn't mean you leave it all behind. Some things stick with you, like the repeated snide comments of your peers and their hurtful actions that make you feel less of a female, less of a person.

"He apologized for looking at other girls and said he'll stop doing it," I finally concede.

"Do you believe him?"

"Sorta. He's a guy, so..."

"Nope. That's not an excuse. We have to hold our men to high standards."

"That's all I'm doing, right?"

Whitney hesitates and then shrugs one shoulder. "Sure. And I'm your eyes and ears. I'll make sure he behaves."

"Thanks, Whitney. Keep me posted. And don't stay up too late. It ruins your mornings."

Whitney groans. "Yes, mom."

We trade smiles before ending the call.

I need to get a grip. I can't spend my life worrying that Hayden is going to leave me for a hotter, more interesting woman. I have to practice letting go of the past and trusting him. The more I practice, the better I'll get. In the meantime, I have Whitney as my spy to give me extra peace of mind while I get a handle on my self-doubt.

Who needs counseling when you can mix a little self-reflection with a best friend who promises to have your back?

With my worries assuaged, the depth of my exhaustion hits me hard, dropping onto my muscles like a twenty-pound weighted blanket. I set my phone on the nightstand, slide deeper into bed, and put my worries about Dad and Hayden to rest as I drift into sleep.

⚜ ⚜

Sunday evening, I find myself in the same spot, top half propped against the headboard, bottom half snuggled under the comforters while a howling November wind whips against the drafty window.

I pull the covers tighter to my waist as I stare at my darkened phone screen.

The day flew by. This morning, my parents and I watched the livestream of church while eating day-old Home for the Hollandaise yeast donuts. Afterward, I insisted I do the Thanksgiving grocery shopping. Mom insisted I not. We ended up shopping together. She used the automated cart, zooming through the aisles and rattling items off her list, ordering me around like a drill sergeant. We bought everything for our upcoming Thanksgiving meal, including a twenty-pound turkey, three pounds of sweet potatoes, and four boxes of Jiffy cornbread mix. I guess Mom wants a lot of leftovers.

Shopping distracted me from thoughts about Hayden and Whitney's eight-hour drive to Maine and Hayden's habitual radio silence. At three o'clock in the afternoon he still hadn't texted me a nice *Good morning* or *How's it going?* No surprise. I pushed through my frustration by dusting the entire house, sweeping, washing and folding all the laundry, and anything else I could find to occupy myself despite Dad's playful jabs to "Give it a rest, Lovebug."

Dad's more alert today, thankfully, but the vacant look in his eyes in the kitchen haunts me now and then. When I recounted the moment with Mom on the way to the grocery, she wrote it off as an after-effect of the anesthesia. "I'm sure it's nothing," she said with finality, which meant the discussion was over.

My phone chimes, interrupting my thoughts and giving me a jolt of adrenaline. I fumble the phone between both hands before stabilizing it. Two deep breaths later, I check the text.

Would you look at that, I marvel.

Hayden texted me first. Miracles still happen.

Have you found Jupiter?

Arthropods. My love language. He knows just what to say. I smile despite the sad pull in my chest at the mention of my missing pet's name and punch back with my thumbs. **No. <frowning emoji> Wanna FaceTime?**

Sure, he responds.

He rings me and a moment later, his gorgeous face melts my heart. He's reclined in bed, one arm above his head, his bare chest exposed.

We catch up on our days, and then I decide to dive into it.

"Whitney said you two are driving up to your parents for Thanksgiving?" I frame it as a question, so I don't sound judgy. I'm totally okay with their Thanksgiving trip. I just need to see the look on his face when I mention it. Is there any guilt? Does he seem guarded?

"Yeah, is that okay?" he answers. The innocent look in his rounded eyes makes my heart skip a beat. I hate being away from him. It makes me go to places I wouldn't otherwise go, wondering if I can trust him, letting my eyes linger too long on Reid's abs. Only a few more weeks and I'll be snuggling next to Hayden in that bed, my life returned to normal.

"Sure. It's fine," I say with a faint smile. "I mean, it's not weird. Is it?"

Hayden returns my half smile. "I can call it off if you want."

"The whole trip?"

"Yeah."

I sink into the bed. "You wouldn't go alone?"

"It's a long drive. I wanted someone with me to make sure I don't fall asleep. But if you're weirded out, I'll spend Thanksgiving with Simon."

Hayden's letting me decide if he enjoys a feast in Maine with his parents or eats a turkey sub with his dog. My body warms despite the threads of cold air coming through the cracks in the wood-framed window.

Why am I acting so foolish? My doubts have nothing to do with Hayden. They're all me, leftover from my gangly teenage years, never mind the *Vogue* cover, the Fashion Week catwalk. Why am I stuck in the past?

Get a hold of yourself, Eadie. Look in the mirror. You've changed. You're hot. Whitney says so.

"Go," I say finally. "On one condition, though. I want us to visit your parents for Thanksgiving next year."

Hayden's face relaxes into a full smile. "Are you sure about that? My dad's turkey is as dry as a rope."

"Of course, I'm sure."

A mischievous look crosses his face. "Tell me honestly. Is Whitney going to drive me nuts the whole drive?"

I giggle. "I've never been in a car with her for eight hours. You're on your own."

Hayden rolls his eyes, but his grin persists.

"Having a travel buddy makes sense," I say. "Even if she does annoy you. I want you to be safe."

"Thanks, Eadie."

I love how he says my name.

We say our goodnights, and then I dream of Hayden wearing a tight flannel shirt and brown Rhinos. When his face morphs into Reid's like the T-1000 cyborg in *Terminator 2*, I jolt out of bed, shake the madness from my head, and resolve to never look Reid in the eyes again.

Chapter 17

Has the bakery always been this small? Between the ovens, mixers, cooling rack, steel prep table, and Reid, there's not much room left to move. Reid's decked out in the usual: an orange and brown flannel, jeans, and boots. An apron covers his bottom half in preparation for an evening of baking. He's ready for this adventure. I'm not.

Last night, I baked pumpkin roll after pumpkin roll, convinced I didn't need any help, especially not Reid's, even though he happily offered. I worked into the wee hours until my feet and shoulders were numb before admitting the job requires more hands. Earlier today, I accepted Reid's second offer to help, and here we are, stuck together in a tiny kitchen until we fulfill the rest of our orders.

"How long until the oxygen runs out of this room?" Reid asks.

I focus on his hair, daring a glance at his lips, which are minus whiskers. He shaved his mustache and beard over the weekend. Now he looks less like a lumberjack, more like the Reid I remember. Kind eyes and a non-descript nose, naturally pigmented lips and a squarish chin with a slight dimple. The only difference is his five o'clock shadow—something he never had when we were in high school—and the two lines between his eyebrows. From frowning during his divorce perhaps?

He notices my lingering gaze. I flick my eyes away. This room may be small, but my powers of avoidance are strong.

"Was that a joke?" I ask as I round the prep table to position my whiteboard against a structural pole that's mostly ensconced in cabinets.

"Not really. It's pretty tight in here. And...stuffy. Why did I wear a flannel?"

"Talking wastes oxygen if you're that worried."

"Touché."

I open cabinet doors, collecting ingredients and depositing them on the table, stopping at the refrigerator for two flats of eggs and the remaining cold ingredients, and then I station myself next to Reid and point to his mixer.

"That's yours. There's the recipe." I gesture at the whiteboard where I scribbled the ingredients for a double batch of pumpkin roll batter.

"What? No. I said I would help. Not work independently. I burn Pop-Tarts."

I pull two bowls and two electronic scales from the bottom shelf and plop one of each in front of Reid. "Just follow the recipe. You're an accountant. This is like math. Make all the numbers match and you'll be fine."

"There aren't any operators."

"180 grams of flour plus 400 grams of sugar equals a double batch."

"That's a lot of sugar." He taps the scale with his knuckle. "What happened to imperial measurements? Cups. Teaspoons. This is more like science."

I fight to suppress a smile while I dump flour into my bowl. "Metric measurements are more accurate."

He's still poking. "Um."

"Are you acting dumb on purpose?"

"I'm trying to flirt, but if you think it's dumb, I'll try a different tactic."

My muscles freeze at the word "flirt." I haven't met eyes with Reid since Saturday. You'd think he'd realize I'm not interested in chummy banter or friendship of any sort.

"I'm kidding. Geez, Grasshopper. Are you ever going to look me in the eye?"

A shiver shoots up my spine. He hasn't called me that since eighth grade.

"No." I measure the rest of the dry ingredients, toss them in and give everything a light mix with a fork.

"We had a little tiff," Reid says. "It's over. *I'm* over it at least."

"I don't know what you're talking about."

"Saturday. When you demoted me to busboy."

"I thought that was a promotion."

"Ha ha. How do I get this thing to measure grams?"

"Press the unit button, genius."

Reid sighs. He continues making random noises—grunts, groans, indecipherable muttering—while measuring his flour, salt, and leavening. I'm well into my wet ingredients, watching them come together in my stand mixer when he plops his dry ingredients into the mixer and sets it to "High."

A poof of fine, white powder engulfs him, sending him into a coughing fit while his mixer continues to throw flour out of the bowl.

"Start with the wet ingredients," I admonish over the hum of our professional-grade appliances. I dive over to his mixer and shut it off.

"You didn't tell me that!"

"Why are you yelling?"

"Because I'm covered in flour!"

I reach over and shut off my mixer before giving Reid a good once-over. His face, chest, and sleeves are dusted with flour, but his glasses gave him a dust-free raccoon mask. His eyes are bright and clear, his expression flummoxed. I can't contain my laughter.

"You look ridiculous," I say between giggles.

"I feel like you're laughing at me," Reid says matter-of-factly as he starts unbuttoning his flannel.

I immediately sober up. "You better have something under that shirt."

"I do."

"I don't want to see your hairy man-chest."

"You didn't mind it on Saturday."

A burst of heat reddens my cheeks. I hastily turn to my mixer and flip it back on, angling my body so my back is mostly toward Reid. I hear him shake out his flannel, making a mess of the floor, no doubt.

He taps my shoulder.

"What?"

"Is my face clean?"

My cheeks are still flaming so I only risk a quick glance. "It's fine," I mumble.

I hear shuffling behind me as he dumps his failed batch of dry ingredients into the trash. "Crisis averted," he says. "I guess I'll start over." More groans and grunts. "I think this would go better if we tag teamed."

"I work better alone."

"Yes ma'am."

"Don't call me 'ma'am.'"

"Yes, Grasshopper."

I grit my teeth. Reid's messing with me, using that nickname. I need to turbo charge my avoidance game. "Be right back, Egg Man," I say as I duck out the door.

I return with my Bluetooth noise-canceling headphones and my phone in my back pocket, the Spotify app already set to my "Loud" mix that's shuffling through Emo bands from the 2000s. Reid glances at my headphones and then at me. When I slide them over my ears, I give him a curt smile and then immerse myself in a cacophony of electric guitars and whiny pop stars pretending to be punk rockers.

With Reid miles away, virtually speaking, I'm able to refocus on the contents of my mixture, slowly pouring in my dry ingredients until I have a loose batter. I grab two sheet pans from the cooling rack and divide the pumpkin mixture between them. A moment later, they're in the top oven and I'm started on my next batch.

I'm on the final spin cycle when I hear a loud *Clack!* My heart jumps to my throat and the adrenaline bolt feels like someone poked me with a cattle prod. I look over. Reid's looking at me innocently despite his obvious guilt.

I rip my headphones off and lay into him. "Did you tap my earphone?"

"I flicked it. Like this." He demonstrates by flicking the air with his index finger.

"Don't *do* that! You about busted my eardrum."

Reid shrinks back, that innocent look still oozing through his spectacles. He pushes them up his nose and collapses his chest even further.

"What?" I spit out.

"You're scary when you're mad."

"I mean, why did you so rudely interrupt the guitar solo in *Na Na Na (Na Na Na Na Na Na Na Na Na)*?"

Reid covers a laugh with his hand. His eyes crinkle with amusement. "How many *Na's* was that?"

"Twelve. And I was rather enjoying it."

He shrugs. "To each her own. Hey, can you check my batter? It looks runny."

"It's supposed to be loose."

"Like *how* loose. And don't start making bowel references."

I scoot over to his mixer and peer inside. His batter looks like a runny bodily expulsion. I think he added too many spices.

I dip my finger in and have a taste.

Reid looks horrified. "There's raw eggs in that."

"I grew up eating raw eggs every Christmas."

"A raw egg down the gullet at midnight to celebrate Baby Jesus?"

"Have you heard of eggnog?"

"Yes. And salmonella."

"Anyway, this tastes like crap. How much salt did you use?"

Reid squints at the whiteboard. "8 grams."

"That's a 3."

His face squinches. "On what planet?"

"You really suck at this, don't you?"

"I survive on frozen meals. Popcorn chicken, skinny fries, Marie Calendar teriyaki noodle bowls. Take out. Uber Eats."

I level my eyes at him. "You need to amend your habits."

He places a fist on his waist and leans into the other hand. "We only have until six o'clock tomorrow morning to fix eighty pumpkin rolls. I can't learn any new habits before then, so I suggest we change our game plan. You measure the ingredients, I mix them. This baby can handle a quadruple batch." He slaps the top of his mixer.

"What's eighty divided by four?"

"I don't do maths in my head. I'm an accountant. We use beans."

"Twenty."

"I knew that."

I eyeball our workstation and do a few more rough calculations in my head including the amount of time it takes a cake to cook in a 350-degree oven. "We can run both mixers at the same time. All you have to do is pour the ingredients in. Can you handle that?"

He raises both hands, palms out. "I'm feeling crazy. Let's do it."

We get to work, me in the middle pouring and measuring, Reid crossing behind me continuously to check on each batch, pouring in the dry ingredients when I give him the go. In short order, the room is filled with sheet pans of pumpkin roll batter waiting for the oven.

I cross behind him, pull out two finished cakes, and slide them into the cooling rack. "We still have to make the filling and roll these things up," I say as a trickle of sweat carves its way down my lightly dusted temple.

Reid doesn't hear me over the white noise of the whirring mixers. I return to my station and start cracking eggs. Each batch takes three. That's twelve eggs for a quadruple batch. Unlike Reid, I can do some maths in my head.

I'm not sure what happens next. I reach over while he swipes up, he crosses behind while I step back. Somehow, the bowl tips violently, twelve raw eggs go airborne, yolks and all, and I catch them with my face and chest, the pre-embryonic goo slapping my shocked expression and quickly dripping down my shirt while visions of the Valentine's dance incident materialize before my eyes like flash bombs. The emotions return too. The embarrassment, mortification, and stabbing betrayal.

Reid's shocked expression matches mine, but his is flavored with guilt and a dash of remorse.

"Eadie," he stutters. "I didn't mean... I'm so sorry. Let me find you a towel." He darts around the small bakery. Finding nothing, he rushes out of the room and returns a moment later holding six hand towels. "Here." He hands one to me and tosses the rest strategically onto my torso until I'm covered in terry cloth, including on my head.

"Um. You can stop," I say.

He grips the final towel in his fist, worriedly searching my face like he's making sure I'm still alive and breathing. A few swipes with the towel remove most of the egg from my face. The rest of me will take more work. Once again, I'm standing in Mom and Dad's café wishing I had a change of clothes.

"I guess I have to go home and change." Not to mention I need time to shake off these decade-old emotions which are suddenly as raw as the eggs on my shirt.

Reid jumps into action and starts unbuttoning his shirt.

"No! I don't need your T-shirt. No cinching at the waist today. Sorry."

"I was going to let you have my flannel."

I give him the side-eye.

"No?"

"It smells like you."

A hint of panic crosses Reid's face. He sniffs an armpit and relaxes. "My Old Spice is holding up."

"That's the problem," I mumble.

"I have no idea what you mean so I'm just going to work on these buttons."

Watching Reid's fingers adeptly expose his white undershirt solidifies my confidence. We need to stop dancing around this. Time has molded us both. We've been punched down, repositioned on the pottery wheel, our walls thinned and refined with each rotation of the earth. My mind is trying to trick me, telling me ten years ago was just yesterday. It's not true. Also, I'm not a ballerina. I can't tiptoe around Reid for long without my strength wearing out.

"Why?" I ask, simply.

Reid stops unbuttoning and bows his head, requiring no further explanation.

I continue anyway. "That day changed my life. I vowed to leave Cold Spring, to prove I was better than this place. Better than all of you."

"I didn't mean—"

"You knew," I cut in, my anger simmering. "You fed me lies, told me you were sorry, told me you had feelings for me. You buttered me up all the way to the pavilion, so I'd feel even worse when your idiot friends assaulted me. Which is what it was, you know. Assault. I could have pressed charges."

"No. Eadie. That's not how it was." He shakes his head and takes a step closer.

"You're gaslighting me now?" I let loose, leaning into Reid and shoving my finger into his chest. "That's not a good look, Reid. I know what happened. I remember every second of it."

He tries to lower my arm, but I jerk it away from his grasp.

"Don't even try it," I snap. "We have to finish these pumpkin rolls, but we don't have to pretend to be friends while we're doing it." I turn back to the prep table and toss a cup of flour into my mixing bowl, ignoring the panicked look on his face.

He's taken aback by my anger. I'm surprised by it too. My undeveloped eighteen-year-old brain seems to be in charge. Again.

"Eadie," he says softly. "You never let me explain."

I pause, both hands resting on the stainless-steel countertop. "There's nothing to explain," I say, resignation dulling my voice.

He touches my arm lightly. "Will you look at me?"

"I really don't feel like it," I say to the mixing bowl.

"I had no idea they were waiting for us in the pavilion. I had nothing to do with it."

"Yeah, right."

"I'm not lying. I tried to tell you the following Monday, but you walked away from me. I tried texting you, but you blocked my number. I tried talking to Gracelyn, but she just told me off. I had nothing to do with that prank."

"Assault."

Reid shuffles his weight. I watch him in my peripheral vision, the white undershirt now fully exposed. "I'm not disagreeing with you. It was horrible. I laid into Jaden after you left. He and I didn't speak for a month."

"But you got back together with Kara within a week."

Reid sighs heavily, rubs his forearms with his dry palms, the raspy sound making my nerves twinge. "I know. I can understand why that sent mixed signals. She and I had issues. Our relationship was never healthy. That's why we're divorced."

He touches my shoulder, and I allow it. I allow him to gently pivot my body so I'm facing him. "She jumped on you and said, 'We did it.'" My eyes defy my feeble attempt to avoid his. "What was I supposed to think?"

"I wanted you to stay."

I capture Reid's gaze, my anger bleeding into the wide blue pools of his irises. "I was covered in eggs and chicken feathers," I say despite my immobile jaw.

Reid wraps his hand around my elbow, giving it a modest squeeze. "Please believe me, Eadie. I didn't know."

"You didn't exactly run after me."

"I was stunned. And..."

"And what?"

"I guess I was humiliated too."

Reid blinks before I manage to utter my next accusation. "Why? Because your buddies caught you with the class nerd? The whipping girl? The 'Walking Stick?'"

"No, Eadie. That's not it at all. When they hurt you, they hurt me."

For an entire decade, I've believed Reid coordinated the most humiliating moment of my life, that he orchestrated it all. And now he wants me to believe he was innocent?

I search his eyes for a lie folded and tucked away in the darkness beyond his pupils. What else is he hiding in there? Most people hide their lies, not their truths. Why has he waited so long to come clean?

I let my eyes drop. "I don't know what to think."

Reid lifts my chin with his finger. "I meant what I said that day."

This time when our eyes lock, the boiling anger in my chest transforms into red-hot flames that ascend my neck and flash down to my toes. Reid's eyes sharpen and his lips part.

I stabilize myself against the prep table and slide backward. The abrupt emotional shift has me searching for solid footing, a rock to stand on based on cold hard facts.

"I have a boyfriend," I mutter.

The intensity of Reid's gaze falters and then loses all potency as he drops his eyes to the floor. "I know."

"Yeah, it's serious," I add, my voice strengthening. "We're getting married." I wince a little at that last part, and again when Reid's eyes survey my left hand. "I don't have a ring. Yet. I will. When the time is right."

With his head still hanging low, Reid looks up at me and runs a hand through his hair. "Yeah. Sure. That's great, Eadie. Congratulations."

And there's cringe number three. I don't bother telling him there's nothing to congratulate me for because I need to get this evening back on track ASAP which includes peeling this egg-soaked shirt off my body and throwing it into the washer.

"I'll take your shirt," I say. "The flannel," I add to make sure there's no confusion. Now is *not* the time for me to see Reid's bare chest. I might incinerate on the spot. And that's...a problem. But I can't ponder a solution right now. We have eighty pumpkin rolls to finish.

"Sure." Reid slides his arms out of his shirt and hands it to me.

I retreat to the bathroom where I will the flames inside me to reduce to embers. I'll worry about fully extinguishing them later.

A quick change into Reid's flannel causes the flames to roll once more. I shut my eyes, take deep breaths, and then I return to the bakery with fresh resolve to recommence operation avoidance. Before touching the flour or sugar or salt, I grab my headphones, slip them on, and turn up the volume.

Reid doesn't argue. We don't talk at all unless it has to do with measurements or oven timers. For the most part, I remain in my cocoon of music. And yet, Reid's presence hangs heavy on me the entire time, the scent of his cologne overpowering the ever-present scents of pumpkin spice and browning sugar.

Chapter 18

I open my eyes at twelve thirty in the afternoon to a fierce pummeling of guilt. It's Thanksgiving. I was supposed to help Mom prep corn cake, broccoli salad, candied yams, green beans, stuffing. I told her we didn't need that many dishes for just the three of us, but she insisted.

"Aunt Bev and Uncle Todd are going down to Florida for Thanksgiving," I said at the grocery store while she tossed nutmeg, cinnamon, cloves, allspice, and ginger into the cart. (Mom likes to mix her own pumpkin pie spice.)

Aunt Bev, Uncle Todd, my cousins, and their kids usually come to our house for Thanksgiving, but this year they're visiting Uncle Todd's mom who is in late-stage cancer. Three generations are driving south to enjoy what may be their last Thanksgiving with her.

I'll miss my extended family, but I won't miss the noise of young children clamoring from room to room while squealing and riling up the dogs. I'm sure I have a mothering instinct in me somewhere, but it burrows deep when I'm around screaming kids. Hopefully, my own kids' screams won't make my mothering skills run and hide.

I throw off my covers and hop out of bed, pretending to be awake and alert, the opposite of how I feel.

Reid and I worked on pumpkin rolls all night Tuesday and then we dove straight into work on Wednesday. After the heady moment between us in the bakery, I was glad the lack of sleep reduced me to an emotionless zombie who only responded to customer and employee commands. Reid spent most of Wednesday in his office, sleeping for all I knew. I wasn't going to poke my head in there and risk another inappropriate moment.

I am not a cheater. I'm not. I will never cheat. My boyfriend is dutifully waiting for me in New York City, and I will not betray his trust. Period.

Whatever is going on between me and Reid, this periodic over-whelm of unwanted emotions, will stop the moment I get my butt out of this state and on a plane. I'm not going to waste time analyz-ing what will soon be a faint memory in my past.

My poor mother. I can't believe I left her alone to manage all the cooking. On a bum hip, no less. I throw on a sweatshirt to complement my gray yoga pants and head into the bathroom to splash my face with cold water.

I may shower today, or I may just stuff my face and roll from table to couch and then up the stairs to bed. I'm feeling partial toward option number two.

As I descend the stairs, the familiar scents of an over-the-top Thanksgiving feast wrap around me. I get notes of turkey mingled with caramelized sugar and fresh yeast bread. I could snuggle up in it, sigh, and go back to sleep, but Mom needs my help. She's probably beyond exhausted.

I enter the kitchen, my tail between my legs. "I'm sorry, Mom. I can't believe I slept so late."

She's at the counter, her back toward me, sucking turkey juices out of the bag and reserving them for the stuffing and gravy. "No worries," Mom says in a singsong voice. Thanksgiving has always been her favorite holiday. She loves to cook, I'm just not sure she *should* be cooking with all the strain it's putting on that hip.

"How are you holding up?" I ask.

"Just fine. I took a pain pill."

I walk over to the kitchen table that's covered in desserts ranging from pumpkin pie to cranberry trifle. A bowl of homemade rolls is among the fare. I grab one and call it breakfast. "Anything I can do?"

"You can tear the bread for the stuffing."

I gladly accept the task, grabbing two grocery-bought French baguettes, a bread knife, and a bowl. "This is a lot of food for three people. We're gonna have to freeze the leftovers," I say while slicing the bread and tearing it into bite-sized pieces.

"There's going to be five of us," Mom says.

I frown at my baguette. "Five?"

"Didn't Reid tell you?"

A buzzing sensation emerges in my stomach, like a bumblebee started doing barrel rolls in there.

"Didn't Reid tell me what?" I say, my tone flat.

"He and his dad are coming over."

The sharp edge of my knife thunks against the counter after an emphatic slice. I peer at my mom over my shoulder. She's dropping green beans into a pot of boiling water to blanch them. "Is that necessary?"

"What? Having guests? Why not?" she asks with a glance, reading the annoyance in my voice. "You and Reid see each other every day in the café."

I refocus on the bread. "*That's* why not," I mutter.

"Are you two not getting along?"

Yes and no. Sometimes too much yes. Of course, I can't say that aloud, so I say, "We're fine. I was just looking forward to eating dinner with you and Dad in my sweatshirt, yoga pants, and messy bun."

"You don't have to dress up for Reid's sake. Unless..."

I whip my head toward Mom. She's looking at me, a teasing smile on her face.

I feel like this is a lose-lose. Now if I spruce myself up, she'll think I'm trying to impress Reid. But if I don't make myself presentable, Reid will see me like *this*. Not that it matters.

My messy bun looks like an inkblot. I can barely subject myself to it, let alone anyone else. Who am I kidding? I was always going to shower and put on a sweater and jeans. It's Thanksgiving, not a snow day.

"Why doesn't he do Thanksgiving with his mom and dad at their place?" I ask.

"His mom left them when you two were in school. You don't remember that?"

"No."

"She's not around as far as I can tell."

I grimace. "When did she leave them?"

"I'm not sure." Mom hoists the turkey and waddles it over to the table. "Must have been over a decade ago. Weren't you and Reid friends in high school?"

"No. He bullied me. Remember?"

"I still can't believe that's true. Reid's such a sweetheart."

Since Mom and Dad were at church when I came home covered in eggs and feathers, I never told them about the incident. Recounting it would have intensified my angst.

"He's changed though, Eadie. You know that." Mom stops in the middle of the kitchen to address me. "And he's been through a lot, with his wife leaving him to pursue acting in New York and his dad moving into assisted living. He quit his job in Indianapolis and moved back here to be closer to his dad. I think he meant to sell the house too, but that hasn't happened yet." She slaps her hot pads together. "Anyway. Be nice. They're our guests."

I give her my "duh" face. "I'm an adult, Mother. I'm not going to be mean."

Mom shrugs and then peeks past me to assess my pile of bread. "We need to get that in the oven. It needs to cook for an hour."

"When is Reid coming?"

Mom taps her knock-off Apple Watch. "They'll be here in an hour. Perfect."

"Perfect" isn't the word I'd use, but it does give me sufficient time to shower, put on fresh clothes, and fuss over my makeup and hair.

I finish tearing up the second baguette and make sure Mom doesn't need more assistance before heading upstairs to pick my outfit for the day. I go with a rust-colored, cable-knit sweater from The Garment Swap compliments of Gracelyn, and a pair of midrise, bootcut jeans.

My shower takes longer than it should while I ponder Mom's revelations about Reid's personal life and the implications of those revelations. I pair these thoughts with Reid's confession that he knew nothing about the egging I received ten years ago. Unable to form substantive conclusions about how all this may have affected him for better or worse, I dry off and get dressed with twenty minutes to spare, all of which I spend straightening my hair and fiddling with my makeup.

The doorbell rings while I'm flicking a rogue speck of mascara with a Q-tip. Never fails. Mascara wands exist to ruin good makeup days.

When the doorbell rings a second time, I realize I wrongly assumed my mom heard the doorbell and welcomed our guests inside. Worry settles in as I imagine her collapsed in a chair unable to move because her hip locked up. I hastily discard my Q-tip and run down the stairs.

The dogs are shut up in the den, which means I don't trip over them on my way to the door. I greet Reid and a very fragile elderly man. David maneuvers into the house with the help of his cane and his son's steady forearm. When he's safely inside, Reid crosses the threshold and hands me a foil-covered dish.

"I come bearing pumpkin rolls," he says, his eyes bright with amusement.

I groan. "Noooo."

"Yes. Turns out we made too many. Enjoy."

"I think I'm allergic to pumpkin spice now."

Reid laughs. "I won't be offended if they end up in the trash."

"Oh, I'm freezing these puppies. Next year I'm gonna give them back to you."

He looks surprised by my comment, and I am too. I just implied that there will be a next year, which is not accurate. I'll be spending next Thanksgiving with Hayden in Maine.

The tiny misunderstanding bears no explanation. I let it slide, putting on my "gracious host" face while taking Reid's coat along with his father's and hanging them in the closet. Reid patiently and gently helps his dad shuffle to the couch.

"Let me find my dad," I say. Because I have no idea what to say to Reid's father, who I remember as a mature, yet well-built man with a straight spine and an honest smile. The man before me is a diminished version of his younger self, yet obviously no less cherished by Reid. Perhaps more so.

Did Reid's mom leave because of their age gap, because she knew she might have to be her husband's caretaker and she couldn't handle the possibility? I can only speculate.

I poke my head into the kitchen and catch Dad stealing bits of turkey as he slices the breast.

"Reid's here," I announce. "And David," I quickly add. "Let me finish up in here Dad. Go catch up with Reid. He can give you my performance review while Mom and I set the table."

Dad is happy to let the women go to work. He pinches my cheek as he walks past. "Happy Thanksgiving," he says as he bends over to plant a kiss on my forehead.

My heart swells with gratitude that I'm able to share another holiday meal with my parents, the two of them together, still able-bodied and in love.

While Dad is entertaining our guests (which he's doing quite well judging by the laughter coming from the living room), Mom and I carry the food to the table. I lay out each place setting, making sure to arrange the silverware the way Dad likes it. We stand arm in arm and enjoy our work—well, mostly Mom's work—before calling everyone to the table.

Once again, Reid hovers near his dad as they make their way to the dining table. He pulls out a chair, never letting go of David's arm as he lowers his father into the seat. Then he walks over to my mom and plants a kiss on her cheek. "Hey, Helen. We miss you at the café."

She chuckles while they embrace. "Don't tell Weston, but I don't miss it much."

Reid feigns being offended.

"I miss you, of course," Mom quickly adds. "And the customers. The nice ones, anyway."

I had no idea my mom and Reid were on cheek-kissing terms. I half expected him to call her "Mom."

"What's the occasion?" Dad asks, his voice booming over the table.

We all laugh. I glance at him, and my humor runs cold. His expression is genuinely confused, his eyes out of focus.

Reid leaves Mom's side and rushes over to Dad. "It's Thanksgiving." He puts an arm around my dad and nudges him toward the head of the table. "Turkey, pumpkin pie, pumpkin rolls."

My dad looks at the turkey and recognition sharpens his gaze. "Well, why aren't you in your seat? The food's getting cold." He pulls out his chair and sits.

Reid meets my eyes for a moment, his expression shifting from lighthearted to serious and then back again.

"Sit, Reid," Mom calls over the table. "Weston is going to say grace."

"Sure." He scoots out the chair across from me and settles in for the prayer.

As Dad is thanking God for our meal and our ability to gather in peace, I say a little prayer of my own. *God, please watch over my dad. I think something is wrong.*

Chapter 19

Everyone eats too much, even my mother who usually eats like a bird. Groans rise from the table whenever Mom admonishes us to pile more food onto our plates. Despite our feasting, we've hardly made a dent in the food. I'm already planning my midnight snack of corn cake and stuffing and tomorrow's lunch: turkey sandwich on a homemade yeast roll.

When Dad throws in the white flag, Mom follows suit. She pushes out her chair and bends over to gather the butter and gravy, but I stop her before she straightens.

"Nope," I say loudly, forcefully.

She twitches before looking at me. "What was that for?"

"Put it down. I'm cleaning up."

"Let her," Dad says. "You've been on your feet too long."

"He's right," I echo.

"Eadie and I will take care of it," Reid says. "You deserve a rest after that delicious meal."

Mom drops her hands to her sides, looking lost for a moment before admitting defeat. "Fine. I bought containers for the food. They're on the refrigerator. Freeze what you don't think we'll eat."

"We got it. Now move." I stand and shuffle her toward the living room. She winces with every step. "Do you need another pain pill?"

"No," she says, fluttering her hand at me. "I never take more than one a day."

I offer her my arm for support, but she rejects it.

"You don't have to hover. I'm not an invalid."

"I'm trying to help."

"I know. I know." She pauses and smiles at me before proving she doesn't need my help by walking swiftly to the couch and sinking into it. "See? I'm fine." Her expression hardens as she tries to hide her pain.

"Dinner was amazing, Mom." I blow her a kiss.

After Reid helps David to the living room, he and I work in coordination, channeling our restaurant experience to efficiently clear the table, rinse the dishes, and load the dishwasher. We stay out of each other's way, predicting the other's movements, maintaining a focused, yet relaxed silence.

He's transferring the corn cake into containers when he finally speaks. "Your mom is an amazing cook."

"She is. She came up with the eggs Benedict variations at the café."

"Really?" He seems surprised. "I thought that was all your grandma's doing."

I dig through the Tupperware in the lower cabinet. When I find a large container, I stand and grab the bowl of green beans. "No, Grandma stuck to the basics. Mom wanted to revamp the menu a little. Make it fresh."

"I'm impressed."

"Why didn't you tell me you were coming over for Thanksgiving?" I grab the spoon from the stuffing dish and use it to coax the green beans into the pink Tupperware container that Mom's had since I was a kid. It has a few melt marks on the inside, but otherwise, it's still functional.

Reid stiffens slightly. "Your mom invited us yesterday, and you and I were... It was just weird." He pops lids onto his containers. "Can I say that?"

"You're free to say anything. I'm not the word police." Even though him *saying* yesterday was weird is just...weird. "Leave one of those in the fridge. I'm going to eat the crap out of the corn cake as soon as my stomach empties. The rest can go into the freezer. I'm not sure how well corn cake holds up to being frozen, but I guess I'll find out." I'm rambling. If I keep talking maybe he'll forget about yesterday's awkwardness, and Tuesday night's emotional intimacy, and that moment in the office when he was bare-chested, and I turned as red as the ketchup on my shirt.

We finish our tasks in silence, finishing by swiping a washcloth over the countertops and hanging the pumpkin-embroidered hand towel on the oven handle.

"Good job," Reid says. "You should work in the food service industry."

"I know a thing or two," I brag even though cleaning the kitchen is hardly difficult.

"Shall we?" Reid motions toward the door and we follow my dad's boisterous voice to the living room.

"How's that son of yours doing?" Dad asks David while we're walking in.

I pause. Reid's an only child like me. I glance at Reid over my shoulder, my brow furrowed. He touches his hand to my back.

"Reid is here," Mom says emphatically, looking more angry than shocked. "You just ate dinner with him."

"Hey, Weston." Reid throws up a hand.

Dad cranes his neck around. "Oh. Hey. I knew that. For some reason, I was thinking you had a brother."

I don't believe him. His eyes look confused, like reality just skipped forward a few frames without him.

Stress overtakes me. I feel the birth of tears. They press against my lungs and start to rise. I can't cry in front of Dad. I don't want him to be ashamed. I don't want my mom to get angry with me for overreacting.

"I could use a little air," I managed to choke out. I grab my coat from the closet and escape through the front door.

When the cold air hits me, my tears halt their ascent. I take several deep breaths to calm the swirling ball of stress in my gut. Or...emotions. I guess.

I'm an adult. I should be able to tell the difference. So, I sit on the porch wall and try to pull the emotions out one by one.

Worry. Grief. Fear.

The door opens and then clicks closed. The concrete swallows most of Reid's footsteps. All I hear are soft repetitive whooshes until he stops beside me. I hike a foot onto the wall and lean against the brick pillar. Reid claims a spot near me.

Just like old times. Reid, Gracelyn, and me hanging out on the porch as we devised new ways to fill up our lazy summer days.

I look at the house across the street. It's a charming Cape Cod with three dormers, green shutters flanking the windows. The dogwoods in front will erupt with pink flowers in the spring.

"Mom keeps saying it's the anesthesia." I home in on the Fire-Rescue marker on the second-floor window. "She says it hasn't worn off."

"Eadie," Reid says. He looks at his hands while he searches for his words. "I should have told you this sooner. I've tried to talk to your mom about it, but I think she's in denial."

I force myself to look at Reid, to face up to the truth, and accept any emotions it might cause.

"I noticed your dad's memory issues when I started, but it was just small things. I thought he might have ADHD. Which could very well be true. But over the last year, they've gotten worse."

He looks at me with his eyebrow slightly raised like he's seeking permission to continue.

I nod.

"I noticed if his routine changed, things got worse. So I made extra efforts to keep everything familiar."

"Like the pantry."

"Yeah. It looks like a mess to you and me, but he knows where everything is. If you move something, he might get confused, and when he's confused, sometimes he lashes out. I don't blame him. I imagine he's just frustrated."

"And when you brought this up to my mom, what did she say?"

"She says he's always been absent-minded. Or she'll blame his blood sugar or lack of sleep."

His words finally register. The tears resume their upward course. I think they're mostly driven by fear, with a boost of disbelief. When they reach my throat, I swallow them back down.

"I'm sorry, Eadie. I should have said something sooner. I wasn't sure if it was my place. I just didn't know."

"It's okay," I whisper. I swing my other leg onto the wall and prop my elbows on my knees. "I think I need a moment." I press my palms to my eyes.

"Sure. It's a lot to take in."

The birds aren't crazy enough to be out in this weather. The only ambient noises are the occasional passing of cars through the neighboring streets and the periodic breeze against the hollows of my ears.

Something strange happens as I sit with my face covered. The emotions seep away as my body gives me a dose of endorphins to stop the tsunami.

"Do you think it's dementia?" I ask.

Reid hesitates before answering. "I really don't know. He'll need to be tested."

"Can he still run the café?"

"He's still great in the café. It's his element. We all assist him now and then, but for the most part, he can hold his own."

That's some good news, at least. Except the café isn't profitable. When will the money run out? What will Mom and Dad do when he needs medical assistance and there's no money coming in? I press my eyes closed again.

My phone buzzes, a momentary distraction. I pull it out of my back pocket.

It's a text from Hayden.

Did you eat plenty of turkey? he asks.

Too much, I text back.

I miss your mom's cooking, he says. **My dad's turkey could be sewn into a purse.**

It's that leathery?

Even worse than it sounds. <puking emoji>

I'm so sorry, I type with my thumbs. **I would bring some of my mom's back to New York but you'd probably die of food poisoning if you ate it.**

It would still be better than my dad's.

I chuckle. Hayden's virtual presence is helping me feel normal. **How's Whitney?**

You forgot to tell me she talks nonstop.

She talks nonstop.

Too late. It keeps things interesting, I guess.

You wanted someone to keep you awake during the drive, I remind him.

And I got it.

I send him a smiley emoji.

Reid stands, adjusts his coat, and gives me a wave.

I flash him my palm. "No. Stay. It's my boyfriend. Sorry. I'll cut him off here in a second."

"No, you guys can talk."

Okay, then, Hayden texts. **I was just checking in. Happy Thanksgiving. Love you. <kissing emoji>**

Thanks. Love you too.

I click off my phone and shove it back into my pocket. "All done."

"All right, then." Reid walks over to the porch swing and sits. "Is he home by himself today?"

"No, he's with my best friend Whitney and his parents."

"Oh?"

"Yeah. It's kind of weird. I said she could tag along with him on his trip up to Maine."

"That sounds...different. Are they friends?"

"They will be after this trip."

"I bet." Reid's eyebrows bobble as he says it.

"What?"

"Nothing. I'm glad you trust them so much."

I squint at Reid while I try to parse his words. Of course, I trust them. Whitney's my best friend. And Hayden's my boyfriend. "Whitney's keeping him in line because I'm afraid he'll have women falling all over him while I'm away," I blurt.

Reid shrugs, his relaxed arms absorbing some of the movement. "I'm not judging. Or prying. It's your business." He leans over and rubs his chin. "Anyway. That's all I can really tell you about your dad. I'm not an expert. My dad has the beginning stages of dementia, so I kind of know what to look for, but like I said, they need to run tests."

I bet. Reid's comment drills through my brain. He's right about it being my business. He doesn't understand the dynamics of my relationship with Hayden. And I'm not going to explain them to him.

So I drop that line of thought and focus back on more important matters. "You're amazing with your dad." I pinch a rogue thread on my knee and give it a tweak. "And with my parents too. So thank you. To know someone has been looking out for them is really…" I glance over at Reid. Our eyes meet and my stomach flutters like the whirligig poking up from Mom's potted mums. "It means a lot to me."

A humble smile spreads across his face. "I'm just doing my job."

"You're going above and beyond."

"I thought I didn't know how to run a restaurant," he teases.

I swing my legs off the wall and anchor my hands on the cold ledge. "Did I say that?"

"You implied it. Several times."

"I—" My thoughts rewind to the busy day during the Fall Festival when Reid and I bickered about who should oversee the queue. Well, *I* argued. He was just trying to help. "I'm sorry about the mean thing I said."

"Which one?"

"Have I really been that bad?"

He tugs on his coat sleeve while he considers my comment. "No. You've just been stressed."

"That's no excuse. I shouldn't have said you're stuck here in a crap job with an ex high school sweetheart. It was mean. And not accurate."

"It's half right."

"Which part?"

Reid dips his head and looks at me sideways. "Guess."

A moderate gust of wind whips up the stray leaves on the porch, their dry edges skittering over the lightly textured concrete until they find a safe haven in the corner where others have already gone to hide.

My shoulders slump. "The 'ex' part."

He levels his pointer finger at me and then leans back against the swing and rests his arm across the back.

"You're not stuck here, though. Mom told me you moved back to take care of your dad."

"I did. Which means I know how stressful it is. So no hard feelings. You have your mom and dad to worry about on top of the café. Taking care of aging parents is no joke without the added stress of a failing business."

His last sentence digs in deep. "You really think it's failing?"

"I mean…"

"Don't say it. We'll figure it out. Or I'll figure it out. Taking care of Dad and the business from New York City is going to be a challenge, but I have to make it work. Right?"

Reid looks unconvinced but he's kind enough not to question me.

"Right," I confirm. "I'll figure it out. Somehow."

The front door opens, and my mom's head peeks through. "It's time for the Peanuts Thanksgiving special and pumpkin pie."

"Okay, we'll be right in," I say as the door closes.

He looks at me quizzically.

"It's a family tradition," I explain. "We watch the Peanuts special while we eat our dessert, which has to be pumpkin pie with lots of whipped cream because that's the rule."

"I couldn't stuff a peanut into my stomach right now."

I lean over and summon my most authoritative voice. "You will eat pumpkin pie and you will enjoy it."

Reid laughs, unloosing a curl. He runs his fingers through it to lock it back in place. "Fine. But I reserve the right to consider this a form of torture."

My expression softens. "Once you taste my mom's pie your opinion might change."

"I suppose I'm willing to trust you."

We trade smiles, both quiet. Neither looking away.

His burnt orange coat pairs perfectly with the brown bricks behind him, the combination paying homage to autumn.

Orange, yellow, brown. The colors mark the end of a growing season when death provides the nutrients for rebirth. Reid's tropical blue eyes are jewels amid decay, an anomalous color on this overcast afternoon. A rebellion against the status quo.

I let my eyes linger for too long.

He punctuates the moment by slapping his knees and standing. "Okay. Let's eat pie."

Inertia holds me to my spot. I'm not sure how to process the moment we just shared. Should I embrace it, file it away, erase it?

"You coming?" Reid says over his shoulder.

I have a boyfriend. I'm taken. Off the market. Erasure is the only option.

I push myself to my feet and follow him inside.

He chooses the couch. Instead of taking the empty cushion beside him, I settle into Grandma's old wooden rocking chair, its narrow seat and curved armrests pinning me in tight.

Chapter 20

After taking Thanksgiving off, I'm back at the café on Friday managing the kitchen. Reid and I are amicable the entire day, but I keep my emotional distance.

Spending Thanksgiving with him was enjoyable, and his honesty about my dad was helpful, but I don't have time for any rogue "feelings" for him. I need to spend my emotional energy cracking my mom's hard shell of denial and formulating ways to save the café.

I have no solution for the latter. For the former, I'll wait until after Mom's hip surgery to discuss Dad's memory loss with her. Before we tackle that touchy subject, I want the anesthesia and the pain medicines out of her body.

Adulting continually proves to be harder than I expected. I could use a prolonged escape somewhere warm with crystal blue water and palm trees. Blue, like the color of Reid's eyes, I muse.

And then I abruptly stop myself.

Anyway...

Instead of a nice beach vacation, I got a gray Thanksgiving Day in Indiana. One day. That's it.

In contrast, Whitney's vacation is still barreling forward. I get to hear the highlights in her barrage of texts. She's holding up her end of the bargain by keeping me posted on Hayden's whereabouts, but I wish she'd omit some of the details.

I receive another text while responding to a customer complaint about overcooked eggs and coffee that tastes like ashes from a wood burning stove.

We decided to stay until Sunday. OMG, it's beautiful up here. We took the pontoon out on the lake and saw a moose on the shore! Hayden's parents ordered pizza last night after we all agreed his dad's turkey sucked.

Great. Let's just make it a four-day weekend. Four days of frolicking in Maine's remote uplands with my boyfriend. Without me. I'm not bothered a bit. Not one bit.

Her texts continue through Friday evening and into Saturday. My phone's notification wakes me up at nine thirty in the morning from a dead sleep.

Hayden is so hilarious! We were up till 12:30 last night playing drunk Pictionary with his parents. I've never seen him act so funny. You need to get him drunk more often.

I don't know how to reply. I'm glad you're having such a great time with my boyfriend? Emphasis on *my*. Could you not get him drunk anymore? Please and thanks.

I putter around the house all day with an undercurrent of anxiety. What's occurring in the hills of Maine that she's *not* telling me? And then I get this:

This town is so *gorgeous*. The town square is straight out of a Hallmark movie and it's *snowing*. Just a little, but the snowflakes are fluffy and fat, *exactly* like Hallmark. Hayden bought me a necklace made by a local artisan. Oh, crap. I shouldn't have said that. When you open your Christmas present, act surprised!

I stumble to the front porch after that one. Mostly to remind myself not to freak out. This was my idea. Whitney is doing exactly what I asked her to do. Sort of. I thought they'd go on a couple of "dates," not spend hours together in a car and have a mini vacation in a romantic and idyllic Maine town. It's fine. I'm fine. I take a deep breath and then go back inside.

My phone is silent for the rest of the evening except for a short text exchange between me and Hayden. He tells me he's having a good time with his parents. He also says Whitney talks a lot and he's ready to come home.

I'm relieved by his last statement. Maybe his experience hasn't been as rosy as Whitney's. I hope that's the case. Part of me hopes he's miserable. Is that mean?

Sunday morning, I receive another update:

We took a walk through the woods behind the house and we saw a bear! Hayden had to slap his hand over my mouth

so I wouldn't scream. He practically had to carry me home. I almost wet myself.

I roll my eyes.

Anyway, we're leaving soon. It's going to be a long night. I'll catch up with you tomorrow!

I give a quick thanks to God that Whitney and Reid will be parting ways soon. I also repent of the jealousy and mistrust that got me into this situation. Maybe I should trust him instead of pushing him into the arms of another woman. Ya think? Lesson learned.

Dad and I take Mom to Harrison Orthopedic Center in the early hours of Monday morning. The waiting room is modern with booths along one side and outlets for device charging. The rest of the room is fitted with comfortable chairs and couches that are oriented toward a flat-screen TV that's playing the news with subtitles.

After they take Mom back, we choose a booth. Dad brought one of his science fiction tomes to read. I rely on my phone for entertainment.

A couple of hours later, Mom's out of surgery. The surgeon assures us everything went fine, and she'll be going home with us soon.

Relieved by the news, I decide I'm ready to confront Whitney. I send her a FaceTime request, and she picks up on the second ring. She's leaning back in her office chair, her forearm weighing against her forehead. "Oh my gawd, girl, I'm so tired. We didn't get home until three thirty. We got stuck behind a wreck for two hours. I almost had to hop out and pee on the side of the road."

Dad looks up at me. I shrug. "But you didn't."

"No. Things finally got moving."

"I'm going to go to the bathroom." I slip my purse strap over my shoulder and start toward the ladies' room.

"Good idea. Let me go hide in a workroom."

By the time I close myself into a bathroom stall, she's already behind glass.

"It doesn't help that we stayed up late Saturday night too."

"Oh yeah?" I ask, trying not to sound too curious.

"Yeah. His parents have a hot tub on the back patio."

"Hmm." I wouldn't know. I've never visited Hayden's parents' house. Small matter.

"We stayed in it for a couple of hours and then we got drunk and passed out on the couch in the game room."

My stomach clenches. "Like together? Or on separate cushions?"

"I was so out of it. I can't remember. I may have to sneak into one of the empty offices and sleep through lunch. Ugh." Whitney groans so loudly it vibrates my phone. "Okay. You were quiet all weekend. How was your Thanksgiving?" She sets down her phone, plunks her elbow on the desktop, and leans into her hand. I have a direct view up her nose.

"It was nice," I say nonchalantly. "Not as nice as yours."

"It really was awesome. Thank you so much for letting me go. I haven't had a vacation in two years. I didn't realize how much I needed out of this city. I can see myself moving up there, you know? It's so peaceful."

"It sounds like you and Hayden got along well."

"I think I annoyed him. I was like a kid in a candy store. I couldn't contain my excitement. He just flashed me an odd look now and then to tell me to tone it down."

I laugh. "Yeah, I know that look. It means, can you please stop talking about the *Dasymutilla Occidentalis* and its common mis-categorization as an ant when it's really a wasp with no wings, and yeah, it can kill a cow, hence the common name, Cow Killer. I would never bore Hayden with such trivia though."

"You're such a geek. That's why I love you. Well, one of the reasons." She flashes me a broad smile. "His parents are amazing," she continues. "You're marrying into a good family."

She knows about my intentions to marry Hayden, even though Hayden doesn't.

"He really loves you. He talked about you a lot."

My ears tingle. "He did?"

"Yep. Eadie this, Eadie that, blah blah blah." Whitney dips her head so I'm no longer looking up her nose. She smiles again. "You picked a good one. Now I need to find one."

Someone flushes the toilet next to me. I wait for the water to stop swirling before I respond. "You know what I think about that."

Whitney sighs. "Slow down. Make them wait. Yeah. I know. It doesn't matter, I've sworn off men for the rest of the year anyway."

"Which is only one more month."

"I can't wait *that* long."

I roll my eyes at Whitney. Despite the "passing out together on the couch" incident, I feel better about Whitney and Hayden's excursion to the hills of Maine.

I change the subject, telling her about Mom's surgery and Dad's apparent memory issues. I also brief her about the café's money troubles, but I never mention Reid. Even though she's exhausted, she listens intently and reassures me that everything will be all right. I choose to believe her. For the moment, at least.

But I still want to put the kibosh on their holiday dating, if only because I set it up with ill intentions. Whitney's eyelids are threatening to close, though. I'll mention it to her later.

"Go find a carpet square and get some sleep."

Whitney yawns. "I may have to go home. I'm not sure I'm going to make it."

"Tell Tabitha you puked. She can't handle vomit."

"I might."

We say our goodbyes and I mosey back to Dad.

When Mom's awake and alert, the nurse wheels her out and we leave, stopping at Culver's on the way home for ButterBurgers, cheese curds, and frozen custard.

That evening, Mom hobbles around with a cane, impressive considering she was cut open with a knife only hours before. Nevertheless, the doctor gave her orders not to overdo it, so I warm up frozen Thanksgiving leftovers and deliver them to my parents while they watch *Star Trek: Picard*.

I eat at the kitchen table because Hayden promised to FaceTime me at six thirty. At six thirty-five the phone rings and I accept Hayden's call.

"Hey there," Hayden says.

He hasn't shaved today. His beard is popping through, shadowing the bottom half of his face. He's sitting at the table in his modern, compact kitchen. Behind him, his hydroponic garden tower is filled with lettuce and herbs. I can hear Simon panting at his feet.

"Hey, stranger." I smile at him and then plop a bite of corn cake into my mouth.

"I'm so glad to be home." He leans forward heavily, giving me a detailed view of the top of his head.

"Whitney said you got home late."

"Next time I'm flying."

"Are there airports in Maine?"

"A few."

"I hear there are moose. Or mooses. Which is it?"

Hayden sits up. "Moose is both singular and plural."

"Whitney said you saw one while you were out on the pontoon."

"Yeah. What else did she tell you?"

"Drunk Pictionary, Hallmark town square, drunk hot tub. Lots of drunkenness." I finish my corn cake and move on to my stuffing. "Oh. And the bear, and you carrying her out of the woods so she wouldn't get mauled."

Hayden rests his chin on his hand in a tired sort of way that squishes the right side of his face. "Wow. She gave you the play-by-play."

"That was her job."

"Huh?"

I freeze mid-bite.

"I'm sorry, what?" Hayden presses.

My mouth is full of food, but I try to talk anyway. "I thought we talked about this. I wanted her to attend the holiday parties with you because I was afraid of gorgeous women hanging on you and stuff."

He looks unimpressed and a bit miffed. "I didn't realize it was her 'job' to keep tabs on me during every second of every day."

I set down my fork. "It wasn't until you translated 'holiday parties' to 'riding up to Maine to spend the long weekend with my parents.'" I mimic his air quotes.

"You said you were okay with her going."

"I was. I am. Why are we fighting?"

Hayden rolls his eyes and then drops his chin against his palm, resuming squish-face mode. "Whatever."

"Don't say that."

"Why not?"

"It's dismissive."

"I'm dismissing this conversation."

"All of it?"

"The parts that annoy me."

"Parts plural?"

"I'm tired."

"Okay. Yes. I'm jealous. Scared. Untrusting. Whatever you want to call it. I was feeling insecure with me in Cornville and you in the gorgeous woman capital of the world—"

"That's L.A. Or Mumbai."

"*Anyway,* I sort of wanted her to spy on you. I thought you knew that."

Hayden stands and steps out of frame. I stare at young lettuce leaves while Hayden rummages around in the kitchen to the tune of Simon's cries for attention.

"I'm sorry. I was stupid. Can you come back?"

He slides into his chair with a beer in his hand. "I'll ask you again, like I have before. Why are you with me if you don't trust me?"

I cover my face. "I do trust you."

"Why can't you look at me when you say it?"

"I do trust you," I say after I lower my hands. "It's not you. It's never been you. It's me. I realize that now. Coming back here has helped me realize how much baggage I've been carrying around from being bullied. I guess...part of me is still that girl who thinks she has to prove herself. But there's nothing to prove. It's silly. I'm silly."

Hayden looks at me quietly. Long enough that I start to feel nervous. Is my own boyfriend going to make fun of me now?

"That makes sense," he says finally.

My shoulders relax. "It does?"

"The past leaves us with scars."

I lean back in my chair and nod.

"But they're what make you beautiful, Eadie."

His comment pumps helium into my lungs. I think I might start floating. "That's the sweetest thing you've ever said to me."

"If it is, I'm sorry. I should compliment you more often." His temples crease as he smiles.

"I'm not going to argue with that."

"You better not. Now tell me about your Thanksgiving."

Even though Mom's recovery should be relatively easy and short, Reid and I agree I should take the week off. (There's the vacation I need? Not quite, but it's something.)

Mom isn't bedbound. The doctors want her to exercise her joint every day, which she does by engaging in light housework and baking the occasional batch of cookies.

By Wednesday, we're going stir-crazy. I suggest tackling the den. By "tackling" I mean cleaning, but I practically have to tackle Dad to get him to agree.

For five days, we sort through boxes, books, magazines, and random Amazon purchases. When we dig down to the deeper layers, we find old pictures and other mementos that bring up memories. Dad is alert the entire time, recounting stories from our past and offering specific details even I had forgotten. He sorts through his hoard with surprising acumen, making me think maybe my worries about his memory were unfounded.

Rather than spoil our bonding time, I stay quiet about my concerns. Maybe it's selfish, but for a few days, I want to pretend my parents are never going to change.

Chapter 21

The weather for Christmas on the Canal is not as favorable as the Fall Festival's. It's not even favorable for an early December day in Indiana. The average temperature for December 2nd is around forty degrees Fahrenheit. Today, the temperature is supposed to top out at ten degrees.

I'm used to the cold, born and raised in Indiana, transplanted to the state of New York. Anything above thirty-two degrees is warm. But as soon as the temperature slips a degree below freezing, it's *cold*. Add in windchill and one might even call it freezing. No bueno for this gal, and apparently for a lot of others because today's crowd is small. Craft and refreshment booths are set up along the canal, but only the brave have subjected themselves to the wind and the cold.

Inside Home for the Hollandaise, business has been steady. We have Brandon and Marlon on the stoves and Annette and Lexis ready to greet diners. I've only had to jump in a couple of times to funnel people to their seats or clear tables after guests leave.

I'm about ready to lock the doors at four o'clock when Gracelyn walks in.

"Gracelyn!" Her name pops out of my mouth at a loud decibel before I can restrain myself. I run into the dining room and greet her with an exuberant hug.

"Hey Eadie," she giggles. She's wearing a knit beanie hat and matching mittens. Her purple waist-length wool coat doesn't look warm enough for this wind chill.

"Are you here to eat?"

"No, I was just shopping and thought I'd pop in to say hello." She bounces up and down to warm herself. "I'm sorry I haven't stopped by earlier. Our operating hours collide."

"Are you open today?"

"My mom's watching the register. She went through the booths but got too cold, so she's in the store warming up."

"Gracelyn!" Reid calls from the pass-through, mimicking me.

"I couldn't help it!" I holler back. "I get excited."

"If Reid joins us, it'll be a reunion," Gracelyn calls into the kitchen.

Reid takes the hint and joins us in the dining room. Around us, Lexis and Annette clear tables and respond to final drink orders.

"Go ahead and close up," I say to Annette.

She hotfoots it over to the door and throws the lock. "Don't have to tell me twice."

"So…" Gracelyn says, shifting her eyes from me to Reid and back again. "How's it going, running this place together?"

Reid points at me. "She's running it. I just follow the orders that she barks at me."

"I wouldn't call it barking, it's more like…" My vocabulary fails me. "Yeah. I bark."

"It's just like old times," Gracelyn says, tilting her head back wistfully.

"Do you want some hot chocolate?" I ask. "Or coffee?"

"No, but I could use some company. Do you guys want to walk around with me?"

"You're going back out there?" I say, aghast.

"It's not as bad as it was. The wind died down."

"We're about to close up," Reid says.

"We are closing up," Annette calls from the other side of the dining room.

"Do you guys got this?" I ask my waitresses.

"Go freeze your butts off," Annette says. "I'm staying in here where it's warm."

I turn back to Gracelyn. "I think that's 'yes.'"

"That's how I interpreted it," Gracelyn says. She tugs her hat down to her eyebrows.

Reid and I grab our coats and join Gracelyn on Main Street.

Gracelyn tightens her scarf around her neck as she surveys the row of festive booths. "I love this town, don't you?"

The trees along the canal are wrapped with Christmas lights, which are glowing in the heavy overcast. Nightfall arrives in less than two hours, the sun already well on its way to the horizon behind the thick blanket of clouds.

"There's something fun like this going on in New York City every day, you just have to know where to look."

She wrinkles her nose. "But it's smelly and crowded and there's no canal."

"There's the Hudson River."

We cross the street and descend upon a booth selling rustic, wooden Christmas signs. The temporary red canopy demarcating the booth is draped in real garland that's giving off a festive pine scent.

"I'd like to visit," Gracelyn says. "But I think I'd go crazy being surrounded by buildings all the time."

I shrug. "You get used to it. But if I start feeling antsy, I go to Central Park."

Reid listens quietly and then follows us as we move to the next booth, which is selling homemade beeswax candles.

"I love these." I lift a caramel-scented candle to my nose.

"I'm thinking about getting a couple," Gracelyn says. The vendor, an elderly lady with a prominent nose, takes note of her comment and emerges from her cozy bundle of blankets. "Oh, not yet." She smiles at the woman. "I'll be back, though."

Gracelyn's phone sounds with a text notification. She digs it out of her purse and swipes up. "Shoot. Mom says there's a line at the register, and the software keeps throwing an error. I need to head back."

"Sure," I say, giving her a quick hug.

We say our goodbyes, and then she sprints off, leaving Reid and me alone amid the holiday cheer.

"Awk-ward," he says.

I swat his arm. "Do you want to keep looking or are you afraid of the cold?"

"I'm afraid of you so I'll do whatever you say."

"Stop," I say, this time nudging him.

"Sure, I'm game. Lead the way."

We continue along the line of booths, walking past the Christmas-themed towels and tablecloths that look shoddily embroidered, taking a moment to enjoy the hand-lathed wooden bowls, and pausing at the metal jewelry artist's table. The artist is wearing a long, black wool coat, a white beret, and a red knit scarf. He smiles at us kindly while standing at a comfortable distance, his hands folded behind his back.

We approach the table dedicated to holiday earrings and necklaces before moving on to a spread of random items including animal keychains. I pick up a sterling silver dog that looks very much like a chihuahua.

"Hayden might like this," I say.

"Is Hayden your boyfriend?"

"I never told you his name?"

"If I recall, you just said, 'I have a boyfriend.'"

"Oh. Yeah. His name is Hayden. We met at a modeling gig and the rest is history."

"And hopefully the present and future," Reid says. He stuffs his gloved hands into his coat pockets and angles his forehead into the slight breeze.

A smile lifts my cheeks. "Yeah. He's pretty amazing. Do you want to see a picture?"

"Will it make me doubt my own manhood? You said he's a model and everything."

"It might." I grin at him so he knows I'm teasing.

We step away from the booth to let other shoppers enjoy the jewelry's fine craftsmanship. When we're out of the way, I pull my phone from my purse and search for Hayden's best photo.

Reid's eyebrows shoot upward when I show him. "Dude. I might even consider dating that."

"He gets offers from guys too."

"I'm sure. I guess I understand why you enlisted your friend to spy on him, to make sure he doesn't take anyone up on those offers."

My eyebrows pinch together.

Reid raises his hands in surrender. "Kidding. Kidding."

Hearing someone else imply that Hayden might cheat triggers me for some reason, but I decide Reid meant nothing by it. "He has easy access to models who are much prettier than me."

"I doubt that."

I shrug. "I smell kettle corn." I sprint in that direction, leaving Reid to gawk at my backside.

He catches up with me at the popcorn booth, which features a large kettle that's letting off a little heat. I hold my hands out to catch some of it, but it doesn't penetrate my suede gloves, only my exposed cheeks.

Before I can order, Reid cuts in. "I got it. Two please?" He hands a ten-dollar bill to the bearded man behind the table, and we grab two long bags of popcorn that are still warm.

I pull off my glove to eat a few of the fluffy kernels. I'll have to save most of it for later so my hand doesn't freeze off. "Hayden would never cheat on me. I know that now. I was just being paranoid."

We're at the end of the row of booths so we pivot to return the way we came.

"Of course, he wouldn't," Reid says. "Why would he? Look at you."

A blush warms my cheeks, but I'm confident Reid can't see it through the ruddiness caused by the cold. "You haven't seen the women I've seen."

Reid laughs. "Eadie, that's weird."

"Some of the women I used to work with when I was a model were weird. They were so gorgeous I was sure they were robots or aliens. Try looking into the eyes of a six-foot blonde with irises the color of topaz and not crumple from sheer unworthiness."

"That tells me nothing. Topaz comes in all colors."

"The yellowish color."

"Ohhh." Reid stuffs his fat glove into his bag of popcorn and pulls out a handful. "That is weird."

"I told you. It's not natural."

"They were probably contacts."

"I have solid evidence that they were not contacts."

"What evidence?"

"I saw her putting in green contacts once."

Reid halts and looks at me for a moment. Then he shrugs his right shoulder and stuffs his fat glove into his popcorn bag, sending pieces to the ground.

"Take off your glove, silly."

"It's *cold*," Reid retorts.

"Goodness gracious." We continue moving along. "So that's why I quit modeling. Or one of the reasons."

"You didn't think you were pretty enough?"

"I wasn't. Not to make it to the top, and I didn't enjoy the job enough to risk not getting gigs and struggling to get by. It looks glamorous, but I assure you it's not."

"Is that why you started modeling? Because of the glamor?" He holds up a finger. "Before you answer, the Eadie I remember wasn't interested in fashion. And, quite frankly, don't get offended, she was a bit of a tomboy."

"A bit?"

"Listen, I'm not judging. There's nothing wrong with being a tomboy."

"No. There's not. I know that now."

We pass Home for the Hollandaise, which is looking rather un-festive despite being a Christmas-themed café. The Christmas lights surrounding the sign are sagging, and there are no decorations in the windows to entice passersby. Today would have been the perfect day to sell ourselves to out-of-towners. Opportunity wasted.

I sigh, and Reid glances at me. The direction of my gaze clues him in.

"We should have put lights up or something," he says.

"Yeah."

"It's fine. There's so much going on."

I sigh again, dropping my eyes to the sidewalk. Unexplored booths approach on our right and we veer that way.

"Okay. I'm ready for your answer," Reid says.

"I forget the question."

"Why did you get into modeling?"

I scrunch the top of my popcorn bag and close it with the twist tie, then I cast Reid a contemplative look. "Have you ever done a thing just because you felt you had something to prove?"

Reid stops and gestures to the length of his body. "Do I look like a football player?"

I admire his sturdy build, evident even through the layers of clothing. Gone is scrawny Reid. Now Reid has muscle. Girth. Maturity. "Back then? No."

"We understand each other."

He resumes walking and catches up with me.

The natural flow of our conversation is leading to a place I'm not sure I want to go. I dive into the nearest booth and examine the cute polymer clay ornaments. He hovers next to me but doesn't ask the question: What did I have to prove?

That I was beautiful enough. Woman enough. Sexy enough. Good enough for a guy from Cold Spring. That I was *too* good for them.

I was on the cover of *Vogue*. I walked the Fashion Week catwalk. I proved it and then some. And I got Hayden out of the deal, so in the end, it worked out.

"Hey," I say. Reid's bent over examining an adorable ornament of a sloth hanging on a Christmas tree. "Thanks for the popcorn. I think I'm going to head out."

He stands. "Oh." His eyes drop to the ground but they quickly return to mine. His expression is different though. More reserved. "Sure. I'll see you Monday."

"See ya." I wave and leave Reid standing alone in the cold.

Chapter 22

Dad does great through the weekend and into the next week. He's out of his chair more, sorting through the den's clutter, checking on the chickens, helping Mom with dinner. It boosts my confidence that maybe the memory blips truly were just the anesthesia, or low blood sugar, or within the normal realm of forgetfulness for a mid-sixties man with undiagnosed ADHD.

Unfortunately, my confidence is broken on Tuesday evening. Dad and I are chatting about the café over dinner when he forgets Reid's name. I watch Dad's anger rise and boil over as he struggles to recall the information, fully aware that he should be able to pull it easily from his mind. He takes his frustration out on Mom and me, yelling at me for fixing dinner too late, and laying into Mom for making him hire a general manager in the first place. He vehemently refuses to let us tell him the name, determined to think of it himself.

Mom leaves the table and hides in her bedroom for the rest of the night. Dad eventually calms down and apologizes to me. An hour later, he joins me in the kitchen while I'm unloading the dishwasher and says, "Reid."

"Yeah, Dad," I encourage. "Reid. You knew that."

"Of course, I did. I just let my blood sugar get too low."

"Did you apologize to Mom?"

"What? No. She's pouting." He opens the refrigerator and pulls out a can of seltzer water.

"She's pouting because you yelled at her."

"She'll get over it."

"Never let the sun go down on your anger," I remind him.

"I'm not angry. She is," he huffs and then leaves the room.

The next morning, I text Reid that I'm going to be a little late, and I position myself at the kitchen table. Mom fixes her breakfast of Frosted Mini Wheats at seven thirty without fail. Today is no exception.

I pretend to be immersed in my phone until she sits beside me, opens her Bible to Philippians, and starts crunching on her cereal.

"Do you want to talk about it," I ask without looking up. I don't want to spook her.

"Talk about what?" she says between bites.

"Last night. Dinner. Dad." I don't need to use complete sentences to jog her memory, which I know is quite fresh. It certainly is for me.

She turns a thin page and squints at the top of the next one. She's either skimming her morning Bible reading or playing dumb.

"I don't know, honey," she says finally. "I'm just trying to start my day."

"How's your hip?"

"Much better than before the surgery, actually."

I nod, take a bite of my bagel, and tap my phone screen. "So, I notice Dad has been forgetting stuff. I think maybe he has the beginning stages of dementia."

Mom sucks in a breath. Her hand trembles midbite. She sets it down and breathes deeply again.

"I think maybe we should make an appointment for him to get tested."

She lowers both hands to her lap. "He's already been tested. Your father has Alzheimer's."

Her words are a punch in the gut. The word "Alzheimer's" is scary enough. Add to it her lack of transparency. I reel from the impact for a full minute before I'm able to speak again. "How long have you known?" I'm devastated. I'm angry. Betrayed.

"Two months." She grabs her spoon again and fishes for a soggy bite of shredded wheat.

"Mother," I say firmly.

"Don't yell at me for not telling you. I needed time to let it sit. I still hardly believe it myself."

I cross my arms and slump in my chair. "Obviously." My tone reflects my frustration.

Mom sets her spoon down gently. She sits unmoving for a moment. "Alzheimer's sounds bad but it's actually the slowest form of dementia. He could still have a decade. Maybe more. It's not like it's a rush."

"It sounds bad because it is bad, Mom. Has he started on medication, therapy, anything?"

"We went to the follow-up appointment to learn the test results, and we haven't returned."

I push back my chair and stand. My feet need to move. My hands need something to do. I pace over to the stove, grab the hand towel from the oven handle, and twist it between my hands. Meanwhile, Mom has tucked her elbows close to her sides and is cradling her forehead in one hand.

Her fragileness strikes me. How did I not notice how thin she's gotten? She cooks, but is she feeding herself?

My anger fades. I rush over to her, pull a chair over, and drape my arm across her back. "It's going to be okay." She's crying silent tears. I feel like a jerk. "I'm sorry, Mom. I'm not mad. I'm just shocked."

"I was too." Her voice wobbles. I just—I can't bring myself to—" She shudders and sinks even farther.

"How advanced did they say it is?"

"It's early." Mom sniffs.

I grab a napkin from the holder in the center of the table and hand it to her. She uses it to dab her eyes and her nose.

"That's good. We have more options, then. They probably have medicines to slow the progression."

"I can't face it."

She might be fragile, but I can't lie to her. Maybe if I remain strong, she can borrow some of my strength. "You have to face it. You have no choice. Dad needs you."

Mom straightens and drops her hands to her lap like they're heavy weights. "I've worked in that café my entire married life. I wanted to retire. Travel. Get out of this town. Do something different." She looks up at the ceiling like a solution is hiding in the cracked plaster.

"You still can. But we have to start with the basics. Set up an appointment for Dad. Get him started on a treatment protocol. Learn ways to help him."

"We have no money to travel." She refocuses on her cereal. Her frown deepens, emphasizing her marionette lines.

I lean over to try to intercept her eyes. "Don't worry about that right now. I'll figure something out."

She sighs again, but this time it's laden with frustration. "You're going back to New York in a few weeks. I have to figure it out myself. And I will. I'm just not ready."

"Mom." I rest my hand on her forearm. "Make an appointment. Please. That's all I ask. You can't put it off."

She looks at me, brushes a lock of white hair from her forehead, and sighs. She looks so tired, but she forces a smile. "Okay."

"Today," I say.

"It doesn't mean I'll be able to make him go."

"If he won't, I'll carry him to the car."

She chuckles and shakes her head. "I'd like to see that. But I'm not sure I'll be able to get in before the first of the year."

"Just see. Okay?"

"If it will make you happy." She reaches up and tucks my hair behind my ear.

I want her to do it for Dad. For her. But I guess I'll take what I can get.

"This was a setup, wasn't it?" Mom says.

"Maybe." I flash her a sly grin. "Are you okay or do I need to stay home today?"

"I'm fine. Bring me back leftover donuts if there are any."

"Sure." I stand and kiss her on the forehead before grabbing my coat and heading out.

During the drive to work, the strong front I wore for Mom starts to deteriorate. My mind travels years into the future. Will he forget *my* name? What if he forgets me? His own daughter? What about the physical effects? Will he become bed bound? Will he become aggressive? How will Mom afford memory care?

The questions pound on me like a heavy rainfall, the deluge leaking into me, fueling the tears that I desperately don't want to let loose, because if I start crying, I'm not sure when I'll stop. I need my daddy. I'll never stop needing him.

I park the Lumina behind the café and try to regain my composure before stepping out of the car. It starts to work. Marginally.

While I'm managing the kitchen, I can downshift into auto pilot. Fulfilling orders will become my sole focus, especially during the lunch rush. I can leave my problems in this car and pick them up on the way home. No one has to know how gutted I feel.

I step out of the car and enter through the service door. Marlon's at his station, steam rising from the browning meat and mingling with the bubbles of sweat on his nose. He turns to welcome me.

"Oh," he says, his inflection dropping off at the end. "Is there something wrong?"

I guess I can't hide. His acknowledgment of my grief unleashes the tears that built up during the drive in. "I'm fine," I say as tears roll down my face. I sprint to the office.

"Is there something I can do?" he hollers after me.

Reid is sitting in front of his computer. He swivels around. When he sees I'm crying, he stands and approaches me. "Eadie, what is it?"

The alarm in his voice makes me cry harder. I collapse into my office chair and cover my face. He scoots his chair beside me and settles into it, placing a hand on my back while I cry. He doesn't ask me to explain, just strokes my back while the tears flow.

When they stop, I raise my head tentatively. I must look a wreck. Reid doesn't flinch. He just studies me with concern.

"It's Alzheimer's," I say. "My mom took him to get tested. She just wasn't ready to tell me. So she didn't ignore you. She listened. I guess she's on her own time line. I'm going to try to be patient."

Reid grabs my hand. He doesn't say anything. He doesn't need to. I know he understands.

The feeling of his palm against mine takes me back to the day we floated down the creek in confident silence. The two of us just existing. Together.

With his hand still wrapped around mine, he leans forward and anchors his elbows on his knees, bringing his face closer to mine. "It's hard. I get it."

His cologne overtakes me, a smell I'm more than familiar with, the essence of Reid. I'm drawn to it. I want it near me. Not just his shirt draped over me, but all of him.

"Thanks," I say, but I've forgotten what we're talking about. I've forgotten everything. His presence becomes my home. His lips are the key that will unlock the door.

As he leans in closer, my eyes track his lips. They're seeking connection. I don't retreat. "Eadie," he whispers.

Hearing my name breaks the spell. I'm back in the office just inches away from a very, very big mistake.

"Oh my... What—" I jump to my feet and spin toward the door.

"Eadie," Reid repeats to my back as I run past the threshold.

The kitchen's bright lights provide the second shock I need to become fully aware. That can never happen again. Ever. I spin back around and trudge into the office, closing the door behind me, but not latching it.

Reid lifts his head from his hands. "I'm sorry," he blurts.

"I'm not a cheater," I state as definitively as possible. Because I'm not. Am I? Was that cheating?

"I know. I'm a jerk. I—"

"I'll never cheat on Hayden."

"It's my fault. You're vulnerable and I took advantage. This is on me. You did nothing wrong."

If he only knew what was going on in my head before we almost kissed. But he's not going to know. "We're friends. Just friends."

"Yeah." He runs a hand through his hair and looks down. "Friends."

"Okay. Now that that's established. Are we good?"

"Yeah."

"Good."

I turn around, tug on the doorknob, and yelp. Marlon and Lexis are standing in the doorway, both bent slightly at the waist to increase the efficiency of their eavesdropping.

"You didn't hear that," I say as I buzz past them.

"But I did," Lexis says. She catches up to me and casts me a knowing glance.

I turn around to find Marlon grinning, the upside-down cross underneath his durag mocking me. "Get to work." I wave him back to his station. "Just. Do work things."

"Sure, boss," Lexis says with exaggerated inflection.

Throughout the rest of the day, when I'm not immersed in fulfilling customer orders, I replay the almost-kiss between me and Reid. Is an almost-kiss cheating? Do I need to confess it to Hayden?

A quiet voice in the recesses of my mind says, "Yes." But I push it back. I'm not ready to go there yet.

Chapter 23

Reid leaves early, mumbling something about an appointment. We didn't speak the entire day, him in the office, me at my post by the kitchen pass-through. With only a month left in Indiana, maybe I can avoid him for the rest of my stay. I'll have to devise an avoidance plan.

By three o'clock, I've only come up with part of a plan. I'll cut Reid's hours to part-time. How long does it take to count beans anyway? Not very. I'll probably email him the new protocol. *Dear Reid, Tomorrow you will begin earning a full-time salary on a part-time schedule.* Voila, he's out of my hair for four hours a day. I'm sure he'll be ecstatic. It's a start.

Lexis locks the front door. I help her wipe down the tables while Marlon shuts down the kitchen.

"Do you want to talk about it?" she asks while we move from table to table.

"About what?"

"Oh, nothing," she says with a sigh.

"I have no idea what you're talking about."

"He really likes you."

I roll my eyes. My back is to Lexis so she can't see it. "I don't know *who* you're talking about."

"Fine," Lexis concedes. "It's your business."

"This café is my business and I intend to run it drama-free for four more weeks." I turn around and snap my washcloth at the air.

She grins mischievously before moving on to the booths.

"I don't know why everyone here is intent on me cheating on my boyfriend." I don't hide the annoyance in my voice.

Lexis stands and crosses her arms over her Phish T-shirt. She sucks in a deep breath. Her shoulders droop on the exhale. "You're right. I'm as bad as Annette. I'm sorry. I'll run defense if you want."

"That's not necessary. I can handle myself."

"Sure. Of course, you can." She unfolds her arms, fluffs her pixie cut, and gets back to work.

I wipe down one more table before the urge to hide becomes too strong to ignore. "I'm heading to the office. Are you okay doing the rest?"

"Yes, boss."

I hurry to the kitchen, eager to duck away from the eyes and ears that heard everything between me and Reid this morning.

"I like working with you, Eadie," Lexis says as I'm pushing through the door.

I pause. "Same," I say over my shoulder with a smile.

She keeps her head down, but I can still read her grin.

In the office, I slump into my chair. Should I tell Hayden? Should I not tell Hayden? The questions swirl in my head, one on top of the other, like my brain is a front-loading washing machine.

I was worried about Hayden cheating on me while I was here. And then today happened. Oh, the irony.

I didn't kiss Reid, so it doesn't count as cheating. Does it?

But I wanted to kiss Reid.

Why did I want to kiss Reid??

Because I was vulnerable. Reid said it himself. He took advantage of me.

I sigh, lean heavily onto the desk, and brace my forehead with my hands. That's not true. He didn't do anything wrong. He felt my vibes. He knew I wanted it too.

Piles of random papers still crowd the edges of Dad's desk. Two drawers won't close in the corner filing cabinet, too stuffed with folders, old bills, and pamphlets. More junk sits on top of the cabinet, broken this and thats from the kitchen that Dad couldn't part with for some reason. I itch to clean it all up.

Instead, I reach over and click off the floor lamp, plunging the room into shadow except for the halo of my desk lamp. Now I know why Reid likes it dark. Out of sight out of mind. Except I still feel like I'm being stalked by a paper monster.

I move the stacks to the floor beside my desk, not caring too much about the structural integrity of each pile. Soon, the desk is clear except for my computer, desk lamp, and Jupiter's travel terrarium. I tap my fingernail against the plastic, imagining Jupiter waving at me with his furry appendages.

What if Jupiter's still alive, still wandering the walls of the Coleman Building? No, he *has* to be alive. I refuse to believe that my pet has perished. He needs me, yet I've been lax in my search and rescue.

I flip the floor lamp back on, turn on my phone's flashlight, and do a quick search of every surface in the room before focusing on Reid's desk, the last place I saw Jupiter. I've checked the desk more than once. Maybe he found his way back?

With renewed focus, I gently open each drawer and carefully dig through office supplies, Reid's very well-stocked Post-it stash, and a pile of fidget toys. When I open the top drawer, I pause, my curiosity piqued by a letterhead poking out of the disarray: *Elite Properties Group.*

I pull out the letter and skim through it.

I am pleased to present you with my appraisal of the Coleman Building... I have attached a detailed report of my findings, including a full description of the property and its features... I'm excited to work with you...

With each sentence, my heart pounds harder. The letter is addressed to Reid. Not to my mom or my dad, the actual owners of this property. Does Dad know about the appraisal or is Reid trying to sell the Coleman Building out from under them?

My anger reaches a boiling point. I need answers. Now.

I stuff the letter into my purse, throw on my coat, and dash out of the office to get to the bottom of this.

I pull up in front of Reid's childhood home, impressed by the new paint scheme. New to me anyway. Yellow trim accents gray siding where there used to be navy and orange. The porch pillars and walls are still brown brick, wrapping around the front and side of the house.

Reid and I sat on that same porch swing on a muggy summer day before our freshman year. We'd just gotten back from church camp. It was the second day of endless rain. I'd brought over my embroidery floss in gradations of blue with yellow thrown in for some punch. I wasn't wearing shoes, my feet feeling every rise and divot in the aging cement.

I hiked one foot onto the swing and looped my carefully curated rope of embroidery floss around my big toe and started tying knots. My other leg was pressed against Reid's. Neither of us acknowledged our proximity. We acted like it was normal. Like holding hands for an hour while floating down a creek was also normal.

It felt better than normal. It felt both sweet and charged, comforting yet dangerous.

"What do entomologists do anyway?" Reid said, continuing our conversation about what we planned to do when we grew up.

"They study bugs. That's what -ology means. The study of."

"They just sit around and stare at bugs all day?"

"I suppose some of them do. If they want to learn more about an ant colony's organizational structure, they'd have to sit and watch."

"And that helps society how?"

I glared at Reid mid-knot. "In case we ever encounter a hive-mind alien, we'll know how to communicate with them."

The plastic cushion shifted beneath us as Reid collapsed in laughter. When he recovered, he sat up and placed his arm behind me, resting it on the back of the swing, not touching me but nearly so.

"But if you insist on my dream being useful, I do have some ideas. I'd like to fight against the release of hybrid bugs into the environment due to the irreparable harm they might cause to ecosystems. Or I could help organic farmers with insect control so they can lessen their dependence on pesticides."

Rain continued to batter the front yard, dredging up a host of smells from loamy to metallic, the water finding the least encumbering path to the storm sewers. The density of the drops created a curtain around the porch, hemming us in and backdropping our conversation with calming white noise.

Reid let his fingers drop from the swing to my shoulder. When his fingertips met my skin, I felt a wave of something I couldn't name. I only knew I liked it.

"Would either of those pursuits be good enough for you, Mr. Judgy?" I asked, not letting the heady moment affect my propensity to tease.

"I'm not judging. I'm just trying to understand your obsession."

"An obsession makes it sound like a problem."

"How many pet insects do you have at the moment?"

"Ten, and two arachnids."

Reid shuddered like he did every time he stepped into my bedroom. He could handle a single pill bug, or the rare ladybug sighting, or a granddaddy longlegs perched on my hand, but too many bugs in his general vicinity? Nope.

"Insects are all around you, everywhere you look." I pointed to a spiderweb in the eaves. He looked at me like I was a swamp monster climbing out of primordial ooze.

I laughed, always taking a bit of satisfaction in making a boy squeamish with my "obsession."

"What about you Judgy-McJudge?" I asked. "What are you going to be when you grow up?"

"No clue." He propped his foot on his knee and began tapping my leg with the bottom of his shoe.

"You got nothing?"

"I know I want to study overseas in college. That's about it. I want to learn a language. Two. Maybe Spanish first. I've heard if you learn Spanish, Italian and French are similar."

I looked up from my friendship bracelet and raised an eyebrow at him. "That would be four languages. What's that? Quatra-lingual?"

"I think that would be multilingual."

"Oh. Yeah."

I went back to tying knots, working my way through the blue, then to yellow, and back again.

"You've never told me that," I said finally.

"It's just something I've been thinking about. It would be a good excuse to get away from here for a while. I don't want to be stuck in this town forever, you know?"

I considered his comment for a moment and decided I might like to be stuck with him on this porch in this rain for a long, long time.

A splotch of rain against my windshield jerks me back into the present. What's happening to me? I can't go all soft. I'm here to yell at Reid for trying to sell the Coleman Building from under our noses. A tsunami of long-buried memories isn't enough to quench my anger.

Neither is this rain.

The longer I sit, the more it asserts itself.

I kick open my door and tromp up the sidewalk catching raindrops with my hair until I reach the security of the porch. After banging on the front door, I wait with my arms crossed and my toe tapping against concrete. Moments later, Reid opens the door. He eyes me warily.

"Did the café catch on fire again?" he asks.

"That only happens on your watch."

My comment evokes visible bristling. "What's up?" Reid asks stiffly. "Do you want to come in?"

I pull the letter out of my purse and flutter it in front of his face. "What's this?"

He goes cross-eyed trying to focus on the paper just inches from his nose. Unable to get a good look, he reaches up and swipes it from my hand.

I swipe it back. "I don't know who you think you are trying to sell the building from under our noses. You know he'd have to sign off, don't you?"

Realization draws Reid's expression southward. He slumps against the doorjamb. "Can I see that?"

"You've already seen it. It was in your top drawer." I hand it to him anyway.

He gives it a cursory glance. "Of course I'd never sell out from under your dad. I couldn't."

I lean into him. "That's right. You couldn't. So why are you trying?"

Reid returns the letter and stuffs his hands into his pockets. "Do you want to come in and talk about it?"

"No!"

"Eadie."

"Don't say my name like that."

"Like what?"

"Like, 'Eadie,'" I say breathily.

Reid rocks slightly at the waist. "That's not how I said your name."

"It's what I heard."

"I think that's a you problem."

I huff and then brush past him into his foyer. The room is divided in two by the stairwell, the living room on the right, a dining room on the left. Despite the home's 1920s Craftsman exterior, the interior is modern with low furnishings and sleek tables. Orange pillows contrast against navy upholstery, and metal art pieces decorate the walls.

Reid follows me inside.

"Hmm," I say, unable to help myself as I survey the room.

"What?"

"Nothing."

"Eadie. I mean, Eadie," he repeats in a much lower, forced tone. "Did you come to talk to me or to make non-descript noises while glaring at my forehead?"

So he noticed. I haven't met his eyes yet. Not once. "I said 'Hmm' because I'm surprised you like modern décor. You seem more...log cabin."

"This is my dad's place. I've just been staying here. I'm supposed to be selling it. Anyway, do you want something to drink while we talk about the letter?"

I give the living room a final spin. "Sure," I say, my anger diminished by Reid's lack of shock at my accusation that he's trying to scam my dad. I should have known better. Conniving doesn't seem to be his jam. Not anymore. Not ever? But I'm still upset that he had a realtor appraise the building without asking Dad. Assuming Dad doesn't know about it. Maybe he does? This wasn't a well-planned ambush.

I meander into the dining room. Reid enters with two steaming mugs of coffee. He hands me one and we sit. The homey scent of roasted coffee beans warms my mood, but it won't stop this interrogation.

"Does my dad know you had the building appraised?" I ask with my eyes narrowed.

He clears his throat before answering. "No."

Ha. I knew it.

"Were you going to tell him?" I press.

"Of course."

"When?" Rain pounds on the windowpane behind me, hammering my questions home.

"When my ducks are in a row?" Reid fingers the handle on his mug.

"Well, are they in a row, Quacky McQuack?"

I doubt a police officer has ever asked *that* during an investigation.

He rolls his eyes at me. "You and your Blanky McBlank."

"It never gets old."

"My ducklings are almost in a row. I wanted to get the numbers back first, which I have, and now I'm ready to write up a report for your dad."

Humph. Not the answer I'd expect from a hardened criminal. And now I'm off my game.

He raises an eyebrow at me. I raise one back.

"Any more pointed questions?" he asks.

"Probably. I need a moment."

While trying to formulate my next attack, I study the dining room. It has the same modern appeal as the living room. Wood and metal combine in the table and chairs to give the space an industrial undertone. I run my nail over the knotty pine tabletop which is held up by two rectangular bands of metal on each end. My anger is dropping like the rain.

"What do you think of the numbers?" I ask. It's not very pointed, but it's the best I have.

Reid takes a sip of coffee and then wraps both hands around the mug. "I'm pleased. Did you look at them?"

"No." I slump in my seat and pull my coat tighter, cushioning myself against the cold rain.

It used to be cozier in here. Plush white microfiber couches, oriental rugs in the living room and dining room, a solid oak table with sturdy chairs, all stained a warm brown. There was no metal to be found, only reed baskets, leather ottomans, and decorative clay pots. All signs of a woman's touch.

When Reid's mom left, did she take her décor with her too? Not that I mind modern. It's clean (can't go wrong there), simple, fresh, a new beginning for Reid and his dad.

And now Reid's taking care of his family home, a dedicated son. And he's watching over the café, a dedicated employee. He knows more about the café's finances than any of us. Maybe I should...trust him.

"Why did you get the building appraised?" I ask.

"You may not like it."

"I know I won't." I nurse my coffee for a moment, letting the heat slide down my throat and warm my belly in preparation for the cold hard truth Reid is about to impart. "Continue."

"The building needs a new roof. New windows. New heating and air. Most of the appliances in the café need replacing."

"Most?" I flick my eyes to the ceiling and sink even deeper into my chair.

"All. The exterior brick needs repointed. The floors need refinished. The upholstery is splitting."

"I get it. The place needs an overhaul."

"But." Reid raises a finger, his palm still anchored on the table. "Companies are looking to invest in Cold Spring. It's close to Indy. The small-town appeal is off the charts. The investment potential is obvious and it's driving up prices."

"You want some out-of-towner to come in and ruin the hometown appeal. Wonderful."

"Eadie." He clears his throat. "Eadie," he says, lowering his voice.

"You don't have to do that."

His shoulders relax. "Good. Anyway, if your parents sold, they'd have a lump sum of money that they could invest, and then they could try to live off the interest."

"*Try?*"

"I'd need to run the numbers."

"But if they keep the café running, they can live off the profits. Then they can sell the building in the future if necessary."

Reid's serious expression doesn't shift. "I've already run those numbers. They'd have to take out an improvement loan to make it happen, and the loan payment would eat up all their potential income."

That's the cold hard truth I was afraid of. The lose-lose. They sell the building, they run out of money. They keep the café open, they run out of money. Neither option leads to adequate financing for Dad's memory care. There'd be no money left for other health expenses that may ensue, or for the home and auto repair costs that will inevitably arise.

I push my coffee mug aside, slide both elbows onto the table, and bury my head in my hands. Beside me, Reid's mug taps lightly against the wood as he finishes a drink.

Before Reid and I split ways in high school, I often had dinner here. The last time I ate in this dining room, his mom had prepared a beef roast with potatoes and carrots. She called Reid's dad to the table, who was visibly much older than her, something I'd always found strange. The four of us filled our bellies with her nourishing home-cooked meal.

His mom left them? Just like that? It must have happened during high school when we weren't friends, when I wasn't there to help him through it.

"I didn't realize your dad liked collecting art," I say. My hands muffle my voice.

"This is all his."

I peek at Reid between my fingers. "He made it?"

"Yep. He took up metalworking after I graduated. There's a shop in the garage."

How much more cathartic, to make your own furniture, your own wall art? The ultimate symbol of moving on.

"That's impressive," I say.

I sit quietly and stare off into the living room while I ponder what Reid's life must have been like after his mom left, and how lucky I am that I've always had both of my parents for support. Reid fidgets beside me like my behavior today has spooked him so much that he's afraid to talk out of turn.

"I'm sorry I jumped to conclusions," I say, but a single apology doesn't seem to cover it. "I'm sorry about everything, including what happened in the office this morning. You didn't take advantage of me." I toss the letter to the table. It slides across the finely polished surface and wafts to the floor.

Reid pushes out of his chair and retrieves it, smoothing out the many wrinkles I placed in it while interrogating him. He's wearing his customary flannel, currently unbuttoned against his white T-shirt, always a little different, but still the same, the attire of someone who likes consistency and sameness. No surprises. Not anymore.

His sleeves are rolled up, his forearms well-defined and capped by broad hands. The hands of a guy who's not afraid to put in the work, even when those around him aren't committed.

He looks up at me, notices I'm studying him, and blushes. When he flicks his head, a lock of hair drops to his forehead, but it's not enough to camouflage his feelings.

He really likes you.

When Lexis's words echo in my mind, I blush, and suddenly I know the answer. I need to tell Hayden.

Reid and I both look down at the table. He slides back into his chair and clears his throat.

"Let's not worry about earlier today. Let's just think about how we're going to make sure your parents are taken care of. How does that sound?"

Raindrops still pound on the window, calming white noise. I dare a peek at Reid, trying not to get caught in his gaze. It mostly works. "You're a good friend, Reid," I say.

Sadness tinges his eyes as a soft smile plays on his lips. "Just friends."

"Yeah."

I grab the letter and tuck it back into my purse. "How many times have you gone over the numbers?"

"Too many times to count."

"What if I looked at them? I'm no accountant, but maybe I'll see something you haven't."

Reid regards me thoughtfully, the tinge of sadness gone, or maybe just hidden. "Sure," he says. "I've stared at them so much it's possible I might be missing something. You have access to everything on your dad's computer. Just go to QuickBooks. I upgraded his spreadsheet system."

"He was still using spreadsheets when you started?"

"Yep."

"Why am I not surprised?" I shake my head and spread my hands out over the tabletop. "Anyway..." My voice goes soft as a surprise bout of shyness overtakes me. "Thanks for the coffee. And for putting up with me." I lean into my hands. "And for looking out for my dad." I lock eyes with Reid. "Really. Thank you."

We hold each other's gaze for a moment before Reid dips his head. "It's been my pleasure."

I stand and jut my index finger against his chest. "Now I'm going to go prove you wrong."

Chapter 24

I return to the café immediately, hunker down in the dark office, and pull up QuickBooks. For an hour and a half, I add, subtract, shift numbers, slash line items, adjust costs, reduce personnel. Nothing works.

Reid is right.

No matter how I look at the numbers they're bad. Depending on how I look at them, they're really bad. Why did I think I could outwit an accountant?

I pick at a hangnail on my left pinkie as I contemplate my findings. The Coleman Building is falling apart. The café's finances are less than stellar. Yet my parents are aging and need a reliable source of income for their retirement years. Reid has been through this thought cycle countless times, no doubt, while staring at this same wall.

Grudgingly, I wheel myself over to his desk, pull out his top drawer, and look for the attachment that lists the appraisal value. When my eyes find the bottom line, I have to grab the armrest to steady myself.

It's more money than I expected. A lot more. Cold Spring is clearly on the up-and-up. How could I tell my parents *not* to sell, knowing the numbers like I do now?

I tilt my head back and balance the appraisal on my face. Maybe it will impart some wisdom, or magic, or help me come up with a way to break the news. It doesn't, and I feel like an idiot, so I stuff the papers back in Reid's desk and sulk.

This should be good news. My parents are sitting on a lot of cash. But I'm not sure my dad will see it that way. I'm not sure I do.

Home for the Hollandaise was Grandma Delores's dream. It has made my family a fixture in Cold Spring, the family everyone thinks they know by simple association. We feed the town. We spread our cheer (or we used to). We give Main Street part of its charm.

I probably spent a third of my life here when I was a kid, coming in early before school while mom helped make donuts, roller skating upstairs after school, stopping in for a cold fountain drink and dessert after a long day of canoeing.

Dad has spent way more time here than me. He not only grew up here, he's spent the majority of his adulthood in the kitchen. His oldest memories are here, solidified by time, deep and rich with history. If the café goes, will his memories go that much faster?

I think I know the answer, and I don't like it. In fact, the whole idea of selling the Coleman Building? I don't like it one bit.

My phone buzzes in my purse. I pull it out and check my notification.

Whitney texted me.

Hey girlie, how's it going?

Things here are weird, not gonna lie, I text back.

Really??? How so?

It's too complicated to explain over text.

My parents might lose their café. I keep having "feelings" for my high school bully...er...friend. Yeah, none of that needs to be immortalized on a random server for the FBI or CIA to rake through. I need to talk to Hayden tonight. I know that. Until then, I prefer to keep my deepest thoughts untraceable.

I'll explain it over FaceTime, I add. I leave it open-ended because I'm not sure when I'll have enough energy for Whitney's energy.

By the time I get home, Mom has already fixed a dinner of ham, northern beans, and cornbread. Mom and Dad sat down moments ago, and Dad is shimmying a square of cornbread from the loaf pan. After dumping it onto his plate, he slathers it with butter and then dollops ham and beans on top.

I hang my wet coat on the rack before sitting in front of the empty plate that Mom already set for me. A gush of air escapes my lungs as my rear hits the seat.

"Long day?" Mom asks.

I take my turn at the cornbread, cutting a square, and depositing it on my plate. "Yep," I reply as a conversation stop, not keen on sharing this afternoon's developments.

"You running the kitchen like a well-oiled machine?" Dad asks.

"Of course."

I prefer my ham and beans on the side, the liquid drained, with a squirt of ketchup on top. When my dinner is fully plated, I dive in, savoring the buttery cornbread first.

Dad wants more details. How's the new cook working out? The felon? *Fine, Dad.* What about Reid? You keeping him in line? *Always.* And so it goes.

Eventually, they move on to other topics including the ongoing clean-up of Dad's den. Mom was ecstatic to find a ten-year-old sewing project underneath a pile of egg cartons. Dad wants to keep the metal sign collection he found tucked between the bookshelf and the wall. Mom thinks he should sell them on eBay. Dad wants to nail them to the den walls.

"They're rusty, Weston," Mom says.

"The patina is the charm."

Mom persists. "You could use the money to buy a new record player for the piles of LPs that you insist on keeping."

He doesn't shoot her down. Mom preens. I have a hunch most of their interactions have gone the same way today.

"Did you make an appointment?" I ask Mom.

Without looking up, she says, "January 15th."

"Appointment for what?" Dad says as he mashes his cornbread and beans together.

Mom flicks her eyes his way. He picks up on her furtiveness. Combine that with my cautious glance and he's got us figured out.

He lets his fork fall loosely in his hand. "Appointment for what?" he says with more authority.

"She knows," Mom mutters. "She figured it out."

Dad's expression hardens. He purses his lips and shifts his eyes between Mom and me. "What does she know?"

"I know you have Alzheimer's, Dad." I almost choke on the word. "I wish you guys would have told me sooner."

"It was just a test. It could have been wrong." He throws up a defiant hand and then shovels a bite of food into his mouth.

Mom reaches over and rests her hand on his forearm. He looks at it as he chews. Eventually, his demeanor relaxes, and he rests his hand on top of hers, giving it a squeeze. A moment later, they let go and recommence eating.

"Did you bring home any leftover donuts?" Mom asks.

And that's that.

Mom starts talking about her sewing group, how they're going to be so excited about her long-lost project. Dad hmms now and then, conveying interest even though I know he'd rather talk about something else.

I tune them out and descend into my own machinations. How exactly am I going to tell Hayden I almost kissed another guy today? How deep am I going to go? Am I going to mention the other times Reid has made my stomach flutter since I've been here? Am I going to keep it high level, play it down, diminish it?

After dinner, I retreat to my bedroom, still undecided, realizing there is no good way to do this. I'll have to play it by ear.

I start by texting Hayden and asking him if he has time to Face-Time. He answers by sending me an invite.

My nerves run like a hamster that's hyped on Red Bull and coffee. I perch on the edge of the bed, struggling to maintain my balance.

"Hey," I say. My heart rate speeds to ten beats per word. I'm surprised I'm not dead. *Play it cool.*

He's already in bed, the muted light from the television flickering on his shadowed features. His tousled hair is standing up straight in front, but he still looks handsome as ever.

We chat about our days. Inconsequential stuff. He tells me he has a break between projects, so when he's not at the gym he's couch surfing with an Xbox controller and a steady diet of gameplay. I tell him about our new repeat customer named Gerard who refuses to tip, searching for a way to segue into confession time.

After fumbling through a couple more anecdotes, I can tell I'm losing Hayden. I decide to get on with it. "There's something I need to tell you."

He perks slightly from his supine position, the back of his head sliding against the headboard. "What's up?"

"You know Reid, right?"

Hayden looks at me blankly. "Reid who?"

"I haven't mentioned Reid?" My voice reeks of false innocence, and I can't stop it.

"Nope," he says. He throws a crunchy snack into his mouth and chomps down.

"He was one of my high school bullies. My dad hired him as the general manager. We've been working together for the last several weeks."

"Oh." Hayden sounds sympathetic. "Yeah. Awkward."

A fluttery laugh escapes my throat, the feathers practically visible as they float out of my mouth. I clamp my lips shut. Then I realize it's my turn to talk. "Yeah. Awkward. I mean, what do you think is awkward about it?"

"He bullied you in high school and now you're working with him? That must be a mindfudge."

I know what he means. He knows I don't like cussing. I don't see the point of it, but it might be appropriate here. Mindfudge, indeed. "Yeah. The cool thing is," I continue, "we're getting along pretty well. In fact, today we were both in the office alone together and, um..."

Hayden furrows his brow and angles his forehead toward the camera. "And what?"

I sit up straighter in bed and get my free hand into the act, waving it alongside my head as I speak. "Don't worry it was nothing. It was just, for a moment there, I thought he might kiss me. And I might have kissed him back."

"You *might* have kissed him back?"

"Yeah."

"Did you, or didn't you?"

"No! We didn't kiss. There was absolutely no kissing, just the thought of it and the kind of wanting to."

Hayden shoots me a confused look as he tries to decipher my grammar. "You're saying you wanted to kiss him?"

"For a second. And then it passed. And it's all over now. So, whew!"

Hayden leans his head back and presses it against the headboard creating a slight double chin. "And you're going to keep working with him?"

Is this where I tell him about my partial solution? Where Reid only works half a day, and when he's there, he stays hidden in the office like a vampire afraid of the sun?

"Yeah" I say. "I guess. I don't really have a choice."

"So..." Hayden draws out the word. "You're going to keep working for the guy you have feelings for—"

"Who said anything about feelings?"

"You wanted to kiss him. You don't want to kiss people you don't have feelings for. You told me yourself. You think kissing is gross otherwise."

"I said that?"

"Yes," Hayden says like a dad correcting his daughter.

We stare at each other for a few moments, blinking.

"Are you mad?" I finally eke out. "Because it didn't mean any-thing. It's been really stressful here. I just found out Dad has—"

"I think you should go for it," Hayden says like it's the most practical idea he's had in his life.

"Excuse me?"

"If you like him, you should go for it."

I drop my hand and clutch the comforter. "I'm not like that," I say, shaking my head. "I don't do open relationships. It's just you and me. Just two people."

Hayden puffs his chest full of air and looks up at the ceiling while pushing it out. "I can't keep doing this."

"Honey," I hear. It's a whisper, barely legible. A female voice.

Hayden angles the phone to the other half of the bed, and I hear the literal shattering of my life as it falls around me.

"Oh my God, Eadie. Are you mad?" Whitney says. The covers are pulled up to her naked shoulders. Her hair looks like she styled it with a balloon.

I can't catch my breath.

"Eadie, honey," Whitney continues. "We were in the hot tub, and we were both drunk, and one thing led to another. But you found someone new. That's awesome!"

"No." I hear my voice, but I don't feel it. I've left my body. This isn't happening.

Hayden trains the camera back on himself. "This was all your idea, remember. You practically threw us together."

"I trusted you," I say breathlessly. "I thought you were my…" My voice falters.

"The waiting thing was kind of cute at first," Hayden continues. "The pure little Christian girl. It was exciting. The thrill of the chase. I couldn't wait to get you in bed, but I'm not gonna lie, the spark wore off."

My jaw drops. The words are like nails into my body. My arms, my chest, my head. The pain is everywhere. "Shut up."

"When you get back to the city, we'll talk, okay Eadie? With you and Reid, and me and Hayden, I think it was meant to be. It's like—"

"Shut up!" I scream into the phone. "Just shut up!"

I end the call and throw my phone across the room. The phone that will cost me hundreds of dollars to replace. I leap from the bed, my hand pressed to my forehead, but I don't make it far. I collapse onto my hands and knees, gasping for breath.

My stomach—not the contents of it—but my actual stomach and the surrounding organs feel like they're pushing past my lungs, lurching up my throat with a finality akin to death. I fall to my side and curl into the fetal position. No tears have emerged yet. Those come half an hour later as I'm naked in the shower, the water temperature set to high, my arms folded around my shins while I rock back and forth under the steady onslaught.

Whitney's voice threads through my head on repeat. *Oh my God, Eadie. Are you mad?*

Chapter 25

I force myself to lie in bed even though sleep eludes me for hours. When I finally fall asleep, I don't dream, like a freight door has shuttered my subconscious—a safety mechanism to keep my mind from destroying itself while it claws for small truths that might fit together to form answers.

In the morning, I push myself out of bed, numb, my emotions still mercifully blocked. I throw my hair into a ponytail, skip the makeup, escape inside an oversized sweater in a feeble attempt to hide from the world.

The motions of my workday are grueling. Each movement, each word spoken is a thousand-pound weight. Annette notices something is wrong. I can tell by the grim line of her lips when she looks at me and the concern etched between her eyebrows. She doesn't ask. I only offer the occasional faint smile to let her know I'm still in the game, barely.

At two o'clock, Reid emerges from the office. He's avoided me most of the day, my expression and demeanor none too welcoming. He approaches tentatively with a stack of Post-it notes in his hand, taps them on the countertop, and leans in with all his weight on one foot.

"I have a little good news," he says.

I redirect my gaze, which was fixed on a pair of crows in the distant maple tree.

"Oh yeah?" I say. I try to lighten my voice but a dullness pervades.

"Our egg supplier came back online. I'm going to switch back to them for our next shipment." He divides his weight and bobs on the balls of his feet.

"That's great." I offer him a glance and then I resume my fixed position at the pass-through, elbows pointed against the counter, chin on my hand, back hunched.

"Are you okay, Eadie?"

"Is anyone?" I murmur.

"What's that?"

"Is anyone in this world really okay?" I say a little louder. "Or are they all just big fat jerks inside?"

"Um." He taps the edge of the Post-its against the counter again. "I'm going to go with big fat jerks, but to varying degrees."

"Hmm."

My phone vibrates in my back pocket. I pull it out and check the notification.

Eadie, will you talk to me? Please? Whitney says. **I want to work this out.**

She's been texting me off and on all day. I have zero intentions of ever talking to her again. How I'll manage to avoid her when I return to my job in NYC, I'm not sure, but I'll figure it out when the time comes.

I stuff my phone back in my pocket, smothering her digital presence with my rear end. It's petty but it gives me some small satisfaction.

Hayden hasn't been in touch with me at all. He's smarter than that.

"Look," Reid persists, "if this is about the café's finances, we'll figure something out, okay?"

"If what's about hmm?"

Reid tilts his head for a better look at my face. "You seem a little off today."

Let's see. What are the odds of me confiding in Reid that my gorgeous model boyfriend from the big city cheated on me with my best friend? A big fat zero. "There's just a lot going on. I'm fine. Really." I give him a weak smile.

He dips his chin and peers at me beneath his brow. "Yeah." Clearly, he's unconvinced.

My phone buzzes again. I rip it out of my pocket, intent on blocking Whitney's number, except it's not her. It's a Gmail notification. Gigi Smalls, my contact at *The Indy Insider* finally responded to my email.

I tap open the reply.

I'd love to come to Home for the Hollandaise to see if your café is a good fit for our Hidden Gems column. I'm available to drive up on Wednesday, December 20th. Will that work?

My chin drops.

"What is it?" Reid asks.

"Did I ever tell you about Gigi Smalls?"

"No, you never told me about Gigi Smalls."

"Well, Gigi Smalls just emailed me."

"What did Gigi Smalls say?"

A small laugh erupts from my throat, a dot of joy in an ocean of gloom.

"She wants to send her editor up here to see if we're a good fit for the Hidden Gems column in *The Indy Insider*. The column appears in their print version, and it goes out to their massive newsletter list."

Reid raises an eyebrow. "Really?"

"Yeah. It would be free advertisement to the Indianapolis crowd. We might coax in a few more Saturday customers. Or even some Harrison County residents on the weekdays."

"Eadie..." His tone could burst a few dozen bubbles.

"I know. I know. I looked at the numbers. This wouldn't solve all our problems, but would it hurt?"

He leans back on his heels, folds one arm across his stomach so he can use the opposite hand to help him think. I watch his finger tap, tap, tap his chin. His expression shifts from wary to adventurous.

"It can't hurt anything," he says, rubbing his palms together. "When does Gigi Smalls want to visit?"

I glance back at the email. "Gigi Smalls wants to come on December 20th."

Reid grins. "We're being annoying."

"Kinda." I grin back.

"It's good to see you smile."

We hold each other's gaze for a moment, and then Reid switches gears. "That gives us…" He looks up as he calculates. "Roughly two weeks to turn this place around."

"Everything has to go."

"Huh?"

"All the decorations. They're old, faded, and depressing. They have to go."

I have some money saved, my nest egg for my future with Hayden. Screw him. It's time to crack that egg and invest in my parents' future. They've given me so much. Some new Christmas decorations for their café are hardly a fair trade.

"All right," Reid says. He thumps the counter. "Let's do it."

Chapter 26

I meet Reid at the café on Sunday afternoon with rubber gloves, mops, wood polishing cloths, trash bags, and every other cleaning apparatus I could find at the Winford Walmart. Reid is waiting for me in the dining room, looking relaxed in a gray fleece hoodie, frayed jeans, and a pair of checkered Vans. Seeing my heavy bags, he jumps up and grabs them from me.

"There are more bags in my car," I say.

"Geez. You didn't have to buy all this. We already have stuff in the utility closet."

"Not enough. I plan on cleaning this place into the fifth dimension."

"You're scaring me."

I force a smile and gently shove him toward the kitchen. I've resolved to be "happy" today, at least externally. Internally, I feel like I've been hacked to pieces by a meat cleaver.

Reid can't know I'm gutted and bleeding. If I tell him, he'll ask questions. Questions will lead to more questions, which may lead to tears. I've already cried so much that I need a Gatorade to replace my electrolytes.

The more I clean, the less I'll think, the less I'll cry. This plan is foolproof. Except for the "happy" part. I'm already worn out by that fake smile. I sigh and start digging through my bags.

When Reid returns, I'm wearing rubber gloves and holding a bottle of degreaser and a cleaning brush.

"Is there a plan here, or..." Reid says.

"I'm scrubbing the chairs and the table bases. You could Pine-Sol the floor and then apply the polish."

Reid surveys the wood floors, which are dark brown in the low traffic areas and tan where Annette and Lexis tread back and forth every day. "They need refinished."

"We can fake it for now. Just polish them up and make them shine."

He nods and then heads into the kitchen, returning with a bucket of water and a Bluetooth speaker.

"Want to listen to some tunes while we work?" he asks.

I offer another fake smile, this one less pronounced so it takes less energy. "Sure."

"Are you in the mood for Christmas?"

I'm in the mood for a bed, a blanket, and dreams that take me far away from here, but I say, with fake holiday cheer, "Absolutely," which takes the effort of two fake smiles combined.

After tapping on his phone, "Jolly Ol' Saint Nicholas" pipes through his speaker. He sets it on one of the built-in tables, and then grabs the mop handle like a microphone and starts singing into it.

I don't have it in me to laugh. Poor guy. I leave him hanging. He switches to humming and gets to work on the entryway floors. When he's done there, we scoot the tables and chairs to one side of the dining room, no communication needed, just the intuition of two dedicated employees working toward the same goal.

I'm thankful for the music. The songs flip through, no advertisements between, no space for random chatting or bonding. Bonding is for animals. I'm human. We can be social or solitary. Our adaptability as creatures is well-documented. I don't need anyone. Never did.

"Jingle Bells" comes on, an instrumental with a jazz treatment. I scrub away years of dirt from the table pedestals, astounded by how grimy they are. Some places can get away with more neglect. Left in shadows, they appear fine until you get a closer look, and then you realize how much they've been keeping you from your potential.

"How's it going?" Reid asks.

"Slower than I thought." I swipe a lock of hair off my forehead with the back of my latex glove. The sheen of sweat on my face feels cool as the ceiling fans turn lazily above.

"I think I'm ready to move everything to the other side."

"Already?"

"Yeah, this stuff dries fast," he says referring to the half-empty bottle of wood finish in his hand.

"Okay." I straighten, feeling a slight pinch in my back.

Reid focuses on the chair next to me, scrutinizing it with a look of disapproval. "That cushion is literally coming apart at the seams."

My shoulders droop. "I know. We need to recover it."

"If we do, it will stick out from the rest."

"True, but at least it won't look like someone ripped into it with an explosive case of indigestion."

He wrinkles his nose as he considers my origin story. "From the One Chip Challenge?"

"Could very well be what happened." I feel a smile tickling my cheeks. A real one.

"How about we check upstairs?" Reid says. "There's extra furniture up there, but I haven't poked around much."

I like his idea better than the prospect of wrangling pleather over two-inch foam with a heavy-duty stapler.

We head up the stairs, my first time climbing them in years.

The room is open, the stairwell surrounded by railings rather than walls. Behind the railing, built-in couches hug the front windows, upholstered in garish 1960s print that's covered with plastic drop cloths. They form U-shapes at even intervals, perfect for Odd Fellows members to sit and chat about...odd things...

The stairway itself pours into the ballroom, which occupies the entire width of the building and most of its length, cut short by a small kitchen in the back. Decorative plasterwork adorns the ceiling, painted shades of greens, yellows, and reds to highlight the tradi-tional details.

Large windows run along North Street on the west side of the room. The east side abuts the neighboring building, thus offering no quaint views. Wooden steps similar to bleachers flank the walls, providing alternative seating.

"This is amazing," Reid says.

"I thought you said you've been up here."

"Several times. And every time I say to myself, 'This is amazing.' My brain goes wild with images of old guys with gray wigs doing secret stuff. What do you think those fellows did up here?"

"Ritual sacrifice. The ceremonial drinking of blood."

"That's dark."

I feel dark. But not *that* dark. "I'm kidding. They did community service and charity work. And then they had meetings and initiation stuff up here."

Reid nods. "I've always wanted to be part of a secret society of manly men. Modernity is boring."

I smile. My second real smile of the day. "I think those are called college fraternities."

"I was in a fraternity and there were no secret rituals, just a lot of beer and smelly guys."

"I'm sorry I missed out."

"Don't be."

We head over to the pile of furniture, which on closer inspection contains a couple of stacks of chairs, two tables, an extra booth seat, and a podium that must have once been in the lobby.

While we're unstacking the chairs, I sneak a peek at Reid. He doesn't seem the frat boy type. Then again, he never seemed the football type either.

Today he looks like he spent two seconds on his hair, ruffling it with his fingers after throwing on his sweatshirt. In New York City, a guy could pay two hundred dollars for the same style and still walk away looking like he was trying too hard. On Reid, it looks organic and natural, like he's impervious to bad hair days.

"Why did you join a frat?" I ask.

"Why did I do a lot of things?" He sets a chair on its base and dusts off the seat, sits and throws his weight around to test the joinery. "This one might work."

"Problem solved," I say, ignoring his loaded question that didn't answer my question at all.

Instead of standing, he stretches his arms overhead, folds his hands behind his head, and crosses his feet at the ankles. Sunlight pools through the windows behind him, illuminating the ballroom's charm as well as its dust motes.

"It's nice up here," Reid says. "A little dusty, but nice. The southern exposure is great."

"I used to roller skate up here."

"Really? How come you never invited me?"

"I grew out of my skates before you moved to town."

"Ah. Why didn't your parents buy you a new pair?"

"I never asked. I guess I grew out of it too."

"That's a shame. This place would make a nice roller skating rink. Or a reception hall. Why aren't your parents renting it out?"

I lean against a table and distribute some of my weight into my hands. "Lead paint. Out-of-date furnishings. Ancient appliances in the kitchen."

None of my reasons lessen the determined look on Reid's face. "They need to start renting this space out for reunions, open houses, meetings, wedding receptions." He throws out a hand. "Heck, you and Hayden could get married up here."

I was thawing, but Reid's comment turns the freezer back on blast. My muscles go stiff and ice lodges in my throat. A second later, the temperature reverses course and my arms, neck, and face become blazing hot. As the ice melts, the floodwaters threaten to return.

I push myself to my feet and dash over to the windows along North Street. Cars take turns at the stoplight, the green light never long enough, creating a perpetual backup. I suck in deep breath after deep breath as car after car passes through the intersection, but the heat and sense of helplessness are unrelenting.

No. No. Not more tears. Not now.

They start as a drip, and then the faucet opens. I cover my face.

"Eadie," Reid says. He touches my elbow. "What's wrong?"

"Nothing," I say between sniffs. I lower my hands enough to find my way up the steps. At the top, I collapse and twist around until my knees touch the windowsill. When Reid enters my peripheral vision, I hide behind my hands again.

"This doesn't look like nothing," Reid says. The step gives slightly as Reid lowers his weight onto it. His hand moves to my knee, and we sit quietly until I regain control of my voice.

"We need to get back to work," I mumble as I wipe my tears.

"Work can wait," Reid says gently.

"No, it can't. We have to impress Gigi Smalls."

"Eadie, what did I say that upset you?"

I scratch my head as I consider ways to deflect.

"Is this about your parents' finances?" he tries.

And there it is. He laid it in my lap. I nod. "Yes."

Reid dips his head to probe my eyes. He looks from one to the other searching for truth. "Turning the ballroom into a rental space could help. I'd have to run numbers, but if they really wanted to make it work, this could become a premiere wedding venue. Just look at that view of the canal. The romance is baked in."

My chin trembles and my eyes start leaking again. I should have brought some Gatorade.

Reid looks stricken by the resurgence of my tears. He leans across the space between us and wraps his arms around me. I find his shoulder and cry into the fleece, pulling in the scent of his cologne with every ragged breath.

Being wrapped in Reid's shirts was intoxicating, but being wrapped in his arms is so much more. My breathing calms. The temperature of my body levels to a comfortable warmth.

"Reid," I say.

He lets go and backs up. Guilt makes him hunch forward and turn away. "I'm sorry. I shouldn't have done that."

I grab his sleeve. "It's okay."

"You have a boyfriend. It's not my place."

"Reid."

He turns his head toward me and raises an eyebrow like a scolded Golden Retriever.

"Hayden and I broke up."

Chapter 27

"I'm sorry," Reid says, looking genuinely upset by my revelation. "If I'd known, I wouldn't have said the thing about you two getting married."

I laugh but it's not joyful. It's raw and biting and bitter. "I can't believe I thought I was going to marry him."

Reid looks at me carefully. "Did you guys talk about getting engaged?"

I laugh again, this time loud enough to fill the room. Reid retreats. I sound like the Wicked Witch of the West and probably look as inviting. "No," I say sharply. "We never talked about marriage. I just had it in my head that he was the one. He ticked all the boxes. Not from Cold Spring. Worldly. Gorgeous." I wipe a rogue tear from my cheek and slide around so my knees are pointing toward the center of the room.

"But did you get along? Did you enjoy each other's company?"

"Sure." I throw out the word like it belongs in the trash along with my pathetic excuse for a relationship.

Reid turns his body parallel to mine and leans his head against the strip of plaster between the windows.

"What?" I say.

His expression was questioning until I called him out, then he flipped into easy-going mode. "Nothing," he says noncommittally.

"You were thinking something."

"I'm always thinking something."

"You were thinking something about me and Hayden."

He leans forward and rubs his palms together. "You don't seem like the shallow type."

I've never been a great swimmer. Maybe I prefer shallow water and a life jacket. Is that so wrong? "You've seen me swim. I'm like a pug with a beer gut struggling to float."

"You know what I mean."

I angle toward him and rest my hands on my thighs in anticipation of a good show. "Actually, I don't. Why don't you explain?"

A nervous laugh escapes Reid's lips. He rubs the back of his neck. "We don't have to talk about this. It's your business, not mine."

"You were going to say my standards for choosing a mate are superficial. I only care about how he'll look on my arm while I'm busy proving to this backward town and to you, and Jaden, and Kara, and everyone else that I can do better than all of you. Believe me, I've had time to glean all sorts of insights into my choices since my boyfriend cheated on me with my best friend."

Reid cringes.

A fresh batch of tears bites the back of my eyes. I collapse into a heap and let them fall. Reid quietly scoots next to me and rests his hand on my back.

"I'm sorry," I say when I've calmed down a bit.

"Sorry for what?"

"I'm sorry for being me."

I hear Reid's breath catch. He lowers himself to my level. "I'm the one who should be sorry." His breath tickles my ear. "I *am* sorry."

Curiosity straightens my spine. Reid joins me. We're side by side, our legs touching. Like it's perfectly normal.

"Why are you sorry?" I whisper.

He turns slightly and grabs my hand. My fingers search his palm, feeling for both familiarity and newness.

"I'm sorry I stood by while Jaden bullied you. I'm sorry I didn't beat him up that night at the park. I'm sorry I made you feel like you had to go out and prove your worth."

Reid let's go of my hand and places his on both sides of my neck, gently bracing me for the intense look in his eyes. "We had a thing going the summer before high school, and I just dropped off the map. I'm sorry."

I break eye contact and let my gaze rest on his lips. They look soft and inviting, no longer off-limits.

He leans in and whispers, "Can you forgive me?"

"I don't blame my stupidity on anyone but myself."

Reid shakes his head and brushes away a tear with his thumb. "You're not stupid. You're a geek." He says it with a smile.

I laugh softly.

His face is inches from mine as we breathe into the silence. I watch his eyelashes bob as he studies my eyes and then my lips. "Reid?"

"Hmm?"

"Are you going to kiss m—?"

Before I can finish, he presses his lips to mine. Confidence spreads through my limbs. I comb my fingers through his hair as he deepens the kiss.

I remember this feeling. On the porch in the rain all those years ago. An inexplicable sense of rightness. Something I never felt with Hayden.

When we part, he answers "Yes" to my unfinished question. We anchor our foreheads together, smiling.

"This is not how I saw today going," I say.

He bites his bottom lip. "Me neither. I hope it's okay."

His comment knocks me back into reality. I just got dumped by my boyfriend and lost my best friend—all in one night. I'm vulnerable. Weak. Not in a position to start anything new.

I pull away from Reid. I can't kiss him again. Because regardless of how many bad decisions led me there, New York City is my home. My apartment and my job are waiting for me. "I'm heading back to New York in a few weeks."

Reid cups my cheek with his hand. "I know, but I've been waiting to do that for years."

"You have?"

"Mmm hmm," he says, unable to utter words because his lips are already back on mine, searching for deeper connection.

So much for not letting it happen again.

Cold Spring may not be my permanent residence, but this moment feels like home, and I pretend I'm here to stay until his warmth retreats and I'm back to being Eadie, the girl who was just dumped by her boyfriend in a way that almost trumps the egg incident. Almost.

"Should we get back to work?" he asks when we part.

I nod and then follow him to the stairs, leaving his kisses in the past where they belong.

Chapter 28

Last year for Christmas, Hayden and I stayed in New York instead of traveling to visit family. A heavy blanket of snow fell on Christmas Eve, quieting the city and giving the streets and sidewalks a needed rest from the rumble of tires and the pounding of feet. We dusted off the chaise longue on his balcony, wrapped ourselves in layers of blankets, and snuggled in a tangle of arms and legs while we watched the snow fall.

"Order up," Marlon says.

His voice snaps me back to the present.

It's been a slow day. Wind chills are in the single digits, fat snowflakes are collecting in layers, and no one wants to experience either firsthand.

Except for the Silver Sweethearts. They arrived at eleven o'clock sharp, shook the snow off their coats, and settled in for the usual.

Since I sent Lexis home early, it's up to me to deliver three plates of eggs Benedict to their table.

I balance two plates on my arm and grab the third, pushing through the door with my back.

"The eggs froze so Marlon had to use vegan egg replacer," I say as I set their plates in front of them.

Mabel makes a face. "I'd never return if you served me something that ungodly."

I chuckle. "You know I'm teasing. These eggs are sturdy. I watched them do pushups this morning."

"Have you been brushing up on your dad jokes, Eadie?" Dottie looks up at me innocently, fluttering her eyelashes. She's still wearing her hat and scarf. Her ruddy cheeks tell me she's a couple of degrees away from overheating.

"It's quiet today," I answer. "I have to entertain myself somehow."

"I don't know why it's so empty," Mabel says sardonically. "The weather is just wonderful."

Jean digs into her eggs. In place of her normal chiffon or silk scarf, she's wearing a heavy knit scarf as well as fingerless gloves.

Dottie lifts a finger. "Um. Eadie, dear. It's looking a little bare in here."

Reid and I have been staying late in the evenings to clean the café. On Monday night, he repaired a couple of booth seats while I polished knobs and light fixtures. From there, we moved into the kitchen and organized the shelves that are visible through the pass-through.

Last night we took down the Christmas decorations except for the 1950s retro tree, including the Santa Claus tapestry with the aid of an extension ladder that Reid brought from his dad's. I held the ladder while it wobbled, visions of him falling to his death making every muscle in my body seize. He survived, and we called it a night.

It hasn't been weird between me and Reid. Which is...weird. After the kisses upstairs, he hasn't made any moves, hasn't even hinted. We haven't discussed our kisses either, which is fine with me. They happened. They were nice. And that's that.

"Reid and I threw the decorations into the dumpster last night," I explain.

Dottie gasps. Mabel pauses chewing and eyes me cautiously. Jean continues eating.

"Why did you do that?" Dottie says, her tone almost accusatory.

"The café was looking a bit shabby don't you think?"

"I think it had a whimsical feel."

I tuck my chin and give Dottie a stern look. "It looked like Santa Claus threw up in here in 1980 and never came back to clean it up."

Dottie rocks her head from side to side, visibly hemming and hawing.

"I was wondering when your mom and dad might upgrade," Jean says in a soft-spoken but direct manner. I appreciate her honesty.

"Now it looks like you're preparing to auction the place off," Mabel quips in a gravelly alto. She's enjoying bite after bite of her eggs and doesn't stop to look at me.

Dottie gasps. She hasn't taken a single bite yet. "You're not selling, are you?"

I've been thinking about Dad, about me, how selling this place would affect my immediate family. I haven't stopped to think about our most valued customers. What would come of the Silver Sweethearts if Home for the Hollandaise closed? Where would they go when their table and their eggs Benedict were no longer waiting for them?

There are other restaurants in town, of course. A handful of fast-food restaurants by the interstate. Mama's Italian Kitchen just out of town to the east. Lester's Steakhouse on the corner. The Golden Wok and The Salty Chick across the street. But I can't imagine the Silver Sweethearts going for Szechuan beef or broasted chicken for lunch.

"Of course not," I say. "We'd never sell this place." I'm overselling it, but it seems best. No need to upset them or start any rumors. Lord knows they fly fast around Cold Spring.

"I have some cash saved up from my modeling days and I decided to use it to buy new Christmas decorations for the dining room. An editor from *The Indy Insider* is coming on the 20th to see if they want to feature us, and I want to put our best face forward."

"Pshaw!" Mabel says. She stops eating long enough to wave a hand at me. "You don't need to spend money on decorations. I have an attic full of brand-new ornaments and decorations that I intended to use around the house, but who has time for that? Especially with no little ones around. It's just me. All I need is a tabletop tree and I'm fine."

"Me too," Dottie says. "I have a garage full of Christmas stuff. I probably bought it while outlet shopping with these two trouble-makers."

Jean raises her hand. "Guilty. I can donate also."

"Reid and I were going to go shopping tonight," I try. Mabel's hardened glare reduces me to muttering. "Or, if you want to donate, um, sure."

"If you don't like what we bring, you can toss it. How about that?" Dottie says. "Just throw it in the dumpster and don't tell me about it so I don't have to feel guilty about wasting all that money."

"Sure," I say.

"When do you need them by?" Mabel asks, her gaze still sharp.

"Reid and I plan to clean the rest of the week and then decorate on Saturday. Would that work?"

"I'll have to ask Stu to climb up into my attic." Mabel pushes up her sleeves like it might take some strongarming to convince her eldest son to help.

"You ladies are amazing. Thank you. It will mean so much to my parents, especially if *The Indy Insider* decides to feature us."

I give them the lowdown on the magazine's Hidden Gems column and newsletter reach. Dottie asks if she can be included in the feature. I tell her not to get ahead of herself. With that, I leave them to finish their lunches, returning only to refill their waters.

When they're gone, I gently tap the office door.

"Yep," Reid says.

He's banging away at his computer when I enter.

"Good news," I say.

"Oh. Sorry. I thought you were Marlon."

"I can see how you might get us confused."

"I heard that," Marlon calls from the kitchen. "You wish," he adds with a hearty laugh.

I plop into my chair, allowing my feet to rest. "We don't need to go shopping tonight. The Silver Sweethearts are going to give us their extra Christmas decorations."

Reid dips his chin, betraying his skepticism. "Do they have enough?"

"Sounds like it."

As he mulls over this new development, he picks up a pen and starts clicking the end in fast succession.

"Is that okay?" I ask.

"Um. Sure." Click, click, click, click. "What about tonight, then?"

I reach over and gently pull the pen from Reid's hand.

He watches me and then laughs. "That was my thinking pen."

"It identifies as a writing pen. Anyway. We could take a break tonight, I guess. Or we could clean."

"Or..."

I lean forward as he draws out the word. "Or...we could dig for buried treasure?"

"Or something less messy. I have something I want to show you."

"I am not playing doctor. No way, no how." I slice my hands through the air.

"Ha ha. No, it's something I've been working on in my dad's shop. You could come over. I could fix you dinner—"

"You can't cook."

"We could order dinner, and then I could show you my project. It's for the café. You're going to be mind blown." He adds the exploding gesture to drive it home.

"I reserve the right to pay for my own meal."

"Sure, if that's what you want."

"This better be good because I really like cleaning."

He crosses his arms and leans back. "Oh, it's good. Trust me."

Reid's porchlight is on and the front door is open, allowing passersby an unencumbered view of his entryway through the storm door. The golden glow of the interior lights promises reprieve from the plummeting temperatures and crunchy snow underfoot. I carefully pick my way up the icy steps, clutching the masonry railing with one hand and my take-out bag from The Salty Chick in the other. Inside my bag is one-quarter white broasted chicken and mashed potatoes made with fresh spuds, not the rehydrated kind.

I let myself in and announce my presence. Reid appears from the kitchen holding a take-out bag and two old-fashioned soda bottles.

He sets everything on the dining room table and grabs my food so I can take off my coat.

"You can toss it on the couch," he says. "I don't have pets. Or bedbugs."

I deposit my coat in the living room, admiring the Christmas tree along the way. Its boughs are artfully draped with silver ribbon, which breaks up the red, silver, and gold glass ornaments. Interspersed among the shiny globes are handmade, tin holiday figurines.

"I'm impressed," I say when I meet Reid in the dining room.

"With?"

"Your tree. Just today Mabel said she doesn't bother with a tree because she lives alone, but you've demonstrated an impressive level of self-care by indulging your festive side."

"You should write self-help books."

"I'd lead millions astray. Is this one mine?" I point to the smaller bag that's more rumpled.

"I believe so. I ordered one-half white with two sides. I assume you ordered less."

"Correct. I can't stomach half a chicken." I round the table and sit with my back facing the darkened windows. Reid comes up behind me and closes the curtains so the whole neighborhood can't watch us eat.

"I don't know how you eat chicken at all since you used to keep them as pets." He sits at the head of the table and digs into his bag.

"After losing a couple dozen chickens to foxes, you become numb to the circle of life. Mostly. PETA probably calls it psychopathy, but chickens eat bugs, and they don't feel guilty about it." I open my Styrofoam container and dig into my chicken breast with a plastic spork.

"Chickens are psychopaths," Reid concludes.

The chicken is still hot, its skin buttery and crunchy. My teeth cut easily through the tender meat as my taste buds drown in savory juices. "Oh my gosh, this is so good. I bet this chicken was on death row for some horrific, remorseless crime."

"Is that how you sleep at night?"

"Yes." I chuckle while spearing another bite.

Reid opens his coleslaw and angles it my way. "Want some?"

"Only if it's the zombie apocalypse after I've exhausted all other food options."

"Well, then." He plops the container back onto the table.

My eyes linger on his hands. They read skilled laborer, not bean counter. The pads of his fingers are thickened by the handling of raw materials and tools.

"Are you moonlighting as a pipefitter?" I ask.

He stops chewing and frowns.

"Never mind."

His confused expression resolves into normal Reid-face.

"I just—you have calluses. Accountants don't have calluses."

"This accountant does." He flashes a palm at me. "These hands do a lot more than push numbers."

We eat in familiar silence, washing our chicken down with soda, and then diving in for repeat bites. I can't stop glancing at Reid's hands, especially the empty ring finger on his left one. Does he still have his wedding ring? Did he sell it, melt it down, throw it into Lake Turtle? I want to ask, but I dig into my mashed potatoes instead.

"How are you feeling?" Reid says, oblivious to my hand-gazing. Hopefully.

"Satiated. But I'm still going to eat the rest of this chicken."

"I meant about..."

"Cheaty McCheater?"

"Yeah."

"It still stings. A lot."

"Of course."

"Staying focused on the café is helping. But..." So many buts. Not the double-cheeked kind. The "but what if I had done this or that differently" kind.

"But you can't bury it because it will come back up. It always comes back up," Reid says.

"Like vomit."

"We speak the same language."

I peek at Reid while he goes ham on his onion rings. There's more to his story. A black box of ten years that I can't see into. We used to talk about everything, no subject off limits. A decade and some change later, I'm starting to think maybe the rules haven't changed.

I focus on my food. A glance might spook him. "Did Kara cheat on you?"

Something between a laugh and a groan erupts from Reid's throat. "No. She didn't cheat."

"Something else, then?"

"Everything else. Everything was about Kara. What Kara wanted, when she wanted it, how she wanted it. There was no room for me. Our dog got more love from Kara than I did."

I take a drink of soda and let my hand slide down the bottle's slender neck. My curiosity isn't satisfied. Also, I could have told him Kara was selfish, self-centered, rude, mean, horrible. But Reid never asked. "I told you so" probably isn't the best look right now, though. Or ever.

"So you decided to end it?" I ask.

Reid wipes his hand with a napkin and then drags it across his lips. After tossing it into his to-go container, he rests his elbows on the table and settles in for his answer. Except it's a question. "I got back with Kara a week after she pulled the egg stunt on you. Do you think I'm the one who filed the divorce papers?"

I pop the lid back onto my box and chance a look at him. His hands are clasped in front of his chest, his head hanging low.

"Why?" I ask.

He looks up and finds my eyes. His eyes aren't sad. They reflect a weary acceptance that comes from countless late nights of soul-searching. The kind of nights I have to look forward to as I process my recent losses.

Reid asks for clarification. "Why did I get back with Kara after the incident in the park? Or why did I marry her? Or why did she divorce me?"

"All of it."

"Okay." He sighs heavily and leans back, rubbing his hands together before folding his arms. The chair creaks under the pressure of his resolve to connect the dots for me. "Where should I start?"

"You could go backwards," I suggest.

"On the surface, she divorced me because she decided to move to New York City to study acting."

An involuntary laugh escapes my throat. "How's that going for her?"

"Let's just say, you're built like a model. You look like a model. You have the goods. She doesn't. But she has a dream, and for her, the dream is enough. She's convinced she can manifest a new reality where she stars in Hollywood movies."

I look at him askance and scratch beneath my ear. "We're almost thirty years old. Hollywood likes them young."

He flips his hands to the ceiling. "It's not my problem anymore."

"You don't pay her alimony?"

"Nope. She said she wanted a clean break. She didn't ask for anything. She just surprised me one night with her lamebrained idea and left the next morning."

It must have been like déjà vu. First his mom, and then his wife. How does a guy deal with profound abandonment, not once but twice?

When I ate dinner here as a kid, his dad sat at the head of the table and his mom on the opposite end. They laughed together, traded stories, made me feel welcome. But there was an unseen rift, lies or omissions hidden under the surface. Did Reid know they were there, or was his mom's exit a complete shock?

"Now, why did I marry her?" Reid continues. "Let's tackle that one." He splays his right hand and studies the back of it, scratches the skin while he prepares for what must be a doozy of an answer. "People connect for different reasons, but all the reasons fall into two categories, positive and negative. People make positive connections, and people make negative connections. I'd argue that sometimes, the negative connections are stronger. They're rooted in complex patterns that crisscross like layers of spiderwebs that are twined together. Try removing one of those webs. It's hard. Really hard. Now imagine having to separate them all. It takes a lot of energy, and sometimes the path of least resistance wins."

"Wow," I say, genuinely impressed by the depth of his insight. Such well-crafted sentences would never form in Hayden's head, let alone come out of his mouth. "Those are astute observations."

Reid curls his finger around and points back at himself. "Counseling. Two years."

"Really?"

"Yeah. I learned a lot about myself."

"Huh."

Color me impressed again. A guy with the self-awareness to realize he needs help and then ask for it. Reid's rough, lumberjack edges are a ruse. Underneath, he's been honed like a gem. How sneaky.

"You moved back here right after Kara left?" I ask.

"Pretty much. My dad had been going downhill for a while. He needed me. And I needed to get out of that apartment."

Reid and Kara had a negative attraction. Makes sense. I chose Hayden for superficial reasons, stayed with him for far too long. Convinced myself I was going to marry him. Acted an idiot and pushed him into the arms of my best friend. Not that his cheating was *my* fault, but I sure helped speed it along.

"You guys broke up. You asked me to the dance. She dumped eggs on me. You two got back together. Why?" This is the question I really want to be answered, but am I being too nosy? "I'm sorry. I'm prying. You don't have to answer that."

"Would answering it help you make sense of that night?"

"And of the decade I spent thinking you planned my utter and total humiliation? Yeah. But..."

Reid reaches over and grabs my hand. My muscles seize upon contact, my rational mind still in charge. I'm leaving in a few weeks. Touching will only lead to eventual heartache. But the firmness of his grasp banishes the future and the past, unwinding my muscles and anchoring me in the now.

"We're friends, right?" Reid says.

I nod, unable to muster a sentence.

"After Kara jumped on me at the park and you walked away, I laid into her. I told her it was over for good. Forever. We didn't talk until the next weekend." Reid pauses to draw in a deep breath. "My room used to be down here, remember? Mom and Dad slept in the suite upstairs. Why is that important, you ask?" Reid smiles. "I see the question on your face."

His thumb brushes back and forth over my hand, each pass sending tingles up my arm.

"It was late, sometime after midnight. She tapped on my window. I let her in and…" A blush rises to his cheeks. He shrugs. "How do I say it…?"

"I think I know."

"Okay." He laughs nervously. "Anyway, four years later, we were married. Note to my teenage self: do *not* let her climb through that window."

I savor a pang of nostalgia as I think of our teenage selves, so flawed, vulnerable yet brimming with a strength afforded only to the naïve. Experience teaches us what we have to fear.

"Anyway…" Reid ducks his chin and rubs his forehead. "Even though we were wrong for each other, we bonded physically, and that intimacy, as immature as it was, filled holes in my heart that I hadn't been able to plug on my own."

Over on the credenza are pictures of Reid and his dad standing tall, some in smaller frames, the pictures blurry and older. Others larger with detailed carving and gilding. Young Reid holding a fishing pole while his dad leans in for the camera. Teenage Reid with a graduation cap and gown, proudly holding his diploma while his dad smiles broadly at his side. Current Reid with his arm around his father as they enjoy the porch swing.

"Did your mom open up the holes?" I ask, feeling emboldened by Reid's openness.

He follows my gaze and scans the old photos, his mom absent from every memory.

"Yeah. She bored into my heart and soul. Violently."

I squeeze his hand and try to gauge his mood. His emotions seem steady. Indicative of acceptance? Although even at his age, the abandonment must still hurt.

His eyes take on a wistfulness. "Your Mom is amazing."

"She really is."

"You're lucky."

"I'm lucky you've been looking after her."

The wistfulness disappears from Reid's face, replaced by a hardening. "My Mom left in the summer. Just before high school."

I suck in a breath. He notices my shock as so many dots connect. "Football," I whisper.

"Right. What better way to stuff your emotions than to pretend to be the tough guy?"

The pain of being abandoned by Reid all those years ago weighs on my chest. I draw my hand away from his. "Why didn't you tell me about your mom?"

"I'd just been burned by the most important female in my life. I didn't think I could handle being hurt by the second most important girl I knew."

My breath catches again.

"I dropped you before you could drop me," he finishes.

I feed my forearms between my legs and hunch over the table. The tangy, spicy smell of sour cream and chives floods my nose. So much to take in. So much to consider. Young Reid just trying to survive. As much as I wish I could have been there for him, it makes sense that he withdrew.

"So," Reid says in an artificially lighthearted tone. "Wanna go look at my project?"

"Why?" I peek at him. "Are you tired of my nosy questions?"

"I'm tired of my answers." He flashes me a broad smile. "I'm sorry I got so deep."

After straightening my back and smoothing my hair, I tease, "I can handle a little depth. I'm not always shallow."

"When did I say you were shallow?"

"The other day before you kissed me. You implied it." My cheeks flame when I realize I mentioned the thing I promised I wouldn't mention. The kisses.

Reid grins at me. There's no hiding this blush. I'm an awkward teenager all over again.

"Let's go to the garage, put on some Christmas music, and then, well... We'll see."

Chapter 29

The detached garage is set back from the house and oriented toward the alleyway, the small concrete driveway leading to it just wide enough for two parked cars. We follow the sidewalk to a door on the side of the stout brick structure.

Reid flips on the lights, illuminating an impressive collection of heavy machinery and hand tools. He lists off their names: chop saw, band saw, press brake, and the granddaddy of them all, the plasma cutting table. He tells me not to ask how much it cost his dad, so of course I ask, almost bumping my chin against the floor when he answers.

"My dad took his hobby very seriously," Reid says.

"Clearly."

Along with the larger tools, smaller hand tools hang on the wall, each moored to the metal pegboard with an appropriately sized hook. Work benches line the back wall, and two large worktables command the center of the room, one covered in a lumpy rectangle of canvas. I'm no Sherlock Holmes, but I'm guessing the secret project lies beneath.

When a living space has been left alone for a prolonged period, it bears the signs. Dust on horizontal surfaces. Spiderwebs in corners. Rusted metal and dingy windows. The workshop has none of that. Reid spends a lot of time out here honing his calluses.

"You've made your dad's workshop your own," I say.

He widens his stance and presses his palms together. Out here, he stands a little taller, his chest puffed a bit higher. "I have. It's why I can't seem to sell the house. I'm enjoying the power tools too much."

"Does your dad need to sell?"

Reid shakes his head. "Not really, no. I was going to sell and move back to Indy, but..." He shrugs. "Cold Spring isn't too bad."

"You were going to leave this place, go to Europe, learn four languages."

"And you were going to become an entomologist."

Reid and I share a look that says more than words can express. Best-laid plans. Immaturity got in the way for both of us. Typical for young adults trying to figure out how to grow up.

"I suppose it's not too bad here." I roll my eyes. "I guess."

"Your parents appreciate having you home."

"My mom is starting to mutter when we're both in the kitchen. I think I'm in her way."

Reid laughs. "She's as stubborn as your dad, just quieter about it." He walks to the worktable and grabs the corner of the canvas.

I join him at the table. "There better not be a body under here."

"I keep those in my basement."

"Good to know."

"Ready?"

"Sure."

He whips the canvas away like a magician revealing his grand finale, uncovering a large metal Christmas tree. A single sheet of metal comprises the back, while four-inch perpendicular strips curve artfully around the edge and throughout, delineating individual boughs. A lip along the back allows room for Christmas lights to thread behind it. Reid fed the bulbs through the holes he punched, and he attached small hooks beneath each bough in preparation for ornaments.

I gasp, overwhelmed by the craftsmanship and attention to detail. "This is gorgeous."

"I was thinking it could replace the Santa Claus tapestry."

"You want to hang it there?"

"When you say it like that, I'm not sure."

"I just—It looks heavy. And it takes electricity. But if you think it will work, I'm all for it. It looks amazing."

"I have a guy coming to add an outlet on Friday. On my dime, of course. And you've seen me work a ladder. I can hang this, no problem."

I flash him a skeptical look.

"Fine. I already have someone lined up to help me on Saturday."

"Good, 'cause I'm not sure Dad has liability insurance."

"He does now. You're welcome. But I won't die. I promise. Do you want to see it lit up?"

"Absolutely."

"If you could balance that side, we'll prop it against the garage door." He wiggles his fingers under one side of the tree. I do the same on the opposite side. It's not as heavy as it looks. We walk it over to the garage door and rest it carefully on its wide stump.

Reid digs through a drawer and pulls out an orange extension cord, attaches it to the string of Christmas lights, and plugs the other end into the wall. The glowing, colored lights give the tree added dimension, emphasizing the 3D effect of the boughs.

"Hold on a second." In a few long strides, Reid crosses the garage and flips off the overhead lights.

"Wow, Reid. It's magical."

He rejoins me and we admire his dazzling display of Christmas artistry.

"I decided to go for multicolored lights over white to warm up the metal," Reid says. "What do you think?"

"Good choice."

"Once it's on the wall I'll hang the glass bulbs. It's going to blow your mind."

"My mind is already blown."

"Told ya." He elbows me.

I elbow him back. "You're full of surprises."

He reaches for my hand and clasps it gently. I glance at him, trying not to notice how the lights warm his face and make his eyes glisten.

A relaxed heaviness drags on my limbs, makes me want to sink into something soft with my arms wrapped around Reid's neck.

My heart thumps against my ribs and my mouth goes dry as his lips close in on mine. I know what comes next. And I told myself it can't happen again.

I slip my hand from his and approach the tree, bending at the waist like I'm studying its minute details. When Reid approaches, I turn and walk over to the workbench.

"What's this?" I ask, referring to another lumpy swath of canvas.

"I'm still working on it."

"Can I see it?"

"Sure."

Reid slides off the canvas, this time with less aplomb. In the dim light, I can tell it's a Christmas village, also constructed from sheet metal, with flourishes that appear carved or cast. He reaches for the power cord and plugs it into the wall, which turns on the white Christmas lights that he's carefully placed inside the buildings to illuminate them from within.

"This is for your mantel," I say. Because he surely wouldn't bless the café with more free art.

"It's for the café."

"Reid!"

"What?"

"This is too much. It's too kind."

"Nah."

Santa's workshop is the largest building, taller than the rest with the most windows. I bend to admire the details and to peer inside. A shadow crosses my vision, and I jump back. "Something's moving in there!"

"No," he says, his tone frustrated rather than surprised.

He moves in and jostles the building. Something escapes and skitters across the workbench. Something *alive*. I shriek while Reid hollers, "I've had about enough of you, you little..." He pulls a hammer from the wall and starts playing Whac-A-Mole with a small mouse.

"No!" I squeal. "Don't squish it!"

"I'm trying to scare it."

He succeeds. The mouse veers left, loses its footing, and tumbles to the floor in a fall that would seriously injure a human. The mouse, on the other hand, is so unfazed that it takes off running. Toward me.

I scream and jump on the closest thing I can find: Reid. With my arms anchored around his neck and legs wrapped around his torso, I hold on for the ride while Reid chases the mouse around the garage uttering expletives that I didn't know he had in him.

He prods the mouse across the floor with the toe of his shoe and finally manages to scoot it to the door, which he promptly opens. With one final scoot, he sends the mouse outside and slams the door behind it.

"Stay out there this time!" he yells. "And stop chewing on my wires you little stinker!"

I burst out laughing. "After all those words you used," I sputter, gasping, "and then you end it with 'stinker?'"

The skin around Reid's eyes crinkles as laughter spills from his throat. "I didn't want to offend you."

"Too late," I say, still laughing. Still holding on.

We notice my compromising position at the same time. My arms and legs wrapped intimately around Reid, the room darkened. His face is in shadow but illuminated enough that I can read the intensity in his gaze and the seriousness of his sudden resolve.

He presses his lips to mine, catching me midbreath, and I feel every bit of his intensity as a jolt of electricity through my body. My back hits the wall. He presses me against it for leverage to deepen his kiss.

The garage falls away and I enter another world where my skin is no longer a boundary, allowing me to experience Reid's essence as it spills into me. My cells spread out like droplets in a gentle spray of water, seeking connection with his.

"I'm sorry," he says when our lips part for a moment.

"Why?" I say breathlessly.

"I shouldn't—You just broke up with your boyfriend. Is this rebound?"

"If I said it might be, would you want to stop?"

He kisses me again, hungrily, tugging my bottom lip between his. "No," he whispers with his lips just centimeters from mine. "But we should probably go somewhere less dangerous." He glances to his left and I follow his gaze to the chop saw that's mere inches away.

A soft laugh confirms my understanding. "Put me down," I say. "But don't let go."

Reid lowers me to the couch, thoughtfully placing a pillow beneath my head. Christmas music plays faintly on the Bluetooth speaker, and the tree glows beside us, painting spiky patterns on the ceiling and walls as Reid finds a comfortable position next to me, stroking my neck as he searches for my lips.

Nothing could have prepared me for the gentleness of his kisses and the confidence of his hands as they press against my back to bolster me against the fervent emotions that come in waves.

"This is really why you invited me over, isn't it?" I ask after pulling in a deep breath.

He lifts his head to get a better look at me. "No. Not at all. Really."

I smile at his gentlemanly response. "I wouldn't fault you if it was."

"No?"

"No."

I catch his lips again and sink further into the couch while "I'll Be Home for Christmas" plays in the background, the relaxed melody weaving through the troughs and crests of our breathing.

Chapter 30

Thursday brings more snow. It piles on top of the old, measuring over eight inches when the sun finally peeks behind the heavy clouds.

Friday's temperatures don't climb out of the teens, assuring a festive blanket of snow for this morning's trip to the Christmas tree farm with Reid. As we drive to North Pole Nurseries, pristine farmlands stretch in every direction, most of the snow untouched except for animal tracks made by stealthy deer, coyotes, and rabbits.

The farm sits just outside of town next to the gentle, picturesque hills of Living Water Farms. The owners, Sam and Beverly Lipsey, have sold trees for over thirty years, enjoying the seasonal boost in sales to supplement their custom woodworking business.

Every year on the first Saturday after Thanksgiving, they kick off the season with their Holiday Extravaganza where they offer hayrides, sledding, hot chocolate, and a petting zoo. Since reindeer aren't abundant in Indiana, they bring in rehabilitated goats, miniature ponies, and alpacas from Cold Spring Critter Care. As much as kids love furry animals, however, the main attraction is the hill behind the cabin that Sam covers in artificial snow (if necessary) so kids can enjoy their first sledding of the season.

When we pull into a parking spot, holiday shoppers are already milling about, winding through the pre-cut trees, and exiting the farm shop with steaming cups of cider and hot chocolate.

The store occupies a portion of the log cabin, which sits on a slight hill overlooking the grounds and gives the tree farm an anachronistic feel and an air of authenticity. Its expansive footprint allows Sam to keep both of his businesses in one space, over half of it dedicated to Sam's professional woodshop. During the summer, he offers free woodworking classes to local teens, always eager to serve the community by sharing his expert knowledge of the craft.

"We're not cutting our own," Reid says.

"Did you mean to phrase that as a question?"

"No. It was very much an imperative statement."

"Wow, big words."

He leans over, smiling before stealing a lingering kiss. "I'm too tired to manhandle a saw. Someone kept me up late last night."

Our faces are mere inches apart. I smile back at him and bite my bottom lip. "And who would that be?"

"You."

"You make it sound so scandalous. We were just kissing."

"I distinctly remember your hands on my chest. And in my hair. And running down my back."

A blush brightens my cheeks as the memory of our nightly make out sessions evokes fresh emotions. "I'll keep my hands to myself next time."

Reid grins. "Oh, no you won't. That's another imperative statement." He pulls me in close for a hug. We end it with another kiss.

Ever since our kiss in Reid's workshop, I haven't been able to keep my lips—or my hands—off him. We've been playing it cool at work, but in the evenings all bets are off. A niggling voice keeps reminding me I'm leaving for New York soon. This can't last, it says. What are you doing, Eadie? You just broke up with Hayden.

But kissing Reid is so...satisfying. What's wrong with a little holiday fling?

We both step out of the car and head to the gated enclosure that holds the pre-cut trees, our boots crunching against snow the entire way.

"We're getting a big tree," I announce as we pass through the gate. "It's for the front of the dining room. It needs to be impressive."

"It has to fit in my truck."

I wave his comment away. "Logistics."

He counters with "Physics. I don't want a stump poking through someone's windshield."

"It'll fit. I promise. My dad does this all the time. They bind them up tight and anchor them down for you."

"Yup. My Mom, Dad, and I used to come to the Holiday Extravaganza every year and pick out a tree."

"Really? Did you cut your own?"

"Dad did. After the sledding, and drinking too much hot chocolate, and giving each pony a name."

"Even when you were a teenager?"

Reid laughs. "Yeah. So?"

"I'm not judging."

"You sound judgy."

"Okay, maybe a little." I grab his hand and we wind through the trees, dodging a dad who is scrutinizing the tree his wife and children insist is perfect.

"What about you?" Reid asks. "Did you guys come to the Extravaganza?"

I pause at a dense tree and inspect its needles. "Nope. Café hours. They always had to work."

"Bummer. We should go together sometime."

My breath hitches. I try to camouflage the sudden inhalation with a cough. Sometime. Such a vague adverb denoting continuity. The continuation of this. I look down at Reid's hand. It's wrapped confidently around mine. Surely he knows this could be nothing. A fling at best. Rebound. What goes up must come down. Am I coming down from a breakup, or...

Reid squeezes my hand. "No pressure. Ignore me. It was just a passing thought."

I gather my breath. "No, it's fine. It was a nice thought." I tug on a limb to see if it's still sturdy, still full of life. "Don't feel sorry for me. My parents own a Christmas-themed diner after all. When I was younger, they hosted a charity fundraiser on the Saturday after Thanksgiving. They sold tickets, hired a band to play live Christmas music. There were games, a white elephant gift exchange. It was a blast."

We move past the tree that I've now thoroughly inspected two times over.

"That sounds amazing. Why did they stop doing it?"

"It took a lot of energy. I think they just burned themselves out with it."

We come up to a tree that's taller than the others, wider, more impressive. I look at Reid and grin.

"That one?" he says, reading my mind.

"Yep."

"It's huge."

"It's perfect."

"Are the needles falling off?"

"I don't know, why don't you check, Ralphie's Dad."

Reid walks up to the tree and feeds his arm through the limbs, getting a firm grip on the trunk. He lifts the tree and smacks the trunk against the gravel. The limbs bounce and quickly return to their upturned position, maintaining their hold on every needle.

"Look at you with your big strong arm."

He lets go and proudly flexes his bicep a foot from my face. Without thinking, I grab it, squeezing the rock-hard muscle.

"Don't swoon in public," he whispers, leaning in.

"Watch me." I let go of his arm, take a step toward him, and press my palms against his cold cheeks before warming his lips with mine.

When I pull away just far enough to smile at him, he says, "Bold move, Kissy McKisser. I see yours and raise you one." He dives in for another kiss that warms my body enough to melt the snow at our feet.

The tree makes it safely to the café, no windshields busted or limbs flopping onto the snowy road along the way. I help Reid place it into a tree stand in front of the window so passersby can enjoy its festiveness, and then I head into the kitchen for a pitcher of water. This tree isn't going to spark a three-alarm fire. Not while I'm around. I plan to remove it from the premises before I board the plane to New York, replacing it with a tasteful artificial tree no matter who balks.

"You're going to need a step stool to reach the top," Reid says as he eyes the tree's height.

"You're not helping me decorate it?"

He gestures to the blank canvas behind us, an entire dining room begging for some Christmas vibes. "I think we're gonna have to divide and conquer. Todd will be here in ten minutes to help me hang the metal conifer."

"Who's Todd?"

"Some guy I know from church." He touches my elbow. "Let me go get you a step ladder."

Reid takes off and disappears into the kitchen. I hear some knocks and bumps and a "Gah!" and then I hear a ding-a-ling, but it comes from the front door. In comes Mabel laden with armfuls of plastic bags. Dottie and Jean follow closely behind, both loaded with heavily stuffed bags threatening to split apart.

"Hello Eadie," Dottie calls. "We're a little early."

I give them a warm welcome, and then they drop their bags on the closest table before spinning toward the door.

"We have more," Mabel announces with her back toward me.

"Lots more," Dottie singsongs.

Before I can open my mouth to object, they're already out the door.

Reid returns to the dining room with a step ladder. He unfolds it and sets it by the tree. "Be careful on this."

"We have liability insurance."

He shoots me a warning look. "I don't want any broken bones."

"Same to you Metal McConifer."

Doubling down on the warning look, he ascends the ladder and descends it, maintaining a steady balance the entire time.

"Show off," I say with a grin.

"More holiday spirit heading your way!" Dottie calls from the front door. She waddles between two heavy loads of Christmas cheer.

Reid immediately snaps to attention and holds the door for Mabel and Jean. "Is there more?" he asks.

"We can manage it," Mabel answers. "But you could help Stu with the Christmas trees."

I slap my palms to my head. "Christmas trees plural? Mabel, what have you three done?"

"It's a big dining room." She walks over and squints at me briefly before dropping her bags and turning back toward the door.

"Mabel! There's more?" I say in an incredulous tone.

"You have no idea."

I follow her out the door and onto the sidewalk where three cars are parallel parked with their trunks open. A pickup truck pulls in behind them with Stu behind the steering wheel. Reid walks around to the back of it and starts tugging on a Christmas tree box.

"Dottie!" I holler because she's the closest to me. "This is too much!"

"Don't bust my eardrum. We're trying to help."

I sidestep while taking a deep breath to temper my emotions. I happen to know how much artificial Christmas trees cost, not to mention the bags and bags of Christmas decorations. Money needs to exchange hands. The café might be struggling, but we're not a charity case. Yet.

What if we sell the place? Will the Silver Sweethearts' Christmas spirit and their money go to waste? Guilt tugs on my stomach. I should have told them the café's days might be numbered.

"How much do I owe you?" I say as Jean walks by with her hands full.

"Don't be silly." She shuffles into the café leaving me to gape at the generosity of our most beloved patrons. Our eighty-year-old patrons, who are carrying heavy bags into the café while I stand here with my hands empty.

I dash over to the nearest open trunk and gather up as many bags as I can handle, huffing them into the dining room before ducking out the door for the next batch. When everything has been transported inside, including three artificial Christmas trees, I survey the pile with a sense of gratitude mixed with heavy doses of guilt and bewilderment.

It must show on my face because Dottie says, "Don't worry, we have a plan. And we have Stu."

She motions to Mabel's son, who is already across the room surrounded by artificial tree limbs and unopened boxes of Christmas lights. He already assembled the tree's base and is working on snapping together the plastic trunk.

Mabel slides off her coat and hangs it over a chair. Jean and Dottie follow suit. Afterward, the three ladies begin methodically emptying the bags, setting boxes of ornaments and lights on the table, stacking up bunches of garland and spools of ribbon. They work quietly and quickly, anticipating each other's next moves like they've known each other for decades. Which they have.

"Don't just stand there with your mouth hanging open," Dottie says. "Help us empty the bags. When Stu's done putting up the tree, grab some goodies and go decorate."

"Sorry," I mutter. I shake off my shock at the abundance of décor spilling from the bags. "I'm just...wow."

Dottie giggles. "We may have done a little shopping."

"You were supposed to clean out your attics!"

"We did that too," Mabel says with her typical matter-of-fact tone.

I join Jean at her table and assist her by unwrapping a few sets of ceramic Christmas villages that will look great on the shelves where the old ones sat. They're connected to small power cords that will plug into the wall, providing warmth and ambiance. Jean tears open a bag of cotton, grabs a handful, and begins pulling it into thinner, smaller pieces.

When the shopping bags are emptied, I choose two strands of colored lights, gold ribbon, a pack of glittery star ornaments, and I get to work on the tree by the drink station.

"Coming through!" Reid calls behind me. I pivot to find him carrying the metal conifer along with Todd. They carry it through the dining room and prop it against the back wall.

Dottie and Jean walk over to investigate, making approving noises as they marvel at Reid's handiwork.

"You did that?" Mabel shouts from across the room.

"Yes, I did, Mabel," Reid answers playfully. "Why do you sound so surprised?"

Mabel's shoulders bounce as she fluffs an angel's dress. "I just never pegged you as an artist. More of a...hunter. With a pocket protector."

"Some of Dad's artistic talent wore off on me."

She stops fiddling with the tree topper, scoots her readers to the end of her nose, and peers at Reid's tree. "I guess it did," she says finally.

He beams at me, and I offer an encouraging nod.

"Thank goodness that Santa Claus is gone," Jean says as she heads back to the Christmas cottages. "He was starting to make me lose my appetite."

"How are we supposed to decorate for Christmas without Christmas music?" Dottie chirps over Jean's comment.

"I knew something was missing," Reid says. He retreats to the office and returns holding his Bluetooth speaker. After setting it on the pass-through counter and syncing his phone, he pipes an orchestral arrangement of "O Holy Night" into the room.

We all fall silent, focusing on our tasks. I try to ignore Reid and Todd as they balance precariously on two ladders, balancing significant pounds of metal between them. Instead, I focus on placing gold stars in a pleasing, random pattern on my tree. When I run out of stars, I grab a handful of silk poinsettias and tuck them strategically among the branches. A dozen more random ornaments later and

I'm happy with my work. I stand back to admire it for a moment before turning around to find something else to do.

An involuntary gasp escapes my throat. I swear the Silver Sweethearts are elves. While I was working on the tree, they were sprinkling their magic around the café, transforming it into a Christmas wonderland. Even Stu is in on it, placing the finishing touches on a masterfully decorated Christmas tree.

The Sweethearts are huddled together on the opposite side of the room. I cross over and scoot my way into their circle, outstretching my arms to give them a group hug.

"You guys are amazing."

"Baby Jesus belongs in the center," Dottie argues.

"He can be off to the side," Mabel counters. "Haven't you heard of the rule of thirds?"

"I think he belongs in the center," Jean offers softly.

"Ladies," I say emphatically to garner their attention. "This place looks amazing. You should host a show on HGTV."

"We'd argue too much," Mabel grumbles. She grabs Baby Jesus and scoots him to the side.

Dottie slaps her hand. "He goes in the center. Majority rules."

"Do you want some coffee? Hot chocolate?"

"Wassail," Dottie answers, not missing a beat.

"Bourbon," Stu calls from his Christmas tree.

"How about hot chocolate?" I say cheerfully, spinning toward the kitchen before they can request eggnog with a splash of rum.

Fifteen minutes later, I re-enter the dining room with a round of hot chocolate. I deliver them personally, except for Reid's. He's still on the ladder, so I place his mug on the nearest table. The room quiets as everyone sips on their beverage while "The First Noel" plays in the background.

"'Bout done?" I call up to Reid.

He scoots the metal tree trunk a few millimeters to the right. Todd backs up to the front of the diner. His graying hair gives him a distinguished look, and the extra weight on his middle denotes someone relaxed and comfortable with life.

"Bingo," Todd says.

I join Todd, nursing my hot chocolate along the way.

"What do you think?" Reid asks, his eyes focused on me.

"It's amazing. It belongs there." The tree's proportions are perfect for the space, and the glass ornaments add splashes of color and the right amount of bling.

Soon there's a crowd around me. The Silver Sweethearts and Stu gawk at Reid's tree while sipping on their hot chocolate.

"Wanna see it turned on?" Reid asks.

In response to our enthusiastic, affirmative replies, he descends the ladder and flips the new switch behind the drink station. The tree illuminates, the light from the bulbs bouncing off the ornaments and bringing Reid's 3D creation to life.

"Well, I guess you really are an artist," Mabel says.

Her deadpan delivery evokes a chorus of laughter. We trade positive comments about Reid's talent while we finish our drinks. Eventually, he tells us to hush and get back to work.

An hour later, most of the room is decorated, yet we've only made our way through three-quarters of the Sweethearts' Christmas haul. I start bagging up the extras, but Dottie stops me and informs me that they'll be taking nothing home with them. "Besides, you still have an entire live tree to decorate," she says.

"We can't hang garland on a Christmas tree, or a Santa Claus nutcracker, or this wreath."

She rests her hand on my forearm. "Save it for later," she says quietly with a knowing look that makes me wonder what exactly she knows. Has she heard a rumor? "My dogs are barking, and I could eat a horse," she adds, reverting to her normal tone. "Who's up for steak?"

Two high-pitched "me's" rise from the room along with Stu's baritone "me."

"Reid and I need to finish up here," I say. "You ladies go enjoy a good meal. You deserve it after all this work."

Everyone grabs their coats and heads for the door. As Mabel passes me, she whispers, "Fix Baby Jesus."

I snicker, knowing I won't comply. Baby Jesus belongs in the center.

When everyone is gone, Reid and I collect shopping bags and do a general cleanup before descending upon the live Christmas tree with copious unopened boxes of Christmas lights and a hoard of ornaments.

I open a box of lights while measuring the tree with my eyes to determine how many strands we'll need. Can a Christmas tree ever have too many lights, though? No. No, it cannot.

"Um, Reid?"

"Yep?"

"We have a problem."

He sidles up to me.

"The tree is too close to the window," I explain. "I can't get behind it to string the lights or hang the ornaments."

"No problem." He crouches and braces the tree stand with both hands, lifting slightly to avoid scratching the floor before transferring the very heavy wooden conifer a few feet into the room. He sets it down, stands, and brushes off his hands.

"Wow," I say, unabashedly admiring his broad shoulders and V-tapered torso. "Teenage Reid couldn't have done that."

"Are you complimenting me?"

"Specifically your muscles, but yes."

"That's the second time you've complimented my physique today."

"I've been remiss, then."

I walk over to him and give my hands free rein to enjoy his capped shoulders and swelling biceps. He wraps his arms around me and pulls me close until our bodies touch. We find each other's lips and I kiss him like we've just been reunited after a tour of duty.

He pulls away but doesn't lessen his hold on me. "We still have a tree to decorate."

"It can wait," I whisper.

"Gigi Smalls," he responds, also in a whisper.

"Gigi Smalls doesn't need a fancy tree."

"The fancy tree was your idea," he says with a tap on my nose. His arms relax to his sides.

I sigh and retrieve the box of lights that I let drop to the floor while my lips were pressed against Reid's. We unpack them and position ourselves on opposite sides of the tree, handing off the strand and adding a new strand when we come to the end.

"I could've moved this tree in high school, by the way. I may have looked skinny, but I made up for it in muscle fiber density."

"Oh? Are you trying to impress teenage Eadie?"

He peeks around the tree. "No. Been there, done that. I already know you had a crush on me."

"Are you so sure about that?"

"You agreed to go to the dance with me."

"I felt sorry for you because your girlfriend broke up with you."

Reid leans around the tree to get a good look at me. His brow is plunging in the center. "Really?"

I shrug coyly.

He furrows his brow even further and then disappears behind the tree. "Who *did* you have a crush on, then?"

"You."

The branches rustle along with his chuckle. We're halfway down the tree with plenty of boxes of lights to go, so I continue stringing them close together. This tree is going to look like a glittering diamond when we're done.

"Reid?"

"Eadie?"

"Do you remember that time in class when you and Kara were sitting in front of me, and Kara said..."

My cheeks flush. Why did I bring it up? I can't talk about my A-cups in front of Reid. We're not there yet.

After a long pause, Reid prods me. "What did she say?"

"Nothing. Forget it."

He steps around the tree, adjusting the space between the cords as he goes. "You have to tell me now. You brought it up."

"It's dumb."

"As dumb as the time I put a tree frog in my mouth on a dare?"

My eyes round and I feel a tickle in the back of my throat, the beginnings of a reflexive gag. "Did you swallow it?"

"No. I spit it back out. It went on to croak another day."

"You could have gotten really sick."

"I told you it was dumb. So..." He stops fiddling with the tree and steps closer to me. "What were you going to say?"

I decide to spit it out. "Kara said 'At least I'm not as flat-chested as Eadie' and you laughed."

A smile creeps onto Reid's face.

"See? You're laughing now!"

He tugs on my arm and scoots me closer. "I was an idiot back then. There's nothing wrong with your...chest."

"How would you know? They could be shaped like dirty socks."

This prompts a belly laugh from Reid. "I happen to know they don't look like Hanes No-Shows."

"Have you been peeping through my window at night?"

"Eadie, you're all over the internet."

"I never posed nude!"

"No, but let's just say...sometimes you weren't wearing much on top."

He's right. I can't argue. My neck flushes. Reid has already seen me half-nude. Wait. Reid scoured the internet for my modeling pictures. He just admitted it.

I rest my hand on his forearm and slowly walk my fingers to his elbow. "You *have* been spying on me."

A self-conscious laugh exits Reid's lungs, mostly a whoosh of air. "I may have kept tabs on you a little."

Was this while he was married or after? I'm curious, but I don't want to pry. Not yet. Maybe later I'll ask him to expound on the depth and length of his crush on me.

Later?

Later when I'm in New York with my job and my lease and he's in Indiana tending to the café and making metal sculptures in his garage? How's that going to work?

It's not. Because this is just a fling. A very, very amazing fling. And I'm going to enjoy it while it lasts.

"Kara was insecure," Reid says. "She lashed out at people she was jealous of."

"Kara was jealous of me?"

"You were prettier and smarter than her. And...just...yeah."

Me. The walking stick. The girl Jaden and his buddies always made fun of. "I'm going to have to let that settle for a while."

Reid and I resume our work, finishing up the lights and encircling the tree with satin ribbons. Before adding ornaments, we plug in the lights and marvel at our workmanship. Then, to the tune of "God Rest Ye Merry Gentlemen," we begin hanging snowmen next to Wise Men and Rudolph next to wooden crosses.

I'm hanging an angel when I feel a sharp prick on my finger. "Ow!"

Reid dashes to my side. "Did a needle finally get you?"

I wrap my opposite hand around my pointer finger, muster my best frown, and show my injury to Reid. A speck of blood pops through the wound. "Should we check my blood sugar?"

He ignores my joke and dabs the blood with the bottom of his shirt.

"Is that sanitary?"

Instead of answering, he takes my hand, presses the pad of my finger to his lips, followed by the rest of my fingers one by one, his eyes fixed on me the entire time. My muscles weaken every second our gazes are locked.

"Better?" he says softly when he's done.

All I can do is nod.

He raises my hand to his cheek and nuzzles my palm before hooking my fingers around the back of his neck. My knees start to buckle but his arms catch me in time. His lips gently meet my forehead, and then he tucks his chin to connect with my lips. My free hand snakes behind Reid's sturdy back, my hand savoring his solid muscles.

Reid couldn't have done *this* in high school. I'm sure of it.

The sound of thumping breaks our reverie. We part and turn our faces toward the window. On the other side, Dottie, Mabel, and Jean are taking in the show with broad smiles. Dottie is jumping up and down and pounding on the window with her mittened hand, while Mabel stands tall and proud like Stu just came home with straight A's. Jean's eyes are wistful like she's remembering a kiss from long ago.

"I think we're busted," I say.

Instead of shirking away in embarrassment, Reid places an emboldened kiss on my lips and the Silver Sweethearts go wild with whoops, giggles, and squeals.

"Well played," I murmur.

Chapter 31

December 20th arrives promising a visit from Gigi Smalls. Reid and I report to work early, well before Annette's and Marlon's shifts are scheduled to begin.

He beats me to the office. I greet his back with a weak wave, too tired and nervous to solicit any morning snuggles. When I move to take off my coat, he spins his chair around and says, "Nope. Leave it on." And then he starts rolling up a black bandana.

Last night Reid informed me that he has a surprise for me, although I'm not sure I can take any surprises today. I want everything to run as smoothly as Grandma Delores's hollandaise sauce.

"Is that one of Marlon's bandanas?"

"Nope."

"Good. I've seen how much he sweats."

Reid ties the bandana over my eyes like we're about to play Pin the Tail on the Donkey. Rather than spin me in circles to make me dizzy, he grabs my hand and leads me out of the office, past the swinging kitchen door, and through the dining room. When he opens the front door, I feel a blast of frigid air and shudder.

"It's cold."

"We won't be out here long."

Cars whoosh by slowly, their tires crunching against the salt-dusted road. He tells me to watch my step, leading me off the curb and across the street. When he has me positioned, he removes the bandana.

The old, uninviting café sign is gone, and in its place is Home for the Hollandaise written in fancy, golden script with touches of red and green in the adjacent Christmas tree. The sign is twice as large, a thousand times more eye-catching, and infinitely more professional. I'm floored.

"Is that neon?"

Reid stuffs his hands into his coat pockets. "Actually, no. It's LED strips made to look like neon. A lot more affordable. And very realistic."

I do a little bounce of happiness and then plant my lips on Reid's. Then I remember my dad's back-and-forth with the Historical Society the last time he wanted to update the café's sign. My joy diminishes exponentially. "Oh no," I say, pulling away.

"What's wrong?"

"Please tell me you cleared this with the town. The Historical Society has their nose in everything."

"As they should, to preserve Main Street's character."

I nod, hedging it with, "Within reason."

"When I sold Home for the Hollandaise as a 1950s diner, they decided it was historically accurate to display a neon sign as long as we turn it off at nine o'clock every night."

"They know Grandma started the diner in the 1960s, right?"

Reid shrugs with his hands still in his pockets. "Eh. I convinced them to overlook that small detail."

"Dad had a heck of a time trying to get a painted wood sign approved. Who did you flirt with to make this happen?"

"I might have worn my tightest flannel and my Birddogs pants."

"Have I seen you in your Birddogs pants?"

"No. You wouldn't survive it."

I jab him with my elbow.

"Do I have your stamp of approval, then?" Reid asks.

"I'll let you know when I see them."

"Not my pants, the sign."

"Oh. Yes, definitely. The sign adds so much character to the outside. And our tree looks amazing with all the exterior lights you strung up. Gigi's socks are going to fly off her feet when she sees this."

He reaches an arm around me and hugs me to his side. "We did a good job."

I face him so I can look directly into his eyes. "*You* did a great job."

He smiles at my compliment and then brushes his hand beneath his nose. "It's freezing out here."

"Yes, it is."

"Let's go make a warm beverage."

"Excellent idea."

We join hands and cross the street.

Reid chooses coffee. I warm up with hot chocolate. Marlon and Annette arrive soon after our mugs are empty.

Since Brandon, our more experienced cook, is out for the Christmas holiday, Marlon volunteered to pick up the slack citing child support, ridiculously high rent, and brakes that need replacing before he accidentally shoves his foot through the floor of his rusty car at a stop sign.

Last night, I made him prepare our signature eggs Benedict and tested it myself. His treatment of my grandma's recipe ticked all the boxes: deep orange yolks infused with our secret dash of spices atop a generously buttered and grilled English muffin.

My staff is here. They're well-trained. The refrigerator is fully stocked with eggs. We're ready.

Almost.

I walk into the kitchen where Marlon and Annette are prepping food for the day. "Team meeting. My office. Now."

My authoritative tone jolts them out of their morning haze.

"Sure, boss," Marlon says.

They follow me into the office, which feels like the Grinch's too-small heart when four bodies are scrunched within it. I should have called Reid into the kitchen instead, but I can't change course. Now isn't the time to appear wishy-washy. I lean against my desk and call the meeting to order.

"Gigi Smalls is going to be here at nine thirty. I want everything to go smoothly."

"What does she look like?" Annette asks.

"I don't know. She might be carrying a notepad, wearing dark glasses—"

"Like *Men in Black*?" Marlon asks.

"I don't think the guys in *Men in Black* carried notebooks," I say.

"They carried those memory flasher things," Annette says. "You know, the metal thing that flashed and erased people's memories."

I glance at Reid. He lifts both eyebrows—a gesture of support. I think.

"I don't think Gigi Smalls will be carrying a memory flasher thing," I offer. "But I do need you to be investigative. We know she's a woman, that cuts down your suspects by half. She'll probably be alone. Another major clue."

"Where do you want me to seat her?" Annette asks.

"By the big Christmas tree, facing the metal conifer."

"I knew a band by that name back in high school," Marlon says. "They were a crappy garage band that pretended to be metalheads." He flashes us the rock-on sign. In sign language, it means "I love you" when the thumb is outstretched. I learned this the hard way after going through a week of VBS thinking we were saluting the devil every time we danced to "My Jesus, I Love You."

"Are you sure it was 'Conifer'?" Reid asks. This meeting isn't going how I pictured it.

"My bad," Marlon answers. "I thought you said 'Juniper.'"

"That's better?" I give Marlon the side-eye.

"I told you they sucked. But your metal Christmas tree is awesome, Reid. I'd like to have one of those in my living room. Just a small one. I don't want to mess with putting up a tree. I get too much Christmas here, no offense. Do you work on commission?"

"Anyway," I say emphatically.

Marlon's eyes go wide like a fly buzzed down his throat. He covers his mouth, lifting his hand just enough to say, "Sorry, I talk too much."

"This is serious, guys."

"She's right," Reid says. "Be on your toes, especially around nine thirty. Do your best work."

"As always," Annette says. She grabs a cardstock postcard offering ten dollars off hairnets and starts fanning her neck. "I'm not saying that to be flippant. I'm just telling ya, we do our best every day because we love the Tucker family, so today won't be any different. You know I'm loyal to a fault, Eadie. I'll go down with this place. You have my promise."

Her comments simultaneously warm my heart and jab a knife into my side. Dad is lucky to have such a loyal employee, but I can't have her betting her livelihood on this place. If we do have to sell, she'll be the first to know so she can start applying for jobs.

"I don't know ya'll like Annette does," Marlon adds, "but you can count on me for sure. I could make your grandma's hollandaise sauce in my sleep at this point."

"I appreciate that, Marlon," I say, offering him a grateful smile. "But promise me you'll stay awake today."

"Absolutely. I slept like a baby last night."

To close the meeting, we all put our hands together and shout, "Hollandaise!" (It was Reid's idea.) Annette and Marlon go back to work and Reid closes the office door softly. He looks at me, shoves his hair back from his forehead, and mouths, "Metal Juniper?"

I flop down in my chair and dissolve into laughter. Reid doubles over, grabbing the doorknob for support, somehow managing to cackle without making a sound.

Now we're ready.

❧ ❧

"Is that her?" I whisper to Annette who is on the other side of the pass-through. Marlon, Reid, and I are standing shoulder to shoulder in the kitchen looking at the woman who just sat down by the Christmas tree that poked my finger four days ago.

"She's not wearing dark sunglasses," Marlon says.

"That was just hypothetical," I say.

"Why would anyone wear dark sunglasses today?" Annette asks, scowling at Marlon. "The clouds are so thick it looks like the sun hasn't even come up. She'd be better off with a memory flasher thing so she can use it to see where she's going."

"The winter solstice is tomorrow," Reid says, adding nothing helpful to the conversation.

"Guys. Shh!"

Turns out shushing is loud, something about the consonants, and the decibel or timbre. I'm not a scientist. I just know, she hears me and looks our way.

"Turn around, everyone!"

Marlon, Reid, and I whip around, leaving Annette hanging in the dining room.

"Are you going to take her order?" Annette asks to our wall of backs.

"Shoo." I swat at Marlon. "Go back to your station."

"Is it her?" he asks as he's scooting away.

"Assume it is. Annette, get in here."

"You're acting like a bunch of fools," Annette mutters.

She rounds the wall and pushes into the kitchen, stopping short of the pass-through. Smart. Reid and I slide over to her, taking advantage of the added privacy.

"What did she order?" I whisper.

Annette lists off four dishes in full voice. Our signature eggs Benedict along with one variation, pancakes, and a loaded omelet. She leans back and twists toward Marlon. "Did you get that?"

"Yup."

"Is it Gigi?" I ask. "Did you ask her name?"

"Who else would order four entrées?"

Reid pushes up his glasses and crosses his arms in a very professorial stance. "I couldn't help but observe that the woman who 'might' be Gigi Smalls is not exactly *small*."

"She's the width of two average-sized women and a head taller than me," Annette clarifies.

"Just because a person's last name is 'Smalls' doesn't mean they have to be small," I say.

"We've never seen her here before and she's carrying a notebook," Annette says. "I'm pretty sure she's our girl."

"She has a notebook!? Why didn't you start with that?"

"Because you three were looking like fools in the pass-through. You distracted me."

I look at Reid. "Do you think it's her?" My forehead pinches into folds of worry.

"Go with your gut," he says.

Annette plants her hands on her hips. "Or...I could ask her name."

"Okay, do that." I wring my hands.

"Relax. Stop acting weird," Annette says before turning to leave.

When she's gone, I shuffle in a circle. "It's her, it's her, it's her."

Reid puts his hands on my shoulders to stop me and smiles with one side of his mouth. "Calm down. It's just a normal day. Let your employees do their work."

"Right. I just need to do my quality control. Like normal."

I take my post by the pass-through, purposefully looking some-where other than the large woman who might be Ms. Smalls. Reid leans against the wall next to me, hidden from the dining room, offering moral support.

While I'm tapping my knuckles against the counter, I hear, "Gigi, that's a pretty name!"

Sly, Annette. Nice work.

Should I go talk to her? Should I introduce myself?

No, she should have the normal Home for the Hollandaise experience, which includes no gawking and no surprise visits by management.

Annette moves on to a table of four and takes their orders. When she gives me the order slip, she bores her eyes into me. Her best attempt at telepathy?

"I heard you a second ago," I say. "It's Gigi."

Her eyes relax along with the rest of her face. "She complimented the décor."

I suck in an elated breath and ignore my desire to hop up and down, opting to drum my fingernails against the counter.

It's a normal day. Everything is normal, I remind myself while Marlon fixes four delectable entrées destined to impress the editor of *The Indy Insider*.

Marlon makes quick work of her order. I instruct Annette to deliver each plate as soon as it's ready.

And then we wait.

Without staring.

We have other customers to tend to, which makes the time pass more quickly. I allow myself only the occasional glance at Gigi. At one point, she stands and takes a few pictures of the dining room before sitting back down. A good sign. Her visit is going smoothly. What a re—

A blood-curdling scream cuts through the dining room sending bolts of adrenaline through my limbs. With my heart in my throat, I frantically scan the dining room for an ax-wielding psychopath in a hockey mask. Instead, I find Gigi Smalls, white as a sheet, gaping down at her eggs Benedict like her poached egg just morphed into a portal to hell.

I run through the dining room, past stricken customers who will soon be demanding answers. When I reach Gigi's table, her chest is heaving, sending bucketfuls of air past her trembling lips.

"What is it? What's wrong?"

Gigi points at her plate.

There's a black dot in the center of Grandma Delores's orange hollandaise sauce, giving the plate a distinct Halloween vibe.

"Jupiter!" I'm both horrified and overjoyed. Mostly overjoyed. For the moment, anyway. "Oh my gosh, Jupiter! I thought you were dead!"

Reid runs up behind me. "What's going on? Is everyone okay?"

"Jupiter came home," I say excitedly, but Reid's alarmed expression reminds me it's not the most opportune time for an emotional mother-spider reunion.

I turn my attention to Gigi. "It's okay. He's my pet. He escaped several weeks ago. I guess he's been crawling around in the walls munching on bugs all this time—"

Reid's hand drops heavily on my shoulder.

"Oh! No. I mean, the kitchen isn't full of bugs or anything. This is just an old building, and you know how it goes. Cracks in the plaster and all that. He's clean though. He grooms himself all the time."

Gigi closes her mouth, but she doesn't look convinced. Or pleased.

"Here, let me..." I lower my hand to Jupiter and flick his legs with my opposite finger, prompting him to jump on my knuckle. "Good boy," I coo. "See, he remembers me. What am I saying? He's not a good boy. He's a bad boy! A very bad—"

Jupiter jumps from my hand, landing on Gigi Smalls, who lets out another scream that could chill Hades. As he crawls up her lapel leaving tiny hollandaise-sauce footprints, she scoots her chair backward until she hits the window. When she can't retreat any further, panic turns her skin ashen. Time slows as I watch her eyelids close like elevator doors, her muscles go limp, and her body teeter and then slide toward the floor.

Reid whips past me and catches her before she hits the wood. His quick thinking jumpstarts my brain, returning my internal processor's clock speed to real time.

"Jupiter!" I squeal. The deepest folds of my brain know I should be more concerned about Gigi than a spider, but for some reason, Jupiter's safety occupies the forefront of my mind.

"Get a cold rag," Reid demands.

"Oh. Yeah. Um." I look both ways, unsure which way to turn, and then I pluck Jupiter from Gigi's lapel and run to the kitchen.

I pass Annette going the opposite way. She's carrying a hand towel and a pitcher of ice water. It's not until after I drop Jupiter safely into his terrarium that I realize the full implications of what just happened, not the least of which is being passed over for the Hidden Gems feature in *The Indy Insider*.

Gigi Smalls is unconscious in my dining room. A *customer* is unconscious in *my* dining room.

"Oh...no."

I press my hand to my forehead and brace my other hand against the desk as the room starts to spin. After a few measured breaths, I regain my equilibrium and my resolve.

I run out of the office, grabbing my purse along the way, because if Gigi is headed to the ER, I'm going with her.

Chapter 32

I rest my chin on my forearms, which are resting on my desk, my top half bathed in the halo of light pouring from my lamp. Jupiter directs his beady eyes toward me for a moment before turning back to the capful of water in his terrarium. I absently tap the clear plastic enclosure with the curve of my fingernail.

Disaster was mostly averted. By the time I made it back to Gigi, she was awake. Not exactly alert. More like, dazed and confused, not sure what day or month it was. After some double-handed fanning with paper plates (compliments Annette), a cold compress to her forehead, and several sips of ice water, she remembered where she was.

She adamantly refused to comply if we dialed 911, hefting herself up via her own power and emphatically shoving her chair under the table. Reid followed her stalking frame out the door. She rejected his offer to pay any medical expenses related to the day's events, telling him she had a mad case of arachnophobia trumped only by her liticaphobia—fear of lawyers—because of her cheating lawyer ex-husband who impregnated their housekeeper. She won't be suing, thank goodness.

Still, Home for the Hollandaise is no doubt on her poo-list now, which doesn't bode well for our chances of being featured in Hidden Gems.

I puff up my lungs and let out a long sigh. Pitying myself feels therapeutic. I'm leaning into it.

Footsteps approach the office door, followed by the scent of Reid's cologne. He helped Annette and Marlon close up the café while I hunkered down in here. I just wasn't feeling it.

The low rumble of castors rolling over tile invades my quiet. Reid pulls his chair next to mine and sits. He rests a forearm on the desk, props his chin on it, and peers into the terrarium.

"I guess today is mostly my fault," he says.

I pivot my head and look at him quizzically.

"Jupiter escaped because of me," he explains.

"I never should have taken him out."

"I never should have asked you to."

I turn back to Jupiter. "Okay. It's your fault. Definitely your fault."

He lets out a gentle laugh and then reaches across my back, anchoring his hand on my shoulder. I sit quietly while he kisses my temple, moving on to my cheek next to my ear, and then my earlobe.

A small thrill tickles my stomach as the sound of his breath sweeps through me.

"I'm sorry," he says.

He doesn't need to tell me what he's sorry for. Today was a disaster. We both know it. "Don't be."

"It was a longshot. And it probably wasn't going to move the dial anyway."

I lower my forehead to my arm. With my nose inches from the fake wood desktop, I say, "I liked you better when you were apologizing."

"I just don't want you to pin your hopes on Gigi Smalls." He squeezes my shoulder.

"Why did you encourage me?"

His fingers comb through my hair, from the top to the bottom and then back again. They pull the hair off my shoulders, trace down my neck.

"You needed the distraction," he says finally.

I lift my head and peek at him through the darkness. He offers a shy smile and punctuates it with a shrug, which draws my attention to his wide shoulders. Solid. Strong. Able to carry more burdens than just his own.

My temple finds the depression between his shoulder and collar bone. I sink my weight into it and let his sturdiness support me.

The Hidden Gems column was a desperate grasp, a way to postpone the inevitable. There's no way around it. My parents need to sell the Coleman Building.

"Can you help me tell my dad?"

Reid pulls my hair away from my neck again and places his broad hand across my shoulders. "Of course."

When we get home, Dad's in his recliner watching a show about ancient aliens. As opposed to young aliens, I suppose. Reid entertains him with work-related talk while I locate Mom.

When I tell her we need to talk, she cranes her neck around, her hands wet from the kitchen faucet, and gives me a funny look. "About what?"

"Stuff." I try to make my voice light, even though dread sits heavily in my stomach. The Coleman Building has been in our family for sixty years. I'm about to tell my dad to sell his life to the highest bidder.

She turns off the faucet with a thunk, dries her hands, and follows me into the living room.

"Can we pause this?" I ask, referring to Dad's show.

He gives me the go-ahead. I pause and the show freezes with a full frame shot of the Great Pyramid superimposed with an alien head.

Mom settles into Grandma's wooden rocking chair. She clutches the armrests, looking worried. Dad looks relaxed and mildly interested.

I sit next to Reid, rest my hands on my thighs, and dive in. "I guess I won't beat around the bush. You need to sell the Coleman Building."

Reid grabs my wrist. Dad's expression flips from mildly intrigued to appalled in a split second. Maybe I should have finessed it a little?

"Wait," Reid says. "I've been running the numbers and I have some concerns. Let's start with that."

"Why didn't you guys tell me you weren't saving for retirement?" Apparently, I'm no good at conveying life-altering news. I just stick the knife in and twist.

"Right," Reid says, trying to rescue me again. "I noticed you're relying on the café's profits to get you through your retirement years. I ran the numbers, and I'm not sure that's going to work. So—"

"So, Reid had the building appraised and it's worth a lot. I mean *a lot*. Since it's right by the canal on Main Street, it's prime property. When you see the numbers, you'll understand."

Dad lowers the leg rest on his recliner and sits forward. "I don't need to see any numbers."

"Dad—I'm sorry. I thought if I got it out in the open quickly, like ripped off the Band-Aid, we could hash it out. I need to leave for New York soon and—"

"I paid you to get my taxes in order, not sell the building out from under me." Dad squints as he points accusingly at Reid.

"He can't sell the building, Dad. You'd have to sign off on every-thing. Just look at the numbers. Please. It's simple math."

Mom looks from me to Dad and then back again. Her eyebrows are arched in surprise, unlike Dad's, which are furrowed as deep as an ocean abyss. There's something else in her expression. What is it? Relief?

"I don't want to look at any numbers," Dad growls, "and I don't need anyone rummaging around in my finances."

"That's what you pay Reid to do," I say.

"As soon as the café is mine again, I'm taking it all back."

"Taking what back?"

"The finances," he spits out. "Hiring. Firing. Inventory. All of it!"

"You can't do it alone anymore, Dad. Your Alzheimer's—"

"That's it. I'm done." He pounds his fist against the armrest and shoots to his feet.

As he stomps into the kitchen, the pendulum clock on the wall behind Mom measures his steps. The ticking continues without him, its volume deafening. I look at Mom apologetically. "That didn't go well."

"It's not your fault, Eadie. I've brought it up time and time again, and he always gets like this. He needed to hear from someone else." She tucks a lock of white hair behind her ear. "You're fine, Reid. Don't worry. You're just doing your job. I appreciate it."

She looks down and I realize I'm holding Reid's hand. I haven't told her Hayden broke up with me. I haven't told her about Gigi Smalls. I definitely haven't mentioned my fling with Reid.

Do flings support you when you're at your worst? Do they stand alongside you when you have silly notions? Do they watch over your parents when you're not around?

I pull my hand away from his and stand.

"Maybe I can talk Dad down," I say.

"Good luck," she warns.

As I'm passing through the dining room, I hear her say, "I'd like to hear those numbers."

Reid answers with, "Sure."

She's in good hands while I try to coax Dad down from the wall of denial that my blunt approach helped him build and scale.

The sound of clanking silverware welcomes me into the kitchen. Dad's at the counter scooping mint chocolate chip ice cream into a bowl.

"I don't want to talk," he says from high atop his wall.

I pull a chair from beneath the kitchen table and sit, take a deep breath to slow down my racing thoughts. *Calm down, Eadie.* I should have spent more time choosing my words instead of letting adrenaline and worry dictate them.

"I'll have some too," I say, deflecting onto the carton of ice cream.

He doesn't answer but moves to grab a second bowl and another spoon. A minute later, he carries two generous helpings of ice cream to the table.

"Whatever you're trying to do right now, it isn't going to work," he says after sitting across from me. To punctuate his sentence, he plunges his spoon into his ice cream, digs out enough for two mouthfuls, and stuffs his face so full he couldn't talk if he wanted to.

"You're going to give yourself a brain freeze."

"Mmm."

Rather than take a bite, I tap the end of my spoon against the tabletop. I like my ice cream soft. I also want to talk without worrying about his retort. "I'm sorry I haven't been around."

This comment surprises him. His features relax slightly. Not enough. There's still an edge there. I need to be careful where I step.

"I should have known you were struggling at work," I try.

The muscles around his eyes squinch.

Nope. That tactic won't work. I try shifting the subject because I don't know what else to do. "I regret going into modeling. I did it for the wrong reasons. I was trying to prove something."

He glances up between bites but doesn't comment.

"I like being a bookings agent better. Much better. I feel more useful. But I'm not sure I like my future when I play the present forward."

"You wanted to study bugs."

"Yeah. But I didn't. So, my twenties are basically a wash. No big deal."

Dad pauses his spoon mid-ascent. "Did you learn?"

"I learned my best angles in front of a camera."

"Did modeling teach you anything else? All the traveling? Living in a big city? Did you learn any lessons that you'll take with you?"

The edge of my ice cream is melting. I carve out a bite with my spoon and deposit it into my mouth. "Yeah. I did," I say after swallowing. "I wish I didn't have to learn them the hard way though."

"Most of us learn the hard way. We take the long way around. Truth is, there is no short way. Life's funny that way."

"Dad—"

"I still have life in me."

"I know."

"Don't count me out."

I don't tell him the Coleman Building's roof needs replacing, the brick exterior needs work, the windows need to be brought up to current efficiency standards. He already knows. "Of course not. I never would. I just want you and Mom to be comfortable. You've earned it."

"I'm comfortable in the kitchen."

"Mom's comfortable on the beach," I say with a smile.

He looks up from his ice cream and offers a small smile of concession.

My ice cream continues to soften. I help it along by mashing it with my spoon and swirling it around. Dad's spoon clinks against his bowl as he scrapes for his final bite.

"The thing is, when it's gone, it's gone," he says. "Your grandma's legacy. Everything the Tucker's have worked for. Gone."

The pain in his voice opens my tear ducts. I stay focused on my ice cream and draw in deep breaths to quell the flood. When I feel under control again, I meet Dad's eyes. "I've tried to think of a way to save the café. Believe me. I know how much it means to you."

He sets down his spoon and rubs the top of Tully's head. She wants to lick the bowl, but chocolate doesn't mix well with dogs. "I don't know what you want me to say, Lovebug."

"Just consider it. Look at the numbers."

He grunts. "After Christmas. But I'm not promising anything. I reserve the right to make up my own mind."

"That's fair."

"I'm sorry I yelled."

"I'm sorry I'm a terrible bearer of bad news."

He lifts his arms to me. I stand and round the table, fighting off the dogs to get close enough to give Dad a bear hug.

"I suppose I should apologize to Reid too," Dad says.

"Probably."

He grabs his empty bowl and carts it to the sink while I settle back in to finish my mint chocolate chip.

"I'm on to you, by the way," he says over the din of rushing water.

My mouth is full of ice cream so all I manage is, "Hmm?"

He grins at me over his shoulder. "I saw how you two looked at each other."

Chapter 33

I ponder Dad's comment for the rest of the evening, taking it to bed with me, turning it over and over in my mind, considering the implications while Jupiter sleeps soundly in his terrarium next to me. I know how Reid looks at me during our private moments. Deliciously. Longingly. How does he look at me when we're sitting on a couch together, preparing to deliver bad news?

How do I look at him?

These thoughts pester me as I'm trying to sleep, and they return when I awaken. I avoid Reid's eyes the next morning at work, afraid he might see something I don't want him to see even though I don't know what it could be. I can only guess. Are my eyes telling him I want more? More than a rebound fling? More than friends with benefits?

I'm not ready for more. The rules of humiliating breakups dictate that I can't be. I can't just bounce back from being betrayed by my best friend and cheated on by my boyfriend of two years. That's not how this works. A person in my position must feel debilitating angst and loss. I'm supposed to feel dehumanized, lonely, broken. And I do.

I think.

When I'm with Reid, the pain disappears with a poof, like it never existed. I feel buoyant and cared for and special. He makes me forget Hayden, Whitney, my life in New York, my Dad's illness. That's the problem.

Forgetting is the opposite of processing. And I know what happens when I don't process. I get sick. Really sick with recurrent migraines and mono. Low-grade depression. Anxiety. Confronting my problems and working to overcome them becomes the only cure.

Reid is bad for me. It seems counterintuitive, but it's true. He's distracting me, and in doing so, he's stunting my growth.

What did Dad see between me and Reid yesterday?

I manage to limp through work. Not feeling myself. Feeling incomplete because I can't find the answer. It's like a torturous game of *Jeopardy* where I can't leave the stage until I've cleared the board myself. I'm terrible at trivia. This could go on for months.

The mood between me and Reid is beyond awkward. He puts up with my cold shoulder until closing time. Exercising his authority, he tells Lexis and Brandon to clean up and lock up, and then he says to me, "Wanna tell me what's up?"

A mere touch to my elbow puts me under Reid's command. With the pads of his fingers, he guides me to the office and shuts the door softly behind us.

"Yesterday was intense," he starts.

I find my chair and sit. "I have a life in New York City."

"Oh." Clearly not the response he expected. Rather than sit, he chooses to perch on his desk with his arms loosely folded in front of him. He's standing over me. Exercising his authority again.

Just what I don't want. A guy who tries to control me.

"I worked hard to fit in there," I continue. "When I first moved to the city, I stood out. 'Look at me, I'm a Hoosier. I look everyone in the eye on the sidewalk and wave like we're passing on a county road.'" I wave for effect.

I'm not sure where I'm going here. Speaking off-the-cuff yesterday with my dad didn't go well, but I'm sure it will work fine today.

You know the feeling you get when you roll your eyes? Well, I feel it now, but I keep my eyeballs locked on Reid.

"I didn't know the local lingo," I add. "I thought people were being rude when they were just being blunt. There's a difference. But I learned. Now I stand out here."

Reid regards me quietly for a moment. "Not really. I mean, I don't think you do. You're still Eadie." He looks uncertain, like he's waiting for my point. Surprise, I'm not sure I have one.

"I have friends. Not texting friends so much. That was only Hayden and Whitney. But I know a lot of people in the modeling industry. I have a lease. I have a church that I go to. Sometimes. And I have a steady job, and my boss said I could move up in the agency."

"People like being around you," Reid says. "You're talented and friendly. None of this surprises me."

"And maybe—maybe I'll finish my degree at Columbia. I have two years' worth of credits. My job at Iconic Models could fund it. I could take evening classes."

"Eadie—"

"I don't want to do long-distance dating again." There, that's my point. Long-distance dating with Hayden was an epic disaster and it only lasted a few weeks. I never fully trusted Hayden and I pushed him away and he cheated on me and now I'll be forever paranoid that the next guy is going to cheat. I need eyes on my next boyfriend. Daily. At least until I learn to trust again.

These realizations are for me. Reid only gets the CliffsNotes version. "I think I'm confused. I think maybe this fling between you and me is keeping me from processing my breakup. I warned you I might be rebounding..."

Reid lowers his arms and presses his palms against his desk. It draws his shoulders forward and collapses his chest. If I look there, I don't have to see the pain in his eyes. The pain I'm causing the longer I run my mouth.

"This 'fling,'" he repeats, his tone muted by disappointment.

"That's what it is. Right?"

His head droops on his neck. For several seconds, he studies his denim jeans like they're infinitely interesting. Then he quietly clears his throat and says, "Sure," pushing himself to his feet mid-utter-ance.

He turns to leave.

"I think we need to wean off of each other."

Reid pauses, his weight on one leg with the other bent slightly at the knee. "We're not puppies, Eadie," he says to the ceiling, and then he leaves me alone in the dark.

Chapter 34

I have an entire evening to think about how bad my talk with Reid went. Plenty of time to formulate what I should have said, how I could have rephrased things or let him down easier.

We're not puppies, Eadie.

Reid's parting line gets a prime viewing spot in my prefrontal cortex. I look at it. It looks at me. Neither of us blink.

My heart has turned to lead, the earth's rotation has slowed, all the extra weight and gravity dragging on my limbs. This is how I should feel after the breakup, the loss of my best friend, the news about Dad, the end of the fling that was numbing me to the pain of it all.

Wednesday morning comes too quickly. I don't want to see Reid. I don't want to feel his reassuring arms around me, but I also don't want to avoid him. I want to rewind to the moment before he kissed me in the garage and stop him. We'd still be friends. Now I have no idea what we are.

I arrive early to center myself in the café. As weird as things are between me and Reid, I'm still in charge. The Tuckers still own this café. This is my territory. Reid is just a guest.

When I step through the service door, I hear a slosh. When I flip on the lights and look down, I curse. A layer of glistening water looks back up at me. The corner of the kitchen is flooded.

Water and electricity don't mix, but I need to find the source of the water, so I risk it. I check the most obvious culprits—the plumbing under the utility sinks and the water heater. They're both fine, which should be good news. Right? I splash over to the walk-in freezer, the appliance I vehemently do *not* want to be broken.

When I open the door, stagnant, warm air greets me. My throat constricts, not from the smell—although it's bad—but from panic. Given how much the temperature has risen, the freezer stopped working overnight, probably early evening, rendering thousands of dollars of food unfit for human consumption. Meats, cheeses, frozen vegetables, pastas. They've all thawed, marinated in the warmth, and exploded with harmful bacteria. We can't feed any of it to customers.

I want to collapse into a puddle, but not a literal puddle, so I limp to the office. Before dissolving into a mess of tears, I call our staff to let them know we can't open the café today. And then I call Reid.

The sound of his voice almost triggers tears. I hold it together, my voice barely trembling while I tell him to enjoy his day off. Then,

I collapse onto the desk and breathe through my racing thoughts. So much money wasted. Money we don't have. What if the freezer can't be repaired?

I grab my phone and pull up Google, only to think better of it and drop the phone back into my purse. Now isn't the time to price a new freezer. More bad news won't help me clean up the mess outside the door.

A mop and a bucket will.

I deploy my legs and force my heavy muscles to do what I should have done before stumbling to the office in a discarded wad of emotions. I check the electrical panel in the utility room.

The breaker to the walk-in freezer isn't thrown, which means there's power running to that ancient thing, it's just decided to file its retirement papers. Well, I got news for it, the retirement age is sixty-seven. Request denied.

Lucky for me, the mop and bucket are two paces from the electrical panel. I grab both, wheel them into the kitchen, and put my arms to work, generating a sheen of sweat within minutes.

I'd like to say the exertion is therapeutic. It's not. My arms and legs feel heavier with each swipe, each squeeze of the mop like a vice tightening around my heart. The ratio of water to blood is heavily skewed, so my heart fares much worse than the cotton mop, voided of blood after a few dull presses while the water is still abundant. My heart is as thin and dry as a sheet of paper, but I balance on my feet and squeeze more and more water into the bucket.

"Hey."

I scream, and it's loud, so loud I'm pretty sure it causes a localized tremor. In the same instant, I toss my mop. The handle makes a dent in the stupid freezer door before clattering to the floor.

"Oops."

I spin around, adrenaline knotting my lips together in an angry pout. "Don't *do* that," I say to Reid who looks like he just donated all his blood to charity. His hands are poised in front of his chest, palms out, probably afraid I might throw something else. "You scared me."

"I'm sorry." His stance relaxes and some color returns to his cheeks. "I just came to see how I can help."

"You can't," I snap.

"Eadie."

"Don't say my name like that."

"Like what?"

"Like that. Just don't say it."

His army green, sherpa-lined coat is hanging open, revealing a black waffle weave shirt with six buttons trailing from the neck. A departure from his normal attire. More clingy than his usual flannel, but still comfortable. That's Reid. Comfortable in any situation. Including a kitchen disaster.

For some reason, this annoys me. I fetch my mop handle and jerk it back to standing. I wish I had an enchanted flute or something. I could play it while the mop dances about effortlessly, shining up the Tucker legacy with a coat of magic wax. Then I could leave for New York City with Cold Spring's rats following along behind me.

"I think it's good enough," Reid says.

Good enough? Nothing about this café is good enough. It's all a notch lower than good, if that, and trending downward. "I don't want anyone to slip," I grumble.

"No one is here."

"You're here. I told you to stay home."

Reid approaches and grabs my mop handle mid-swipe. I try to tug it away, but he rests his hand on mine and works my fingers loose one by one while I relax under the spell cast by the trail of electricity shimmying up my arm.

"It's going to be okay," he says to my temple because I haven't turned to face him.

"No, it's not," I say to the wall. "We're losing the café, the place where all my dad's memories are stored."

My face scrunches up. Even under Reid's reassuring touch, a knife stabs my heart and I feel the blood trickle. I thought my heart was dry. I thought there was nothing left.

I bury my face in my hands, and before any tears spill from my eyes, I feel Reid's strong arms around me, hugging me close in a sideways hug. I turn so our chests are facing and find myself surrounded by his coat as he pulls me in. Tears stream from my cheeks to his shirt, and he supports me until they're dry.

"I bought my plane ticket," I sniff.

Reid leans back to see my face. His mouth drops open to say something, but he quickly closes it. He draws my head to his shoulder, and I angle my face toward his hot neck, made so by his winter coat and our closeness. His head drops to my shoulder.

The scent of his cologne overtakes me, and my mouth's proximity to the skin beneath his ear—to the place he dabs the musky, woody scent—proves too tempting. I press my lips to his neck, my senses ignited by the heat transference. As I search his skin, he lifts his head, buries his face in my hair, and then brushes it away to kiss my temple.

Our cheeks touch, and then our lips find each other, melding into a long, roving kiss. When we part, I lift my chin and gasp.

"What are we doing?" I whisper.

He intercepts my lips, tracing his fingers down my neck.

"Reid."

"Eadie," he says.

"I'm leaving in a week."

"I don't care," he murmurs into my hair.

"This isn't weaning."

He pulls away again so he can see my face. Bracing my neck with both of his hands, he says, "Eadie..." And somehow I know what's next. The sincerity mixed with a deep fondness. I *know*.

"Don't," I try, but he's unfazed.

"I love you."

Heat flashes through me from head to toe. The bomb Reid just dropped burns me so thoroughly that my skin feels singed. While my body is reacting to the flames, my mind is screaming danger.

"No," I say. I drop my arms and step back. "No."

"Eadie."

His baritone treatment of my name tempts me to return to his arms, back to the danger zone.

"No, no, no."

I veer left, round the prep table, and close myself into the office, leaning against it to barricade myself in. He revived my heart—I'll give him that—because it's plump and red again, back to pumping blood so frantically that I feel lightheaded.

I love you.

No, no, no.

A soft knock vibrates through the door. "Can I come in?" Reid's voice is muffled by the decades-old wood.

"This was supposed to be a fling," I call out.

Seconds pass.

"It was never a fling for me," he says. "I know it's a lot. Can we talk? Just a minute and then I'll leave you alone."

I close my eyes and breathe deeply. I kissed him first. I kissed his *neck*. I ravaged his musk-scented skin when I was the one who said we needed to end it.

What are you doing, Eadie?

Before answering my own question, I spin around and open the door. Reid's expression brightens when our eyes meet.

"Thanks for letting me in—"

I tug on his neck, pulling him into the office, and shutting us both inside. He looks surprised and pleased as I place my hands on his chest and press him against the door before pinning him to it with my lips.

I melt into him, my body weight easily shifted by Reid's strong hands. He coaxes me over to his desk and props me against it, our lips never parting. I work off his coat and drop it to the floor, my hands obeying their desire to explore his wide back. They find the hem of his shirt, and I tuck my fingers beneath it and press my palms against his bare skin.

His lips lose their curiosity, and he pulls away. "We should talk," he whispers.

I grab his shirt collar and bring him back to me. He expands his lungs and exhales heavily, kissing me deeper as his breath feathers past my cheek. His lips travel to my earlobe while he reaches around and slides my hands off his back. "We need to talk," he says softly into my ear.

"I don't want to talk."

He stands and takes a step back, creating an ocean of space between us. "We should."

I pull in my bottom lip and graze my teeth over it.

"I don't want you to regret this."

"I don't regret it right now."

Reid grins at me as I stand and wrap my arms around his neck. I press my lips to that grin, unable to help myself. He lowers one hand to my waist, the other anchoring my mid-back. "I know you're leaving. You have a lease, and a job, and friends, and a church, but I'm willing to try long distance. I love you, Eadie."

His words pour a cold glass of water over my head. What am I doing? Long distance? No. I'm leaving. I'm broken. Betrayed. Processing.

He dives for my lips, and I feel like I'm floating. Floating away from my problems.

I enjoy the escape for a moment longer and then force myself back to earth, pulling away.

Reid won't be in New York City. I'm going home alone, with just my thoughts, which aren't nearly as pleasant when he isn't around. Hence the weaning. No, not weaning. Weaning implies a kiss here and there, less every day until there are none. I'm so confused I can't even get my metaphors right.

"What are you thinking?" Reid asks, searching my eyes.

"Th—This was all my fault," I stutter. "I'm sorry. I'm not being fair. I can't."

"Can't what?"

"Long distance. I can't."

He holds my gaze for a moment. I watch the shift in his emotions as he digests my words, and then he looks down. His hands slip to my hips before glancing off.

"I'm sorry, Reid."

His shoulders drop and hunch forward.

"I'm really sorry."

"Yeah. Umm..." He takes a step back, casts his gaze to the floor, failing to hide his disappointment. "I guess there's nothing else to talk about, then."

I bend down, grab Reid's coat, and hang it on the back of his chair. His sadness permeates the cramped room, doubling the weight that has already returned to my arms, my legs, and my lungs.

"I'm going to go clean out the freezer," I mumble, closing the gap to the door in three short steps.

"Wait."

I rest my hand on the doorknob, but I don't dare turn around. If I do, I might run back to him for more, confusing him further.

"I'll clean out the freezer," he says. "I'll get it fixed. Take a few days off and enjoy Christmas with your mom and dad."

I don't know if he's handing me an olive branch or devising a way to avoid me. It's definitely a way for me to avoid him, and I think that's what I need. What we both need. It's not weaning. It's ripping off the Band-Aid.

I peek at him over my shoulder. "Okay."

"Eadie." He stuffs his hands in his pockets and ducks his head. "I just wanted you to know."

"Thank you." My voice sounds stilted.

Thank you? That's the best I can offer after that epic make-out session? But what else do you say when a guy tells you he loves you and you can't say it back? You don't fall in love with a fling. Flings end when the vacation is over.

"Goodbye, Reid," I say in the same stilted tone, and then I cringe all the way to my car.

Chapter 35

My plane to New York leaves in five days. I have time. Too much time. Too much time after letting Reid down hard—*again*—to ponder my life choices, from this morning's glazed, dipped, crème-stuffed donut which gave me a monster headache, to waiting until two days before Christmas to shop for my parents, to leading Reid on by devouring his lips.

Distraction is a must. I achieve a good dose of it by zipping down the interstate at seventy-five miles an hour to *The Aughts* playlist on Spotify, rummaging through disorderly sweater displays at Macy's, struggling to find Dad something he won't politely thank me for and then bury in his den.

I find my mom the perfect sweater and my dad an Italian leather wallet, Mom a sapphire necklace and Dad a pair of Yaktrax and flannel pajama bottoms. Armed with shopping bags and brown sugar boba milk tea, I speed walk through the December cold with "parum-pa-pum-pum" on my lips and an inkling of Christmas spirit in my heart.

Until I shut myself into Mom and Dad's faded Chevy Lumina under heavy gray clouds, freezing my nose off with rush hour traffic looming on my horizon. The Christmas spirit floats away like a ghost and all I have left is my headache.

I pull up Spotify and search for a Christmas playlist to distract me. Memories of decorating the café with Reid surface, followed by memories of kissing Reid by the tree, kissing Reid on his couch, attacking his lips in the office. Where the Christmas spirit was, now resides an empty ache.

So, instead of Christmas "cheer" I click on the *This is Muse* playlist, crank up my tiny Bluetooth speaker, and let the clashing of drums and electric guitars fill me with distracting amounts of dopamine.

At home I wrap presents, clean the kitchen (every surface, cabinet doors and all), check on the chickens, ignore a text while I'm dusting and conditioning the dining room furniture, check the text and nearly spit my lemonade across the kitchen table.

Merry Christmas, Eadie. I'm sorry. I hope you can forgive me. I can't wait until you're home.

Whitney. She hasn't texted me in days. I thought her angsty groveling was over. Apparently not. I click on her Contact card and smash my thumb on "Block this Caller."

I can forgive. Sure. Eventually. Doesn't mean we have to be friends. Doesn't mean I have to look at the face of betrayal every day during lunch breaks. I have my limits, and some pride—

a gram of it left, but it's still something.

Angry at Whitney and angry at iPhones and cell towers for deepening my already bad mood, I embark on another cleaning spree, stopping only to eat a few bites of Mom's lasagna.

Mom knows I like to clean. She also knows something is up by how frenzied I am. "I want the house to be spotless for Christmas," I say.

"I thought it already was," she replies.

"I'm deep cleaning."

"That's what this is?"

"Yes. I'm finishing the den tomorrow and I might get to the basement. We'll see."

"Really, Eadie. Just sit down and relax. You're making your dad and I nervous."

"I can't relax when everything is a mess."

She leaves me alone with my ShamWow and my half-empty bottle of Murphy's Oil Soap. This stuff doesn't smell very Christmas-y but the citronella oil is opening my sinuses and the mosquitos are leaving us alone.

Sunday, Christmas Eve, I make good on my promise to make Dad's den shine without the help of an enchanted mop. Elbow grease, Murphy's, and linseed oil are all it takes. Who needs magic?

Mom forbids me to enter the basement, blocking my way with her hands on either side of the door. I take my ShamWow upstairs instead and occupy myself until the afternoon when I'm finally left with nothing to do but think.

So, I go to a movie. And when the movie is over, I go to another movie. And when that movie is over, I lean back in my chair, watch everyone leave, and then I cry because nothing feels right. The heaviness in my muscles isn't just fatigue. It's defeat. The game's over, and I'm not sure I want to play again.

A good cry doesn't solve my problems, but it does help my mood. I leave the theater determined to push past my emotional funk and enjoy Christmas with my family.

On Christmas morning, I put on a bright face. With Dad's Alzheimer's, I'm not sure what next Christmas is going to look like, or the next, and I don't want to frown my way through these precious moments. Before descending the stairs, I take a deep breath and coach myself with positive affirmations. I can't dictate the future, I can't change the past, but I can make the most of the present.

As usual, Mom has the Royal Philharmonic Christmas album playing amid the scents of mulled cider and melting sugar cookie candles. Just like she forbade me to clean the basement, she forbids me to enter the kitchen.

A little after ten o'clock, she fills the dining room table with dishes—French toast casserole, cinnamon coffee cake, egg and sausage biscuits, fruit pizza. We eat together, taking our time to enjoy her hard work and relish each other's company while our presents wait for us under the tree.

Eventually, she fills mugs with peppermint hot chocolate, and we retreat to the living room where the tree glows brightly in the corner. Dad is impressed with his new wallet—I think he may actually like it—and Mom gushes over the sweater. Even Dad offers his approval.

They're far too generous to me, heaping on five presents, including a Home for the Hollandaise sweatshirt in the same script as our new sign.

"Reid helped me out with that," Dad says proudly. "He sent me the graphic and a link to some site."

"It's great," I say, plastering on a smile as the ache returns and spreads its tentacles through my heart.

The sweatshirt *is* great. And thoughtful. And generous of Reid, which is his style. Always looking out for my dad. Designing a new logo when no one asked, paying for a new sign when it wasn't his financial burden to bear, despite knowing the café's days are numbered.

I fold it carefully and tuck it back into the gift box. I'll wear it proudly in New York whenever I need a little reminder of home.

❦❦❦

Christmas day at the Tucker household includes two meals, brunch and dinner only, because dinner is Thanksgiving Part Two. Think turkey, stuffing, cranberry sauce, the works. Again, it's Mom's thing.

She won't let us help her cook, but she will allow us to enter the kitchen to steal a Christmas cookie or two. Or five.

Mom's in the kitchen basting the turkey and I'm munching on an iced snowman cookie when the doorbell rings. I don't think FedEx or UPS run on Christmas so I can't imagine who it would be. When I see Reid through the front door's beveled glass window, I nearly choke on my cookie. Surely Mom didn't invite him to Thanksgiving Part Two.

"Mom," I holler over my shoulder. "Reid's here." He's staring at me through the fancy window, his face like diamond puzzle pieces. This is awkward. "Did you invite him to dinner?"

"Let him in, Eadie," Dad says from the living room.

"Did you guys invite him?" I repeat.

Dad pushes himself out of his recliner, grumbling. He waddles over, bent at the waist like he doesn't want to be upright. "No, I didn't. Why are you making him stand out there?"

"Why would someone come uninvited on Christmas?"

I grab the door handle before Dad reaches it, causing him to grumble some more. "I got it, I got it," I say. I wave him away and open the door.

"Reid!" Dad says chummily. "Come on in."

Reid steps into the foyer, and Dad gives his back a solid slap. "I didn't think she was going to let me in."

"Sorry to make you wait out in the cold," Dad says to Reid while gluing his widened eyes to mine.

I glance at Reid and shrug. "Never hurts to be safe. This neighborhood is crawling with hoodlums."

"Reid!" Mom joins us in the foyer and wraps her arms around Reid. Man, are my parents happy to see him. "Merry Christmas! Are you enjoying your holiday?"

"Very much so."

He is? I mean, I'm glad he is, but shouldn't he be mourning our breakup, or obsessively cleaning his house, or finding a myriad of other ways to distract himself from the fact that I'm leaving for New York and it's over? It's so over.

"Can I take your coat?" Mom's voice cuts through my weird thoughts. I'm sad because Hayden cheated on me. *That's* why I'm sad. It's why I'm cleaning maniacally and blaring Muse for dopamine hits.

Moments later, Dad's in his recliner, Mom's in Grandma's rocker, and Reid is on the couch. I'm leaning against the pony wall that divides the living room from the foyer.

"Get over here and sit," Dad says.

"I'm fine," I say. "I'm going to be doing a lot of sitting on the plane."

"That's three days from now." Mom casts me an exasperated look, but I'm more interested in Reid's jaw muscles that flexed when I mentioned New York. He keeps his eyes on Mom and Dad as he swallows through the tension. "What brings you here on Christmas?" Mom asks.

"I come bearing gifts." He pulls two red envelopes from his pocket. They're decorated with festive stickers and glitter and closed with wax seals. He hands one to my mom and the other to my dad.

Mom eyes the envelope curiously and turns it over in her hands.

"You didn't have to give us anything," Dad says. "I just wish we could have given everyone Christmas bonuses."

"No worries. Just open it. You first." He nods at Mom

I walk a few paces and perch on the couch's armrest, still a cushion and a half away from Reid.

"I hate to open it," Mom says. "It's so fancy." She pokes at the wax seal before tearing the paper around it. Inside is a simple sheet of paper. Her eyes move side to side as she reads. "Wh-what is this?"

"What's it say?" Dad asks.

"I—I don't..." Her mouth gapes and she lifts a hand to cover it.

"Well, what is it?" Dad asks a little more impatiently this time.

Mom hands Dad the paper. As Dad takes it in, he leans back and rubs his bald head. "Well, I'll be... Is this legit?"

"Absolutely," Reid says.

"Anyone care to fill me in?" I ask.

Dad ushers Reid ahead with his hand. "You better tell her. I'm speechless."

Reid looks at me and our eyes lock for the first time today. My stomach fizzes and sparks. I clear my throat and will my face not to betray the tiny fireworks going on inside me.

"It's a grant award letter from the State of Indiana to restore the structure and façade of the Coleman Building."

I jump to my feet. "What!?"

Dad flings the letter at me. I grab it from him and skim for the most important detail. When I find the award amount, my eyes nearly pop out of my head like I'm in a cartoon. This definitely feels like fiction. I spin toward Reid. "Are you kidding me? How did you do this?"

"I've been working on it with the Community Development Coordinator for over a year. I received this letter yesterday. Talk about a Christmas present, right?"

I press my palm to my forehead and drop to the couch. Now there's only half a cushion between me and Reid. "So do we need to have the work done before we sell or—"

"Your dad needs to open his letter."

Dad needs no further prompting. He rips open his envelope and pulls out the letter, skimming the text to find the meat.

"What is it, Weston?" Mom asks nervously. She leans over her armrest for a closer look.

Dad looks stunned, and he's truly speechless this time, so Reid explains. "It's a small business development grant from the Horace Byrd Foundation. He owned a lot of property in downtown Indianapolis and wanted to support his tenants, many of whom were small—"

"How much is it for?" I interject.

"Enough to upgrade the kitchen and make other cosmetic repairs, upstairs too if you want to start monetizing that space."

I didn't know I could squeal. Turns out I can. My cry of joy peals through the living room. I wrap my arms around Reid's neck and pull him into a hug, and while I'm there (why not?), I plant a kiss squarely on his lips, which turns into a second, longer kiss. And then he goes for a third. After the fourth, I realize it's conspicuously quiet.

Reid and I turn our heads toward my mom and dad. Dad is grinning from ear to ear. Mom looks downcast, her countenance strained. I let go of Reid and face forward. "What's wrong, Mom?"

Tears spurt from her eyes. She tries to hide them with her hand. It doesn't work.

"Helen," Dad says, "what's wrong?"

She answers by springing from her chair and darting out of the room.

***

I tap lightly on the bedroom door and ask Mom if I can come in. She makes an indecipherable sound, which I interpret as my permission to enter.

Decades-old floral wallpaper wraps the room, once in style, now a reminder of how finicky trends are. Mom is sitting at the foot of the queen-size bed, her back hunched as she nurses a tissue.

I sit beside her and sink into the memory foam mattress without disturbing her posture. "What's wrong, Mom?"

She responds by sniffing and heaving out a shuddering breath. "We were going to sell," she whispers finally.

Her words settle between us. She's right. The grants change things. They give us options. We could still sell, sure. Or we could keep the café running.

"I was excited for your dad to retire," Mom continues. "I wanted to travel before his memory fades too much. Nowhere fancy. Maybe up to Lake Michigan, or a cabin in the Smoky Mountains, but now..."

"With the grants and the improvements, he'll never want to leave work," I say. "He'll want a Tucker in the kitchen."

Mom nods into her tissue as a soft sob escapes her throat. With Dad chained to the kitchen, she'll be robbed of time with him as he slips away, little by little, year after year. I imagine myself working dutifully for decades with no end, no reward, just more work and profound loss.

I rest my hand on her back. "You want some time of your own with Dad. Free time, just the two of you."

She nods again and sits a little straighter.

"Maybe Reid should have told you he was applying for the grants."

"I would have preferred that," Mom says.

I rub Mom's back for a moment, and then I drop my hand and tap on the comforter. "If you make the improvements before you sell, you'll make a lot more money, and then—"

"I don't care about the money," Mom snaps. "I just want your dad." The final sentence sends her into another round of tears. I grab a tissue from the dresser and hand it to her. "It's been so nice having you here," she says between sobs. "Your dad hasn't been worried about the café. He and I have had more time together, and I haven't felt nearly as lonely."

Her words send a little shock through me. From my perspective in New York, my parents have been working happily at Home for the Hollandaise, solidifying their marriage bond by spending their days together at the family-owned business. Instead, Mom's been second fiddle to Dad's work ethic, feeling lonely despite being right beside him?

"I didn't realize you were feeling lonely. I should have come home more often."

Mom waves away my comments. "It's fine. I'm fine." She's calmed down again, her crying reduced to the occasional sniff.

"You're not fine."

"I'll be all right. We'll just keep going on like we did before. Nothing will change. Nothing ever changes." She sighs heavily like she's been holding her breath for a long, long time.

"Mom." I put my hand on her shoulder. "You should talk to Dad about this."

"Don't you think I have a thousand times, and if he was going to listen, he would have done so by now? You're the only one he listens to, and then only sometimes."

"Do you want me to talk to him?"

"About what?"

"About...you being lonely. I don't know."

Mom pats my knee. "I'm an adult, Eadie. I can fight my own battles. I'll be all right. I'm better now, in fact. I was just having a moment."

"I think it was more than that, Mom."

"You didn't tell me you and Reid are kissing now."

"We're not. Not anymore."

"It sure looked like kissing to me."

"I thought we were talking about you and Dad."

She pokes me in the side. "Not anymore. I want to hear about you and Reid."

I spring up from the bed. "Um. Heh. It's a long story. There's nothing to tell. Anyway. Okay, bye."

I flash her a wave, and then duck out of the room as she hollers after me, "If it's a long story, how is there nothing to tell?"

Chapter 36

A Rhode Island Red pecks at the end of my tennis shoe as I push myself back and forth in the chicken swing. It's below freezing, but I'm blanketed in Dad's goose down coat with the hood cinched tightly around my chin. The occasional snowflake lands on my sleeve, displaying its unique geometry until my breath eventually melts it or the wind scoots it along.

After leaving Mom's room, I couldn't make my feet turn into the living room where Dad sat chitchatting with Reid. I veered left instead, and since the kitchen didn't feel far enough away, I ambled down to the chicken coop and gave the chickens a speech about being thankful they're not turkeys. They weren't impressed.

"You're surrounded by psychopaths."

I turn my head and peer up at Reid who's standing outside the gate. He stuffs his hands deep into his coat pockets, not inclined to come in with the chickens.

"They've been let out for good behavior," I answer.

"That one is trying to dispatch your shoe."

"I think she just likes the way her beak bounces off the rubber."

"Ah. Thus saith the Chicken Whisperer."

"Something like that." I shrug. A snowflake slides off my sleeve and falls to the dirt, lost among the pebbles, never destined to amount to much. "Together everyone achieves more," I announce to mother nature.

"Tell that to Lexis," Reid says. "I think she'd disagree."

"Lexis is too young to know any better."

Reid pulls his hand from his coat pocket and thumps the gate with the edge of his fist. "So... I feel like a jerk."

"Did that not end the way you were expecting?"

"No. It didn't. Your mom came back into the living room looking all chipper. I think she was faking."

I scoot sideways so I can look at Reid without craning my neck. "She convinced herself she's okay. For now."

"What did she say to you?"

"That she was looking forward to selling so Dad would pay more attention to her and she wouldn't have to be lonely anymore."

Reid winces and gives the gate another wallop with the side of his fist. "That's not what I wanted to hear."

"Did you know she was unhappy? Could you tell?"

I watch Reid shuffle through two years of memories in a few seconds. "Honestly? No. I had no idea."

"You should have told them you were applying for the grants."

"In hindsight, yeah. I've been holding onto the small-business grant for four months, but I'd given up on the State of Indiana. I didn't want to get their hopes up. Then, the second letter came, and I decided to surprise them. I really thought she'd jump for joy."

"I jumped for joy."

The wind musses his hair as he grins at me. Reliving our recent kisses on the couch, no doubt. I keep giving him what he wants, then taking it away.

Wait. What?

"You've known about the small-business grant for four months?" I pause to blink. "Like, the entire time I've been here?"

"Yeah," he says, unaware that he's just implicated himself in the world's shortest criminal investigation.

"You were manipulating me," I say like I just solved a whodunit.

He shoves his hand back into his pocket. Appropriate. He doesn't want to show his hand. Reid Avory, the Poker player, secretly collecting his Royal Flush to surprise us at the end, swooping in to save the café and the girl.

"I don't need saving," I say.

He cocks his head. "What do you mean?"

"You wanted me to think all hope was lost so you could swoop in and save me."

Reid shifts most of his weight to his left leg, letting the other leg relax. "I'm not trying to save anyone. I just want to help."

"Why didn't you tell me about the grants?"

The wind gusts and blasts Reid's cheek. He pulls up the collars of his coat to fend off the cold. My cheeks feel the sting, but the rest of me is still warm inside Dad's bulky coat.

"I didn't tell you because I didn't want to get your hopes up."

"I've been worried about the café's finances for weeks. I redecorated the entire dining room on a fool's errand."

"It wasn't foolish. The dining room needed an upgrade."

"I thought the world was ending when our walk-in freezer busted and ruined all our food. And you just let me stand there and cry."

"That's not how I remember it."

"You swooped in and enjoyed the show."

"You attacked me with your lips."

"I did not attack you!"

The freezing December air is no match for Reid's icy glare. Yet, I continue. "You knew we won the small-business grant, and instead of telling me, you took advantage of me and made me fall—" The word lodges in my throat, an aspirin tablet wedged between my larynx and my spine. I swallow a few times to ease the discomfort and erase the acrid taste. "You lied to get me into that dark garage and—"

"That's not true." The furrow between Reid's eyebrows is as deep as the Grand Canyon. "I was protecting you."

"I don't need protecting, Reid."

"Everything was still up in the air. The small-business grant pays out over three years. I didn't know if it was best to sell, or start remodeling the kitchen, or wait for the response from the State of Indiana."

"You could have told me. I could have helped you decide. But you wanted to be the superhero who saves the café before the credits roll."

Reid's frigid glare pricks my already stinging cheeks. "I was trying to help your family. That's all. I'm sorry I didn't do it the way you wanted."

He turns stiffly and stalks away, bypassing the house to make a quick exit, leaving me alone with a bunch of clucking psychopaths.

When I fall through the back door, the heater's warmth is an inferno against my frozen cheeks. I tear off my gloves and press my hands to the raw skin.

"What were you doing out there?" Mom asks from the kitchen table. Dad's next to her with his elbows propped on the tabletop and his arms crossed.

Why are they sitting there with no food, no beverages, no bowls of ice cream? Just sitting? I narrow my eyes. "Were you spying on me?"

"No," Mom answers quickly. Too quickly.

"You're both sitting at the kitchen table with nothing but your guilty faces."

"She made me," Dad says, pointing at Mom.

"We thought he was going to propose or something," Mom says.

"Mother!"

"She thought," Dad says, pointing again. "I said, 'Who proposes to a woman in a chicken coop?'"

Mom shrugs innocently. She's faking. "Why didn't you tell us you two are dating?" she says, fake innocent voice in full force.

"We're not dating."

"You kiss men who you aren't dating?" She raises an eyebrow at me.

"I don't make a habit of it."

"That's good," Dad says. "You never know how many other mouths he's kissed."

Mom nods. "Herpes, the mouth variety. It's very common. Abstinence is best."

My parents are in rare form. I understand Dad's giddiness. He just got his café back. I suppose Mom is happy because she thinks Reid and I are an item. Time to quash her hopes. I drop heavily into the seat beside her. "Reid and I aren't dating. I'm going back to New York in three days. I'm not about to try the long-distance thing. Not after the Hayden disaster."

"What was the Hayden disaster?" Mom asks. "You never told us you two broke up."

I groan.

"What happened, honey?" Mom prods.

"He cheated on me with my best friend. In a hot tub. Or after the hot tub. Or maybe both. I don't know the logistics."

"When was this?" Dad asks.

"Thanksgiving weekend."

"Ohhhh," Mom says, my revelation turning her into a little song-bird.

"Yeah, he cheated on me with Whitney. The one who's lactose intolerant that I had spying on Hayden while I was gone."

"Well, that backfired," Dad, a.k.a. Mr. Obvious, says.

I purse my lips and look down at the dulled and scratched wooden tabletop. "I realize that," I say after recovering from Dad's barb. I know he didn't mean anything by it. "Anyway, I was devastated. I still am."

"You seemed pretty devastated earlier on the couch," Mom says.

I purse my lips again and become even more acquainted with the timeworn table. "I lost my boyfriend and best friend in one night, and it was partly my fault, so yeah. It stung. A lot. I mean, it *stings*."

"I never thought he was trustworthy," she mumbles under her breath.

"Translation, you thought he was too good for me."

"Eadie! Not at all. He just had a look about him."

"You got that right," I say with an exaggerated eye roll.

"Reid's trustworthy," Mom quips. "And he's a good kisser."

"Mother! How would you know?"

"It looked like you were enjoying it."

Dad snickers.

"You two are in quite the mood."

Dad reaches over and grabs my hand. "We just want you to be happy, Eadie."

"And you seem happy around Reid," Mom adds. "Except for a moment ago."

"Were you using Dad's binoculars? The ones I bought him for birdwatching?"

Mom pinches the right corner of her lips. Guilty.

"Guys." I squeeze Dad's hand, and then I splay my hands over the tabletop, leaning forward to emphasize what I'm about to say. "Mom. Dad. I *am* happy. I'm happy in New York. You need to come visit. You'd see me in my element and then you'd understand."

"You seem in your element here too," Mom says.

"Helen," Dad warns.

"I'll do everything I can to help with the grants," I say to shift Mom's focus. "Or with selling the building, whatever you decide. Just because I'm hours away doesn't mean I can't help."

"I think we're going to be fine," Mom says with surprising confidence. She grins at Dad, and he winks at her.

"If 'fine' means leaving a dried-out Christmas tree in the dining room for months, I don't believe you," I say.

"While we were in the bedroom talking, your dad and Reid agreed to put Reid in charge of the renovations. And..." Mom's grin widens into a full smile. "Reid is going to start working in the kitchen so your dad can go part-time."

My jaw wants to drop, but I clamp it shut. My parents are the happiest they've been since I arrived in Indiana. All because of Reid. Once again, he swooped in and saved the day like a...

Like a...

"Is he going to clean the cobwebs?" I ask.

"He's going to be in charge. Your dad is going to manage the kitchen when he feels like it. So, yes? I assume cleaning cobwebs is part of the deal."

"And make sure we have enough eggs, and keep the Silver Sweethearts happy, and change the light fixture in the office?"

"Yes, yes, and yes?"

There he goes again. Reid Avory swooping in like a...

Godsend.

I slap my forehead.

Mom looks at me hesitantly. "Do you need some DEET?"

"I chased off all the mosquitos yesterday with the Murphy's Oil Soap."

"Did I miss something?" Dad asks.

I groan out a long "No" and then I collapse into a heap while Mom grins beside me.

❦❦❦❦❦

The clothes Gracelyn gave me won't fit into my suitcase. I don't want to return them. Not now anyway, so I leave them neatly folded in the dresser to deal with later. I'm not sure when I'll return to

Indiana, but a few items left behind in the guest bedroom won't hurt anyone.

As I'm choosing which pieces to take with me, I pull out my grasshopper slippers and make a face. Every time I look into their beady eyes, I'll think of Cheaty McCheater. They have to go.

I tromp to the bathroom and chuck them into the trash can. On the way out, I catch a glimpse of myself in the mirror and lean in for a closer look. The day's events distracted me from the heaviness that's been pressing on me for days. Now, in the quiet of evening, the weighty burden asserts itself again. Whenever I think of my plane ride, it doubles down.

But it's not the plane ride, really. It's returning to a life that used to revolve around Hayden but has lost its center. It's walking into Iconic Models and having to look at my backstabbing ex-friend.

My bee pendant hangs from my neck, the silver glinting in the light. The bee pendant Hayden gave me. Another reminder. I grab it and I almost rip it off my neck but think better of it. The bee did nothing wrong. It was Hayden and his stupid face that made a mess of everything. So, I remove the necklace by the clasp, let it drop into my hand, and head back to the bedroom, depositing the necklace on the dresser for my future self to contend with.

Before tending to my suitcase, I pause at Jupiter's terrarium. He perches on his back legs, his black eyes glittering at me beneath the heat lamp.

"I'll protect you from the mean TSA agents," I say.

He stretches his pedipalps toward me like he's reaching up for a hug. I've been hesitant to take him out of his terrarium, afraid he'll jump down again and get lost under the crooked baseboards. My apartment is less drafty with fewer crevices and cracks for a small spider to get lost in.

"We'll get to snuggle soon, okay? Just a little longer."

My phone rings, interrupting our bonding session. I walk to my bed to check the caller. "You've got to be kidding me." Why is Cheaty McCheater calling me now? On Christmas? I am not talking to him. Not gonna do it.

The phone continues to ring. Hayden wants to FaceTime.

"Fine," I growl. I swipe the phone from the bed and answer.

Hayden appears, his face aglow in flattering lighting, every perfect angle of his face highlighted to perfection, every shadow painted with an artist's brush. Objectively, he's as gorgeous as ever.

"Merry Christmas," he says. Hydroponically grown plants form a green halo around his head.

"Is this what we're doing now? Calling each other on significant holidays? National Bubble Wrap Appreciation Day? National Hairball Awareness Day?"

A faint smile causes Hayden's dimple to appear. The sight evokes no emotion. No longing, sadness, anger. Nothing.

"I deserve that," he says.

"That's the least you deserve."

"True. I'm not going to argue."

"That's good because if my ex who cheated on me with my best friend called me on Christmas to argue with me, I'd think he was a special kind of pathetic."

"Don't you think that already?"

I blink at his 2D image. What do I think about Hayden? What do I really think? After two years of dating a gorgeous model hunk who cheated on me, how do I really feel? Since I'm not feeling much for him at the moment, I'm going with "ambivalent."

I hunch over my knees and reposition the phone. My chin looks like a barge from this angle. I don't care. "How's your girlfriend?"

"Whitney?"

"Seriously? Who else? Unless you got rid of her already."

Hayden leans back, runs his hand through his hair, and clears his throat. Oh no he didn't.

"Actually..."

"What the heck, Hayden?"

"It was mutual. Honestly, Eadie, after that night in the hot tub, she started getting on my nerves. I'm not making excuses for myself, but I think it was the alcohol. That woman never stops talking."

"So you... Both of you were in the hot tub, and then..."

"Do you really want to go there?"

"How does it work, actually, because I thought the hot, chlorinated water made things—"

Hayden clears his throat obnoxiously.

"I deserve to know," I continue. "You were mine then. Supposed to be anyway."

"Let's just say, it's not as romantic as it sounds."

"Hmm."

"Eadie."

"What?"

"I didn't mean what I said."

My brain flips through his recent comments, trying to fathom what he's talking about. I find nothing interesting or memorable. "About what?"

"When I said waiting on you was getting boring. I wasn't bored. But I was pretty darn frustrated, to be honest."

"With me?"

"No. With...*things*." He tucks his chin and bugs his eyes at me.

"Hayden, I'm not going to lie, this conversation is weird. You cheated on me. We broke up. Why are you calling me at seven o'clock on Christmas day?"

He clears his throat again, less obnoxiously this time. "I wanted to tell you that Whitney and I broke up."

"Stop the presses! The relationship didn't last!"

Hayden covers his mouth, but I hear his soft laugh. "I deserve that too," he says through his fingers.

"Yeah, sorry, but my give-a-crap reserves are pretty tapped out."

"I guess that means you don't want to try again."

My laughter hits me so hard that I fall back on my bed. I lose track of my phone's camera while I'm clutching my stomach. I have no idea what he sees. I don't bother sitting up when I'm done. I hold my camera, my arm outstretched, and let him see me from an angle that he will never, ever see again.

"I take it that's a 'no,'" he says. He looks more amused than heartbroken, which causes a flicker of anger in my gut.

"Of course it's a no." I glare at myself in the top corner of the screen to make sure my angry expression is on point.

Hayden runs a hand through his hair again and then shakes his curls back to his forehead. "Yeah. I figured. But I had to try."

He thought his gorgeous face and his muscled body and his broody stare would be enough to make me run back to him. Ha. I sit up and scoot my legs over the side of the bed. "You need to find a woman without a spine who doesn't talk much. I think she's your perfect match."

Hayden's confident grin falters, and his eyebrows dip toward the center. I struck a nerve. Mission accomplished. "Okay...well..." He falters a moment before resetting his shoulders. "So you're coming home soon?"

His comment jars me. I am home. I feel like I'm home. But I'm not home. Am I?

A leaden weight drops onto me, liquifying on contact and spreading through my arms and chest so fast that I can't breathe. When I manage to pull in air, my lungs are constricted, confined by the pooling metal.

"Um. Yeah. My plane leaves in three days."

"Whitney quit her job."

"She did?"

"She said it would be too weird with the two of you working together. She still thinks you two can work it out."

I should be relieved by the news, my lungs a little freer, but the pressure keeps clamping down. The sidewalks of New York City teem with people, yet the thought of walking those streets conjures a deep loneliness, like I could tread them for miles and never be seen.

Reid would see me. He'd recognize my pain and whisk it away with a gentle touch and a kind word. He'd wrap his arms around me, whisper in my ear, "It's going to be okay." And it would be okay, eventually, because Reid is trustworthy, loyal, selfless. A godsend.

But Reid is in Cold Spring. And my plane is headed to New York.

Oh no, no, no. I'm not going to cry. Not in front of Hayden. "Hey, nice chat." I shake my head at myself. Nice chat? So decidedly not true.

Hayden leans forward, refining his focus. "I'm sorry, Eadie."

When I think of losing Hayden, I'm ambivalent. When I think of losing Reid, I'm buried under a ton of lead and I can't breathe.

"Don't be," I say absently. "It's fine."

"It's not fine, Eadie. What I did to you is not fine."

"It is. Really."

"How?"

"Because I think I'm in love with someone else."

Chapter 37

Darkness surrounds me as I ascend Reid's porch steps, pumpkin roll in hand. Not expecting visitors this late on Christmas Day, he's turned off his porch light and snuggled in for the night. His glowing front window is a portal to his living room, giving me a clear view as the ever-changing images on the television flicker on his face.

My soft knock on the front door causes him to perk up and walk over. He opens the door and locks his eyes on mine.

"Eadie." The breathiness of his tone gives away his relief. He clears his throat. "Eadie," he repeats in a deep baritone that nearly buckles my knees. I grab onto the doorjamb with my free hand.

"Did I say your name right?" he asks.

"You can say it however you want."

One side of his mouth turns up in a smile.

"Are you going to invite me in? I'm freezing."

He jerks his hands from his flannel pajama pants to welcome me in—the pajama pants that look better than anything I've seen him wear. Or maybe it's because I'm finally allowing myself to look. *Really* look.

I flick my eyes to his face and double my grip on the doorjamb as I step inside. The foyer smells like cinnamon mixed with the woody tones of Reid's cologne. It's all I can do to *not* attack his lips.

"I brought you something," I say, trying to coax my voice out of swoon mode.

"Oh?" He raises his eyebrows and reaches for my gift.

"It's a pumpkin roll."

His eyebrows drop with a thud. "Oh," he says, concern sending his tone off a cliff. "One of ours?"

"It's been in the freezer since Thanksgiving."

He winces. "Um. Thanks?"

I smile at him broadly. "I told you I was going to give it back."

"You did." He scratches his forehead before pivoting toward the kitchen. "I better put this right back into the freezer."

"Uh oh." I follow him through the dining room.

"Yep. You'll be seeing it again." He glances over his shoulder, long enough for me to catch his worry. "I've heard these things keep for years," he adds with a touch of uncertainty.

In the kitchen, he slips the pumpkin roll into the freezer and closes the door carefully, staring down at the handle before turning to face me. "Eadie—"

"I'm sorry."

He falls backward, catching himself with the quartz slab.

"I'm sorry I said you were trying to save me," I continue. "And for saying you were trying to be Mr. Superhero and whatever other dumb things I said. Are you still mad?"

With his chin tucked, he gazes up at me. I've known Hayden's eyes to smolder, but Reid's smolder outburns them by infinite degrees. His eyes are blazing so hot I feel like I'm roasting. In a good way. "Do I look mad?" he asks.

"Uhh..."

He approaches slowly, wraps an arm around me, and presses against the small of my back. "I don't care about our fight," he whispers. "I don't care about New York, about how long the distance is. I only care about you."

His lips descend onto mine and an explosion in my core renders my arms and legs useless. He holds me up with his strong arms and presses me to his chest. "Are you okay?" he murmurs.

"Am I okay with what?" I ask breathlessly as his lips travel down my neck.

"With this?"

I lift both hands to his cheeks and direct him back to my lips. "Do I look okay?" The scruff on his chin tickles my face.

He grins at me mischievously. "Let's go somewhere less dangerous."

"The kitchen is dangerous?" I giggle.

"How I feel about you is dangerous." He nuzzles my neck, and then in one deft movement he picks me up.

I let out a small yelp in surprise, but I quickly settle into his arms, relishing his embrace.

Reid's body tucks perfectly next to mine as we both lie on the couch, my head propped on his arm, his free hand stroking my cheek as he gazes into my eyes before going in for another kiss. I close my eyes and enjoy being this close to Reid. Why did I ever think I belonged anywhere else?

When his lips leave mine, he adjusts his position and rests his head in the nook between my chin and my shoulder, draping his arm protectively across my chest. I bend my arm and play with his curls.

"I should have told you about the grants," he says.

"You did what you thought was best. I can respect that."

We're quiet for a moment as we enjoy the in and out of each other's breaths.

"My parents are happier than they've been in years, even despite Dad's Alzheimer's. You did that."

"I like your parents," he says matter-of-factly.

I admire the light patterns on the ceiling made by Reid's Christmas tree while I consider my next comment. "Does your fondness for them have anything to do with your fondness for me?"

A breath escapes Reid's lungs, a silent laugh. "Maybe. A little."

"Well, I'm forever indebted to you, Reid Avory," I say, chuckling.

"Forever?" he says with a hint of surprise. "I like the sound of that."

I turn and bury my face in Reid's hair, breathe in the manly scent of his shampoo, enjoy the tickle of electricity that travels all the way to my toes.

"I changed my mind," I say.

He pops his head up, "About what?"

I shift my weight and sit. Reid follows my lead. His eyebrows are knitted together in worry.

"I changed my mind about long-distance dating," I explain quickly. His expression relaxes, but pain lodges in my chest. "I have to go back. I have six more months on my lease, and I can't just quit on Tabitha. Not after she was so accommodating."

"I understand."

"But—" I take Reid's face in my hands and place a gentle kiss on his lips. "I don't know if I'll be able to stand it."

He pulls me closer. "We'll figure it out."

Reid isn't Hayden. Reid isn't Hayden, I remind myself. But still, an inkling of worry is there. "Maybe I'll have Gracelyn spy on you," I joke.

Reid puts his hands on my shoulders and turns me so we're facing.

Tears burn the back of my eyes.

"I'm not like Hayden," he says softly.

I clench my jaw trying to hold back the tide, but it doesn't work. Saltwater drips down my cheeks. Reid catches it with his thumb first, and then his lips.

He levels his eyes with mine. "I'll never hurt you."

"Never?" I sniff.

"I may annoy you sometimes, but..." He grins.

"I'll annoy you back," I say with a laugh.

Reid's expression turns serious. "I love you."

The words don't scare me this time, but I'm not ready to repeat them. Not yet. "I—" Reid places a finger on my lips.

"It's okay," he says. "You don't have to say it back."

"I want to try this out for a while."

He kisses my forehead. "Me too. There's no rush."

His voice calms me, the reassuring words even more so. I sink into his embrace, press my cheek to his chest, feeling at home against the pattering of his heartbeat.

Epilogue

"**O**pen it," Reid says.

I look down at the present, test its weight again. Heavy. I have no idea what it could be. Also, it's New Year's Eve, not Christmas. Why the Santa Claus wrapping paper? Why a gift at all?

"You didn't have to do this," I say.

"I wanted to give you a going away present."

I pushed my flight back a few days so I could attend the New Year's Eve party that Dad arranged on a whim. He announced the grants to the staff after Christmas and said we needed to celebrate. The doors to Home for the Hollandaise have been open since six thirty. We had a rare dinner rush, invited customers to stay for cards and a dessert bar. We've had a surprising number of takers, including the Silver Sweethearts who received special invitations.

It's an hour until the ball drops. Reid invited me upstairs, and we settled into one of the U-shaped couches along the front windows.

"Open it," he repeats.

I tear at the paper and reveal a nondescript box. When I pull off the lid, my jaw drops. "No way."

"Yes way. Your mom told me your shoe size. They should fit perfectly."

I pull out one of the teal and purple roller skates, admiring the silver accents on the wheels.

"I cleaned and shined the floors, popped in a few lightbulbs. It's a regular roller rink up here. For now, at least. Work isn't going to start up here for another year or two, so you still have some time."

"I can't believe you bought me roller skates." My tone bubbles with giddiness.

"And..."

Reid walks over to the old podium and pulls a box from one of its built-in shelves. He sits next to me and opens it. A pair of black and yellow skates are snuggled among yellow tissue paper.

I cover my laugh with my hand. "You're going to put those on your feet?"

"Should I not?" he says with a grin.

"No. You should. Right now."

We both dive into our boxes and pull out the shiny new skates, tugging them onto our feet and threading the long laces through the eyelets. When each skate is tied tightly, Reid offers me his hand.

"Wait. I have a present for you too."

He looks at me curiously. I grab his hand and angle my body toward his.

"I got out of my lease."

Despite the shadowy room, Reid's face brightens. A swell of laughter travels up from the dining room, capturing my mood perfectly.

"I talked to my landlord. He told me he has a waiting list, and he was able to find new renters in less than an hour."

Reid's hand tightens around mine. "That's amazing, but—"

"When I get back, I'm going to put in my two-week notice. I hope Tabitha doesn't hate me, but I have to do what's right for me."

"Which is?" He raises an eyebrow expectantly.

"Which is, finding a rental here and helping you at the café until I decide whether or not I want to go back to school."

Before I can pull my next breath, Reid gathers me into his arms and kisses me long and hard. "That's amazing," he says, his lips still inches from mine.

"It's not as good as roller skates, but it's something."

"It's everything." He kisses me again and I melt under his hands.

After a few more kisses for good measure, he says, "Do you want to skate?"

"My legs feel wobbly."

He smiles proudly at his ability to render me like a thick slice of bacon. I elbow him playfully.

With his arm as support, I stand on eight wheels and try to remember how not to land on my butt. We both scoot forward cautiously. After a few minutes, we get the hang of it and start doing circles around the wide space.

"What are you two doing up there?" Mabel calls up the stairs.

"Nothing," I holler back.

"Doesn't sound like nothing," Dottie chirps, followed by a giggle.

I grin at Reid and grab his hand. We do a few revolutions, and then I lean too far back and lose my footing. Reid tries to help me stabilize, but I take him down with me. We fall into a heap, me flat on my back, and Reid hovering over me.

"Oops," I say.

"Are you okay?"

"You said you would never hurt me."

"Does roller skating count?"

"Umm..."

"Does this make it better?" He dives for my lips, and I turn into a mere puddle on the floor.

As his kiss lingers, I hear Dottie call up, "I know what's happening up there now!"

Reid and I both dissolve into laughter. He falls onto his back, and we admire the ornate plaster ceiling until our giggling subsides.

I'm the first to move, propping myself on my elbow to get a good look at Reid's impossibly gorgeous face.

"What?" he says when he notices my serious expression.

"I love you."

Reid sits up to meet me. His face softens with fondness as he traces my features. "I love you too." He encircles me with his arms and pulls me back to the floor.

My lips press against his as gravity tugs on us both.

I'm finally home.

Follow Erin!

There's more to come! To stay up-to-date on Erin Lucy's new releases, **sign up for her newsletter** at www.erinlucy.com.

About the Author

Erin Lucy is partial to beaches and corn fields. She loves small towns, quaint cities, and places that feel cozy. Her social media of choice is Instagram. She's also on Facebook, or you can stop by her website to see what she's up to.

She has a day job, three kids, a husband, and some pets. If she's not writing, she might be reading, going to church, going to the gym, or drinking way too much boba tea.

Long ago she received an English degree with Honors from a college in the Midwest.

9 780989 880893